An Exceptional Adventure

A Tale of Magic, Love, and Betrayal

Other books by this author:

Arianna A Tale from the Eleven Kingdoms

Mystic Highlands Love Story

Mystic Highlands Wedding

The Shapeshifters' Bride: A Love Story

An Exceptional Adventure

A Tale of Magic, Love, and Betrayal

GC Sinclaire

Printed in the United States of America

GC Sinclaire
Gig Harbor, WA 98329
www.gcsinclaire.com

An Exceptional Adventure: A Tale of Magic, Love, and Betrayal/GC Sinclaire--1st ed.

Print Edition ISBN 978-0-9994627-2-0
E-Book Edition ISBN 978-0-9994627-3-7
Hardback Edition ISBN 978-0-9994627-4-4

Library of Congress Control Number: 2023906914

Dedicated To:

The Universe
for sending me this
incredible story,
my wonderful readers,
and
all those
with
Magic
in their Souls.

Contents

Enjoy!

Chapter 1

A Sudden Shift

Nothing could have prepared me or any of us for what was to come. Had I even had an inkling, a hint of a premonition, I might have just stayed in bed. Not that it would have made a difference! Somehow, the spell would have found a way to collect me, even hiding under my covers! As we all know, some things are just meant to happen. My exceptional adventure was one of these. However, the incident left me with some thought-provoking questions. Did my presence and actions change the past and the future? And if so, was this part of some Divine plan, or was it entirely accidental? The answer to this I might never know.

That eventful morning, I was looking forward to spending several hours working on my latest book. Fate, however, had other plans for me, ones that would affect not only my life but those of many others related to the Magnuson Clan. Fortunately, in the end, the change was for the better. But, it did not start out that way. In the beginning, the situation looked rather bleak and caused me some serious heartache. Worst of all, it separated me from Phillipe, my husband, my rock, and the love of my life.

The day started out like many others, pleasant and peaceful. When the rays of the bright sunshine outside found their way around the floor-length curtains and started dancing through the room, our dogs began getting restless. Bear, our male German Shepherd, came over to see if I was awake. He stuck his large head on the bed and gave my face an exuberant licking. I gave him a gentle petting, and he settled back down.

Our pets know the routine and are always patient with Phillipe and me. For just a moment, I laid there without moving, bathing in the delicious sensation of my husband's strong arm draped comfortingly over my slender waist. As usual, his warm body was pushed up tight against my bare back. I felt so safe, so secure, so protected. With him around, I had nothing to worry about, ever.

Phillipe was the most caring, loving, devoted husband I could have asked for, a true blessing. As always, I could not help myself - I started smiling. How much I cherished this remarkable man and our peaceful but passionate life together! I would have done anything to keep it this way, as would he. Therefore, as a rule, we made sure to never go to bed angry and to resolve issues openly and honestly.

The word 'love' actually seemed inadequate to describe the depth of my emotions for Phillipe. He was everything to me, and I to him. Silently, I gave thanks. I could not think of a better way of starting the day than filled with such feelings of love and deep gratitude. We had just celebrated nine years together, and our relationship was just as exciting and romantic now as it had been when we first got together. That is saying something since it started with quite a bang!

Once my mate realized I was no longer asleep, his well-muscled arm tightened possessively around me. There would be no slipping out of bed now! Not that getting up was on my mind anyway! I had a completely different agenda! Melting against Phillipe, I gave my rear a seductive wiggle, producing a sharp intake of breath. Even after all this time, this playful act never failed to yield the desired result. The game was on!

Being squashed up against him suddenly was not enough. Yes, it sent fire racing through my veins, but I needed to see him, to connect on an even deeper level. I wanted to drown in his loving gaze. Guessing my intention, Phillipe relaxed his grip just enough for me to turn around. Finally, I came face to face with my handsome mate.

Affectionately, we smiled at each other. We were only too aware of each other's bodies and what the other craved. I was so grateful to see that Phillipe's gorgeous green eyes reflected the same depth of happiness and desire I felt. Having my love returned in full measure was something I deeply valued. Never, as long as I live, will I take this for granted; it was special to me beyond words.

Phillipe and I had both known heartache before we found each other. What we shared was special, magical even. I just adored him, and he me. Often, we finished each other's sentences or reached for something before the other even asked for it. Being so in tune, so deeply connected, felt incredible to us both. We wanted more, so we continued exploring what that link could do and actively worked on strengthening the bond we shared.

We knew how different the situation could be. Before we became a couple, we had relationships that were nothing like this. They had been with nice enough people, but something had been missing. We had both longed to take things to a whole new level. But, none of our partners had been willing to work on achieving this. They were prepared to settle for what was.

Phillipe and I had made our love grow and last. After regarding me for a long moment as if he was following my train of thought, my husband pulled me closer. He dove in for a kiss that started out sweet and gentle but quickly turned passionate. Our desire for each other flared up brightly, and one thing led to another. I was not very patient, I wanted him, and I wanted him now! Phillipe was only too happy to oblige me. To his credit, I cannot remember a time that he turned me down. Another thing I loved about him!

Keeping my hands off this magnificent hunk had never been my strong point. Good thing that he was just as attracted to me! And that we were well-matched in bed! We loved exploring each other, teasing, touching, and finding new ways to increase the other's enjoyment. Phillipe saw it as a personal affront if he did not drive me positively mad, and nothing turned me on more than hearing his moans of pure pleasure.

Being in no hurry, we took our time. Slowly and deliberately, we drove each other toward the brink of madness. A stroke here, a pat there, some kneading somewhere else, a circling with the tongue, a lick here or there, all designed to increase the other's desire. By now, we knew just what to do and what felt best, and we switched things up to keep our lovemaking fresh and stimulating. No way were we going to allow this to turn into something boring!

We had discovered that being completely and totally present heightened all these delicious sensations even more. All that mattered for the next few minutes was giving and taking in a most intimate and satisfying manner. Everything else was put on the back burner. It could be dealt with once we were done. This allowed us to enjoy the other's ministrations to the extent that they deserved.

To my delight, talking dirty often had quite an effect! It added spice, as did the costumes and dresses I wore for date nights! Over the years, we have acquired quite an assortment of outfits, and both of us have gotten very comfortable slipping into different roles. Anything from innocent milkmaid to smoldering seductress was fun for me, while he liked being my knight in shining armor or a darkly seductive gent, human or other.

Those kinds of activities, however, were usually reserved for those special nights, but that made this morning's lovemaking no less of a turn-on. Once we were both well-sated, we showered together. This took a few minutes since Phillipe liked to hold me against him while seductively washing my body, including those special parts! He gave them extra attention since he was an expert at satisfying me and enjoyed doing so.

When he finally decided I had enough, my legs felt like jelly. He was rather pleased with himself, but turn-around is fair play. As my fingers played over his soap-slicked skin, his moans of pleasure were a welcome reward. Since I relished the feel of him, I took my time in getting him to a climax. Now, the drying-off fun began.

My husband and I could talk about anything. Being so masculine, he brought out more of the feminine side in me. Feeling safe and protected made it possible for me to be as sensual and sexual as I cared to be, naturally, within limits. Setting boundaries in a relationship is vital, and we each had ours. Since we adored each other, we respected those limits and stuck to the things the other genuinely enjoyed.

I had blossomed like never before since we got together and was genuinely thriving in our marriage, in no small part due to Phillipe's encouragement and support. He was always there for me, ready to help, advise, or just listen. He had my back, no matter what, and I had his. I felt truly blessed to be his wife. And I loved that, like that morning, our life together was never dull.

Once we had dried each other off, we got dressed. Our light-hearted banter had us both laughing before long. Finally, we headed downstairs. After letting the dogs out, we started on breakfast. Harmoniously, we worked together, just as we always did. Phillipe prepared the pets' meals while I fixed ours. It was so routine that it took very little time before the food was ready. After the pack got their bowls and the guinea pigs their salad, my husband and I sat down at the table to enjoy our food.

While we were eating, we talked about the upcoming day. A legal dilemma was giving him trouble. Without providing specifics, he ran the case past me. I might not have a law degree, but sometimes it helps to lay the facts out to someone else. Eventually, we got around to discussing my work. My husband usually had valuable input to give that I greatly appreciated. His suggestions made my stories even more fun and generally found their way into the books. Since it was so different from the others, he was genuinely intrigued with the setting for my latest tale.

Right in the middle of editing an entire series, this one had appeared in a dream. It had insisted on being written. To my delight, I was having a lot of fun with it. I loved sharing some of the details and talking about my progress. Once I got started, however, my natural enthusiasm for my craft took over! When it came to my work, I could go on for hours! I had to watch that since not everyone was as patient as Phillipe!

He had a keen interest in this tale, and we discussed several possible scenarios. Between flirting shamelessly with each other and being interrupted by the pets, that is. The dogs, as usual, were all around us, entertaining us with their antics. Laughter filled the room like sparkling sunlight. Phillipe, our pack, and I were genuinely happy. As usual, I could not stop smiling and felt like I was on cloud nine.

Everything was as it should be; warmth, harmony, and love filled our home. Life was good!

But then, from one instant to the next, something shifted. The hair on my neck felt like it was standing up. I looked around, trying to figure out what had just happened. Things were not as they had been, of that I was certain! For one, the sunlight streaming in through the windows had lost much of its brightness. And, the air in the room suddenly brimmed with a sense of malice that was affecting everyone and everything within reach.

Our pets, who usually get along great, started growling and snapping at their buddies! I noticed that their eyes looked strange, somewhat glassy, almost like they were in a trance! Or drugged! Their pupils were huge, and their usually so gentle gazes were wild and fixed. Phillipe and I could not get their attention no matter what we tried. They were too focused on snarling and circling each other, ready to attack!

We were afraid that someone would get hurt. Cautiously, my husband and I grabbed the two pups by the neck. We shoved them in their crates, keeping them carefully restrained so we would not get bitten ourselves. Arianna, we managed to secure by backing her up into the pantry and closing the door. That left Micha, who was snarling at Hella Rose and Bear through the bars of their cages. I was glad that the little guy was small enough to pick up by the scruff of the neck as long as you supported his legs. We locked him in another room, then separated the guinea pigs, our boys, Teddy and Orion.

However, to my dismay, we were not immune to whatever was happening either. Phillipe's eyes looked odd as well. He seemed somewhat disoriented, almost like he was drunk or high. What could have caused this? Was there something in the water? Or the food? A quick glance in the mirror showed me that I was also affected but not as much as the rest. I had drunk a large glass of water just a few minutes ago, which eliminated that possibility. The dogs had not shared our breakfast, so it was not the food either!

My husband had snapped at me while we dealt with the pets. Whatever it was, it hit all of us at about the same time! Phillipe was still griping at me even now! When I continued to answer him calmly, he ratcheted up his verbal attack. After a few more minutes, I was tempted to respond in kind. Enough was enough! Somehow, I seemed to be the only one with an ounce of reason left! To keep quiet, I bit my tongue. The pain helped to stave off the flood of words about to spill out.

My deep love for Phillipe was holding me back, at least for now. When he landed an especially low verbal blow, I finally had it. Turning around, I fixed him with a glare that would have made most people cringe. I don't yell; I get calm and cold when angry. Oh, and my eyes get bright green, a sure sign of trouble for that unfortunate person who has managed to get up my ire. By now, I was not just a little mad; I was absolutely furious!

As can be expected, things escalated from there. Phillipe blamed me for the pets' behavior and accused me of starting the argument. And the coffee had been too weak, the smoothies too runny, and the story I was writing was just plain stupid. Nothing I did or said was right anymore. Somehow, in some way, a profound shift had occurred. My usually so loving and supportive husband had become his polar opposite!

His harsh criticism continued to rain down on me unabated. It seemed my mate was striving for maximum damage to my self-worth and self-esteem!

Phillipe even looked different. His handsome face was cold and aloof. I barely recognized this person berating me and felt extremely hurt and downright confused. What had happened to bring about such a change? Just a few minutes ago, we were making love! To my horror, the situation got even worse! The man I adore went from being downright mean verbally to outright combative! He started to poke me with every ugly point he made as if trying to goad me into hitting him back.

In vain, I attempted to diffuse the situation even though I was pretty furious myself. Unfortunately, with all the provocation, I was getting closer to losing my cool by the moment. Desperately, I tried to hold onto reason. We had been so close just a few minutes before! This was all wrong, but my pleas to stop this arguing fell on deaf ears. Unlike his usual reasonable self, Phillipe was distant and unreachable. He continued his verbal attacks as well as the shoving.

I had no idea what to do. We all have moods, but my husband, he was my rock! He was the most solid, stable person imaginable! Not in all the years I have known him had he ever acted like this! He was not abusive, not with his words nor with his actions! Never before had I been afraid of him, but I was now. That realization pierced my heart like a spear, and the sudden pain in my chest made it hard to breathe.

How could I make him switch back to the man I had married? Right then, I needed the comfort of his loving arms more than ever before! Phillipe was the one who helped me through the jitters before book signings. He was at my side during all my public appearances. He was steady, calm, and loving. I had never even suspected this kind of viciousness was in his nature!

What had happened to the man I knew and adored? The longer all this went on, the more I despaired. And the more the tightness around my chest increased. Panic had set in. Being treated in such a manner brought up distressing memories from the past. With them came the feeling of being helpless, of my life being out of control. Phillipe's cruel words wounded me so deeply that I fell back into old patterns I had thought were long gone. I retreated into myself and just stood there, letting the onslaught continue unchecked.

Usually, and with anyone else, a situation like this would not have fazed me. I would have handled it in stride. Quickly, I would have told the offending party in no uncertain terms where to get off, even my brother or parents. I was quite capable of standing up for myself and have not allowed my husband's protectiveness to make me weak or dependent on him to fight my battles. If pushed hard enough, I turned as fierce as a lioness!

But this was the love of my life! Any disconnect between us felt awful, even at the best of times. We were both sensitive people and did not like conflict between us. Therefore, we usually talked about issues before they became a problem. Our getting into a fight was very rare. Until this morning, Phillipe had been kind and gentle, no matter what. We had always been fair and treated each other with love and respect.

This was the first time he had ever snapped at me like that, spoken to me this hurtfully, this cruelly. It hit me hard, especially since the things he accused me of were totally unfair. I knew very well that I had not started this and that I was the one trying to reestablish goodwill, not him! I had no idea why he was behaving this way or what I had done to make him so very angry.

The way I saw it, I was trying to be the voice of reason. Still, needless to say, I did not handle the continued barrage very well. Especially since my own temper was about to boil over! My hands were shaking, and I was terribly on edge, and not just from the arguing! There was more to it! I finally noticed that alarm bells were clamoring in my brain and had been for a while!

Something was awfully wrong! Trouble was brewing; I just knew it! And, instead of facing it together, we were pulling apart!

The abrupt change in my beloved Phillipe had brought up deep-seated insecurities I had not faced in years. Add to this the sense of imminent danger. As a result, suddenly, I was terribly afraid that my entire life was falling apart. I had never had reason to feel this way in all the time we had been together! My husband understood me so well and spoiled me with all his love and attention. Our relationship had been the envy of many of our friends.

Being in conflict with him, the person I loved most in this world, seemed incredibly wrong. On top of this, my emotions were out of control, vacillating between great sadness, disbelief, confusion, and extreme rage. The depth of my fury, my desire to hit, hurt, and destroy Phillipe, had me recoil in horror. This was not like me! I could not recall feeling like this, even at the worst of times!

The fighter part of me was itching for battle. I cringed, for I had never known it and me to be this vicious and vengeful! We usually work well together, and I am much stronger since I have embraced that aspect of myself. At that moment, however, any semblance of decency and rationality was rapidly slipping away. Noting this, I grew even more worried.

Unchecked, the warrior in me is a mindless killing machine. And I am well-trained in self-defense. I realized I would not be able to hold back much longer. I needed to get out of here before things escalated, and I did something that could not be undone! There was no time to spare! Due to feeling such deep hurt and overwhelming panic, my self-control was slipping away rapidly!

Pushing Phillipe away from me, I raced for the door. I did have the presence of mind to grab my phone and a light jacket as I fled the house. I desperately needed time to get the turmoil inside me calmed down before I did or said something I would regret forever. In my rush, I did not even think of taking one of the dogs along. Usually, they are my constant companions, and I rarely go anywhere without them but not that day.

In that instance, I was not thinking clearly at all. I was in full fight or flight mode. Loving Phillipe with all my heart and soul, I had

chosen the latter. Dashing out of the door, I hurried toward the rear of the garden and the path that lay beyond it. Once out of the gate, I intended to break into a run to put as much distance between my husband and me as possible. And, as quickly as I could. Since I was in good shape, that was not going to be a problem.

Chapter 2

Emotional Meltdown

Any time something bothered me, I turned to my husband. He was my shoulder to lean on, my support, and my best friend. His unwavering encouragement was a blessing that I was deeply grateful for. He was always there for me, or at least had been until that morning! From one moment to the next, he had turned into someone I needed protection from! This was beyond my comprehension since it was so alien to his nature. Phillipe was never mean or violent! How did things get out of hand so quickly?

Reviewing the incident, I became aware of my own emotions. Why had I been so irritated with him even before he started laying into me? This made no sense! I felt like I had just entered a nightmare. Or the Twilight Zone! All I wished for, with all my heart, was for things to return to the way they had been! Why can't life have a reset button? I could have used one about then! I would have loved it had I been able to undo that entire ugly scene!

Now that Phillipe was not right in front of me anymore further infuriating me, my anger was ebbing. Some reasonability was asserting itself, and my panic was starting to subside. My breath no longer came as fast and was deepening; my pulse was still racing but was slowing. Even my hurried flight toward the back gate lost some of its urgency. I seriously thought about returning to the house and trying to make peace between us one more time.

But my mate's hurtful comments continued to echo in my mind. Like an unstoppable force, they were drilling their way into my heart, leaving devastation in their wake. I was still in disbelief that this had happened between us and mystified as to what had sparked this nasty fight! How had we, two calm, respectful, reasonable people, gotten so out of control in what seemed like an instant?

By then, I was more than halfway along the path to the rear gate. Sorrow flooded my heart and soul and drove out the last remnants of fury. My steps faltered. Turning around, I glanced back at the charming home I shared with my husband. I was not surprised to see Phillipe standing at the window, watching me. With hope in my heart, I returned his gaze, searching for some softening in those gorgeous green eyes, for any signs that things between us could be repaired.

I longed to reconnect with my mate. Raising my hand, I gave him a tentative wave. But, if anything, those beautiful orbs I had allowed myself to drown in during our lovemaking that very morning grew even colder. With a pang of deep sadness, I realized there was no reaching Phillipe. He looked at me as if he hated me. The glare he was giving me was so fierce that I involuntarily took a step back.

It seemed that my marriage was over. The pain that shot through me at this realization took my breath away, and I doubled over. But, with a vengeance, it also reawoke my own anger! I was not so weak that I would collapse just because this man no longer wanted me! I had been on my own before and had survived previous breakups. I would make it through this one as well! Straightening up, I met his glare with one of my own.

Fury washed through me, and the fight impulse kicked in full force. As I had been trained, I automatically dropped into a boxer's stance, my fists balled, ready to let fly. My body language screamed rage and defiance. I would not allow anyone to treat me this way, not ever, not even him, whom I loved most in this world! I had held back, mostly, but he had hit way below the belt! Those awful things he had been spewing at me must have been festering for a long time to come out with such viciousness!

My hostile posture was not lost on my husband. He had not moved away from the window and was still glowering at me. I could almost physically feel the loathing he was projecting in my direction. It further incensed me. I was no weak female who would beg or plead for forgiveness when she was the one who had been wronged! He would have to apologize first or at least meet me halfway! And that, from what I was sensing, was not about to happen!

Then, after a moment, Phillipe actually snarled at me! That truly stunned me! My suave, well-mannered, highly evolved husband was behaving like an animal! That was so unlike him! I gave him a look that clearly stated my disbelief. Seriously? Could he get any lower? Or meaner? I was glad to have distance as well as the glass pane between us. Since I was not in immediate danger, continuing to act bravely was doable, even in the face of such a flagrant display of hostility!

Inside, however, I was quaking with anxiety, but I was not about to let Phillipe see that. However, had he even taken one step out the door, I would have run. Not now or ever was I going to get into a physical altercation with my husband! Just the thought of hitting him, even in self-defense, made me sick to my stomach. You don't harm the ones you love! This was all so silly! Why had he not talked to me before all this resentment boiled over?

After several seconds of shooting visual daggers at me, Phillipe stepped away from the window, only to reappear an instant later to flip me the bird. I could not believe it! We had gotten as low as that?

His gesture, however, caused such a wave of fury to bubble up inside me that I saw red. I almost marched back into the house. My hands clenched so tightly they hurt. For a few seconds, all reason fled. I wanted to punch something, preferably Phillipe. The urge to hit, utterly destroy, and pulverize him was almost overwhelming! He was going to stop hurting me one way or another! How dare he treat me like this? To cast me away?

Taking some deep breaths, I calmed down a little. Suddenly I realized the danger my being in such a state represented to my mate and anyone near me. After years of self-defense classes, I knew only too well what I was capable of. For my own sake, I had to get away! Whipping around, I raced for the gate and then down the path. I needed to get some of this extra adrenaline out of my system before the warrior inside me took over, and we started something we would regret!

I had no doubt that my husband could stand his ground against me. A battle between us would have been brutal. Since we met, Phillipe and I have trained together. As a lawyer, he had seen enough violence and what people did to each other. Therefore, he wanted me to be able to protect myself from any attack, physical or other. As a result, I was a decent fighter with fists, staff, and sword. But I also had magical abilities!

Never before had I used them for harm, and I did not intend to start doing so now! With so much fury inside me, it was hard to hold back. The magic was right at my fingertips, ready to be deployed at the slightest provocation. If I was startled, I might just act on instinct. Some things could never be undone, and it was best to prevent them in the first place! Determinedly, I sprinted down the path as fast as I could, needing to put distance between Phillipe and me before I let lose my powers on him, accidentally or not.

However, since I had eaten breakfast not long ago, I quickly ran out of breath and had to slow down. But at least I had made it past three of the large yards of our neighbors!

On a primal level, hitting him for hurting me this badly would have been rather satisfying. That primitive, enraged part of me still wanted to turn around and attack. Thankfully I was a little more in control of myself even after such a brief exertion, and my better nature was taking back control. Violence is never a good choice unless you are defending yourself from a physical attack and are in imminent danger. Then, it is best to incapacitate your opponent as quickly as possible!

I was rather good at protecting myself, making me a formidable opponent in a fight. Phillipe and I were sparring partners and well-familiar with each other's moves. If we engaged in a clash, one or both of us could get seriously hurt. I loved my husband and wanted to avoid that. Therefore, as long as my emotions were running this high, it was not a good idea for me to return home!

Also, I had experienced enough rudeness and cruelty for one day! I needed a place to think, somewhere I would be undisturbed. Several possibilities were available to me, and I considered my choices. I could go see my friends, but as on edge as I was, I really did not want to be around anyone. Nor was it safe until I figured things out.

Besides, this was between my husband and me. It was not my way to put someone else in the middle! People usually felt compelled to take sides, and that was neither fair nor did I want that. Also, considering the sudden shift in mood that I had experienced that morning, who knew if I would not get just as irate with one of them?

Staying clear of all others seemed the best and soundest thing to do until I had more of an idea of what had caused all of us to behave so irrationally. Hella Rose and Bear were siblings and played together all the time! They had never acted this way toward each other! That alone pointed to some outside influence, and I could only hope they would calm once it waned.

I wished I had taken them with me, or at least one of them. After this confrontation, I felt lost, rejected, and abandoned. Also, I was not sure if things could be fixed between Phillipe and me. Usually, when someone voices complaints and resentments in the manner he had, they have been smoldering underneath for a long time. Had all his affection that morning been an act? Did he really want a divorce? The thought alone caused a sob to bubble up from deep inside me.

Tears started to roll down my face. All I wanted was to curl into a ball and let the grief out that was choking me. Since I could not return home, I needed to find another place to hide out for a bit and lick my wounds. The seashore and my favorite cove were nearby. As was the marina where our sailboat was docked. After weighing my options, I decided that I would head there. For one, I loved the sea, and being rocked by the waves would help calm me.

The yacht also had additional advantages. Since I craved privacy, being on board with the curtains drawn was the easiest way to avoid others. No one would even know that I was there! And it had some of the comforts of home. We kept clothes, food, water, and a small computer on the vessel. If I felt like it, I could sleep there and even work. It really was the perfect place for me to hide! Determinedly, I headed down the path toward the harbor.

I had not gone much further when the remainder of the fury boiling inside me bled away just as quickly as it had arisen. My frantic gait slowed as a sense of mortification, then hurt, and eventually, hopelessness and deep shame washed over me. I had not said as much as Phillipe had, but it had been enough. My words had not been nice or kind. They had probably been equally as spiteful as the things my husband had hurled at me! Remembering them, I cringed.

What had gotten into me? I usually treat others how I want to be treated myself, with respect, graciousness, and kindness. Even when I was confronted with rudeness, I kept my cool. If I had to make a suggestion, I did so gently, phrasing it as a question. Being only too aware of how devastating criticism can be, I used praise of people's good points to encourage them; I built them up and applauded their accomplishments. I did not tear them down!

By nature, I am not a destroyer. I prefer to be a cheerleader for my friends and loved ones. But I make sure to do so with honesty and authenticity. Phillipe said I cannot help but bring out the best in people, and he loved me for the ease with which I made friends. He tended to be much more reserved and not as outgoing as I am, which is not surprising for an attorney.

Our differences, however, were precisely what made us so perfect for each other. Neither Phillipe nor I are without flaws, and we accept that. Instead, we concentrate on each other's many strengths. Over the years, we have acquired excellent conflict-resolution skills. Therefore I still could not fathom what had caused us to behave in such an awful way!

Usually, my husband and I made an incredible team. We even have our own way of dealing with obnoxious individuals all worked out. I got to be the enforcer when everything else failed. On those occasions, he enjoyed watching me put someone in their place. I was quite good at it too! Also, since it was so unexpected, they never saw it coming.

Because I was happy, bubbly, polite, and blonde, people tended to underestimate me. Most believed that Phillipe was the one they had to look out for, and they were right. However, I was his secret weapon. People don't suspect the steel core under all my sweetness and that I am a force of nature when necessary. If needed, I can be much fiercer than my soft-hearted husband!

He often called me his 'Holy Grail.' I adore that, by the way, and cherished him in equal measure! What had happened to that? After the fight we just had, how would we find our way back to each other? I, for one, would need a few days to process all this and for my heart to heal. Right then, the hurt I was feeling was pretty intense.

Phillipe had been out of line, but I did owe him an apology for my part in the debacle. Someone must be the first to take responsibility for their behavior in a fight between lovers! It might as well be me. I did not want to live with the guilt that I had failed to do so. Stopping, I quickly sent him a text.

'My words were neither true nor kind. I should not have responded like that. My heart aches at having hurt you. I love you.'

That was all I could think of saying, but it should be enough. Having extended an olive branch to my mate, I went back on my way. I still felt the need for some time by myself. Also, I wanted to examine why some of the things he had said had affected me so profoundly.

Anything I reacted to that intensely pointed to underlying issues, probably based on childish, outdated beliefs.

As upset as I was with him, the thought of being on our yacht without Phillipe still felt odd. He and I usually went to most places together. Deep down, I missed him already but was not about to turn around. Any fight we had affected me physically, and this one had been a doozy. From all the emotional upset, I not only felt nauseous, but my head hurt, and I was feverish.

At this point, I was so physically ill that I just wanted to get to the boat. After drinking some water, I could curl up on our bed and let the tears flow, maybe even sleep for a while until my body calmed down. As I walked on, as if wanting to torture me, memories of better days flowed into my mind like film clips. The images caused such immense pain that they took my breath away. Our life together had been so blissful until just about an hour ago!

How could everything change so suddenly? How had I ended up in this nightmare I could not wake up from? Our life together had been everything I had ever dreamed of and more! During the summer months, whenever the wind had been just right, we had walked along this same path down to the marina to take the dogs and us out for a sail. Afterward, we had 'napped' before walking into town for dinner or returning home.

On other days, we had hiked and explored the island. Phillipe and I loved living here. We had picked the Isle of Arran as our home because it was stunningly beautiful and met our needs. We both wanted to have forests and the sea within walking distance. Grocery stores and restaurants could also be reached on foot. That and the magnificence of our surroundings had been among the deciding factors for us settling in this location.

My parents would have preferred us to be a bit closer, but, in the end, they had respected our choice. Phillipe's folks, on the other hand, saw our new location as an improvement. At least we were still in the Highlands and not in London!

Being so upset, much went through my mind. Deep in thought, I made my way along the path that lay behind our home and those of our neighbors. It ran all the way down to the marina and the beach. Usually, I loved checking out all the plants in the well-tended, fenced-in gardens on my left but not this day. Nor did I notice the tasteful, stucco houses on their large lots or their latest improvements.

Right then, none of it mattered. My eyes were turned inwards, not out. Feeling utterly miserable, I was totally blind to the beauty around me. My heart was aching, and my throat felt so closed off that I could not have spoken had I tried. Like a runaway train, my thoughts kept spiraling out of control, going down, down, and down. Realizing I was wallowing in self-pity, I decided to stop this descent since it was going nowhere good. THAT I knew from experience!

To distract myself, I ran the problem through the conflict resolution module I had learned in one of my self-improvement courses. Create Your Destiny, by William Whitecloud, had helped me make a fundamental change in my life. Not only had my relationship with my family gotten closer as a result, but, entirely unexpectedly, I had met up again with Phillipe shortly after.

We had been friends as kids but had not seen each other in a couple of years. On that occasion, we had 'clicked' instantly. That he had even attended the festivities had been unexpected. A business meeting in Ny Havn that had prevented him from going to the solstice gathering had fallen through at the last minute. Therefore, being in the neighborhood, he had decided to drop in on the solstice celebration.

Had I manifested that? It had sure felt like it at the time! All that night, we had eyes only for each other! It had been the beginning of something truly magical! One of the sobs I was trying to hold in so desperately tore itself free. My hand instinctively flew to my mouth to prevent the others from escaping. I needed to get to the boat and privacy fast! I was not sure how much longer I could maintain my composure. Therefore, I increased my pace.

My body, I might have been able to control, but no matter how much I tried, I could not stem the flood of memories.

After we got together, Phillipe helped me with marketing my work. Before long, my books started selling like wildfire, catapulting me into fame and fortune rivaling his. Once he and I decided to remain a couple, we bought our beautiful home on the Isle of Arran. Being so in love and genuinely enjoying each other's company, we spent as much time together as possible. This was easily done since, most days, we both worked from home.

Being able to set our own hours had a lot of perks. We got started when we wanted and could keep going until late if need be. We would take our dogs for a walk or go for a sail when we felt like a break. Another heartbroken sob escaped me. Good thing that there was no one here to hear me! No Magnuson cried in public! It just was not done! To regain some control, I recalled the first time Phillipe and I had visited here.

The research we had done led us to believe that the landscape in this area was spectacular. People from all over the world came to the region to see the island. We were looking for a place to settle, and the Isle of Arran topped our list. Phillipe and I had therefore come here on vacation. We had instantly fallen in love with the place. It was perfect for what we had in mind, and we cherished the rugged beauty of the isle.

Even the temperature was to our liking. Not too cold in the winter, nor too hot in the summer! And, it was great for sailing and hiking!

Usually, I would have genuinely enjoyed the lush green forest on the hills to my right. My eyes would have been combing its depth, watching for what I was not sure. To me, these woods were just plain magical. The many hiding spaces under the tall trees fired up my imagination. Over the years, they have given birth to more than one of my stories. The mix of wild spaces and more manicured ones, maintained lovingly by the local foresters, was gorgeous and struck just the right balance between human needs and wildlife habitat.

The result was stunning and created the perfect backdrop for my fantasy to take flight. Not that this took much! This place was so enchanting that I would not have been overly surprised if unicorns, fairies, or other beings of legend had stepped out from behind one of the tall trees! I could envision dwarves digging for precious stones or mining gold in the mountains and colorful dragons flying overhead, surveying their domain.

This day, however, I could not see the wood's delights and wondrous possibilities. With my head lowered, I moved along the path on autopilot. I wanted to get to the boat as quickly as possible before my meltdown worsened, and I could no longer hold in the tears. Against my will, my thoughts were drawn back to that ugly fight. Going over the awful scenes in my mind, I was trying to figure out what had happened that morning.

I was so preoccupied that you could have exploded a bomb next to me. I would have walked on, utterly oblivious, completely absorbed by the threat to my marriage. Moving along almost at a run, I was deaf and blind to my surroundings. Luckily, getting to the marina did not require my attention; my feet knew where they were going!

Unnoticed by me, an odd stretch of dense, greyish smoke suddenly appeared just ahead. It had a strange purplish tint to it and emerged out of thin air. One second, there was nothing; the next, this weird mist created a curtain that hung from the ground up to far above my head. It stretched across the pathway and beyond, making it hard to avoid. The most peculiar thing was that it just sat there, totally immobile.

Once it had fully materialized, it seemed frozen in place. Unlike a regular cloud, the gentle wind from the shore did not affect it in the slightest. It stayed just as it was. Its outline was well-defined, and the haze seemed uniform in its consistency, creating a wall of sorts. A diffuse, rather insubstantial one at that but a barrier nonetheless.

Unfortunately, its presence never registered. Therefore, I walked right into it. I was desperately searching for a way to fix things with Phillipe. Part of me longed to run to him, to have him make it all better, but that was not an option. At this time, there was no solace to be had from my husband. I would have to soothe my own wounded heart.

When I reached the other side, the scene around me had changed drastically. But not even then did I become aware that something was wrong. I kept right on going. My need to understand why the argument had happened was all-consuming. If I was going to prevent such an incident in the future and have a chance of undoing some of the damage that had resulted from tempers getting out of control, I had to know what had sparked it in the first place!

On their own accord, my steps slowed. But by then, it was too late.

Chapter 3

A Fateful Night

Completely devastated and utterly preoccupied, I was totally oblivious of my surroundings. I had walked right through that unusual cloud without it even registering that something odd was afoot. Since I was determined to find an explanation for the sudden shift in our behavior, I kept examining the morning's events. Finally, I concluded that it could not have been natural. What were the odds of us, the dogs, and the guinea pigs all getting into a fight at the same time? That was more than a little suspicious!

How could a solid, stable marriage fall apart within minutes? Some outside influence had to have been at play to impact us to such a degree! What exactly had affected us, I was unsure of. Then, another possibility occurred to me. If this was not due to some outside force, it must have been brewing for a while! Was my head so far in the clouds that I had missed the warning signs? I had been so sure that Phillipe was happy!

How could that change so suddenly? And what had made the dogs so very aggressive? And the guinea pig boys, Teddy and Orion? These questions continued to whirl through my mind, consuming all my awareness.

Unable to find answers, my thoughts drifted to the past, to that summer solstice night when Phillipe's and my love affair began. The last time we had been together had been a couple of years back. We had talked then, but it had been more like old friends who had not seen each other in a while, nothing special. I had no expectation that this meeting would be any different.

Being rather bored, I had been delighted to spot him, never suspecting the turn things were about to take. To our surprise, the attraction between us was intense, electric, and magical from the moment he came to greet me. That was new for both of us and unanticipated but not unwelcome since we already shared a deep bond and understood each other well.

I loved Phillipe's aptitude to instinctively pick up on all my suppressed emotions and his capability to make me feel at ease. To me, he was like a calm lake. Just being near him was soothing, especially when I was upset. It was part of his magic. His other gifts are seeing through people's masks and intuiting what they are trying to hide. His abilities served him well and made him an effective attorney and a wonderful husband.

But being so successful also had its drawbacks. Phillipe was in high demand and not just by our people and the Mackays. Anyone facing off against a formidable opponent in court wanted him by their side. This, however, made it possible for him to write his own ticket with MPC, the Magnuson Procurement Company, the clan's trade business. He and my father had come to an agreement that suited them both.

Once we got together, I felt truly blessed that spending time with me was more important to him than making loads of money. But

Phillipe also liked to help people, something I wholeheartedly supported. Occasionally, he took on pro bono cases, often defending an innocent person accused of a crime they did not commit. Some were facing impossible odds. Being brilliant and having certain capabilities, he usually won.

Picking up precisely what the villain was concealing gave him an edge that few other lawyers had. All he needed was some time in the same room with a person. Phillipe never divulged secrets, nor did he abuse his powers. But they did make it possible for him to send his investigators to dig up the proof he needed to tip the scale in his client's favor.

Something I truly admired about him was the high standards he held himself to. Phillipe refused to defend those who were guilty! He did not care how much money they offered him; he would walk away from any prospective client who was lying about the case or had committed the crime fully aware of what he or she was doing. His reputation for honesty and keeping things above board preceded him in every courtroom.

Villains cringed, and victims rejoiced when he entered. I liked to accompany him and watch him work. When my husband interrogated witnesses, he kindly and gently got them to tell the truth, even if they did not want to. The newspapers found this quite impressive and usually attributed it to his skillful questioning. They would not have believed the real reason had they known!

It is pretty incredible what a little bit of hidden magic can do! Even when we were youngsters, folk found it impossible to lie when Phillipe was around. His mere presence made them tell it as it was. I must admit that any chance we got, we used this shamelessly to our advantage. Another reason why my parents were so against us playing together! We discovered all kinds of things the adults were trying to keep a secret from us!

In addition, my mother and father feared Phillipe would teach me to be more independent and to rebel against their rules and archaic ways. In the end, I did that all by myself and in such a manner that it often escaped their notice!

Due to us being kin, my folks could not officially object to us playing together. For that, I was immensely grateful. Phillipe and I were distant cousins from the same clan, except I carried the Magnuson name and Phillipe his father's, Mackay. We both lived in Ny Havn for most of our childhood. Our similar upbringing gave him an insight into my life that no outsider would ever have.

Despite having much more self-determination, he understood how I felt about my parents' often unreasonable expectations of me. Even as a boy, Phillipe tried to help me carry some of the daunting responsibilities that came with the status I was born into. Not many other people would have volunteered to do so or did.

He was allowed to have more freedom than I did. Thanks to the Highlander influence from his father's side, his family had been far more relaxed than mine about the perfect way to behave. My mother thought this absolutely abhorrent and did not want some of his more casual manners to rub off on her precious daughter.

Phillipe's parents decided to leave Ny Havn when we were teenagers. He and I had been heartbroken to be parted, but there was nothing we could do to change the situation. I missed him bitterly. We had been close friends and had spent much more time together than my folks knew. I could talk to him about anything and be myself for a few moments when we sneaked off to our hiding places. Even then, he was my pillar of strength.

Once Phillipe moved away, we did not see each other very often. Having established a life for themselves with the Mackays, neither he nor his parents attended many of our celebrations.

As the direct descendants of the original chieftains, my family was among the aristocracy of the clan. My mother and father, along with a small circle of others, ran everything in Ny Havn. This bunch lived and breathed all things Magnuson. They demanded the same of their children. Therefore, we were expected to set a good example for all the rest.

Many revered my parents due to their business acumen and all they had accomplished in the company and at Ny Havn. The hotel they oversaw was booked out months in advance, MPC flourished, and the teaching academy was filled to the gills. Having an older brother, Oliver, saved me from being forced to follow in their footsteps. He was the 'heir to the throne,' and for that, I was grateful.

Early on, he and I were taught to hide our feelings and think twice before saying or doing anything. Spontaneity was discouraged. We had to present a calm, competent façade that inspired confidence in the kin no matter what was happening inside us. As far as my father was concerned, we would be the future leaders of the business and the clan.

Therefore, we had to act accordingly, even in private. My parents saw this as good practice, as did those of my closest cousins. We wanted to rebel against all those rules we had to follow, but none of us dared to step out of line. At least not when we could get caught! We each found our own sneaky little ways to have some freedom!

Phillipe had been luckier than us. His mum and dad had allowed him to experience life in a way the rest of us could only dream of. I had loved secretly joining him in his adventures, my one and only rebellion against all the rules imposed on us children.

He and I spent as much time together as the circumstances allowed. Mostly, we managed to sneak around unnoticed, but on rare occasions, we got into trouble. Never with the law or anything like that; we just had fun and did things many other kids could do without repercussions. Usually, I was the instigator, but my mother and father always blamed Phillipe for being a 'bad' influence on me!

Had they only known how much we really did! Climbing onto the roof of the hotel had been a real treat. We knew exactly how to do it without getting caught. You could hide among the chimneys, and no adult would ever find you! The view from up there was spectacular. You could see all the way to the mountains and far out to sea! To this day,

I still go up there on occasion, just because. And I showed my brother Oliver. He needed a refuge.

Knowing the consequences of some of our exploits being found out, Phillipe and I learned to never let our guard down. We always kept a lookout for any grownups. In addition, we practiced moving about without being seen. This was great for getting around undetected, a skill that still served me well. And, since my mother was clairvoyant, we worked on shielding and projection. It was the only way to slide anything past her!

While growing up, around Phillipe, I could be free to do some of the things my heart desired. I could be a child and run wild for a few stolen minutes. But I was just as happy to sit quietly and study together, something my parents fully approved of. He encouraged me to follow my heart, to become who I wanted to be, something I have never forgotten. However, all our fun and outings ended when he and his folks moved.

After that, Phillipe and his parents attended the family gatherings less and less. Having a bit of a crush on him, I missed his presence. Through rumors, I followed his exploits, and, I have to admit, I envied him. He was free to choose what to do with his life! That made me resent my parents' heavy hand even more. Outwardly, I was docile and did most of what I was told, but the seeds of rebellion were growing in my heart.

Eventually, knowing that my cousin was following his bliss gave me the courage to object to my parents' plans for my future. I was keenly aware that this would not go over well and that I would have to fight them all the way, but I did not relent. This was my life, and I intended to live it the way I wanted. Who gave them the right to decide what I should study or who I should marry?

Not only did I reject the two choices of husband they had presented me with, but I also nixed the career in management they had planned for me. Instead of working for the company as they had intended, I became an author, which was my true calling. Naturally, my folks were deeply disappointed. They made sure to voice this numerous times. But, in the end, we worked out a compromise that gave each of us something we wanted.

For my part, I agreed to help with any brochures and promotions. Our family would continue to present a united front which meant showing up at every function. I was expected to act as if I was actually enjoying these events. That was easy since I had plenty of practice hiding my real emotions. In return, I was allowed to acquire a small cottage in a quiet setting on the outskirts of a nearby village and to follow my chosen profession.

Filled with excitement, I moved out of my folks' grand house. To my surprise, my father even loaned me a couple of cousins to assist with the furniture. After they left, my mother came by to see if she could help. For the first time I could remember, we spent a pleasant couple of hours together. We decorated and chatted, then had tea. My parents being so supportive was unexpected. It surprised me, but I was grateful for their graciousness. It went a long way toward easing the tension between us.

My new home gave me freedom for the first time in my life, and I just adored it. Then Phillipe and I started dating, making things even better. My eyes teared up when my thoughts were drawn to that fateful summer solstice night nine years ago. My steps faltered, and I sat down where I was, not caring who witnessed this moment of weakness.

Like a movie, the scene unfolded in my mind's eye, and I was there, reliving it all.

The fragrant night air washing in through the open windows cooled the building and diluted the smell of alcohol and sweat from the dancers. The party had been in full swing for a while, and things were getting pretty wild. Comfortably ensconced at one of the little tables on the second-story balcony, I kept an eye on the revelers below. As usual, I was one of the few still sober. However, that did not bother anyone since they knew I did not judge them.

My spot had been strategically chosen. I was sheltering in the shadow of one of the thick columns holding up the roof of the sair, the ancient mead hall we used to this day. This made picking me out from below hard and gave me a semblance of privacy. Thus I could watch and act without being obvious. So far, no fights had erupted, but I was ready just in case one did.

If I was not going to participate in the revelry, my parents expected me to help keep the peace at these events. I had gotten pretty good at it over the years, and the self-defense classes I had taken gave me the confidence to stand up to any of these brawny brutes. Still, I hoped not to have to dash down the nearby stairs to help break up an argument.

Thankfully, most of such unpleasantness could be prevented by sending a spell of calm and peacefulness through the building at regular intervals. As soon as I could feel it waning, I would renew it. And I was not the only one. Several of us guardians were scattered throughout the building doing just that. Thus people were having fun without unwanted drama.

Another benefit of my location was that the noise from the music was not quite as loud up here. Slowly sipping a glass of water, I let my eyes travel over the space down below. Then, suddenly, movement by the entrance drew my attention. It was Phillipe walking in. He was late, and his showing up at all was unexpected. When I spoke to his parents earlier that evening, they mentioned that he could not make it due to an urgent meeting.

His timing was perfect. By now, the summer solstice celebration was in full swing. Thanks to the freely-flowing alcohol, inhibitions had dropped. People were enjoying themselves, each in their own way, some a little too much, and with persons other than their spouses. Keeping an eye on those coming and going was one way the guardians prevented unnecessary conflicts.

If need be, we would follow and intervene. Knowing the clan members well, we were aware that anything could happen when they got too far into their cups. We have saved many a lady experiencing a temporary lack of judgment from waking up the next day with regrets!

As soon as Phillipe entered, he came to a dead stop. He did not notice when the guy behind him ran into his back. He just stood there, sensing. Then, his eyes unerringly found me. He had no problem locating me up here on the balcony, even concealed in the shadows. I was surprised. He had known instinctively where I was hiding! Our eyes locked for a few long moments, and the world around us seemed to fade away, leaving only him and me. Finally, he smiled at me.

The flush of pleasure spreading through me caught me unawares. I detected an echo of my own amazement from Phillipe. With difficulty, he tore his gaze away. I felt an instant sense of loss that was so intense that it stunned me, and I shivered. Leaning forward a little, I followed Phillipe's progress through the crowd. He was stopped by someone every few feet who wanted to speak to him. Laughter and goodwill followed in his wake.

It was evident how well-liked and respected he was. Many here owed Phillipe since he was the one who had bailed them out when they got in trouble. I liked his friendliness and the sincere way he shook hands. He was very different from the two cousins my parents had chosen for me! I could not imagine married life being pleasant with either of them, at least not for someone like me!

Once Phillipe located his parents, he greeted them affectionately. After a short exchange, he took his leave. Once more, the handsome man wove his way through the hall, this time toward the stairs furthest from me. Quickly, taking two steps at a time, he made his way up to the balcony. My eyes remained glued to him as he slipped along the tables, working his way closer, unseen by the others who had taken refuge up here.

The grace and efficiency of his movements were mesmerizing and had quite an effect on my body. We had just been childhood friends the last time we saw each other. What had changed? Maybe we had grown up a bit, and the time was right for something more between us? I had always had a bit of a crush on him but had never acted on it. But then again, I had never felt such an intense attraction to him either!

Naturally, I did not fail to notice how tall and handsome he was. The pictures I had seen in the newspapers had not done him justice, not even in the slightest! My heart started beating ever faster the closer he got. All his attention was focused on me, and his gaze only left mine when he needed to negotiate around something.

Finally, he reached the spot I had claimed as my own. Without hesitation, I rose from my chair and stepped toward him. Our eyes met, and he pulled me into his arms. We are cousins, after all, and all the kin hug. But, this turned out to be anything but a casual embrace! We gasped as a sharp pang of intense desire shot through us. His gorgeous green eyes darkened, and suddenly, something hard was poking at me.

The effect had been almost instantaneous. Surprised, we took a step back. But, Phillipe was as unwilling to release me as I was to put more distance between us. Hesitantly, his hands slid from my shoulders down my arms. The slight touch left a trail of fire behind. My sharp intake of breath made him realize the impact he was having on me. However, I could tell I was not the only one reacting by the bulge in his pants!

Backing off just enough to break the physical connection between us, we looked at each other. Neither of us had an explanation for this sudden and magnetic attraction. We had hugged hundreds of times over the years! This kind of draw to each other had never happened before! Still, the need to touch was overwhelming. We did not dare to get too close again, so we tentatively raised our hands. Palms out, we slowly moved them toward each other.

Just before our fingers touched, arcs of sparks appeared between his digits and mine! We looked at each other in wonder. Could this be the magic of the summer solstice, or were his powers reacting with mine? We thought this rather intriguing and decided to find out just what it could do.

Phillipe and I played with the electric current between us. We tried to work out how close our fingers needed to be before the interesting effects popped into existence. The more we experimented, the more distance it reached. Eventually, we managed to increase the sparkling stream of energy to a full six inches! We laughed like delighted children at this accomplishment and the pretty display all those flashes made. My job of watching the merrymakers was utterly forgotten.

Since the power flowing between us did not hurt, we decided to see what would happen when we tightly clasped hands. We immediately felt the buzzing in our palms and looked at each other in wonder. This was really something! Neither of us had ever experienced anything like this before! After a moment, the current started running back and forth between us. Curious about what would happen next, we held on.

After a couple of minutes, our bodies seemed to equalize, and the flow faded and finally stopped. We were a little disappointed. This had been interesting and fun! Since the excitement was over, we sat down at my table. Taking a quick look over the banister, I spotted my father. I signaled him that I was done for the evening, but I did send out one last spell for peacefulness. Now I could give Phillipe my undivided attention!

We started talking and catching up on events since we had last been together. Finally, we got around to our love lives. To our surprise, we discovered that neither of us had been dating for a while. I have to admit that I was relieved to hear that. Phillipe was as well, and he was not afraid to say so. Or show it! Without hesitation, he moved his chair even closer and took my hand.

The absentminded circles he was drawing on my palm with his index finger while we talked were incredibly sensual. The light touch left a host of sensations in its wake that made their way up my arm and spread throughout my body. Soon, the sexual tension inside me grew to such proportions that I was starting to have difficulty concentrating on his words!

His eyes never left mine during our conversation. At times, I felt like I was drowning in that bottle-green gaze. Being with him in this manner felt just right, as if it was meant to be. Never in my life had I felt this drawn to a man, had my body responded to even the slightest of touches, had I wanted someone so fiercely. Now I understood the frantic matings that tended to happen on solstice nights like this! There was magic in the air, and I was not immune to its effects!

My desire for this handsome man at my table was over the top! It took everything I had not to act on it! I had been to many of the clan's celebrations over the years and had never felt that way! Not about anyone, not even Phillipe! So why now? What had changed to trigger this current between us?

And where was this going? Casual or sex without an explicit agreement of exclusivity was not my thing! However, I was just about ready to make an exception in this case!

Chapter 4

Summer King and Queen

Odd things were known to happen during the summer solstice celebration here at Ny Havn. Maybe we should not have played with forces we did not understand. But, Phillipe and I have always been curious. We had been absolutely fascinated by the strange phenomena. He and I just could not help investigating and got caught up in the moment, forgetting that actions during this night had consequences, some good, some not so. People have been healed from deadly diseases, and infertility has been reversed, even in some who had lost all hope.

Every year, a number of babies arrived nine months later, so one had to be careful! The kin believed the births and recoveries proved that the old ways were still the best. Evidently, the event and the clan were blessed by the Gods! As long as we all celebrated these special occasions together, just as our forefathers had, things would always turn out well!

Also, giving the deities their due was a great excuse to really let loose, especially since most of those present were family!

During our experiment with that current flowing between us, a special bond formed between Phillipe and me. Without us realizing it, fate had declared us mates, and it would not be denied. Utterly oblivious to this development, we continued to chat. After a while, we went down to the dance floor and joined the throng of bodies writhing to the music. To my astonishment, I began to really enjoy myself. For the first time in many, many years, the summer solstice celebration was turning out to be fun!

When we had danced enough, we grabbed plates of food and an unopened bottle of wine. My parents had drilled into my head not to drink anything else here. You never knew what had been added! Since the night beckoned us, we found a quiet spot under the trees near the creek. It was just perfect for a picnic! Phillipe had even thought to bring a blanket, and we settled in once we had spread it on the soft ground.

While eating, he regaled me with some of the mishaps which landed his clients in trouble or had happened to him. I loved that he managed to see the humor in most of his daily interactions! And, Phillipe had a way of presenting the tales that was just plain fun. I don't think I have ever laughed so much in my entire life!

How much I had missed his company! Being around him was just as wonderful as I remembered. Or maybe even more so with this new electricity crackling between us! It added an entirely new dimension to our relationship! At the time, I attributed this to us being young adults with certain natural urges. And neither of us was immune to the sexual tension in the silky night air all around us!

Since this was often the case during these solstice celebrations, I did not think much of it, even if it did seem more intense than usual. However, if I moved too close to Phillipe or him to me, it did increase to a rather uncomfortable level! Since we are empaths and especially sensitive, I figured that the carnal undercurrent wafting about was affecting us both.

In any case, we had eyes only for each other. Neither of us was interested in the goings-on around us. Every time Phillipe looked at me, and our gaze met, I felt a stab of such desire that it was rapidly getting hard not to act on it. When the temptation to run my fingers through his hair, touch him, kiss him, and more became too great, I suggested we rejoin the party in the mead house, the rebuilt sair.

Phillipe, realizing that I was getting uneasy, immediately agreed. This erotic tension between us was all new for both of us. Quickly, we packed up the remains of our meal, folded up the blanket, and set out toward the hall.

The way back was definitely interesting and quite educational! I am no prude and was by now used to these kinds of shenanigans, but still, some of the activities of the couples we walked past made me blush from head to toe! But, it also increased the fire in my blood and in his! The desire to step behind the next bush and let nature take its course was gaining more power over both of us by the second! But, Phillipe respected me and knew this was not like me.

So, to defuse at least some of the growing sexual charge, he started making whispered comments about the more unconventional and inventive antics we caught sight of. Some of what he came up with was so hilarious that I struggled not to bust out laughing right then and there! Even the memory brought a smile to my face. Phillipe had such a talent for lightening the mood!

'Treeburn' was only one of the remarks he came up with that night, but it would stick with me, especially since he uttered it with such seriousness. Every time the words popped into my mind from then on, they would conjure up a vision of this adventurous pair's frantic efforts and unusual positions. Neither of us had seen anything like it, and we exchanged an incredulous glance.

Who would have suspected that one could have sex that way! Phillipe and I were so fascinated that we stopped to watch for a few minutes. And we were not the only ones! The spectacle was utterly mesmerizing! They had to have been into gymnastics or yoga to achieve such flexibility! There was no way I could contort my body like that!

Eventually, the show came to an end, and we moved on. By the time we reached the sair, my education in the art of lovemaking had been expanded considerably!

At the mead hall, things had also gotten louder and wilder. Some more inebriated couples were going at it wherever they could find some slight concealment. Or not. One pair did not seem to care at all who watched. He had her up against the wall and was pumping away. Good thing all the kids had been put to bed! The action around here was definitely X-rated! That was one of the reasons that the little ones were having a supervised sleepover in the cottages furthest away.

My mother usually set up a magical barrier that kept the children from sneaking back to the party. Unlike some of our other celebrations, this event was not suitable for minors. Or outsiders, for that matter! Not surprising with spirits flowing so freely! For many, inhibitions had long since dropped away. Since this was their night to let loose, they were taking full advantage of the occasion.

Having already gotten an eyeful outside, Phillipe and I moved toward the middle of the hall. There, things seemed to be a little tamer. After finding an ample enough space, we easily fell back into the familiar pattern of our own steps and style that we had developed when we were younger. That we had not danced together in a couple of years made little difference.

We had so much fun that we stayed on the floor until we were practically dripping with sweat! We finally decided to head for the table with refreshments. Just as Phillip and I were weaving our way out of the throng, we heard the next tune begin. Boy, was I glad we were no longer out there! That song was rather bawdy, and the dance extremely sensual. If we had taken part in that, my precarious self-control might have teeter-tottered right off into oblivion!

As it was, with all the sexual goings-on around us, my state of arousal was already higher than usual. It would not take much more to tip it over the edge and for me to give in to my attraction to the handsome Phillipe! The touch of his hand in mine was electric, sending tingles all through my body. I could have pulled away, but we would have lost each other in the frantic melee. So I let him lead the way and followed behind in a bit of a daze.

After some searching, Phillipe and I located a couple of drinks we deemed safe. A few minutes later, we went back to dancing. Since it was so crowded, we stayed close together and ignored everyone else. Neither of us wanted someone to cut in. All our attention was on each other. It felt natural to be together, comfortable and right. As best we could, we ignored that out-of-control desire flowing between us.

I was glad I had drunk sparingly and was still mostly in control! Making love that night was not something I intended to do, no matter how tempting! I wanted this new feeling between Phillipe and me to blossom, to grow over time. If we were going to enter into a relationship, it had to be built on a solid foundation so that it would last. If we had sex right now, I would no longer be able to be as objective as I needed to be. From past experiences, I had learned that this was something to be avoided.

In addition, knowing myself well, I had no desire to give my body casually, not even to someone I had known most of my life. For me, exclusivity was a non-negotiable requirement. Agreeing on such a thing was not done in one night, at least not in my book. I wanted wooing and the fun and excitement of a real courtship first. We had talked about this, and Phillipe understood.

He was willing to respect my wishes. Unfortunately, our pairing off had not gone unobserved.

Finally, the time came to elect the summer king and queen. The horn was blown to call all those enjoying themselves on the grounds back to the sair. Once everyone was assembled, the ballot box was placed on a table in the center of the room. Phillipe and I cast our votes for a couple spectacularly dressed in perfect Highland fashion, which our clan had adopted ages ago to fit in. The two were stunning, and we expected them to win. How could they not? They looked amazing!

Phillipe and I were dressed smartly, but nothing like these two! But he did look very roguish and handsome! His loose, white linen shirt was covered by a dark grey, superbly tailored vest ornamented with silver stitching. The semi-tight black pants perfectly set off his splendid physique and accented his tight rear and long, well-muscled legs. Shiny, knee-high boots rounded out his ensemble. His hair was ruffled from all the dancing, but I thought he looked just beyond tempting.

I was wearing a long cream-colored underdress with a dark-green silk overdress decorated with bands of silvery moons around the front, neck, and arm-holes. I had several such gowns, but this one was my favorite. Moon-shaped emeralds, surrounded by diamonds, sparkled on my ears, and the matching necklace showed off my slender neck. The embroidery on my beautiful shoes had the same theme. I loved this pair since they looked perfect while still being comfortable!

I knew we looked great, but nothing like the couple we had voted for. Those two deserved to win after all the effort that had gone into those gorgeous costumes! Expecting this as well, they were already sidling toward the stage. Therefore, Phillipe and I were more than a little stunned to hear our names called. This was completely unexpected! We exchanged an incredulous look.

How could we have won when the competition's outfits outshone ours by a mile? Besides, they were much better suited to represent the clan this night! Before we could object, however, Phillipe and I found ourselves surrounded by a throng of people. Quickly, we were pulled along to separate rooms.

The laces of my bodice were undone with alacrity. I was still stunned by this turn of events and stood there in a daze. My dress and undershirt were slipped off before I could even protest. Then, my bra and underwear followed in rapid succession. Giving me no time to grow self-conscious, I was pushed down on a table. Amidst much laughter, perfumed oil was massaged into my body by several of the ladies. Some got awfully close to sensitive places!

Once I was sufficiently anointed to fill the room with the heady smell of roses, I was guided to a chair in front of a mirror. One of the women brushed out my hair and pinned it over to one side. Another renewed my makeup, using the most gorgeous shade of pink I had ever seen on my lips. Being pampered like this was really something! Next, a sheer linen shift, somewhat too see-through for my taste, was pulled over my head.

After some last-minute touch-ups, I was hustled out the door and over to the dais to stand beside Phillipe, dressed only in a loincloth. It was then it truly dawned on me what was to come. Everybody was really getting into this, and any protests would have done no good. Anyway, after getting a good look at the Summer King's well-muscled form, I was unable and unwilling to voice them.

Seeing Phillipe practically naked had tipped the scale too far. One look had been enough to chase all rational thoughts right out of my head. We had desired each other already, and only my self-imposed rules had prevented us from stepping behind some hedge and giving in to the attraction between us. Now, those objections lost all importance. Pure, hot need filled me, and I could not take my eyes off him nor he off me. The effect my bare body, covered only in the light material, was having on him was rather noticeable.

We just stood there staring at each other. Finally, gentle hands turned us around to face my father. Did he have anything to do with this? I eyed him suspiciously. In response, he gave me a guileless smile. He appeared a little drunk and none too steady on his feet. That reassured me. If he was inebriated to that point, he probably was not plotting! But with him, you never knew. He would do anything if it benefitted the clan or our family!

I was distracted from that train of thought by our kin clapping rhythmically and calling our names. It was really quite loud in the hall, and the feel of the place was different than a few minutes ago. It seemed that the seductive charge in the air had intensified, had become even more powerful. This further heightened my want for Phillipe. I assumed that the wine I had consumed earlier was to blame for all this. What else could it be?

Not being sober, however, made it easier to play along. Still, I would have run if I had been up there with anyone but Phillipe. He suddenly wrapped a possessive arm around my waist as if reading my mind. In a way, this was comforting. But it also made me wonder if he had picked up on my thoughts of flight and wanted to keep me here with him. To reassure him, I moved a little closer to him.

The next thing I knew, he was squashing me against him rather tightly, increasing the sexual tension between us even further!

Distracted by Phillipe's nearness, I waited for the crowning ceremony to begin. Usually, my father officiated, but he stumbled over to one of the tables. I guessed he had imbibed too much and wanted a cousin, Doug MacPherson, to take his place. I only vaguely remembered the man. It seemed that this fellow was rather straight-laced and seldom joined in with the drinking. Also, I did not believe that he attended the fetes very often.

Most likely, he was the only sober person left in the room! After a brief discussion, the new officiator made his way up to the dais with a steady step.

Chapter 5

A Different Sort of Ceremony

Doug's arrival on the dais was greeted with thunderous applause. The assembled spectators had been growing impatient. As much as they loved the summer king and queen crowning, all these delays kept them from some of their own fun. As expected, the drinking continued. But, some were anxious to get back to some of those more private activities that had been temporarily put on hold for the ceremony.

"Good evening, Magnuson Clan, and welcome to our annual summer king and queen celebration!" Doug MacPherson shouted.

A roar of approval greeted his words. Finally, things were moving along! Then, the hall grew expectantly quiet. Pushing himself between us, Doug grabbed one of my hands and one of Phillipe's. He raised them high.

"I present to you Cara Magnuson and Phillipe Mackay, our duly elected summer king and queen!"

Loud cheering followed his words.

"Let the ceremony begin!" the cousin announced.

Stepping back, he took a goblet from my dad, who seemed to have decided to assist despite being inebriated. Doug handed the cup to me. I raised it to my mouth, intending to take only a very small sip. However, my father managed to bump into the chalice at just the right moment. As a result, I ended up swallowing a large mouthful. I was so surprised that I almost choked. Had this been on purpose?

The glare that I shot my offending parent was greeted with an unrepentant smirk. Now I knew I was in trouble! What was my father up to? Was there something in that wine? Before I could figure it out, Doug drew my attention back to the ongoing ritual. Taking the goblet from my shaking hands, he handed it to Phillipe, who had not missed what had happened.

The observant man looked at me questioningly before raising the cup to his lips. He was not about to go through with this if I did not want to.

I realized that Phillipe would get me out of there that instant if I so desired. That warmed my heart, and I gave him a grateful smile. Had it been anyone but him, and had he not given me the option to flee, I might have walked off the dais, regardless of the consequences. My parents, naturally, would have seen this as a major embarrassment and would have been pissed! But I would have stood my ground, especially after my father so glibly forced a good amount of that liquid down my throat!

Phillipe's eyes met mine over the rim of the chalice. I gave him a subtle nod to let him know it was okay to proceed. Only then did he take a drink. With a gesture that brooked no refusal, he handed the vessel back to MacPherson, the master of ceremony, who passed it on to my dad without hesitation.

Doug kept watching my father with a frown on his face. For a moment, I got the impression that he was somewhat puzzled and not at all that happy about something. However, when he turned back to Phillipe and me, he was smiling again. My mind was beginning to feel a bit fuzzy, but this still struck me as odd.

With that first part accomplished, Doug placed our hands together. Then quick as can be, he tied them together with a red ribbon.

"My lady, do you give your body, heart, and soul to your king?" he addressed me.

"Hey, those are not the words!" someone yelled from the back of the hall.

Quickly, some others shushed him. Things were finally moving along, so let them proceed! But he was not the only one muttering that something was off.

"Everybody does the rites in their own way! Let him proceed!" my father shouted back, squashing any further comments.

"My lady, do you give your body, heart, and soul to your king?" Doug repeated the question.

Feeling flustered and a bit dazed all of a sudden, I barely comprehended the words. So at first, I did not answer. Alarm bells were clamoring in my brain, but I perceived this and my surroundings as if through a fog. For some reason, I could no longer think clearly. But, even then, it registered that something was not quite right. Finally, it dawned on me. The phrasing was quite different from what it should have been! Was this due to a personal preference, or was there more to it?

Not even my father glaring at me got me to comply, so I looked up at Phillipe. That, however, was my undoing. The desire and affection on his face were plain to see. This sent such a wave of longing through me that I was speechless for a few seconds. With a sense of wonder, I met his gaze. The next thing I knew, I felt like I was drowning in those gorgeous green eyes. The world around us ceased to exist. There was only he and I.

A moment later, without any conscious thought on my part, I distantly heard myself saying:

"I do."

"Do you, our Summer King, accept this lady as your queen? Are you willing to let her into your heart and soul and promise to honor her?"

"I do." His answer came without hesitation, his eyes never leaving mine.

"I give you your Summer King and his wife, the Queen! Meet Cara and Phillipe Mackay! You may kiss the bride!"

A roar greeted his pronouncement. I was too distracted by the handsome man before me to pay those words much attention. All we saw and heard were each other. Phillipe moved toward me as if drawn by magic, and his mouth claimed mine. I let out a moan of pure yearning as he pulled me tightly against him. Something hard pushed into my stomach, making me want him even more.

As our tongues engaged in an intimate dance, my attraction to this handsome man continued to grow. The current sparking between us was different from the one we had played with earlier, much sweeter but also more powerful and much more heady and seductive! The dice had fallen! This force of nature brewing between Phillipe and I would not be denied!

The loud clamoring of our kin barely even registered as the kiss fanned the flames of fervent desire between us.

The entire ritual had been different from the ones the years before. But at that moment, I did not care. When the awareness managed to push its way into my mind, I chased it away by attributing the variation to Doug having a different style from my father. For some reason, however, the notion that it reminded me vividly of the handfasting rite still used occasionally to join two people together kept intruding. Well, this had just been for fun. It was not like it was legal. Or was it?

I was not sure and too far gone to work it out since I seldom touch alcoholic beverages. The two bottles of wine Phillipe and I had shared had already dulled my senses, but I had downed several glasses of water since. Somehow, that last drink had made things much worse. My father had been here on the dais, and I did not think he would let me come to any harm. So, how could I suspect foul play? Maybe the wine they used for this ritual was just exceptionally potent!

But, however much I tried to ignore it, something continued to niggle in the back of my mind. It was desperately trying to get my attention time after time. Unfortunately, I was too intoxicated by the wine and the delicious sensations sweeping through my body to pay attention. Phillipe's nearness was setting my body on fire!

His gorgeous eyes regarded me hungrily when we finally came up for air. We both knew what the inevitable outcome of this situation would be. Neither of us minded one bit. We craved each other to a point that was all new to me. Since we had been officially pronounced a couple, he pulled me even closer. My entire being responded to his nearness by sending such a wave of need through me that my knees threatened to buckle.

All of me was totally focused on him. The heat of his bare skin penetrated the sheer shift in an instant. I gasped softly. Hearing that, Phillipe's eyes turned dark with desire.

Watching his handsome face and noting his reaction was the final straw. I was done for! I could hold back no longer. Pushing hard against him, I raised my face to his, not caring who was watching. I was hungry, starving for him, and I wanted him now! Just as Phillipe lowered his head to claim my lips again, I caught a brief glimpse of my mum wiping away tears. More alarm bells started ringing in my sex-addled brain, enough to give me pause for an instant.

This was just too odd. My mother was not the emotional type! There was no reason for her to react that way to a mere summer king and queen ceremony! Women cried at weddings! If only I was not so befuddled, I could figure this out! Then, Phillipe's tongue exploring my mouth drove all rational thoughts away before I could further explore these concerns. The sensation of detachment, floating, and unreality also grew more intense.

More than ever, I could feel his hard length against my stomach. All my concentration wandered toward that insistent throbbing. My focus now was entirely on his member. After a moment, I realized that my parts were pulsing in sync with his. I wanted, had to have him inside me to quench this insane heat. It felt like it was going to consume me, burn me alive! I had to do something to get some relief!

Therefore, I started climbing Phillipe like a tree.

Somehow, all our inhibitions had dropped away. Desire so intense that it would not be denied drove both of us. The strength of the need for each other left us breathless. Our audience had been completely forgotten. Wrapping my legs around Phillipe's waist, I began rubbing against him. He was holding me up, guiding me to where it felt best. I could feel him pulsating against me, separated only by the thin cloth. Urgently, I moved up and down, eliciting a frustrated moan. The shift was in the way, preventing his ingress.

He wanted me as badly and as eagerly as I wanted him! Was his blood burning like mine? His eyes told me all I needed to know. Never in my life had I experienced something like this before! I am my folk's daughter. We keep our emotions in check and are big on privacy! Usually, I am bubbly but also calm and collected. I am the figure of decorum they expect me to be and appropriately restrained when in public! This was not like me!

My subconsciousness was screaming at me at this point. Snap out of it! Something is wrong here! But, all the warnings were in vain and never even penetrated the fog shrouding my brain. At that moment, I wanted this man in front of me so badly that I did not care who was watching! I was ready to have him right then and there, in front of the entire clan and my folks!

Vaguely, I noticed my brother arguing with my parents whenever I caught a glimpse over Phillipe's shoulder. The next thing I knew, my outraged sibling cold-cocked our father. I saw this clear as day, but none of this actually registered or took my attention away from this gorgeous man in front of me for more than a few seconds. All higher-level thinking seemed to have turned off, and only base instincts remained. The urge to mate superseded everything else!

Had I been able to think, I would have realized something was wrong. Neither Phillipe nor I would have ever behaved like two animals in lust. That was just not like us! Had I been sober, I would have been completely appalled at this display of public wantonness on my part! And, I would have run for the hills! Instead, I continued rubbing against Phillipe like a horny cat, increasing our need.

Who knows what would have happened had we not been separated just at that moment! With much laughter, we were pulled apart by our kin. Neither Phillipe nor I were pleased with this development, but our protests fell on deaf ears. Instead, we were picked up by some of our more strapping relatives. A bawdy procession, making all kinds of lewd comments, carried us to the lovingly decorated suite that had been prepared for the Summer King and his Queen.

On the way, someone pushed something into my hand and told me to sign it. I obeyed without conscious thought or paying attention to what I agreed to. My entire focus was on that delicious man, and my eyes were glued to Phillipe. He was the object of this insane, primal hunger, and I ached with a want that was totally new to me. All I could think of was taking him inside me, time after time, and riding him hard.

In the suite, we were deposited on the large bed. This was done with much hilarity. Those lovely cousins of ours counted down before turning us loose on each other. The second he was free, Phillipe reached for me. I met him eagerly, slid against him, and started pushing my body against his. This spurred him on, and I moaned as his hands roamed hungrily over my slender body.

Determinedly, he made his way to the sensitive area between my legs. I arched up when he made contact, inviting him to slide inside me. I was so fully in the throes of passion that I was totally unconcerned that others were still in the room. Opening my legs wide, I allowed his fingers to explore me through the thin cloth. The sensation was so delicious that I could barely lay still, especially when he pulled the shift up to my knees and moved down so that his mouth could access my sweetness.

Those of our relatives who were left in the room barely managed to shut the door behind themselves before Phillipe yanked the thin gown up to my waist. I raised up to help him. Stradling me, he pushed against me, despite his urgent need, asking for permission to drive his member inside me. Unable to form coherent words, I ground against him, encouraging him to penetrate me, to claim me as his.

I screamed his name as he slid inside. Placing my hands on his tight rear, I bore down hard to pull him in deeper. His moan turned me on beyond all reason, and I started shifting beneath him. I wanted every last bit of him, all his glorious length. Frantically, we moved together, him pounding inside me harder and harder. Finally, blessed release washed over us, and Phillipe collapsed on top of me, his head buried in my hair and his shaft still inside me.

We stayed that way for a few minutes, but then Phillipe turned his face just enough so that he could get to my neck. Seductively, he ran his tongue over my flushed skin, and I shivered deliciously. This seemed to encourage the lusty male, and he aimed to increase the effect. Therefore, he began to alternate between licking and sucking. It did not take long for my whole body to start vibrating with renewed need. I began arching beneath him, inviting him to take me once again!

But he was not quite ready yet for another round! Pushing against me almost regretfully, he watched his flaccid member slide out. Laying down next to me, he supported his head with one hand while his fingers found their way inside me. Phillipe watched my face with fascination as he moved his digits in and out or rubbed them across my most sensitive areas. Whatever elicited the most response was what he focused on.

The sensation was so overwhelming that I needed to touch him to keep from going insane. His shaft jerked at the first contact, and I wrapped my hand around it. Picking up the rhythm he was setting, I started squeezing and releasing while Phillipe continued to stroke and tease. As the sweet torture he was subjecting me to ratcheted up the pleasure inside me, my hold on him became almost a lifeline.

His groans told me when I grabbed him too hard. Not wanting to hurt him, I tried to maintain better control. But it was difficult to concentrate on anything except the sensation of him doing such enticing things to my body! His ministrations took me higher and higher, and before long, I exploded again.

Trailing his wet digits over the glistening skin of my flat stomach, Phillipe playfully drew first small circles, then larger ones. His light touch was the perfect combination of almost tickling and seductive. My body responded instantly to those incredibly sensual strokes. A wave of heat accompanied the contraction of my vagina. Then, to mix things up a little, he began kneading the insides of my thighs.

I rested, my head on his forearm, soaking up all this attention and enjoying the sensations raging inside me. It had been a long while since I had been intimate with anyone, and being with Phillipe was like nothing I had experienced. The chemistry between us was out of this world! Every touch elicited such a delectable sensation that it sent rays of delight through my entire body! Wanting to return all this pleasure in equal measure, I leisurely allowed my hands to explore his muscular form.

Before long, this turned into a game. We copied each other, then tried to best what the other was doing. Phillipe won, hands down. His butterfly touches all over my torso just about drove me mad. My body arched, and my head was thrown back as he let his fingertips do their magic. I gave myself over to the delicious sensation, but then my desire to have the real thing inside me put an end to the playing.

That time, however, we proceeded a little bit slower and less frantic. We explored what felt best until we climaxed once more. But, that was not the end of it! All night long, we touched, teased, and made love. We pleasured each other time after time. The passion between us was so all-consuming that it eliminated all rational thought.

Only when the first rays of dawn found their way into the room did we finally fall into an exhausted sleep. We were still wrapped around each other from our latest round of lovemaking, unwilling to let go, to put distance between us.

The morning was beautiful, bright and clear. I woke up sometime around 9:30 AM. Phillipe's arms were wrapped so tightly around me that I could not move. My face was pressed against his chest, and I was firmly held fast against his bare front. After a moment, I noticed that something hard was between my legs. This sparked instant desire. When I wiggled just a little in the hope of bringing him inside me, I realized just how sore all that activity from the night before had left me. I might be willing, but my parts needed a break!

Phillipe woke up when a soft moan of pain escaped my lips. He quickly realized that he was not in much better shape. We were both pretty raw from all that sex! So, instead of making love again, we cuddled for a while. But, that seemingly unquenchable fire between us ignited once more. It burned brightly, demanding action of some sort.

Was this just our chemistry, or was something more to this? Never in my life had I been so out of control, unable to hold back, to resist my partner. My need for Phillipe was overwhelming! He felt the same about me! This frantic, fierce craving was something utterly alien to both of us. We were behaving like we had been given a massive dose of some aphrodisiac! My father would not dare, or would he?

That thought faded away rather quickly in the face of my ravenous desire. But when Phillipe slid inside me, the pain was more than either of us could bear. Thankfully there were other ways to delight one's partner! Working his way down my body while leaving a trail of kisses and licks, he gently pushed my legs apart. Expertly, he used his tongue to drive me to insanity and then release. At least that did not hurt quite as much!

Once he had taken care of me, I did the same for him. I took my time, teasing him, driving him so wild that he was squirming on the bed, moaning with pleasure. I loved it! Just watching him in the throes of passion and being able to give him such pleasure really turned me on. I had to be careful not to aggravate things, but this was doable.

Even before he exploded, I had already reached the point where I needed his attention again. This was not normal!

Eventually, we had enough, or so we thought. Getting cleaned up in the bathroom sparked yet another round of careful ministrations. I was highly perplexed. We were behaving like animals, our urge to mate all-consuming! What was up with that? I was extraordinarily attracted to Phillipe, but that did not explain our intense craving for each other to the exclusion of everything else! We had not yet eaten, so we were decidedly hungry by the time we finally made it out of the bathroom.

Imagine our surprise when we discovered someone had been in the room while we were in the shower! They had placed coffee and a few croissants on the nightstand. Also, our clothes had been left on a chair. Staying some distance apart to minimize this magnetism, we quickly got dressed. It would be safer to have a few layers of material between us! Then we made short work of the hot beverage and delicious pastries.

The mead hall was still quiet when we opened the door. Most were likely still asleep or passed out from too much drink. It would be a while before breakfast was served, and we were hungry now! But, on the other hand, this was the perfect opportunity for us to slip down the back stairs! Something inside me wanted to get as far away from this place as possible. And quickly!

What had happened the night before? I had only vague memories of the ceremony and what came after. The ones that finally emerged were somewhat fuzzy but clear enough to mortify me. Had we really behaved like that? I knew that the king and queen got rather bawdy, but to that extent? How could I have cast off every last bit of restraint and acted this way? A display like that, in front of the whole clan! How was it possible that my parents had not interfered and put a stop to that?

The more I thought about it, the more I realized something was seriously wrong here. What I remembered of the event was too unlike me! I had been raised to behave like the perfect lady, always! Until now, I had been the 'good' example for all the other young women of the kin! I was so embarrassed that I did not want to run into any of my relatives at that moment or anytime soon! Phillipe seemed to feel the same way. Hand in hand, like a pair of ghosts, we slipped through the building and out to the parking lot.

We had one close call, but in the end, we got lucky! Phillipe and I let out a sigh of relief. We understood each other only too well. We needed time to work out what exactly had happened. Since it affected us both, we decided to head to my house and do so together. Using the other vehicles as cover, we made it to our cars without meeting any of our kin. When I drove away, I felt like a weight lifted off me.

I was relieved that we had made it out of there without being roped into something or another the 'summer king and queen' were supposed to attend to. And without having to act like nothing unusual had happened the night before. Neither of us had felt like dealing with our folks or the lewd comments that were sure to be tossed our way. As usual, the celebration would culminate with a scrumptious breakfast and maybe even a light lunch. After that, people would start heading home.

As hungover as I expected most of them to be, they would not miss us. As long as there was food, coffee, and tea to be had, life was good. We were not the first pair to get away successfully the next morning and take themselves elsewhere! Besides, I was not sure if I could be civil to my parents. They had witnessed the ritual but had not interfered when things got out of hand. They should have!

To be honest, I felt betrayed. What kind of world was this when you could not trust your own folks to look out for you?

Phillipe followed me to my cottage. We worked together to fix breakfast since we were starving by now. This time, however, for food and not each other's bodies! After a substantial meal, we crawled into my bed, mainly to sleep. At least for a while!

Chapter 6

A Coming Together

My mind emerged from the memories of that night long ago. I was sitting on the side of the path, my arms wrapped around my legs. Tears flowed freely down my face, and I could not keep them from coming. The sadness I was feeling at that moment was too overwhelming, too all-encompassing. I missed my husband so much that it caused me severe physical pain. Not being able to cope with such agony, I allowed the events that followed that fateful summer solstice night to unfold in my mind.

To my delight, Phillipe settled in with me at the cottage. He did not return to London two days later as he had planned. Instead, we took a vacation right there in my home. We talked, cuddled, made love, and went for long walks with my dogs. The more time we spent together, the less we liked the idea of being parted. The feeling of belonging, being safe, and being able to talk about anything without being judged was so very precious to us. Phillipe and I felt extremely lucky to have each other. We wanted more and could not bear for our togetherness to end.

Once we reached my house, Phillipe and I started to relax. We were still reeling from the events during the solstice celebration. We remembered more as the hours passed and compared notes. By that evening, we had arrived at the only possible conclusion: there had been more than wine in the chalice we had been handed! We suspected that someone had added a powerful aphrodisiac. That explained why it had tasted a bit off!

Until that night, I had always believed that the couples elected summer king and queen had been play-acting for the clan's entertainment. But now I knew better! They had been under the influence just like us! Those parties were always wild. But for someone like Phillipe and me, who tended to be more conservative even then, being so out of control due to being drugged was a shock!

My father had been right there. He must have known that there was something in that wine! And, he had made sure that I took a large swallow of the stuff. That pointed to my dad having been in on the whole thing! To say I was furious with him is putting it mildly. He was lucky if I ever spoke to him again! Had my parents not raised me to be all lady? Expected me to be perfect at all times?

How could a strict and rather stuffy upbringing like that prepare me for participating in such a ceremony? Phillipe had also never attended a ritual such as that. We would have preferred it if the attraction between us had been allowed to flower naturally, without coercion. But there was no sense in crying over spilled milk. What was done was done.

Our growing attachment and the continued, almost magnetic attraction to each other made me wonder. What was so different about this cousin beyond that he was so unlike the rest of the family? For one, Phillipe was one hundred percent his own man. He worked for the clan's business but on his terms. Since we had been childhood friends, I trusted him completely. I had kept all others at arm's length since my last relationship but had allowed him right in. I could not explain it, but being with him just felt right! But why?

The answer evaded me, something that I found unsettling. But, after stewing about it for a bit, I decided to go with the flow. As the week went by, I opened up to Phillipe more and more. We had some honest, deeply intimate conversations whenever we managed to make it out of bed for a few hours. I loved that he could accept me just as I was and me him.

Also, our sexual chemistry was really something. I could not resist Phillipe, not for a moment! That man set my body afire time after time and still left me wanting more. Even without an aphrodisiac. Good thing that the feeling was entirely mutual! And that we were once again best friends. Except now it was on a much closer level than ever before.

All we had to do was look at each other, and we knew exactly what the other was thinking. That was almost more incredible than the animal magnetism between us!

When the inevitable parting could not be avoided much longer, Phillipe grew unusually quiet and rather withdrawn. I left him to his contemplations and worked on the book, having learned long ago to never follow a man down the rabbit hole. Doing that was the perfect way to drive him away! If he required space, I was secure enough to give it to him. Being needy or clingy was just not me.

The past had shown me that things would always turn out the way they should. And it helped that I firmly believed that what was meant for me would never pass me by. Was I a little anxious? Sure! But I made sure to meditate on that and to surrender to the Universe instead of stressing about Phillipe and my relationship. Later that afternoon, I took the dogs down to the beach. We had a great time playing fetch. The salty air and the sea wind blew all my worries away.

Before too long, we saw a familiar tall figure heading our way. My dogs, Maxine and Sweetie, greeted him enthusiastically. Phillipe led me to a sheltered nook and pulled me close. The next thing I knew, he was making love to me with an urgency I had not seen since the summer solstice! Good thing that we had the beach to ourselves, but the sand got into everything!

Once we were sated and our clothes restored to some order, we cuddled up close together, watching the restless waves. Phillipe's thoughts were far away, but he was holding me close. As usual, I very quickly succumbed to the mesmerizing effect the sparkling sunlight on the water had on me. There is nothing like it, thousands of diamonds shimmering on the sea. In my opinion, that has its very own magic!

After some time, Phillipe cleared his throat. I turned to look at him expectantly.

"Sweetheart, I do not want to leave, but I have to. I have pushed my work off as long as I can. Would you be agreeable to moving in together? It would make getting together so much easier!" he asked me expectantly.

The happiness I felt at that moment must have shown on my face.

"It would certainly be much more convenient," I agreed teasingly.

"Is that a yes?"

"It is," I responded with a smile.

Phillipe's mouth descended on mine, and he kissed me with such ardor that I suggested returning home. I needed a shower and some desanding before any more lovemaking was going to take place! Ultimately, the wait and continued building of that sexual tension between us added something extra. We ended up spending a very long time in the bath, and my legs felt like limp noodles by the time we were done.

That evening, over a leisurely glass of wine and a delicious dinner, we talked more about our plans. We had known each other so long that we mostly agreed on how best to achieve them. After the last week together, I genuinely looked forward to cohabitating with Phillipe. Neither of us liked the idea of being separated by such a long distance. Getting a place together was undoubtedly the most elegant solution!

London and my home near Gairloch were too far apart for our liking! It was impossible to reach each other without a lengthy trip, making it difficult, but not impossible, for Phillipe to drop by for a weekend. Since I could work from anywhere, Maxine, Sweetie, and I ended up spending a lot of time in London. That was a whole new experience for the dogs as well as me!

When Phillipe and I were apart, we talked every night, sometimes for hours. We liked having the phone next to us and going to sleep together. And, naturally, texted each other first thing in the morning! I was in love like never before, and it felt amazing. Especially since my affections were returned in the same measure! All that happiness had me floating on cloud nine; he was always on my mind.

Missing each other rather severely when we were not together, we were both in a rush to find a place. And Phillipe was growing more and more tired of his life in London. Before that fateful summer solstice celebration, he had kept himself busy. He had taken on so many cases that often he was so busy that there was no reason for me to stay with him. Besides, I had a house and garden to care for, and I missed my little sanctuary after a couple of weeks of all that hustle and bustle. The dogs were not overly fond of city life either; they were used to running loose.

To speed things up, we did some extensive house hunting on the internet. We wanted to settle somewhere where we could sail and hike, with a climate that did not get too hot or cold. But, at first, we had a hard time finding just the right spot.

All this changed when I had a dream that gave me a new story. After writing it down, I got on the internet to find the locations of the events I had been shown. One was definitely Gairloch, but the other? It was harder to pin down until, totally by chance, I came across the Isle of Arran. While perusing the local website, the image of the magnificent mountain on its main webpage immediately spoke to my heart. This looked like a place where I would love to live!

From the pictures, the place was just plain beautiful. The more I researched the island, the more I wanted to see it for myself. If nothing else, for the book. Having been there, I would be able to describe it much better. When Phillipe called me late that night, I shared my discovery with him and gave him a brief outline of the new tale. From his voice, I could tell he was tired but also so intrigued that he continued asking questions. I loved him even more for being so interested in my work.

Wanting to hear about his day, I finally changed the subject. I inquired about what was happening at the office. Phillipe had good news himself. He was making progress with wrapping up his latest big case! So that he could fully concentrate on the proceedings, I had gone home to my cottage. Anyway, with all the preparations he needed to make for their days in court, Phillipe would not have had much time! He was so relieved it was over and that they had won.

Since he really missed me, Phillipe decided that we should go on vacation to celebrate. So he immediately booked our lodgings on the Isle of Arran for a week later. The next morning, he told his secretary to clear his calendar. We could both hardly wait! When the day finally arrived, he came in from London via plane and train.

Since I love driving through the Highlands, I took the A9 down from Gairloch. We had agreed to meet at the resort where he had made our reservations if one of us was running late. But, I made great time as did he. Therefore I waited for him at the ferry dock since I arrived just a few minutes before he did. I was still amazed that it worked out that way! So often, it is hard to calculate just how long a trip will take!

As the ship neared its destination, we got our first look at the island that was to become our home. Phillipe had his arm around me and was just as excited as I was. Arriving there together made it so much more special! In absolute awe, we stood near the bow and watched the Isle of Arran come closer. The pictures had been magnificent, but the reality was even more so! Even Maxine and Sweetie seemed to approve!

The next day, we went exploring. Since we had my car, we were able to go all over. The more we saw, the more we fell in love with the place. The island just felt right, to both of us. By early afternoon, we had made our decision. A local realtor was only too happy to show us some available houses that day! The third one we looked at was just perfect for us. Phillipe talked me into buying it on the spot. Everything was coming together like it was meant to be!

Our move-in date was five weeks from then. To be honest, I was a little surprised that Phillipe was so quick to decide on a place so remote and different from what he was used to. He had been in London for several years now and was well-established there. Since he worked for the Magnuson Clan mostly remotely, this allowed him to have other clients. He had seemed happy there.

I decided to bring this up since I did not want Phillipe to move somewhere for my sake where he would not be happy. I loved him too much for that. As it turned out, he was more than ready to leave the city. Having a soft heart and no woman in his life, he had taken on way too many cases. He confessed that he would be only too happy to sell his share of the practice to his partner and let him continue the business.

Phillipe had plenty to do looking after the clan's enterprises. Wanting a life beyond work and some freedom to travel, he also intended to cut back on that. He had put aside money for years, and I had inherited a tidy sum from my grandmother. Between us, we had more than enough savings, so we might as well have some fun!

The move would not affect my circumstances very much since I was already living in the Highlands. Phillipe's, however, would change drastically due to our purchase. But, he was as excited as a little boy about the whole thing! I found this incredibly endearing. He could not wait to start our life together and settle in our new home. I realized he had loaded himself down with so much to keep busy. Getting together with me had major league shifted his priorities.

The minute we signed the paperwork for the house, he started thinking of ways to extricate himself from his current situation in the city. At the time, a good part of his handling of the Magnuson Procurement Company's legal concerns was done online. However, he would still need an office nearby since he did not want all his assistants in our home. Wouldn't you know it, but it did not take us long to find one? It had just become available the day before!

Soon, we had it all settled. When I asked Phillipe if he was absolutely sure about all this, he opened up more about his feelings. When he had first moved out of the Highlands, he had liked London. Growing up around Gairloch, he had enjoyed all the excitement of a city that size. But, even before we became a couple, he had started getting tired of it. He did not like all that traffic and missed the beauty and clean air he had grown up with.

Besides, Phillipe liked that the Isle of Arran was several hours closer to the Magnuson lands. We could drive up to Gairloch together and combine business with visiting our families. Since he had no intention of being gone from our new home more than he had to, he considered pulling out of London altogether. I would have never asked him to do this, but I was glad all the same.

In a way, the move made good sense and came at the right time. Over the last couple of years, the affairs of the Magnuson Clan had demanded extra attention. The focus of Phillipe's practice had therefore shifted. Some of the matters had required his presence, and he had to make the long trip to Gairloch more often. This, in turn, had forced him to put his pro bono work on the back burner or pass it on to his partner.

Phillipe had one case he needed to finish but intended to have it wrapped up within the next few months. His office and his personal employees, however, could move before then. Since MPC had long tried to entice Phillipe to live closer, they had a standing offer for housing for him and his people. And workspace. After electing to live on the Isle of Arran, this suddenly sounded very tempting. He decided to take them up on it.

This would give him two offices, but he only needed his secretary and a clerk for the one near our home. The rest would work in Ny Havn. He hoped most of his employees would choose to leave with him, but they were city folk. The Highlands were very different from the glamor of London! If they wanted to stay, Phillipe was sure his partner would be happy to have them.

Caring about his staff and wanting to provide them with job security, Phillipe made their hiring a condition for the sale of his part of the practice. That way, everything was laid out plainly and above board. Hearing him talk about all this was a real insight into his inner workings. And, he even asked my opinion! To say I was hooked is putting it mildly!

After five magical, wildly successful days on the Isle of Arran, our vacation was at an end. Phillipe returned to London. He still had much to think about and more decisions to make. I drove back up to Gairloch, taking my time. I had a discussion coming up that I dreaded.

In a way, it was funny how confronting my folks still made me feel like a child!

Chapter 7

Shocking Discovery

When I informed my parents a couple of days later that I was moving, I expected fierce opposition or at least a lecture about renigging on my responsibilities to them. After all, I had agreed to show up at their functions. To my surprise, I got neither. However, they were not particularly thrilled when they learned about my new home's location! Still, after some token resistance, my folks offered to send some cousins over to help me pack. Now that I had not expected!

My parents' congenial behavior instantly made me suspicious. This had been way too easy! What were they up to? What was their motive for being so nice? It is sad when one cannot trust their folks, but I knew mine too well. Something was going on here that I was not privy to. But what? Being in the dark made me uneasy. This was my life, and I was determined to find out!

Maybe it was time I looked into why Oliver cold-clocked our father at the summer solstice celebration. My brother had been evasive when I had brought up the subject before, but for him to hit someone, especially our parent, was more than a little out of character!

My car was parked in front of my folks' manor-like Ny Havn home. As I was getting ready to get in, one of the kin called my name. The elderly woman hurried up the circular driveway to chat with me. My heart sank. This cousin was known for being a gossip, and I was sure she had been waiting for me. I knew what was coming and was on high alert. One had to be very careful what one said around this one! She was always fishing for something she could spread around!

It was a relatively long driveway, and cousin Bertha was rather rotund. Huffing and puffing, the woman eventually reached my vehicle. The delay had given me enough time to put Maxine in the backseat of my car and hook her in. She was usually very well-mannered but could not stand this particular individual. Neither could Sweetie! Good thing that I had left him at home! Maybe they picked up on my dislike of this shrew? Phillipe thought that likely, and he was probably right.

As Bertha gasped for air, I waited patiently for her to speak. I would have met her halfway, but Maxine had spotted her and had started growling ferociously. She is a Doberman and usually as sweet as they come. In this case, however, I was not sure if she would remember her manners! My priority had been securing her since I did not want her to threaten or bite the cousin.

Once the dog was in the car, for a moment, a tiny instant, I had considered driving off. But that would have been rude, and that was just not me. I believed Bertha had to be very lonely and unhappy to need rumors to make herself feel important! As it was, she lived all alone. These days, she kept an eye on things from her window. I had seen the glint of her binoculars as I drove down the main street.

Coming all this way was most likely more exercise than she had gotten in months, and I eyed her with concern. Her face was red, and her chest heaving! Quickly, I opened the back of my RAV and bid her take a seat. This was far enough away from Maxine to be safe. Bertha accepted this gratefully and, once she found her voice, started to regale me with the town's latest news. Not that I cared, but I paid attention anyhow. Sometimes one could learn something from her, even if it was only how to be patient!

Eventually, Bertha maneuvered herself onto her feet. Relieved, I thought that she was finally ready to move on. The cousin said goodbye, then took a few steps toward the street. Suddenly she hesitated. The trek ahead of her had to be daunting! The road was a long way off for someone like her, and I considered offering her a ride home. She was really too out of shape to go very far!

Just as I was about to speak, she turned back and innocently asked where my husband was and if we would live in Ny Havn. For a few seconds, I was too stunned to respond. Husband? Then it dawned on me that she must mean Phillipe! I am sure my face spoke volumes because Bertha tottered down the long driveway with a very satisfied smirk on her face! At that moment, she vividly reminded me of a Cheshire Cat!

So that was what she had been after all along! Phillipe and I were a couple and had been elected summer king and queen. But my husband? Where had she gotten that idea? That tidbit on top of my parent's reaction was an interesting coincidence! The lady had not even made it halfway down the drive when I stopped my vehicle next to her. I smiled politely and mentioned that Phillipe was in London. Divulging that could not hurt.

Unable to help myself, I offered Bertha a ride. She was only too happy to accept it. I felt sorry for her but good thing that she did not live very far! She had a beautiful home and plenty of money but no one to share it with. She had been married long ago, but he had died. The couple never had children. Bertha, with all her wealth, was all alone in the world. I thought that was rather sad. But I was still not inclined to reveal more information.

That we were moving in together was none of this busybody's concern. Pulling up her driveway, I stopped in front of her house and got out to help her out of the car. The disappointment when I drove off with just a friendly goodbye was clearly written on her face. Was it only because she did not learn much, or was there more to it? Maybe I should check in on her on occasion! She was a second cousin and family, even if she was nosy and somewhat annoying!

Still, I sighed in relief once I was on the road to my cottage. Bertha required a tremendous amount of tolerance. And a nimble mind to stay ahead of her trick questions! But she was a master at collecting information and always had the town's pulse. I suspected she knew more of what was happening than my parents and their friends in their ivory towers! My mind was racing. What did the old lady know that I did not? She was very shrewd. Had her question been a hint?

Had more than Phillipe and I remembered happened the night of the solstice? Pulling over, I shut off the car. I needed to think this through and might want to return to Bertha's to ask her some questions. Getting into a meditative state, I went over what I recalled of the events of that night. Could the wine alone account for all the holes in my memories? I had not had that much to drink! Blacking out like that had never happened to me before! Nor to Phillipe!

From what I had heard, some date rape drugs prevented recall. But we had been among our kin! It had been a wild party but no different than the years before. However, I was sure that there was a good reason my parents had advised me to never drink anything at the solstice celebrations that did not come in a sealed bottle. Therefore, something added to the wine in addition to the aphrodisiac was well within the realm of the possible.

My recollection of that night had so many holes! Try as I might, I could not fill them in! Things got really fuzzy shortly after I took that gulp from the chalice. Vaguely, I remembered signing something while we were being carried to the suite. But mostly, the events after the kiss were dreamlike and blurry. It seemed my body had been a mass of such intense need that making love to Phillipe had been the only thing on my mind!

That brought me back to my behavior that night. Never before had I coupled with anyone during one of the celebrations! I was highly selective when it came to sharing my body and very picky with whom I went on a date. Losing control like that, even with someone who turned me on as much as Phillipe did, had been totally unlike me.

Phillipe had been no better. What all had been in that wine? I remembered feeling the effect very quickly. It had to have been a substantial dose to work so fast! My father would not allow someone to drug me, or would he? But then again, he had bumped me rather conveniently! As a result, I ended up with a large swig instead of the tiny sip I was going to take!

The summer solstice was the day of the year when most of the kin got together. The clan's account paid for the food and drink, and there was always plenty. It was the one occasion when our people could really let loose. Some were known to spike their beverages. Having seen how out of hand things could get during the celebration, I was always extra careful. I had no intention of accidentally ingesting something that would wrest control over my actions from me!

Drugging others without their consent was not allowed, even if the old customs got to rule for a night! But that did not stop people from imbibing themselves and letting go of conventions. For some, having wild, passionate sex was part of the fun. That was one of the reasons few strangers were ever allowed to attend. The later it got, the more the inhibitions dropped, much like during the pagan festivals of long ago! Who could blame my kin for having fun?

The weather in late June was usually perfect. That time of the year, the night air felt like silk on one's skin, and the moss was soft and inviting. There were plenty of hidden places to sneak off to all around the mead hall. Those convenient spots did see a fair bit of action. Just as in ages past, children tended to be born about nine months later, even to couples who had been trying in vain.

Honoring the old Gods seemed to bring about many blessings, which helped to keep the custom alive. The hotel was closed for the week before and the one after. Only invited strangers were allowed in or near the village during that time. Even if most of those having sex were partnered, their uninhibited behavior might still meet with some fuddy-duddy's disapproval. Therefore, it was best if the word did not get out exactly what happened during these celebrations!

After all, we behaved perfectly well the rest of the year! The monthly full moon ceremonies were open to all, our equinox parties were relatively tame and public, and the winter solstice festivities were family oriented. In December, Havn was just magical and a huge tourist attraction. Everything looked very festive with all the snow softening the lines of the ruins and the houses. Some of the pictures I snapped after a fresh snowfall are now sold as postcards!

The summer solstice, however, was all ours. I had chosen long ago not to participate in some of the activities. As part of the deal with my folks, I had agreed to be there, but that was it. Therefore, my behavior that night was totally out of character for me. Also, the sexual hunger Phillipe and I had felt for each other had not been natural. It had taken until the next day for it to reach a more normal level! By that time, both of us had been in pain.

For the past few weeks, I had been so happy that I had not dwelt on negative things. My embarrassing behavior after the summer king and queen coronation had been something my mind had shied away from. But Bertha's words had hinted that there had been more to the ceremony than Phillipe and I were aware of. She had called him my husband. Could that be true? If it was, my father had to be behind that! Would he dare to marry me off without me knowing?

I considered this for a few minutes and concluded that he just might! Maybe it was time to take a close and more objective look at that night! I went into a deep meditative state that I hoped would help me remember more details. Determinedly, I brought up everything that I could recall. As a result, my suspicions were not allayed but increased! The memory of signing a document on the way to the suite was vague, but it was there. That was not part of any crowning ritual that I had ever witnessed! What had that been all about?

Needless to say, I turned the car around and made my way to the Magnuson Clan Archives. Thanks to our competent leadership, it was very well organized. Usually, you can locate any desired paperwork quickly and easily. I had no problem finding the pertinent folder and started going through it. At first, I discovered nothing out of the ordinary. All that was in there were the no-liability forms that all those attending the event had signed.

My instincts, however, prompted me to keep looking. I could sense that something was hidden here and that it was important. It was just not where it should be. I trusted my senses; they never stirred me wrong. If they said something was there, I would continue searching until I found it! Therefore I checked in all the sleeves around that folder. I found nothing out of the ordinary pertaining to Phillipe and me.

But I am tenacious. If my gut told me that a clue was here, somewhere, then it was. It was just a matter of thinking like my father. Where would he hide something he did not want me to see? I decided to try the personnel section. I looked in my folder, then checked Phillipe's. Nothing! Where else could I look? I pulled out my parents' file, but it was not there either. The logical approach was not working; it was time to use my magic!

I recalled as much as I could about the document I had signed. Holding the image in my mind, I moved my hand over the outside of the first of the many file cabinets in the room, top to bottom. Then I moved on to the next and the one after. I kept going, hoping to detect something, anything. If that piece of paper was here, I was sure my magic would find it!

The certificate was not among the festivity records. Nor was it with the files for the clan members or hidden in the personal files for the business side of the clan. That left the shelves containing the Magnuson history and other odds and ends. Why would it have been placed with those? That made no sense! Maybe the document had not yet been filed and was in my father's desk? Or in the clerk's office? The possibilities were endless!

For a moment, I was just about to despair. I sank down on one of the chairs and put my head in my hands. Frustrated tears were welling up in my eyes. I needed some answers! After all, this was my life! If my father had interfered somehow, there would be hell to pay! He had no right, none whatsoever! I was a legal adult! Furiously, I glared at all the well-maintained file cabinets and shelves. If only I had a baseball bat! I was angry enough to do some real damage!

Rage washed through me, and the desire to take some sort of destructive action was almost overwhelming. I visualized dumping all those folders on the floor in one huge, disorderly pile. But, that really was not me. Since I had been forced to help out here one summer, I knew how much work went into this impeccable organization! Undoing that would not hurt my father but the clerk responsible for the filing! And whatever kids could be roped in to help clean up the mess!

I needed to get my temper under control before I did something I would regret! Kicking off my shoes, I grounded myself to the earth and centered myself. I slowed and deepened my breaths, then found the location in my body where I could feel the rage. As expected, the tightness in my neck and shoulders was out of this world! Putting all my attention on that area, I stayed with the sensation until it released and ebbed away.

It took me a few more minutes to calm down all the way. I realized that I was also afraid, so I acknowledged and stayed with that until the knots in my stomach dissolved. Determinedly, I entered a state of surrender. Suddenly, now that I was more receptive and not hampered by emotions, the sense that the piece of paper was in this room grew to a certainty. Fine, I would keep looking!

With renewed resolve, I eyed the history section. It spanned an entire side of the room, reached from the floor to the ceiling, and consisted of thousands of folders. This was indeed a daunting task! The method I had used on the file cabinets would not work here; I needed a different plan! Maybe, to start with, I should find out what shelf the document was on and then work on pinpointing the exact location? That would most certainly speed things up!

To my surprise, I detected a faint vibration when I reached the third shelf from the bottom. I could not help but feel a sense of incredulity but also of renewed fear now that I was getting closer to the truth. Moving my hand up and down, I confirmed my finding. Slowly, I walked along, trailing my fingers over the files. The sensation was strongest toward the middle, so after making it all the way to the other side, I returned to that section and worked on narrowing down the number of folders by defining the endpoints.

The section between the slightly pulled-out files I used to mark my efforts grew smaller and smaller. Finally, I was down to three records. I hauled them out and laid them on the floor side by side. I got down on my knees and tested each. One vibrated stronger than the others, so I concentrated my efforts on it. Leaning back against the shelf for comfort, I started going through it page by page. Eventually, I located an envelope that had to contain the paper Phillipe and I had signed. I did not even have to open it; I just knew.

Why had it been misfiled so far away from where it should have been? For what reason had it been hidden? I was sure that it had been done on purpose. The clerk was not this incompetent! The envelope was addressed to some distant cousin, but the name told me little. All this was very mysterious, and now that I finally had the document within my reach, I felt rather apprehensive.

I wished Phillipe could have been here with me, but maybe it was best if I saw this first. I was almost afraid to get verification of what my father had done. A few minutes passed before I steeled myself and dared to pull out the page. I took a deep breath, unfolded it, and looked down. One glance was all it took for my suspicions to be confirmed. Even though I had suspected this, it was still hard to believe!

The certificate was witnessed by my father and mother and signed by the cousin who had conducted the ceremony. Maybe he was related to the person whose name was on the envelope. From the appearance of it, it was all perfectly legal. How could they? How dare they interfere with Phillipe's and my life like this, rob us of free choice?

To say that I felt betrayed at that moment is putting it mildly. This was over the top, even for my heavy-handed parents. For quite a while, I just sat there, stunned. My mind was busy weaving all the information I had collected together. In light of this discovery, some of their recent behavior took on a whole new significance! No wonder my folks had been so nice and had not objected to me moving in with Phillipe!

I sat there, staring down at the document for a long time. I was absolutely furious. How could my mother and father manipulate us in such a way? We were both adults! I seriously considered returning to their home and confronting them. Of all the underhanded things to do! It would have been nice to have been given a choice in this, even if I was already very much in love with Phillipe by the time we had returned to the party!

If this had just affected me, I would have had an easier time accepting this affront. It took me a while to calm down, but eventually, I faced the fact that done was done. We were married! But I was determined we would find a way to undo this if Phillipe wanted out. I loved him too much to hold him to this against his will. He was a lawyer and a good one. If there was a loophole, he would find it!

That night, we had consummated the union. To my mortification, almost before the kin had left the room. Therefore it was perfectly legal. There was no denying that. But nobody liked being tricked! How would Phillipe react when I told him what my father had done?

Knowing his parents, I seriously doubted they had been in on this dastardly deed! Most likely, it had been all my folks! That my dad had planned this was perfectly clear. It was just too convenient that Phillipe's meeting in Ny Havn had been canceled at the last minute, allowing him to attend the summer solstice celebration! I did not believe in such coincidences, not where my family was concerned!

My parents knew how much I liked Phillipe and that we had been best friends growing up. He had been my secret first crush. My mother, an expert at noticing such things, had probably shared that juicy tidbit with my father. Since I had turned down all the son-in-law prospects they had sent my way, my childhood playmate must have suddenly looked good! After all, he had turned out to be an exceptional young man!

Fearing I would remain single forever, my dad must have decided to resort to subterfuge. He must have had it all in place long before the celebration! What else had he done? The connection between us when Phillipe entered the room had been instantaneous. Had that been his doing as well? I examined my memories of that scene more closely. After a thorough check, I concluded that, at least in that instance, no human influence had been at play, only fate's.

My father must have been watching us all night. I bet he had seen us slip out together and had congratulated himself on his plan coming together so beautifully! Here I had thought that he was too inebriated to plot something devious! How wrong I had been!

The switch to a different grandmaster presiding over the coronation ceremony, the wine spiced with a cocktail of drugs powerful enough to wipe out our memories and to not just lower but eliminate our inhibitions, my mother's tears - now it all made perfect, awful sense. I was so angry my entire body was vibrating with fury. Pulling myself together, I carefully laid the offending piece of paper on the floor and took a picture of it. My hands, however, were shaking so badly that it turned out so blurry that I had to do it again.

For a moment, I considered making the document disappear. Two could play this game! I could file it somewhere where it would never be found! Or retrieved, for that matter! Let the river wash it out into the sea! But sanity reasserted itself, and I remembered who I was dealing with. My father was always prepared! He would have considered such an eventuality. And, he knew me well enough to realize that I believed in a couple choosing each other knowingly and out of their own free will, not by trickery.

My dad's sneakiness, competence, and ability to anticipate the actions of others made him a great businessman. Everything my parents oversaw was highly successful. But, until that summer solstice, he had never turned those abilities on me. Having watched him, however, I knew just how carefully he planned. If I had thought for a second that I could get away with it, destroying this piece of paper would have been precisely what I would have done. But, he probably had another copy stashed somewhere!

Resignedly, I took the document over to the copy machine, almost tripping over Maxine, who had curled up next to it and had gone to sleep. Then, I returned the original to the envelope, stuck it in the folder, picked up all three files, and placed them back in their spot on the shelf. Not wanting my parents to know just yet that I had figured it out, I meticulously went over the room to ensure it was like I had found it.

What was I to do? On some level, I did not object to the end result of my father's interference, but having someone else make such an important decision for Phillipe and me was just wrong. That smudged and somewhat crumpled piece of paper would affect the rest of our lives! We should have had more time to get to know each other and the freedom to decide when and if to take this momentous step!

Good thing that I loved Phillipe! We were crazy about each other and were planning a life together anyhow. Still, it smarted that by clan law, that fateful solstice night, completely unbeknownst to us, he and I had not only been crowned summer king and queen but we had been legally married!

How was Phillipe going to react when I told him?

Chapter 8

Breaking the News

Once I stopped shaking with suppressed fury and had calmed down a little, I used one of the computers in the archive to check online. My father was always exceedingly efficient! In all his dealings, he made certain to leave no loopholes for one to slither through, at least if he could help it. A small part of me was still hoping to be able to destroy the document. But, sure enough, the marriage certificate had been officially filed with the local district! As I suspected, he had boxed Phillipe and me in most efficiently. It was difficult to stomach that he would do this to me, his own daughter. I saw it as a betrayal of epic proportions.

Tears started flowing down my face, and my whole body shook with gut-wrenching sobs. Maxine came over and pushed her head against my leg. I slid off the chair and wrapped my arms around her.

Holding her close usually helped me but not that time. I had to tell Phillipe what my father had done, but the mere idea was too much. As a result, my insides started to rebel. Everything I had eaten that day wanted out. I just barely reached the nearby bathroom before getting violently ill.

A few minutes later, with my stomach empty but my heart feeling just as heavy, I slipped out of the Magnuson Archive. The copy of the certificate, I shoved into the glove compartment. With getting so sick, I had almost forgotten it! Feeling rather morose, I put Maxine in the backseat. After buckling her in securely, I slid into the driver's seat. For a bit, I sat there, my head in my hands. Pulling myself together, I started the car and headed for home.

It was almost time for Phillipe to call me. How would he react? I could not blame him for being angry and feeling entrapped. I most certainly did! We were both victims of foul play, but my parents, not his, had been the instigators. Thus, I was dreading the upcoming conversation. Had my father permanently damaged my wonderful relationship with this amazing man? If he had, I would never forgive him!

Figuring I would have a few more minutes and could at least make it home, I drove slowly through Ny Havn. But the connection between Phillipe and me had grown very strong. We could usually feel each other's emotions, even over a distance, but especially powerful ones! Those were like beacons! Therefore, I had not gotten very far when I heard the unique ringtone I had for him.

I almost threw up again right then and there! Phillipe must have sensed that something had happened and that I was terribly upset!

"Hi, love! Are you alright? I would have called you earlier, but I was in court until now!"

"You could sense that I was upset?" I asked him with a sense of wonder.

"Yes, and it took everything I had not to storm out of the room and call you! What happened? Are you ok?"

I could hear the concern in his voice, and it warmed my heart, but the fear of losing him was so great that my hands started shaking.

"I have something to tell you, but I need to pull over first," I told him sadly.

"Oh, oh! That bad?"

"Yes, that bad!" I stated flatly.

The resignation to the worst possible outcome was clearly audible in my voice. How could I blame Phillipe if he never wanted to see me again after this debacle?

"Sweetheart, whatever is going on, we will face it together! You are not alone in this!" Phillipe told me reassuringly.

"Hold on, I see a spot where I can stop safely!"

After pulling over, I turned the car off and checked that it was locked. The area was safe enough, but still! Next, I engaged the emergency flashers. This would ensure that I was clearly visible on the dark country road. And it gave me another moment to collect myself.

"Ok, I am parked. Please, do not be angry with me! I had no idea!" a sob escaped me.

"Honey, I am not going to get mad at you! I love you! Please, tell me what has you so upset!" it took a few minutes for his soothing voice to calm me enough to proceed.

"Remember when we thought that the ceremony was different at the summer solstice?"

"Yes, it definitely was. So what about it?"

"For one, the wine might have been drugged with more than just the aphrodisiac."

"That would explain some things! I could feel the effects almost immediately!"

"Me too," I responded. "And I am pretty sure that my father knew about it."

"Maybe, maybe not. That chalice went through a few hands, love."

I had not considered that and had to concede his point. We had no proof that my parents had anything to do with drugging us. Phillipe and I had been so attracted to each other already that we would have made love even without chemical encouragement, just not as often. The marriage would have been valid one way or another.

"Well, that was not the worst of it. I am so sorry, but the cousin performing the ceremony is an actual clergy. The paper we signed …."

"Was a marriage certificate, wasn't it?" Phillipe stated calmly.

"Yes, it was. I am so sorry!" Once again, I started sobbing. "How could they do such a thing? They had no right to interfere! If you want to, we can fight this!"

"We are truly married?" Phillipe wanted to know, with a sense of wonder in his voice.

"Yes, registered at town hall and everything! I am so sorry!"

Phillipe let out a loud whoop! I was stunned! Now, this I had not expected! Was he actually happy about this? That was one reaction that I had not dared to anticipate!

"They took your right to choose …."

"Love, I agree, what they did was underhanded, but I cannot find it in my heart to be angry about this! I love you, and we are already moving in together!" Phillipe reassured me.

Then, something seemed to occur to him. He grew very quiet. Now it was my turn to sense how troubled he suddenly was and how apprehensive! But, before I could say anything, he spoke again.

"Are you upset about us being married?"

The question had been asked hesitantly, flatly, and without emotions as if he feared my reply. They pierced my heart. He was as scared of losing me as I was of losing him! This momentous question needed to be responded to very carefully! Obviously, he needed just as much reassurance as I had!

"Phillipe, I love you. I want to spend my life with you. I am just sad that the choice to decide this for ourselves was taken from us, from you!" I answered him gently.

"Ah!"

I could sense his relief and then a sudden resolve. At least he was no longer concerned about me hating the idea of being married to him!

"My sweet, I really wanted to do this in person," he said with a sigh. "But oh well!"

Phillipe paused for a bit to find just the right words.

"Sweetheart, I love you. Cara Marie Magnuson, would you please do me the honor of becoming my wife?"

I sat there for a minute, too stunned to answer. This caught me completely off guard. We had known each other most of our lives but had only been a couple since the summer solstice! All the tension that had built up in my system gave way to giddiness. He really loved me and wanted to be married to me! The happiness of the moment had me in tears.

"Yes!" I finally managed to push out, joy filling my heart as the answer left my mouth.

"I am so glad to hear that! You had me worried there for a second!" Phillipe joked.

"You made me the happiest woman in Scotland!" I responded with a huge smile on my face.

"I am delighted to hear that! But, we will do this again properly. I want my proposal to be something that you will never forget!"

His promise sent several ideas flashing through my mind. Some, however, were much less appealing than others. For one, I was still very angry with my parents. As far as I was concerned, I did not want to socialize with them any time soon! Phillipe knew me so well! He picked up on my apprehensions and laughed.

"Not too public, I promise! And away from Ny Havn! Also, if you do not mind, I would like us to have an actual wedding ceremony someday. Is that agreeable with you?"

"Phillipe, you wonderful, amazing man, I would love that!"

"Consider it done," Phillipe stated firmly. I could hear the smile in his voice.

"Where are you right now?"

"A few miles outside of Ny Havn."

"On that dark country road?"

"Yes."

"Hmmm. Are you feeling better now? Good enough to drive home?" Phillipe asked me with concern.

"Yes, thanks to you," I assured him. "However, I am still mad at my father. He had no right to do this. I intend to give him a piece of my mind, and my mother too! I will not tolerate their interference in our lives again!"

"That I agree with. But, we will confront your parents together, my love," Phillipe stated determinedly. "You do not have to fight your battles alone anymore. You have me now!"

"Thank you, Phillipe! That means so much to me!"

"Now, please, make your way home. And call me as soon as you get there! I do not like the idea of you being out there all by yourself! Do you at least have the dogs with you?"

"Only Maxine," I answered contritely. "Sweetie got into the mud this morning and needs a bath before going anywhere!"

"I wished I was there with you, my love. Please get going and call me as soon as you arrive at the cabin, will you?"

"I will," I promised.

Starting up the car, I put it into gear and checked the road. No headlights in sight, so I pulled out cautiously.

"How far are you from home?" Phillipe wanted to know.

"About 10 minutes, love."

"I will be waiting for your call. Please be careful!"

"I will," I assured him and hung up.

I could not help smiling. Phillipe was determined to keep me safe, to protect me. I really appreciated that!

Personally, I did not mind driving while talking. But it worried Phillipe when I did so on these winding country roads, especially in the dark. His concern warmed my heart. Humming a happy tune, I expertly maneuvered my car through the tight turns. I had grown up here and was well familiar with the place. The biggest danger was the wildlife, so I kept a sharp eye out for the unexpected deer or other creatures. You never knew what could run into the road out here!

I was so relieved that Phillipe had taken the news much better than I had expected! Still, I felt terrible about the stunt my family had pulled. But I was also deeply grateful that my worst fears had not come true. That he would actually be happy about the whole thing had never even entered my mind! How many men would have been good with finding themselves married without their consent? No one else I knew of!

His love and forgiveness of my parent's manipulation were my final clue that Phillipe was my 'One.' And I was his wife, legally! That, to me, was really quite stunning! Now that the much-dreaded conversation was behind me, I relished the thought. I would keep my own name since that is what I published my books under, but maybe, just maybe, someday, I would add Mackay. I was so deeply in thought that I was surprised when I arrived at my home.

As promised, I called him as soon as I was inside. After talking to Phillipe some more, I was floating on cloud nine. But I was still upset with my father, furious, really. I had no intention of speaking to my folks for a while. Being as busy as they were, we did not communicate very often as it was. Most likely, they would never even notice. My parents and I would have words but at a time of Phillipe's and my choosing.

We moved to the Isle of Arran shortly after. My little cabin, we had decided to keep for now. It had been steadily increasing in value and was still going up. Holding on to it for a while longer made good financial sense. Also, it provided us with a place to stay that was independent of the company and my parents. We both felt this was a good idea, just in case Phillipe decided to work for someone else or the conversation with my parents went wrong.

Therefore we would leave it furnished, just like Phillipe's flat in London. We had a lot of fun picking out stuff for the house. Once all of it had arrived, hauled in, and placed, Phillipe, the pets, and I settled happily into our new home. Over the next few weeks, we met our neighbors and began our integration into the friendly community of the island.

Initially, my husband had to return to London a fair bit to wrap up his pro bono cases. But as the weeks went by and more and more of his business there was taken care of, all that changed. Instead, we started heading north to Gairloch more often. I would go with him on those trips to see my friends and to check up on the little house.

My parents, we avoided as much as possible. Neither of us was feeling that benevolent toward them. We did spend some time with my brother Oliver on occasion since he had not been party to the deception. Father had sent him on an urgent errand that night to make sure that he would not interfere. By the time my sibling joined us, the dirty deed had been done.

Phillipe and I would have probably gotten married eventually, even without my parent's interference. But I resented their actions. I felt forcing our hand had been wrong and a total Neanderthal move. Seriously, who nowadays would even think about doing such a thing to their daughter? Only my folks and some of their equally high-handed friends!

My husband finally convinced me to give my mother and father another chance. The four of us had a lengthy talk during which Phillipe and I established some firm boundaries with these two. I made sure that they understood that disrespecting our wishes would have consequences. The days of the chieftain deciding everything were long in the past, and it was time that they accepted this.

Strangely, we got along much better from then. Now THAT I had not expected! My relationship with my parents was warmer and more loving than ever. Standing up to them had gained me the respect I had always longed for but never gained while I did most things I was told. Who would have figured that? Not me!

Chapter 9

Wedding Times Three

That fateful summer solstice happened over nine, mostly blissful, years ago. Since the clan really likes a party and we wanted to repeat the vows our own way, and fully conscious, we had an official wedding a few months later. My mother and I arranged it together. Knowing this was one of her strengths, I accepted most of her suggestions. To my surprise, maybe to appease his guilty conscience, my father insisted on paying for everything.

As a result, the event got much grander and more involved than Phillipe and I had expected! Despite the many details that had to be addressed, the planning turned out to be much more fun than I had anticipated. My mother was cooperative, and we interacted peacefully. For once, she was listening and hearing me! That in itself was a miracle! We worked well together, and I got really good at delegating from watching her.

Since I had never been involved in organizing this size of an event, it would have been daunting without my mother. Had it been up to me, I would have been just as happy to have a small, private ceremony on the seashore. One day, when we were rushing from store to store, I wistfully shared that sentiment with her. We both knew that our standing in the clan came with a price. One did not always get to do as one wished. Quickly, I dropped the subject and did not think much more of it.

My mum, touched by my sharing that secret wish with her hugged me. She had gotten to know me well enough in the last few months to understand me much better. And I her. That alone was worth going through all the preparations. For the first time in my life, we were actually close! Phillipe and I had dinner at my parents' home several times a week when we were in Ny Havn. The four of us got along famously now!

That meant much to me and was the best wedding present of all! Even Oliver joined us on occasion, as did my husband's folks. Still, we were a little surprised to get a formal invitation from my folks for the night before the big event. My mother even had a dress sent over. It was magnificent! I immediately fell in love with the light seafoam-green creation of lace, silk, and tulle. Stars, moons, and sequins attached to the outer layer gave it a sparkle that appealed to the little girl in me.

This was a gown fit for a princess! It was absolutely gorgeous! As were the matching necklace and earrings, a gift from my father. We had no idea what to expect, but they had gone all out! Phillipe chose a superbly cut black suit with a white shirt and a light gray tie with flecks that complimented my dress. We took great care to look our best. It was the least we could do since my folks had gone through so much trouble!

We had just added the last little touches to our outfits when the limousine showed up to pick us up. Sedately, we were conveyed through the town, then past the turnoff to my parents' house. Soon after, we veered off in the direction of the seashore. We were heading for the beach house! Phillipe and I exchanged a puzzled glance.

The chauffeur helped me out of the vehicle when we arrived. No one was to be seen, but tiki torches lit the way down toward the sea. Since this was obviously the way we were supposed to go, we followed along the lightened trail.

When we rounded the corner of the cottage, and I caught my first glimpse of the surprise awaiting us, tears filled my eyes.

An arch decorated with flowers had been placed near the tideline! Phillipe's parents were standing near it, as was my family, including my brother and his new girlfriend! Cousin Doug was also waiting, dressed in a kilt with just a few special touches characteristic of the Magnuson Clan. My mother had not only listened and understood, but she had set out to make my wish come true!

Hand in hand, we walked toward the others. Once we had said hello to everyone present, we came to a stop in front of Doug, who had moved to the other side of the archway. He greeted us solemnly and, once we were ready, went right into a simple handfasting ritual. The fiery light of the torches, the silvery illumination of the moon, and the heady aroma of the flowers in the arch intermingled with the light breeze from the sea – it was magical!

The rite was beautiful, everything I could have asked for. I was incredibly moved by this thoughtful gift. My mother had truly heard me and had given me the ceremony dear to my heart. And not just mine. Phillipe was just as touched. To say our vows in a setting just as this had been our dream, one we had sacrificed for the good of the clan and convention. This meant much to us both and was truly special!

We had a lovely party afterward, just us and our families. After a delightful dinner together, we sat around and reminisced over drinks. Later that evening, my folks announced they were sending Oliver to the art school of his choice. My brother had been unaware of their plans and looked like he was about to faint. Then he jumped up and rushed to our mother and father to thank them. He was so excited and pleased that he hugged everyone else as well!

Oliver loved to draw and paint, and he was good at it. He had been prepared to work for the clan because that was expected of him. That he would be encouraged to follow his own dream was something that he had never expected! Phillipe and I were so happy for him!

The next day was the big event. Almost every member of the Magnuson Clan came to celebrate with us. Cousin Doug presided over this ceremony as well. Later, while making a toast to us during the reception, he joked that this was the first time he had married the same couple three times. I realized right then and there that this was significant! Numbers are important, especially things that come in threes! Without ever expecting or intending this, our union had been uniquely blessed.

An ornate arch had been set up on the dais in the mead hall, the sair, and the entire room had been decorated with flowers and boughs from the evergreen trees around Havn. My mother and her helpers had done a fantastic job. It looked just gorgeous! Rose petals had been strewn down the center aisle. Their delicate fragrance wafted up at me with every step. The effect was just enchanting!

For this ritual, we did things according to our age-old tradition. This event was more for the benefit of the clan than Phillipe and me. However, I had balked at stark white. Instead, I had chosen a wedding dress that was an absolutely stunning creation of creamy silk, lace, and pearls. It was strapless, leaving my shoulders bare. Formfitting to the waist, it flared into a voluminous skirt with some extra length in the rear.

My hair was held back by a sparkling tiara and allowed to tumble down my back in shining blond waves. My mother would have preferred a more classic do, but, at the time, I did not like putting that mass of locks up or confining it in any way. That changed once we got Bear and Hella Rose. Those two loved to cuddle. Having a large dog step or lean on the strands was just downright painful! Braiding it helped to minimize some of that.

After that little detour, my mind returned to the memory of the wedding. Phillipe looked incredibly attractive in his black tuxedo. He wore it well, and my heart just melted when I saw him. He had to be the most handsome man in the world! I did not have eyes for anyone but my husband that day or ever since and have never regretted marrying him, not even now.

As part of the ceremony, my father got to walk me down the aisle and present me to the groom. He did so with much aplomb and a huge smile for Phillipe. Then he took his seat in the front row of benches that had been brought in just for the wedding. I have always wondered what church they had been swiped from! They were very old, and the carvings were unusual but exceptionally beautiful.

My father actually beamed with pleasure! I don't think that I have ever seen him so proud! My mother cried, yet again, just as she had on the previous occasions. Once the ritual had been concluded, the magnificent benches were placed along the walls. To one side, a table was set up for the reception.

Once everything was in readiness, the cake was brought out with much pomp. It was an incredible piece of art! The three-tier creation was almost too magnificent to cut into! But Phillipe and I did our duty. We shared the first slice and then started passing out pieces. It tasted just as good as it looked! After some dancing, including the traditional Ceilidh, a buffet was set up, and we all took a break to eat that delicious food.

Everything was planned down to the minute, very stylish, and classy, and our kin loved the celebration! But then again, they did most parties! People continued to congratulate my mother on a job well done. Naturally, she adored all that praise. I did not mind. She deserved it for all the work she had put into this!

Phillipe and I thrived in our partnership. After a few months, he had concluded much of his business in London and was no longer putting in such long hours. Since we had enough money coming in already, my husband primarily worked for the Magnuson Clan. He had become highly selective about what outside cases he would accept.

Surprisingly, he ended up being in higher demand than ever before! This allowed him to pick and choose who he represented.

Being happy and content benefitted us both. It flowed into my craft. As a result, I was even more prolific as an author than ever before. The words streamed into my mind and sent my fingertips dancing across the keys so rapidly that, at times, it was hard to keep up. And, having Phillipe as my calming pole helped when I edited a story I had written. After all, how can my readers feel the emotions of the scenes unless I do while I am spinning the tale?

When we had moved in together, Phillipe and I had made the deal to always put each other first, before anything and everything else. I came before his job, and he before my books. With a few mutually agreed-on exceptions, we had stuck to this. It had served us well. We were best friends and still had amazing sexual chemistry, even after nine years. Until this awful morning, we had been extraordinarily happy.

Nothing could have prepared me for all this changing in an instant! There had been no hint of trouble, at least none I had noticed. I had believed that we had a solid relationship that would withstand the trials of life. How wrong I had been!

Chapter 10

A Strange Place

Sitting there on the path, I was utterly despondent. The life I had known seemed to have come to an end, and the sense of loss I was feeling was overwhelming. Phillipe and I had been in the worst fight of our marriage, one that had gotten really nasty, at least for us. I knew that some couples argued like this all the time, but that was not us. I was too sensitive for that, and such a thing affected me too deeply. My heart hurt, my stomach was churning, and my entire body ached.

Looking back, I clearly see that my emotions were out of proportion with what had happened! But right then, I was totally unaware of this fact! Huddling there, my nerves felt raw and frazzled. That stupid argument seemed to have brought about the end of my world. The grief I was feeling was tremendous. I could not imagine my life without Phillipe. He was my love, my rock, my security.

How had he gone from being a loving husband to someone who seemed to despise me in an instant? This had to have been brewing underneath for some time! How could I have missed that? Had I been so blinded by love that I had been unaware of my husband's emotions? I thought we talked openly and about everything? Had he truly been such a consummate actor?

These thoughts and others like them occupied me fully. They just kept coming. Had I been in my right mind, I would have never reacted to a mere exchange of a few ugly words to such an extreme. And I would have realized that something was really wrong with the entire incident to start with!

At that moment, however, I was close to hysterical. The security of a future with Phillipe seemed to have evaporated inexplicably. I felt utterly forlorn. Loving my husband so very much; I could not imagine my life without him. Even the thought of losing him hurt my heart. How could something that our goddess had blessed be torn apart so suddenly, so quickly? I just could not understand any of this, nor why it had happened.

Everything was off that morning. Very unlike myself, I had fled my troubles mindlessly. I tend to confront problems head-on. One of the reasons our marriage is so happy is because Phillipe and I continue to improve our conflict-resolution skills. Usually, I chose to work things out instead of running. That day, however, my fight-or-flight impulse was in full force, and all rational thinking was entirely absent.

Somehow, my thought processes still felt muddled and unclear. My pulse was racing, my head and chest hurt, and I could not concentrate. Every time I had an opposing thought to the panicked ones running through my mind, it would slip away before I could examine it closer. To my further annoyance, this very effectively kept me from getting a grip on the root of the problem! But, I tenaciously kept worrying at it, going over the scene again and again. I needed to understand what had really happened and why!

To do that, I had to change my state of mind. Nothing good ever came from riding the runaway train of hurtful reflections down that descending spiral. In that direction lay only desperation and pain. I needed to get off this crazy ride into the abyss! Determinedly, I concentrated on my breathing, bringing my mind back on task every time it tried to flit away.

Eventually, I was calm enough to look at things more objectively. I concluded that Phillipe's and my enraged behavior had been absolutely irrational and made no sense, especially when our dogs and guinea pigs had also acted oddly. They had been much more aggressive than I had ever seen them, just like us! I still had no idea what had caused this or why I was so terribly upset. Or why my senses kept telling me something was wrong and that I was in danger!

Nothing much ever happened on the Isle of Arran! It was a safe place! But, my training and experience had taught me not to ignore my instincts. Trouble was brewing; I just knew it. And, for once, it scared me. Life had been so easy and pleasant these last few years, with little adversity! I had become spoiled. Even on those rare occasions when there had been growth opportunities, Phillipe and I had dealt with them together, as a team.

We were a genuine power couple, and there was little that we could not handle. But without my mate by my side, I felt very alone and utterly lost. Had I had an inkling of what was being aided and fed by all these unhappy emotions running rampant in my mind, I would have found some way to stop them cold!

As I would discover momentarily, there was a good reason for my being on edge. I had walked through the wall of smoke, oblivious of its presence. At that instant, the damage was done, and the trap was sprung. I had kept going for a few more feet, totally oblivious that I was no longer on the path to the boat. Only when memories came flooding in full force had my feet stopped of their own accord. Suddenly weak, I had sunk down to the ground.

For the last few minutes, I had been utterly blind to my surroundings, seeing only those things of days long past. Eventually, however, an awareness that trouble was stirring trickled through, and

I jumped to my feet and looked around. Utterly astonished, I blinked, then rubbed my eyes. Was I seeing things? How was it possible that I was not on the path? And where exactly was I? What had happened to the forest, the houses? All the things that should have been there?

For a moment, I was totally perplexed. How could I have gotten lost on a track that only led to places I knew? I had been this way countless times! Never, not once, had I seen this place along the way! And, where was the sun? It had been shining on my shoulders just a little while ago! The slight breeze that had cooled my feverish skin was also gone. To top it all off, everything around me seemed weird and out of focus!

It took me a few minutes to come to terms with what I was seeing. This appeared to be an entirely new reality! And it was not a pleasant one either! In some ways, it reminded me of that old American TV show we watched occasionally, the Twilight Zone. Taking in all the weirdness had the hair on the back of my neck bristling.

Suddenly, I was afraid. If this place's appearance was an indication of things to come, they would not be good!

Everything around me seemed leeched of color, dark, kind of dirty, and unkempt. The scenery was odd and unwelcoming, eerie even. The path was still there, but it was no longer smooth pavement. I noticed it was now cobblestone pavement, broken in spots and with some disgusting-looking, slimy growth between and over some of the cracked blocks. And that was not the only change!

The more I took in, the surer I was that I was no longer on the Isle of Arran, but somewhere I would have preferred not to be. To my left, where the neighborhood homes should have been, was a dilapidated, white rail fence. It surrounded a sad-looking meadow with several emaciated horses. Those poor animals looked so skeletal that my heart went out to them. They seemed to be just barely alive and moved sluggishly. I feared that they could drop dead at any moment!

Right then, I made up my mind. If at all possible, I was going to find a way to help them! For the time being, however, there was nothing that I could do for them. First, I had to figure out what was going on here and where exactly I had ended up! Hopefully, they could hold out a bit longer until I was able to get them out of here!

Letting my gaze move on, I took in a driveway some distance away. The deeply rutted lane led to the remains of a small house. It was in terrible shape! The poor thing was in dire need of a whole lot of maintenance or, alternatively, a tear-down! The roof was missing shingles and had several large, gaping holes. It had to leak something fiercely! That was if it even rained in this strange place!

And that was not all! Several of the windowpanes were broken, and a couple of the frames had shifted and deformed. The mottled and cracked front door hung at an angle. There were signs of long-standing neglect everywhere, and most of the paint had long since flaked off. A few remnants of it were still visible in the more protected spots on some of the boards. It was a sad sight! That little dwelling had most certainly seen better days!

The state of the place made the one sign that someone might live there even more incredulous. Greasy, greyish smoke was issuing forth from the chimney! The odd plume drifted down and snaked its way low across the field. The horses were as far away from it as they could get. That alone was suspicious. When I focused on the haze, I realized that it was not only surprisingly dense but, judging from the consistency and the color, a purplish gray, it was not natural.

This was a clue and required further investigation. Carefully, I extended my senses out toward this miasma. The closer I got to it, the more I felt an aversion. This stuff was spawned by magic! Curiously, I let my eyes rove over the unpleasant spell-generated smoke. Only then did I realize that it was completely immobile, hanging in midair like it was frozen in place. I was stunned and took a closer glimpse at the sad-looking pasture.

Now that I examined it closer, I noticed that besides the almost imperceptible movement of the unfortunate animals, nothing else was in motion here either! The tall, sickly, yellowish grass stood stock still! Not a blade wiggled or waved! How had I missed this the first time? I must have been really dazed! Good thing that my head appeared to be clearing!

Being in some sort of almost stasis did not bode well for helping the poor horses! Even being in such a sad state and so thin, they would be too heavy for me to move easily! Nor was I sure I could even get near them with the spell on the meadow! And there was no way to tell from here if they were real or part of the landscape. Finding that out would require getting in there, and I was disinclined to do so any time soon!

Thoughtfully, I regarded them for a few minutes. I decided that when the time came, I would have to use magic to fetch them. Maybe once I had more information, I could devise a plan, but for now, I would have to leave them where they were. That went so against my nature! I absolutely hated to see something suffering and would have preferred to resolve the issue this minute!

But I had to figure out what I had gotten myself into first. Sadly, I turned and took stock of the rest of the scenery. Further down the path, a short distance beyond the driveway, was some sort of fog. It was so dense that it made it impossible to see any further. Did this extend all the way around? I verified this by checking beyond the house. The scenery faded out just about the same distance away!

The border of thick, white mist added to this strange place's eerie atmosphere. It made it seem like this bizarre world just came to a stop there! I could even see that haze above me! That distinct cloud appeared to be the limitation of this mysterious, enchanted space! Suddenly, something occurred to me. This reminded me of being caught in the center of some spooky snow globe! That observation made me shiver since it did not seem far off.

Having established the boundaries, I investigated further. An old orchard was located to my right. It gave me the creeps. Dirty, yellowish, roiling vapor was completely concealing the ground. The trees themselves were spindly and oddly shaped. Each one was gnarled and heavily covered in moss, indicating they had been there a very long time. They reminded me of people frozen in weird, painful, contorted positions. The effect was quite disconcerting and very unsettling.

My imagination as a writer was in full gear by now, which was not necessarily good! Looking at all the shifting, swirling fog, I would not have been surprised if it hid all kinds of awful creatures lying in wait for the unwary! I made up my mind right then and there. If I could possibly help it, I was not about to set foot into that terrifying grove!

Looking around once more, I examined everything in more detail. This was definitely the strangest place I had ever seen! What had I walked into in my stupor?

As I stood there taking it all in, suddenly, the ground shivered, almost knocking me off my feet. Lightning crackled overhead, and I heard distant thunder. Then, everything around me became transparent and diffuse, like it was disappearing into thin air. I crouched down, panicked, making myself as small as possible while also being coiled like a spring, ready for action. I was prepared to defend myself if I had to. No way was I going down without a fight!

After a few seconds, my surroundings came back into focus. I let out a breath of relief. It appeared I had survived whatever this had been, but it had been peculiar! When I thought back on the sensation, I realized it had felt like a wave of some kind had just passed through this horrid globe. For an instant, it had made my surroundings appear even more unreal. Or had I seen what was actually there? Could all the backdrop be fake?

Could this entire scenery, or at least part of it, be an illusion? Eyeing the unpleasant landscape around me, I weighed my options. I could leave the pathway and find out for sure. But, everything in me screamed that doing so would be a giant mistake. In this instance, I was only too happy to heed my inner senses. Besides, none of what I saw made me want to explore.

Actually, the idea of setting foot into that ghastly, roiling fog of that loathsome orchard seemed downright stupid! That revolting miasma blocked out any view of the ground! Who knew what was underneath it! Once again, I let my gaze play over this appalling vista. It appeared downright menacing in some spots. This place was wrong on so many levels that it had my senses on high alert. The path seemed to be the only safe space.

Then a thought struck me. Was it purposely designed to keep one on the trail? Somehow, this seemed right! Now I was curious and decided to examine this notion further. I applied the scientific method to the situation and came up with a working hypothesis. If I was right, this place was meant to keep one on the walkway and herd one into two specific directions, almost like a TO and FROM!

Looking back to where I had come from, I took stock of what lay behind me. It seemed that I had walked only a short distance after crossing the barrier before my memories had brought me to a stop! Had that been the intent of this dreadful globe? Maybe so! This was a place created by magic. Could it have benefited from all those negative thoughts and emotions? Maybe even fed off them?

My gut told me that I was onto something. Once again, I shivered. I had walked in easily, but could I get back out?

Where I had entered this nightmare, the peculiar, unmoving smoke extended across the footpath and beyond. Great! It effectively created a barrier that would have to be crossed to reach what lay beyond. Not a thought I cherished!

Home, however, was on the other side! There was no way to avoid it. If I was going to figure this out, I had to take a closer look!

Chapter 11

A Need for Information

Resolutely, I made my way toward the plume of thick smoke. I stopped just about a foot away. Carefully, I bent forward until my nose was within inches of the mysterious haze. Very cautiously, I took a brief sniff. That is all it took. I backed away immediately. Hazel! As I had suspected, this was witchcraft! Was I trapped in this enchantment, or could I leave? That would be the next thing I would have to ascertain!

It would be foolish to jump to conclusions without knowing more about this globe-like place. What I had seen so far, was that the full extent of the spell's environment? Or was there more? I would have to experiment and investigate further to find that out, but first things first. Would I be able to return to my home by walking through the cloud of smoke? Somehow that seemed too easy and out of character for this place! I had a niggling suspicion of what I was dealing with and was hoping with all my heart that I was wrong!

I could have kicked myself as I stood there regarding the barrier before me. The crisis in my relationship had put me in such a stupor that, despite being trained in such things, I had walked right through a cloud of hazel smoke! What kind of idiot does that? I could only shake my head at myself, feeling utterly incredulous and totally exasperated with myself. How could I have been so oblivious? I knew better than that!

Then, something occurred to me. Had my distraction and the fight been part of the spell? Without being in such high emotional distress, I would not have left home in the first place! Nor would I have walked through that haze! I would have seen it for what it was! And what easier way to achieve the ultimate distraction than causing a rift between Phillipe and me?

A threat to one's relationship was equal to an existential threat. It had hit me where it hurt the worst and had caused me to be extremely dismayed. That was enough to put anyone in a fog! I loved my husband! Just the thought of parting ways with him made my heart ache! Whoever designed this enchantment must have known a fair bit about psychology! They had used my affection for Phillipe against me! How could someone be so cruel?

Now I was no longer sad but absolutely furious. I vowed that if I ever got my hands on the person responsible for this, I would hold them accountable. I might just give them a taste of their own medicine! I stood there fuming for a few more minutes before it dawned on me that I also bore some responsibility. No one had made me walk through the smoke! I had done that all on my own, and I had run when I should have stepped back and thought first.

As a result of my carelessness, I was no longer in my own time and place. As far as I knew, this could even be a different dimension. In light of all this, the morning's events took on a whole new meaning. The spell caused Phillipe and the dogs to become aggressive and downright mean. On the other hand, I had managed to retain a modicum of niceness. This, in a way, had put me in a victim position and at a disadvantage.

Now, this actually made perfect sense. I had fled to avoid further ugliness and not wanting to inflict more damage on someone I loved. This had gone according to the incantation's design! Obviously, I was meant to end up here! And why only me and not Phillipe? That was something I needed to figure out. What had I ever done to anyone that they would want to harm me?

Or had this something to do with my parents? Obviously, I had been the intended target and not Phillipe. I hoped he had calmed down and that he, the dogs, and the guinea pigs were alright now that I was where I was meant to be. A strong feeling that this entire thing had something to do with the Magnuson Clan welled up in me. I let out a sigh. Since I seemed to be caught in this enchantment all by myself, it was up to me to figure out how to get out of this!

If only I had been able to avoid this in the first place! My senses had caused me to be so very on edge. That had played right into the spell's design by increasing my anxiety! My instincts had been trying to warn me but in vain. Under the influence of this malicious incantation, I had done all the wrong things! I had reacted instead of thinking and had run when I should have stayed put! How had I missed that something strange was going on?

The sudden aggression in all of us had been too out of character and had come on too abruptly to have been natural! I should have seen that! Under the magic's influence, Phillipe had attacked me verbally. His words had wounded me deeply. We knew each other so very well! It had been easy for him to hurt me enough to send me running mindlessly. How sad! We had forgotten that we were best friends!

That was not our usual way of dealing with each other! But, obviously, our spat had been orchestrated from afar by a vicious and devious mind. Hopefully, that awful fight had nothing to do with real trouble between my husband and me! That at least made me feel considerably better! And maybe there was aid coming from the outside!

By now, unless Phillipe was meant to come here as well, he must have felt the danger. Once he calmed down, he would immediately realize that I was no longer on Arran. Since I could not sense him, I was sure he could not detect me either. Poor thing! He must be utterly panicked! If only I could send him a message!

This situation was really unbelievable! With all my training and abilities, I should have noticed that our uncharacteristic behavior was due to an enchantment! But I had not, and that was that. Beating myself up about it was useless. Having clarified that, I wondered who could have done this. Could this be someone we knew? Or was the magic capable of finding the easiest and most efficient way to get the desired person into the trap?

If it was one of our friends, the person was close enough to us to be aware of what would trigger our darkest emotions and cause the desired effect. That, in itself, was highly disconcerting. In my mind, I ran over all those in our inner circle since they were the only ones privy to such information. I came up empty. No one stood out. So if it was not one of them, then who?

Could it have been a stranger? That felt right. You did not have to know someone intimately to cause them pain. When I thought about it, I realized that most people in a loving relationship would not react well when their marriage was threatened! That was definitely one of my weak points! Another was my pets. Those I loved almost as much! I was very protective over my little family and would defend my husband and them with my life if I had to!

Most other things I could handle, but losing Phillipe or them? Not so much! The spell had hit me where it hurts, and a lot of power and malice had gone into its creation! But who would do this? And for what reason? I quickly discarded the possibility that it had anything to do with my husband's court cases. On occasion, someone did get angry when things did not go their way due to his brilliant representation of his clients. But most of those individuals did not have access to magic! And it just did not feel right.

Try as I might, I could not come up with anyone who might have a grudge against us. Phillipe and I were careful how we treated folks. Regular people and those with the gift! We worked hard to be fair to everyone we did business with, and we loved our friends! Offhand, I could come up with only a couple we might have offended over the last years and none that we had hurt on a level that would warrant an act of revenge such as this!

I could sense that this construct was pure malice. If this was the kind of enchantment I suspected it was, it could contain many exits leading to different places and maybe even times. If I was not careful, I could get stuck somewhere far from the Isle of Arran, Phillipe, and my pets. Finding my way home might not be easy!

If my hunch was correct, this enchantment was meant to trap and keep me here in this hideous, alternate reality. Or possibly another one of its choosing. Neither option appealed to me in the slightest. The only way to verify this was by walking through that cloud of smoke. I suspected that every time I headed through that barrier, I would end up somewhere else. There was no telling where and the possibilities were endless.

One could spend years or maybe even a lifetime in this nightmare, trying to get home! If I was to ever make it back to my little family, I would need a plan.

The who had done this and for what reason would have to wait for later. For the moment, I had more immediate concerns. This place had many dangers for the unwary. I needed to carefully consider every one of my moves before doing anything. My legs were aching from all the emotions I was experiencing, and I needed to sit for a bit. Thankfully I spotted a convenient log that did not look too disgusting next to the path.

Running my hand above it, I ensured it was free of magic. When this was confirmed, I took a seat and made myself comfortable. Now I could give the problem at hand my full attention. In my mind, I carefully went over everything that I could remember about spells such as this. Once I realized what I might be facing, my heart sank. There were several varieties of such traps! Which one had I stumbled into due to my inattention?

All of them sucked you in, one way or another. Some used more sophisticated magic tailored to the victim, as had been the case with me. The end result was the same. The person was caught in a globe like this, usually referred to as the nexus. From there, the different enchantments diverged. Some were worse than others, and I truly hoped this one would give me a chance to return home.

The first and most malicious sort stranded you someplace far from home when you crossed the smoke again. I had vaguely remembered this while examining the barrier. Therefore I had not given in to my impulse to rush through it to get back to my family. The possibility of being lost forever was the most terrifying of all. I would never see Phillipe again, nor my parents, my brother, or my pets! That notion was plain heartbreaking!

But, on the other hand, I could not just sit here forever, either! Eventually, I would have to give crossing that boundary a try. Only then would I know for sure what sort of a set-up I was dealing with.

The second and less malevolent types would send me to a different location when I made my way through the smoke but would allow me to return to the nexus. The only thing that changed when one walked through the portal was that far side. The third variety would send me to a new place each time I crossed without returning to the original node. That category had no constant of any kind.

To complicate things further, time could be an additional factor. The thought of ending up somewhere far in the future or the past also sounded less than appealing! Plus, there could be odd combinations of all the forms. To learn more about this particular spell, I would have to do some experimenting, no matter how much I feared the outcome. Remaining here forever would gain me nothing. It would get me no closer to home and my husband!

The fear of losing my family forever would only grow if I waited. That would make it even harder to take action! I could end up too paralyzed by anxiety to do anything! I refused to entertain the possibility of not returning to my loved ones! I was going to make my way home!

Therefore, determinedly, I devised a plan.

1. First, I would find out what happened when I crossed through the smoke. This would tell me more about the trap. I was hoping that the strange place I was in was a nexus.
2. Then, once I had gathered all the information I could, I would work out a way to make it home.

Having laid out a course of action, I felt considerably better. Quickly, I got to my feet. I might as well get this over with, and there was no time like the present!

Chapter 12

The Crossings

Steeling myself, I walked through the cloud of smoke to the other side. When I emerged, I gasped with surprise. This I had not expected! The view before me was absolutely stunning! I was immediately enchanted by all the beauty around me. Gently rolling hills, lit up by warm summer sunshine, reached all the way to the horizon! The predominant vegetation was tall, colorful grasses interspersed here and there with bright yellow flowers and stands of trees. The effect was magical.

Near me, a few tall, ancient oaks with immense trunks provided inviting shady areas to linger. Majestically, they stretched their branches into the clear blue sky dotted with the occasional puffy white cloud. I stood and stared in wonder. This place was gorgeous! It radiated a peacefulness that made it incredibly appealing. The setting was calling to me, encouraging me to come and run up and down the slopes like an exuberant child.

The urge to move away from the smoke was immense. I could stay here and rest under one of the giant trees once I was tired of racing around. What would it be like to explore all this magnificence? I could be happy here, and forget all my troubles! This magical setting promised to alleviate the hurt weighing down my heart. The grass under my feet was so soft, the sun pleasantly warm. Remaining here was so very tempting! Especially since this scenery was in such stark contrast to the ugly place I had just come from!

The thought of losing myself in all this beauty was so very enticing! I was just about to take that first step into this glorious landscape, but then, I hesitated. Something did not feel right about this! Suddenly I realized that something wanted me to stay here! Most likely forever! This was part of the trap! I started fighting the compulsion to move away from the smoke.

Once I had shaken off the overwhelming urge to head into these lovely hills enough to reestablish my will, I turned and ran back into that hazel cloud. I was in a hurry to get away from the charming spot that had almost become my permanent prison. Having been so close to succumbing to the enchantment, I was deeply shaken. Despite being aware of the possibility, I had almost fallen into this trap!

I had come so close to walking away from my entire life, from everyone and everything I loved! The pull had been immense. I was grateful I had the presence of mind and the strength to resist it. Giving in would have sentenced me to an existence in a magical stupor! The place was magnificent, but that was not life, not for someone like me! The lack of stimulation, of interacting with people, would have done me in after a while!

The experience left me more cautious than ever. As I made my way through the smoke, I could not help but wonder what I would have to deal with on the other side. Where would I end up?

To my relief, I found myself in the same disturbing, nightmarish backdrop I had left a few minutes ago. That was the information I had been looking for. The globe was the nexus, the anchor spot of the spell. Now I knew more about the type of trap I had run afoul of. Having a fixed locus gave me a FROM, and I knew my TO. It was always easier to get somewhere when one knew the starting and endpoint!

Now, all I had to do was find a way to dial in the right place on the other side of that awful smoke. There had to be a way to do this, to call in that one spot among many that was my home! Returning to the log, I sat back down to evaluate what I had learned thus far. More systematically this time, I began to sift through everything I could recall about this kind of sorcery.

Having been a rather solitary child, I had been interested in a variety of subjects. Also, my memory was close to photographic. Anything I read, watched, or heard could be called up when needed. That came in handy now. I sorted through the data until I had a clearer picture of my prison. This kind of enchantment was a very efficient trap that did not like to give up those it collected. Especially since most used its victims' life force to power themselves!

This did not look promising! I had to conclude that my chances of getting out of here were not good! But despite the odds being stacked against me, I was not about to give up. There had to be a loophole in the spell; I just had to find it! There usually was a way to get around things; it was the nature of this type of magic. I recalled reading that, if done right, a construct of this sort could be influenced.

With the right motivation, it could be diverted from its purpose of keeping the prisoner away from his or her home. I was determined to come up with something. This trap would not defeat me!

The fact that I had read so much of the forbidden section in our library now served me well! I had sneaked in there any chance I had and had systematically read tome after tome. Some of it had been rather repulsive but fascinating nonetheless. That my mother had frowned on anything that she saw as dark had made these books just the more interesting!

Being young and secretly a little rebellious against my parents' heavy-handedness and high expectations, I had seen it as a worthy challenge to circumvent some of their ridiculous restrictions. And not just where the books were concerned. Just for fun, I had made it my personal mission to get around all the magical barriers my mother had put in place around our home.

Getting caught was just plain stupid, and I was anything but. Therefore, I managed to maintain the outward image of the obedient daughter, at least most of the time. I did have to stand up for myself on occasion. Had I not, my powerful parents would have run over me like two bulldozers. They really did not mean to, it was just their way, and they did it to everyone.

Once I made it to university, I experienced a yet unknown freedom. I watched other kids of the clan go wild away from all that parental supervision. But, this was only a temporary reprieve unless I learned to make my own way in the world, independent of the Magnuson kin. Therefore, I studied hard. I was determined to have my life the way I wanted it, on my terms, and not how it had been laid out by my folks!

Having a reputation for being a good and conscientious student, it had been easy to convince my professors to allow me access to that coveted advanced section among their books. Since I was not known for abusing my powers, I was granted the privilege halfway through my very first semester. That I was an upper-echelon Magnuson and my parents had attended the college probably helped!

Instead of partying, I spent the evenings closeted in that sealed-off section of the library, working my way through text after text. My father had always emphasized that knowledge was power. That was one of the few things we agreed on. Not that I wanted to use what I read against anyone; I just wanted to be able to keep myself safe and independent. After several incidents at our home, this had become almost an obsession.

My parents were among the ruling board members of the Magnuson Clan, the Magnuson Procurement Company, and the kin's other businesses. This had made our family the target of several magical attacks. It was nothing my folks could not handle, but I almost ran afoul of one of these on a night-time excursion to the library. Therefore, I had gotten extra careful while sneaking about. I should have applied the same caution when I was not!

As luck would have it, I got caught up in a couple of these nasty spells. The first one snagged me as I was heading to the kitchen for a snack. For once, my actions were all perfectly innocent and above board. Thankfully, the little charm's magic was pretty amateurish. Therefore, it took me only a few minutes to unravel it and proceed with my errand.

With the second one, curiosity got the better of me. It was much more potent and way more malicious. Having just gotten home from school, I noticed an ornate envelope on the doormat of our house. I picked it up since it was raining, and I did not want this pretty gift to get ruined. Only then did I notice that it was addressed to me. But, it had not come through the regular mail, which was suspicious.

Still having the innocence of a child, I thought that a tiny peek at the contents would not hurt. And how could such a beautiful item be dangerous? However, the second I touched the seal, it triggered the enchantment, and I ended up fighting for my life. The petrification spell enveloped me instantly, taking down all my protective barriers.

All I could do was delay the inevitable. Sending everything I had against it, I did manage to keep my vital organs from shutting down for almost an hour. But I was only a kid. In the end, it was stronger than me. More and more of my body was turning to stone!

I would not have survived if my mum had not saved me. Unexpectantly, she arrived home early that day. She nullified that menace in the nick of time! However, having to be rescued did not sit well with me. Especially not by my mother!

She reminded me how she had saved my life for years and never failed to bring it up at the most embarrassing moments! I hated it and, on occasions, her, but that incident sent me on a determined search for ways to protect myself. Circumventing her rules to do so did not bother my conscience, not in the least. It was my clandestine way of getting even with her.

My peaceful life with Phillipe had allowed me to relax. After a while, I had stopped my obsessive reading of protective and attack magic treatises. I sort of kept up on such things on the internet, but living on the Isle of Arran, we were far from any library with occult texts. Occasionally, I had slipped into the one in Ny Havn, but opportunities had been few and far between. Therefore, it had been a while since I had looked into such hateful things as this enchantment.

However, I accumulated a vast amount of knowledge during my days at university. Several sources I had read spoke of this kind of construct and how to deal with it. I now had several possibilities. One I discarded outright. Reentering the cloud time after time until I found home would be demoralizing and exhausting. And it could take a very long time. Also, it was too haphazard an approach for my liking.

In addition, there was always a chance that I might inadvertently step into another world meant to keep me there. Just at the thought, I shivered. I got very close to never seeing my husband, family, and pets again! That was just unacceptable! There had to be something, some way, that would enable me to stack the odds in my favor!

Try as I might, for the moment, nothing viable occurred to me. I finally had to face it; I needed to collect more information to locate the loophole in this spell.

Once again, I made my way through the smoke, but this time, I counted the steps from one edge to the other. After 18 paces, I came out on the other side. To my dismay, I arrived somewhere in a busy city. The sidewalk was extremely crowded, and people were all around me. Being used to my quiet life on the Isle of Arran, all this sudden humanity was daunting! The most bizarre thing, however, was that no one moved!

Being surrounded by so many immobile folks was more than a little eerie! I felt like an interloper, like someone who did not belong, which was accurate in this case. This was not my home and maybe not even my time, judging from the clothing and the vehicles on the road. Turning around to head back through the smoke, I almost panicked. It was gone! I looked around frantically, but detecting the haze took me a bit. It had been hidden between all these inert people!

Trying to get back to it, I jumped when I bumped into something hard and solid. One of the cars! It was way too close for comfort to the sidewalk where I had emerged! And it was about to hit a young woman who had been pushed off the walkway a few feet away! She had frozen in midfall! Good thing that the vehicle too was motionless! Maybe I could do something to save her? Putting my plan to reenter the smoke on hold, I determinedly headed her way.

The petite brunette had a perky nose and sparkly brown eyes. She was beautiful and barely older than me. Her build was very slender, and she probably did not weigh all that much. But when I tried to move her, she would not budge, not in the least! However, I was not about to give up. Now that I had gazed into her face, I could not bring myself to leave her to get hurt or possibly killed!

Looking around, I located a hardware store. Pushing my way between all these frozen folks, I browsed the aisles until I found just what I was looking for. A block and tackle pulley! Without hesitation, I reached for it, but even it turned out to be much heavier than it should have been. This led me to conclude that some sort of resistance to my interference was at play here! Still, that was not about to stop me!

Using all my strength to lift the mechanism, I carried it out to the street. A convenient lamppost would give me the leverage I needed, but getting the rope to her and back with all the people in my way would not be easy. Finally, I managed to reach the young woman and wrapped the line around her in such a way that she would be pulled back on the sidewalk.

I started to reel her in once everything was prepared to my satisfaction. Even with the extra leverage, overcoming that initial inertia took me a bit! Still, she moved back onto the walkway relatively smoothly once I did. I pulled her in just a bit more and, just in case, decided to leave the rope in place so she would stay where she was and not fall again. To make sure that she was secure, I tied the end of the cable to the lamppost.

Finding her attached in this fashion would cause some surprise, but it was better than the alternative!

My task accomplished, I headed back toward the place where I had last spotted the smoke. It felt eerie and somehow wrong to move among all these stock-still persons. When I took a moment to catch my breath from all that exertion, I looked around. The metropolis was not one I recognized. The street names were in English, but this was not Europe. The style of dress and the cars were all different. My eyes fell on a newspaper stand.

What better way to gain information! Slipping around several people, I made my way there. It was the 18th of May, 2018! Five years ago! And I was in Philadelphia, a city in the United States! If I ever made it out of here, I would have to look in the archives to see what happened to the young lady. I really hoped that I had managed to save her! She was still securely tied to the sturdy lamppost and out of harm's way. Since there was nothing else I could do, I made my way into the smoke.

What a relief when the city faded away! I even welcomed the purplish smoke that now surrounded me. It was much more soothing than all that immobile humanity had been!

Chapter 13

New Friends

Counting the steps, I made my way back toward the nexus. To my surprise, as I neared it, I spotted an indistinct outline of something that had not been there before, right at the edge of the haze. Carefully, I moved closer until I could just make out the two richly dressed ladies huddling there. I stopped and watched them for a moment. I was not about to make my presence known until I figured out if they were friends or foes. However, it did not take long to establish that they presented no threat to me!

The pair was sitting on the path like they had collapsed on that spot from sheer exhaustion. They were clinging to each other and crying, a picture of abject misery. I felt for them. Who knows how long they had been caught in this trap? With a quick glance, I took in the scenery beyond them. As I had surmised, I was back at the nightmarish house, orchard, and meadow with the worn cobblestone path.

The only difference this time was the girls. Looking them over, I noted that they seemed as out of time and place as I felt in this cursed place. Being so distraught, they were oblivious to their surroundings. Curiously, I examined them closer, then looked down at myself. Glancing back and forth between them and me for a few minutes, I discovered something vital. The three of us looked different from our gloomy surroundings!

We were like bright spots in this sickly, frozen landscape! Our clothes had retained their vivid colors and stood out in stark contrast to our environs which seemed to have been leached of vitality and pigment. Their skin was a little pale, most likely from the shock of finding themselves here, but it still had a healthy tone. One of the girls was blonde, like me, and the other was darker. Their hair was a bit disheveled but shiny and vibrant.

But there was a slight distinction between us. The hues of my clothes were more vivid than the young ladies' dresses. Was this due to the time they had spent here? That caused me some concern. Would we end up just as bleached as the rest of this nightmare if we stayed here too long? That was not a pleasant thought! More information was needed! I would have to talk to these girls to find out their story and how long they had been here!

From the sad state of their magnificent gowns, I would say it had been a while. My heart went out to them. They were so young! What an awful situation for them to get stuck in! I would not wish this dreadful place on anyone! Were there others besides these two? And was this globe the nexus of the entire spell or only of the portion affecting me? Then how had they gotten here? And what did we have in common to get caught up in here?

Every time I found a couple of answers, they left me with more things I needed to know. This was most frustrating! I had narrowed down what type of trap I was dealing with. Also, since the girls were here, it might be safe to assume that the spell had not been specifically created to capture me. Why, then, had Phillipe and I drawn the magic's attention? That was a question that I really wanted an answer to! And could I get back to the island?

Crossing the barrier twice had confirmed that this spot did not change. That was important. Akin to using a GPS unit for directions, a fixed point of origin was part of the equation. Once I figured out how, I intended to use this to get to the desired destination, my home. I had the beginning of an idea. All life, but especially magic, consists of energy. Each person, thing, and place has a specific vibration.

Therefore there had to be a way to influence what location appeared on the other side of the hazel smoke! I would have to think about that more, but first things first. Moving out of the haze, I knelt next to the slender young women. The pair were sobbing disconsolately. Honestly, I could not blame them for feeling so desperate and lost. Who knew how long they had been trying to return to their loved ones!

"Excuse me, ladies, can I help you?"

The two flinched, looked up sharply, then jumped to their feet. When they saw how calm and confident I appeared, their eyes lit up with hope.

"Do you know how we can get home? Away from this awful place?" the shorter and obviously younger one asked me immediately.

Now that they were no longer huddled together, I could finally get a good look at the girl. I instantly liked what I saw and wished we had met under different circumstances. Her wide, cerulean eyes were full of fear, and her delicate face very pale. Still, even this distressed, she was stunningly beautiful. The blue flax woven into her long, blonde curls perfectly set off the deep azure of her irises and enhanced the appearance of innocence and youth.

She must have been an incredible sight before getting caught in this mess! I figured that the girl was maybe 16 years old, a teenager. What could she have possibly done to deserve getting stuck in this awful place? She looked too sweet and innocent to have hurt anyone! I did, however, detect a hint of pain in this amiable person. It told me that even with her apparent genteel breeding, this young lady had experienced more than her fair share of adversity.

The taller girl eyed me with more suspicion and reticence. They were both very young, and this one had also known hurt. From the similarity of their facial features, I assumed they were related in some way. My interest was piqued. What did the three of us have in common to end up here? That I needed to find out!

Since I had the two's undivided attention, I repeated my offer of assistance. Naturally, the young women had questions and started shooting them off rapidly, both talking at the same time. I tried for a few moments to make sense of this garble but to no avail. Finally, I gave up, and I held up my hands.

"Ladies, please, one after the other. I am Cara Magnuson, by the way."

"My sister and I are also of the Magnuson clan! I am Hilda," the little blonde introduced herself.

"How can we be of the same clan? How is this possible? We know all our people!" the taller, darker, and obviously more mature of the two enquired. She eyed me suspiciously. "And why are you dressed so strangely?"

"That is the way people dress where I'm from."

"Seriously? You go out in public like that?" Hilda gasped, eying my black leggings, teal blouse, and dark-blue windbreaker with interest. She was obviously shocked, but I also detected a hint of intrigue. This little one was nowhere near as naive or innocent as she seemed!

"Yes," I replied with a smile. "Usually, I would dress a little nicer to go out, but I was in a hurry."

"How can that be? We have never even seen clothes like yours!" the elder girl protested.

"I guess I come from a time in your future."

"We have met others from our future, but none of them were dressed like you!" the brunette scoffed.

"There are others here besides you two?" I exclaimed with excitement.

"Yes, all from different times," Hilda acknowledged.

"This is really quite extraordinary. I believe that we are caught in an enchantment that stretches through time. Since all three of us are Magnusons, it could have been specifically designed to ensnare those of our family!"

"You are telling us the truth? You are not part of this whole setup?" the older one demanded, scowling something fiercely.

"Yes, I am from the future, and some of us dress like this. I have no reason to lie to you."

"I guess," she admitted reluctantly and with rather bad grace. "But that does not mean that you are not!"

"Eldred! Be nice! She is the first person we have met who seems to have some understanding of this place!" Hilda admonished her ill-tempered sister.

"My point exactly! How does she know what no one else does?"

"Eldred!" Hilda repeated with a fair amount of exasperation in her voice. She turned toward me.

"Please forgive my sister. She is a bit overprotective at times," she explained.

"I understand," I assured her, smiling. "However, we are better off working together."

Hilda agreed, nodding enthusiastically. Her sibling, however, was not yet convinced.

A spirited discussion broke out between Eldred and Hilda. I left them to it and just watched. Something kept niggling at me. Since they were occupied, I examined this closer. Either their names or appearances were vaguely familiar to me, but why? What was so important about these two? Searching my memory, I finally recalled a painting in one of the ancient family books.

It was of one of my distant ancestors. For confirmation, I looked at the older sister more closely. She was tall and slender, with glowing skin, forest green eyes, and waist-long, shining chestnut-colored hair. The strong set of her jaw was unmistakable. It reminded me very much of my mother, especially when she had made up her mind about something! Even the hair color was similar. The resemblance between the two was quite uncanny!

From their clothes and demeanor, I guessed that these two were well-bred. Eldred's magnificent gown was decorated beautifully with sparkling, clear gemstones. It was obviously incredibly expensive. The material alone must have cost a small fortune, and it must have taken months to decorate. Hilda's dress was beautiful but not as elegant. It was befitting a younger girl of around 16.

Still, if they were from the era I figured, most people would not have been able to afford something this exquisite and expensive. These two were obviously nobility. Then, all of a sudden, it hit me.

"Are you the Eldred Magnuson?" I gasped.

"Yes. Why?" Eldred answered with rather bad grace.

"Seriously? One of my ancestors was an Eldred Magnuson!"

"Ancestor?" Hilda gulped. "Honestly? What year do you come from?"

"2023. How about you?"

The girls were taken aback by this revelation. This they had not expected, and they exchanged a startled glance.

"Long before you. We are from the year 1616. Do you know who that Eldred was married to?" the chestnut beauty asked.

"Yes. Her husband's name was Cedric Magnuson."

"That was our husband-to-be before we ended up here!" Hilda exclaimed.

It was my turn to be filled with wonder. I looked at Eldred. We did have a fair amount of resemblance, much more than I did with Hilda, despite the shade of my hair being much closer to hers.

"Could you be her?" I marveled.

"I bet she is! I can see the resemblance between you two!" Hilda announced.

"I very well could be," Eldred finally grudgingly admitted. "This is a strange place."

"Yes, it is!" I agreed.

"You would not believe all the things we have seen!" she told me with a shrug.

"You went through the smoke?" I asked immediately.

"Yes," Hilda told me rather sadly. "More times than we can count! And we have been in a bunch of these cells! All we want to do is get back home!"

"Me too," I agreed. "Me too!"

After realizing I was who I claimed to be, Eldred was more friendly toward me. Building on this, I told her I needed as much information as possible to devise a plan to get us out of here. The sisters decided they would help if it meant they would have a chance to see their loved ones again. Therefore, we made ourselves comfortable on the log. With a bit of prompting, the girls started telling me about some of the adventures they'd had since getting caught in the trap.

I listened with rapt attention. As I had figured, Eldred and Hilda had been here for a good while. In their desperation to find a way home, they had gone from one nexus to another and through the veil of smoke many, many times. They had seen a lot of different places, and not much surprised them anymore. But, it was obvious that they were weary and had just about given up hope.

"How did you get here?" I asked when they had caught me up.

"We were on the way to be presented to our husband when this cloud of stinky smoke appeared on the path. Naturally, we all stopped. After some hesitation, one brave man went through it. Nothing happened to him. He waved to us from the other side that it was safe. So the rest of us followed. Those in front of us passed through just fine," Eldred explained. Before she could continue, her sister broke in.

"We ended up here, all alone! Our friends, the entire wedding party, all were gone!" Hilda wailed. She threw herself into my arms and started sobbing.

"We have been trying to find a way back!" Eldred added, also breaking into tears. "It is awful here!"

When she met my eyes, I clearly saw her despair. She had been strong for her younger sister's sake for so long but had reached her limit. Having someone older present who seemed to have a bit of a handle on the situation lightened the burdens on the slender shoulders of this brave young woman. She broke down as well. Before I knew it, I held both the sobbing girls in my arms, gently rubbing their backs to help soothe them.

These two were barely out of childhood and had obviously led a life of luxury. Eldred was not sure how long they had been here, but it had been much longer than me. This place was so depressing that it was not surprising that they had started to despair. They were so worn out from stress and fear that they were about to give up. Who could blame them? The more I lingered here, the more I missed Phillipe. And the pets!

Bear and I were so very bonded that I seldom went anywhere without him. His absence left a hole in my heart. I really hoped that he was ok and had settled down. In a way, he is my familiar. His gentleness, sweetness, and intelligence most certainly set him apart. His sister, Hella Rose, was even more brilliant, but she preferred to stay with Phillipe.

The other two were old enough now that they had reached retirement age. To our amusement, they still disciplined the younger ones when Bear and Hella Rose got too rambunctious. Little Micha usually stuck with me, while Arianna just adored my husband. The dogs loved the two guinea pigs, Orion and Teddy, and watched over them whenever we took them outside.

Each of our companions was so different but wonderful in his or her own way! How much I would have appreciated their comfort! To say that I missed them bitterly is putting it mildly. My heart ached with longing for Phillipe, my furry family, and home! And to think that these poor girls had been here for weeks! No wonder they were in the state they were in! It said much for the sisters that they were not in worse shape!

While I held them close and let them cry, I had the chance to compare our coloring unobserved and at my leisure. There was no denying it. Eldred and Hilda's clothing and hair had lost some of their vibrancy and hue. This confirmed my hypothesis that our life energy was being used to power this nasty construct. When my new friends finally calmed down, we decided to continue our exchange of information.

"What was it like for you when you passed through?" I inquired.

"We tried to talk to people on the other side, but they were all frozen in place. Everything was!" Eldred exclaimed.

"I noticed that as well. Did you come across any place where things moved?" I asked curiously.

"No. Did you?" Hilda asked wide-eyed.

"Yes, and I believe those places are designed to entrap us if we explore them!" I stated.

The girls turned pale.

"Forever? With no way to get home?" Eldred squeaked.

"It seemed that way," I affirmed.

"We were lucky we did not come across one of those!" Eldred told me. "We kept hoping to find someone to speak to on the other side!"

"We never did, but we did talk to others stuck here!" Hilda informed me.

"How many have you met since you got here?" I asked immediately.

"Well, there was the old lady, the young couple, ...," Hilda began.

"Twentynine," Eldred interjected. "I counted them all."

"That many!" I exclaimed.

"Probably even more," Eldred said tiredly.

"There are so many of these cells!" Hilda agreed. "We have not visited them all!"

This globe was empty except for Eldred, Hilda, and me, so there was most likely a nexus for each person! That would make for a rather large cluster of horrid prisons! This was not good! No wonder this enchantment was so powerful! It had plenty of people to feed off!

My heart sank at this unwelcome news. The problem was much bigger than I had anticipated! And, according to the girls, I was the only one they had met who had some idea of what we were dealing with and a vague notion of what to do about it. Could I go home and just

abandon the rest to their fate? No, my conscience would not allow that, not when there was a chance that I could help.

My heart sank as I realized I would not be making it back home anytime soon!

Chapter 14

The Plan

Eldred and Hilda's adventures provided me with a lot of valuable information. Some of the conclusions I had drawn from my experience in the city were now confirmed. After thinking about this for a while, I came up with two possible explanations for this phenomenon. We were either out of sync with time and space or were vibrating at a different frequency to all the frozen locations. None of us could exist in those places! We would starve to death since it was so hard to interact with any of the objects!

The lack of anyone to talk to would also wear one down after a while. Suddenly, another possibility occurred to me. We could be dealing with a combination of time, space, and frequency! And it may vary every time we crossed the veil of smoke! That would most certainly complicate things! Add to that the first location I had come to that would have trapped me for life!

We could survive there, but, except for the vegetation, it had felt devoid of other life. Staying there would have made for a very lonely existence! No animals, no people – what an awful thought! I had seen the wind move the grass and the branches of the tall trees but no birds in the sky, no insects, nothing! Pleasant to look at, but that was about it!

That dimension, for lack of a better thing to call it, had been very different from all the ones the girls had encountered. I was confident the portal would have closed behind me if I had walked further in. Permanently! Luckily, I had not followed the compulsion to wander those gorgeous sunlit hills!

When I shared my misgivings with the girls, they turned pale. To be trapped in the aggregation of nexuses was bad enough, but to be the only living being in a place such as that could only lead to madness! Both were grateful that they had never encountered a single location like that on all the occasions they had crossed the smoke. Eldred and Hilda had entered some of these frozen landscapes, not even considering that they could get stuck somewhere!

Hilda, very thoughtfully, voiced the opinion that the tempting spot might have been meant just for me. At the time, I had still been extremely upset. I had craved solace and to get away from it all. I stared at her in shock. This I had not considered! Eldred, not to be outdone by her sister, then speculated that maybe, to a point, this enchantment responded to our emotions.

What an interesting suggestion, but one that made sense! This meant we had to be careful what we thought, felt, and wished for! But those were valuable insights! The longer we talked, the clearer the picture of our situation became. We finally concluded that we were out of sync with all locations except home or those meant to trap us permanently. This was huge! If we could find a way to somehow affect the vibration of the space beyond, we might be able to call in our homes!

But how? We tossed around several ideas. After discarding most, the beginnings of a plan began to take shape. If we could pull it off, we would return to where we belonged! I could go home! But first, I had to take care of Eldred and Hilda. They were not much more than teenagers and needed my help! I was not about to leave them here to languish in despair!

Seeing their distress had kicked my protective instincts into high gear. And I had been raised to put the needs of the clan members and others before my own. Eventually, I would be reunited with Phillipe, but it would have to wait. My conscience would not allow me to abandon Eldred and Hilda to their fate. Their groom was waiting for them back there in the Havn of 1616!

A disturbing notion swam into my mind at this point. Both my husband and I were descendants of these two young ladies. If they remained trapped here, would we even be born? I mentioned this to Eldred and Hilda, and we discussed the ramifications of their continued imprisonment in this magical trap. While we talked, I remembered that their influence had improved living conditions and had been vital for the survival of the Magnuson Clan during the witch trials!

Getting them back home suddenly took on a whole new urgency! I had to take care of them before returning to my family! Besides, how often does one have a chance to spend time with one's distant ancestors? I was starting to really like the girls. They had been so brave and had continued trying to return to their space and time when many others would have given up! I was pretty impressed with their resilience and perseverance!

Since I was older than them, I felt responsible for Eldred and Hilda and their welfare. This gave me even more incentive to find a way out. Also, this malicious construct could not be left to draw in even more people. According to the girls, I was the first person they had met in their explorations who knew what we were dealing with.

In a way, that put a lot of responsibility on my shoulders. It looked like it was up to me to return all the prisoners to where they belonged and to disable the spell! But, for now, I did not have to do so alone! The sisters were more than willing to help! Therefore, I put our rather impressive minds to work.

Magic was tricky. When an enchantment was performed with such ill will as had been the case with this trap, a set of complicated rules came into play. Most of the time, however, there was a loophole somewhere. We just had to find it. Eldred, Hilda, and I went over everything I remembered reading about such spells. We fished out those facts we felt applied here. It was nice to have their feedback!

As long as the spell was this strong, going home without the assistance of others would be impossible. The three of us together might be able to affect the location on the other side, but there was no way to dial in both destinations! Obviously, I did not belong in the girls' time, nor did they belong in mine! And it would not be fair to the rest of the people stranded here to just abandon them!

Good deeds, thankfully, have a special magic all of their own. I remembered reading two accounts of persons who had escaped similar situations. Both believed they won free because they were selfless, kind and followed their hearts. They had assisted others where they could. When I mentioned this, Hilda wondered how many people stayed stuck because they only cared about themselves. That was a sobering thought!

I did not intend us to be among their number! Being blood relations did have benefits! Since these girls were my ancestors, it would allow us to create a connection more easily. And, it would be stronger than with just a stranger. Thus, we would have more power to use against the construct. Together, we should have no problem calling in the frequency corresponding to the sisters' home.

However, one of my biggest concerns was the large number of people Eldred and Hilda had met during their captivity here. If each of us was supplying life force to this horror, it had to be well charged with such a supply of energy to draw on! That was not good news! I assumed there were even more people here than the 29 the girls had visited. With so many, the resistance to bending this spell to our will and getting the hazel smoke portal to do our bidding could be significant.

Conversely, the opposite should apply. With each person returned, the enchantment was deprived of one of its power sources and should weaken. Eventually, it should collapse in on itself, hopefully spitting me out where I had entered. Not that I would take that for granted with this nasty construct! When the time came, I would use every bit of magic at my disposal to ensure that I ended up in the right place!

In a way, we were in luck. In a trap this malicious, any deed committed with good intentions and a pure heart was like a shining star. It had quite a ripple effect! One hero, or heroine in my case, could turn the tide. More would be better, but I could not ask the girls to make such a sacrifice after all they had been through! The sooner I could get them home, the better! I had been here nowhere near as long and would remain behind.

There had to be others imprisoned here who would be happy to help me. Putting all reluctance aside, I decided to embrace the challenge. Not that I had much of an option. I, for one, would not be able to live with myself knowing that someone was still ensnared in here and that I had left them behind. Freeing them all became my main goal, trumping going home to my beloved Phillipe and my much-missed pets.

After debating with myself for another few moments on how best to achieve my objective, I decided to share my conclusions with the girls.

"I have an idea," I told the young ladies.

"Will it get us home?" Hilda asked, almost afraid to hope.

"I am willing to try if you let me."

"But how?" Eldred wanted to know.

"I have your magic," I explained.

"Magic? How can you have my magic? I do not have magic! I am not a wise one!" Eldred objected.

"It shines brightly within you, both of you," I insisted.

"You said you remembered seeing Eldred's picture in one of your books. What did it say about her? About us?" Hilda asked shrewdly.

She had not forgotten my earlier comments and correctly assumed that the archive would also contain information about them! Should I tell them what was recorded there? Would that change history, or would it bring about the events mentioned? I battled with myself for a moment, then decided to go with my gut feeling.

"I remember reading that all those born of your bloodline will inherit your powers. Your sharp instincts and circumspect guidance will help your husband in difficult times. Together, you ensure the survival of the clan!"

"Seriously?" Hilda asked immediately. Eldred, for once, seemed to be speechless.

"Yes, both of you are very powerful, and you will become even more so with time," I assured them.

The two looked at me with wonder, then at each other. Eldred and Hilda were silent for a very long time, mulling this over, testing the validity of my statements. When my words rang true, they stood up straighter, and their smiles got brighter. Neither had ever seen themselves as anything special, and they liked the idea of having the gift.

If I remembered correctly, her abilities had made their mother an equal to their father in their marriage. Could it be possible that they did not know?

"Your mother never told you?" I asked curiously.

"No," Eldred answered rather brusquely.

Ah, here was a sore subject! It was evident that I was missing something important.

"Then you were not trained?" I inquired, not understanding how this could be possible.

"We were taught some spells, but our parents were too busy to do much else. Many in the clan can do what we do; we just never called it magic," Eldred explained.

"And we were strictly forbidden to do it in front of anyone!" Hilda added.

"Now that makes more sense! Both of you have the potential to be very powerful, but with the witch hunts, your parents were trying to keep you and the clan safe! That was very wise of them!"

"They are hunting people like us?" Hilda gasped.

"Yes, all over the world. People fear what they do not understand. You will be fine if you are careful! And, according to our records, you will have long, happy lives and serve your clan and your husband with distinction!" I assured them.

Judging from the history in the archives, Eldred and Hilda's husband had utterly adored them. Cedric had trusted their counsel over all others. The three had made an incredible team. Together, they had positively affected our clan and a good part of the region. The trio had always advocated for peace and cooperation. This brought prosperity to the whole area.

"Since we ended up here, I do feel different, like I have been touched by the fey or something has awoken inside me," Hilda said thoughtfully.

"Yes, now that you mention it, I do too. Maybe we can help you get us home?" Eldred enquired.

"Sure! Three are always more powerful than one!" I told the girls.

Now that I had Eldred and Hilda's undivided attention, I explained what we needed to do. They would be the first to leave this magical prison. This, however, would make it the hardest to dial in their home. But I had every intention to persevere. We would find a way! Failure was not an option, especially since it meant we would all be stuck in this dismal place forever. Or until we had been deprived of enough vitality to become shadows of our former selves and then fade away!

"Please, dry your tears," I encouraged the sisters. "If I have anything to say about it, you are going to your wedding! And soon!"

The two exchanged a worried glance, their eyes sad. I understood. After being here this long, Eldred and Hilda were afraid to hope. Every time they had crossed the barrier, they had been disappointed.

"Girls, what do you have to lose? Come on, you can give this one more try!"

To motivate them, I made my words sound more optimistic than I was actually feeling. But it worked. Finally, the two brightened up. Hilda and I redid Eldred's hair and neatly put it back up. Next, we detangled Hilda's. Just being 16 yet, she would wear it tumbling down her back like all the other teenagers her age. It was lovely to start with and reached just past her waist. Then, we worked on the clothes, rubbing out any spots and adjusting the laces.

As much as possible, we needed to restore their appearance to how it looked before disappearing from the wedding procession. Soon, we had managed to bring back a semblance of their former glory. They still seemed just a little more faded, which increased my ire with this awful spell. Not only did we need to take them home, but I also intended to reclaim the vitality stolen from them!

A little while later, we were almost ready. Some of the damage done to Eldred and Hilda's outfits was still visible, so I started using magic to fix it. Naturally, the girls wanted to learn the spell. Within minutes they were practicing on each other. Between the three of us, we made rapid progress. Unless someone looked closely, they would never notice a difference.

Confidently, I marched up to the smoke. I was ready to take this spell on! For what it was doing to Eldred and Hilda, I felt enough anger at this enchantment to sustain several people! The girls followed more slowly. They were still somewhat apprehensive. Not that I could blame them. It was hard to allow oneself to hope again! When I smiled at them encouragingly, they did cheer up a bit more.

"Are you ready?" I asked them after giving them one last going over.

"Yes, we are," Hilda stated bravely. "Do you really think this will work?"

"Yes, I do. Please, remember there is much we do not know. As a precaution, we should hold hands," I reminded the two. "While in the smoke, if you let go of me or each other, you might end up somewhere else!"

My gut told me that this was important, very important. We had to be in physical contact until we were through the cloud. I made sure to impress this on my companions once more. Another advantage to holding hands was that the energetic connection this established would make it easier to combine and channel our powers. We had never worked together before, so every bit helped!

Since I was not certain how far beyond the portal I needed to take Eldred and Hilda, I intended to personally deliver them to their husband. I was reluctant to admit that my motives were not entirely altruistic. My burning curiosity about the man they were about to marry might have had much to do with this!

The balcony area of the mead hall had copies of paintings of some of our ancestors going back hundreds of years. Many times, people had commented how much my beloved Phillipe resembled this Cedric Magnuson from so long ago! I had to see this for myself!

Chapter 15

An Alliance is Formed

Grabbing a solid hold of each other, we stepped into the cloud of hazel smoke. Instead of walking all the way through, however, we stayed within its plume and stopped just a bit shy of the other side. It was time for the first part of the process. I had explained it all to them in detail, but neither Eldred, Hilda, nor I had ever done anything like this. We would be learning as we went.

"Close your eyes, girls. Now look for sparkling threads leading away from us," I instructed the young ladies.

"Do you see any?" I inquired after a few minutes.

"I do not see anything no matter what I do!" Hilda responded unhappily.

She was very tense and most likely trying too hard. Hilda had the ability and an abundance of power. She should have been able to easily detect the shimmering gossamer strands of our life force!

"Sweetheart, relax! You got this! Take some deep breaths and calm yourself, then let it come to you," I instructed. "Remember, do not try to force it!"

I could sense my companions following my instructions, and I gave them a couple of minutes to get into a more meditative state. Both of them were familiar with spells and how to cast them, and this was really not that much different.

"Better?" I finally asked them.

"Yes, but I am still not seeing anything!" Hilda complained.

"Give it another minute! Just flow with it; allow it. Do not try too hard. Instead, let go of any expectations! You can do this!" I assured her.

"I got something!" Eldred exclaimed. "Thin threads of lights like cords are coming off all of us! Mine and Hilda's are all going in one direction!"

"So are yours, Cara!" Hilda gasped.

We were making progress! Good! These girls had a lot of magical abilities, and they were smart! Too bad that they had not been trained more!

"In that direction must lie the center of this spell!" Eldred mused. "Can we go there and smash it?"

"I wished it was that easy, but no," I told them regretfully. "For one, I suspect it is way too strong for us to overcome, and if we undid the spell, we would trap all the other people here!" I explained.

"It would not send them back home?" Hilda asked, horrified.

"No. The enchantment collects the victims and creates the globes. In a way, they are miniature dimensions, and if the spell feeding them is gone, they would just collapse with the person inside them."

"How awful!" Eldred gasped. "Where would these people end up?"

"I have no idea. I think they would just cease to exist, so we need to be careful when we try to regain some of our life force so that we do not damage the enchantment itself!"

"Oh!" was all Eldred could say.

"Concentrate on those shimmering cords and start pulling them in," I instructed.

The three of us got to work. I reeled in the last of my threads long before the girls were done. I gently tugged the end free. I was now no longer connected to the enchantment, which should make it easier for me to pass from globe to globe once Eldred and Hilda had been delivered to their groom. Having my full power available to me without that constant, slow drain felt so good and was such a relief!

Since they had been here so long, my companions, especially Eldred, had much more of a fight on their hands. Therefore, I went to her assistance. Between the two of us, we were gaining ground fast. To my surprise, Hilda seemed to manage quite well on her own. Still, it took us a while, but eventually, we reclaimed all the vitality stolen from us. Now, it was time for the second part of the plan.

"Think of your home as hard as you can!" I advised them.

With my eyes closed, I reopened the connection to the girls. I allowed their memories to wash over me and immersed myself fully in the images of their lives. This allowed me to get a feeling for the area. Carefully, I studied the vibrations of the place they had come from, then worked on holding them in my mind. When I felt sure I had it just right, I turned my intention outward.

However, when I sent my attention beyond the cloud, I was in for a disappointment. All I could sense were blurry images. Try as I might, I could not get a clear fix on the location we were trying to dial in. Finally, it dawned on me! It was so simple! We needed to be closer! Pulling Eldred and Hilda along, I cautiously moved us a little bit further toward the edge of the plume.

Since the girls had the gift, I continued explaining what I was doing to my companions. To my pleasure, these two were quick learners. After a couple of tries, they managed to bring their vibrations into the correct range. This was great and incredibly helpful! Working together like this significantly amplified our abilities! We were now a power of three instead of one!

Having achieved this second step, I showed them how to get a feel for the place beyond the veil. Once we had mastered this, we moved on to the final part. We applied our will to the portal portion of the spell with a vengeance. We needed to encourage it to home in on the location of our choosing instead of its own. The initial resistance we encountered was immense, but we kept at it. At first, nothing happened, but then we felt a subtle shift. Finally!

Keeping up gentle but firm pressure, we started to nudge it into the right frequency range. Once it began to move in that direction, all we could do was watch and wait. A few moments later, we noticed that the place just beyond us, outside the smoke, was changing! It was responding to our will! We continued to push it toward the frequency of the desired location, not letting up our relentless pressure for an instant!

With relief, we observed that we were getting closer and closer to our destination. Then, we could sense a faint echo of the vibrations we held in our minds! This small success gave the three of us just the boost we needed. We concentrated on the end result even harder! With increased speed, our goal kept getting closer and closer! When the girls' home came into full focus, we felt something snapping into place. Our minds and the space beyond were now vibrating together!

The sensation was one of homecoming. Eldred and Hilda were smiling with pleasure. I needed to remember this for the next time I called in a destination. Having achieved our objective, the three of us opened our eyes. We got our first glimpse of the scenery beyond and prepared to step through.

Excitedly, the girls took a small step into the landscape before us pulling me along. They were so happy to be back and out of the nightmarish environs of the enchantment that had entrapped us all. But then, they stopped. Almost as one, the sisters gave me a concerned glance. Frankly, I was puzzled. What was going on in those pretty heads? Weren't they glad to be home?

Looking from one to the other, I noticed how thoughtful their faces appeared. I watched as Eldred's jaw set with determination. All I could think was 'Oh, oh!" before she retreated into the smoke instead of moving forward. After a second, Hilda did as well. Puzzled, I followed their lead. What had just happened?

"What about all the others? It took all three of us to do this! Cara cannot do this on her own, Hilda!" Eldred addressed her sister.

"This was really hard, even doing it together! You are right, Eldred. She cannot get home without our help!" Hilda agreed.

"Remember the old lady we met, Hilda? She was kind to us! How can we leave her behind?"

"We cannot," Hilda agreed with a sigh of resignation.

Their minds were made up, and I was not about to argue with them. Having made a similar decision for their benefit not long ago, I understood their motivation only too well! They could no more abandon me than I could have left them in the trap!

"Can we find our home again?" Hilda asked me.

"Yes, I have its vibration. I believe it should be easier next time," I assured Hilda. "But, your wedding!"

"It can wait. Eldred is right. You need us!" Hilda decided.

Her face now displayed the same stubborn expression her sister's sported. Still, I had to try!

"But girls, are you sure? You are so close to home and your Cedric!" I protested.

"He can wait a little while longer. We are not yet bonded to him like you are to Phillipe. If you can make that sacrifice, so can we! Right, Hilda?" Eldred stated firmly.

"Yes," Hilda agreed, equally as resolved.

The sisters had made up their minds. I could sense that there was no way to change this. Secretly, I was immensely relieved to keep them as my allies. Our combined powers could weaken this malicious construct in record time! But they deserved recompense. I would make sure that they benefited from this immense sacrifice! It was time that they learned more about magic!

Together, hand in hand, we returned to the nexus.

"I propose forming an alliance of Magnuson women to combat this evil!" Hilda suggested formally.

"I second this notion," Eldred announced.

"Then we are now the Magnuson Alliance against Evil!" Hilda cheered. "And you, Cara, are our third member!"

"Thank you, both of you! I am most honored, and I am so very proud of you! Staying with me to help was a courageous and selfless thing to do!" I told them with a grateful smile.

I was delighted to have the privilege of their company for a while longer! And to be part of their alliance! Hilda, always the more impulsive, threw her arms around me. To my surprise, Eldred followed suit.

We stood there, holding onto each other for a very long moment. When we pulled apart, all three of us were grinning broadly. We were absolutely elated, especially me. I guess I had finally managed to win over the standoffish Eldred!

Chapter 16

Important Revelations

Unfortunately, Eldred was absolutely correct in her estimation of the situation. Tuning in to the girls' home had been difficult even with our combined powers. On my own, it would be impossible. To have any chance of succeeding, I would have to find others with magical abilities. This could take time. And first, I would have to figure out how to get from nexus to nexus. The girls had done it but had no clue how. They had not taken the time to experiment.

The delay while I was figuring things out would allow the enchantment to pull more people in, growing ever more powerful and harder to overcome. Time was of the essence. Eldred and Hilda had manipulated the portal along with me and knew what to do. Having experienced assistants would be incredibly valuable. The three of us should be able to clear this place out in record time! Therefore, I gladly accepted their offer to help me.

Our task would become easier with each person delivered back to where they belonged. We decided that the first individual we would rescue would be the old lady who had befriended the girls. It was now a matter of locating her among all the cells!

From the girls' description, I had formed a picture of the layout of this nightmarish place. Eldred had mentioned that it reminded her of a beehive. Each party had its own cell, separated by something like a corridor. The sisters had to push through a membrane-like substance to enter or exit any of these prisons.

Hilda did not like the way it felt when they passed through. She described the sensation as highly unpleasant and admitted that she had panicked a few times. Getting in and out appeared to be easier for Eldred, but even she revealed that it took her breath away and made her nauseous. Both shared that it had been becoming more challenging the longer they were here.

It was safe to assume that their loss of life force to the incantation was at least partially responsible for the increased resistance they had encountered. I admired the girls for having been so persistent in their exploration of this construct and in their search for a way home. Maybe now that we had reclaimed our energy and were no longer directly attached to the spell, these walls would present less of an obstacle. One could only hope so!

Passing through did sound pretty awful. Clearly, this nasty enchantment liked to keep all its prisoners apart. Hilda mentioned that she believed that this atrocity also fed off our emotions. Keeping us in seclusion, therefore, yielded additional benefits. Being away from their home, missing their loved ones, and all alone in such a gloomy and depressing environment was bound to increase a person's misery. On top of that, there was nothing to do here. Everything outside the path was frozen and, according to the girls, almost impossible to interact with.

My dismal cell offered no shelter since getting to the dilapidated house would not be easy. There was no food here nor anything to drink. The dreariness in itself was depressing. This truly was the perfect place to push even the most cheerful person into the depth of despair! If Hilda was right, this would add to the dark energy of this awful hex, making it ever stronger.

Hilda believed that most of us here could not overcome the part of the trap meant to keep us in isolation. Only her sister had discovered a way to enter and exit the globes. For some unknown reason, Eldred seemed to have a knack for finding her way around in this nightmarish setting. She would lead us now. Determinedly, she guided us down the path, past the driveway, and toward the area where the scenery ended.

To my amazement, when we reached the barrier, the fog parted before us. The way forward revealed itself. Needless to say, I was stunned. It had not done that for me, but then I had not walked right up to the mist with the impunity and determination Eldred had. Her sheer will alone forced the vapor aside, revealing the membrane that separated us from what lay beyond. She was about to grab our hands and push through, but I stopped her.

"Eldred, let's try something first. You guys always held hands when you entered or exited, right?"

"Yes," Eldred answered, clearly intrigued.

"Let me try it on my own first," I declared, walking up to the wall.

My admiration for the girls rose even higher as I got a good look at the barrier. It looked alive! I shuddered. Carefully, I reached out and touched it. It felt warm, kind of leathery, and sort of like skin, definitely repulsive. Now I saw why the girls had called it a membrane! That was precisely what it was! Could this entire complex of cells be made up of organic material? And where had it come from?

Steeling myself, I pushed against this disgusting obstacle, first lightly, then with increasing force. Soon I put my shoulder against it and used the weight of my body. The barrier might have stretched a little, but that was it. It was not about to let me out! Next, I asked Hilda to try. She made no more headway than I had! However, when Eldred walked up to it, the wall gave way on its own accord. An opening into the tunnel between our nexus and the next appeared.

One after the other, we stepped through into the passage filled with a white mist that gave way before us. We did so without holding hands. To my surprise, there was no nausea or anything else like that. I might as well have walked through a door! The strange barrier began to close silently behind us. As we watched, the material just flowed back into the empty space! Soon, there was no sign left that a hole had ever existed.

"Well, that was easy," Eldred stated drily.

"It was," agreed Hilda. "It was you all along!"

"Eldred, you are just as powerful as the stories say!" I exclaimed. "I am so glad that you and Hilda decided to stay! I would have been stuck in there!"

"No, you would have found a way," Eldred disagreed with a grin. "It is not in your nature to let a little something such as this defeat you!"

We smiled at each other, and an understanding passed between us. In some ways, Eldred and I were very much alike.

While Eldred led us toward the cell where she believed the old lady to be, I had a discussion with the girls about magic. As it turned out, they knew much more than they were aware of! It just had never been called that and for a good reason! Their time was a dangerous one for anyone considered to be a witch! Their parents had done their best to not attract undue attention to the village!

For the first time in their lives, Eldred and Hilda could talk about the subject freely with someone who had the privilege of an extensive education in magical things. They were burning with curiosity not only about their powers but also about my life! Initially, I hesitated, but then I answered their questions in great detail. After what they had been through, they deserved some compensation!

It was sad to hear that the sisters never had the opportunity to explore the full extent of their abilities. As was the custom passed down from our ancestors, their education in the use of their powers had been done in great secrecy. Their lessons had been conducted only behind closed doors. Unfortunately, the practice of more complicated spells and such had been kept to a minimum.

No one could know that those living in Havn were different! In the past, the consequences of such information leaking out had caused nothing but sorrow! Since most of the members of the clan had capabilities of some sort, neither of the sisters believed that they were anything special. The construct, however, was showing them that this was not the case.

Eldred and Hilda would eventually grow into the most powerful sorceresses of their generation, but no one outside the clan would ever know this. They would find clandestine ways to help their neighbors to avoid drawing attention to the village. I was grateful that we no longer needed to be as afraid of persecution during my time. Folks were much more accepting, and the days of the witch hunts were over.

Still, we were careful. People fear what they do not understand. As cute as magic appeared on television, folks often reacted differently when encountering such forces in real life! With our neighbors, the Magnuson Clan had carefully cultivated an image of New Age hippies instead of the powerful beings we were. Any odd occurrences were easy enough to explain away.

However, caution around those who were not like us was too ingrained in my people to fade away overnight! Too many years of fearing persecution had left its mark.

Their intelligence and ability to grasp abstract concepts made teaching Eldred and Hilda a pleasure. The sisters picked up on the principles I presented fast and easily. Eventually, it sank in that they really did have the gift. That moment was like an awakening for the siblings. From then on, they were determined to learn everything they could. Thus, we managed to cover the basics very quickly, even though we practiced each bit thoroughly.

Before long, we reached more advanced topics. Now we really started to have some fun! Since this construct was large and we had a ways to go, we stopped several times to rest. We used those breaks to delve deeper into some of the subjects that Eldred and Hilda found especially interesting. Some of it was just too hard to explain on the go, and the girls found it helpful to be able to watch how I performed a particular enchantment.

To my immense surprise, once they fully understood the principles behind a spell, these two would devise different ways of accomplishing the end goal. The first time they did this blew my mind. My parents had discouraged experimentation, so I had never even thought about trying to rearrange an incantation in that manner! This was amazing, and I loved it! Magic, for me, would never be the same!

Just as I had enlarged the sisters' world, so did they now expand mine! As we strode toward our destination, the three of us worked on honing our instincts. Thus we gained more information about the construct and the people imprisoned within. For the first time, we got an estimation of the actual size of this awful place. We were stunned. It was huge and still growing!

Eldred had been right; the trap was hivelike. Therefore, we decided to call it that. The awful enchantment had created a construct that was much larger than we had anticipated. And it contained a lot more people than the girls had met, probably about double! This was unpleasant news! But we were determined not to let this discourage us. So it would take a bit longer to take everyone home! We would make good use of the time!

The three of us would keep learning as we went, starting right then. Hilda and I watched how Eldred did the focusing in on her target. Like a bloodhound, she was following a trail neither of us could perceive, at least not at first. We kept asking her how exactly she did this. Finally, Hilda started getting the hang of it. She took the lead and pinpointed the direction we needed to go within this maze of prisons.

I kept trying but failed. Eventually, we figured out why I could not home on our target. Hilda also knew the lady we were heading for, but I did not! That was the difference! I could sense people around us, but without previous contact, I could not use my instincts to find a specific person within the strange world of the spell. Finally, we decided to link.

Suddenly, everything fell into place for me. I could tell we were getting closer to the woman, but we still had a way to go.

Another piece of important information that we discovered was that the hive existed outside of time and space. It was in what we believed to be its own pocket dimension. Due to the large number of captured occupants, it was honeycombed with many nexuses like the one I had found myself in. However, search as we might, we discovered no empty cells beyond the girls' and mine.

Therefore we had to assume that every time it captured another person, it created a new space to imprison them in! This would expand it even further! Since it was being sustained and powered by all those it kept within, it could continue to grow indefinitely. Now that was a terrifying thought!

Our path continued to weave between the large cells. As we went, the white mist that filled the passage kept parting in front of us and then closed behind us. It was eerie! We were in a bubble of sorts that moved along with us. I was so glad that I was not alone in this strange place! As were the girls! A good part of the time, we walked holding onto each other. The physical contact gave us a sense of security that we bitterly needed!

I continued showing Eldred and Hilda how I did the various spells to distract us from our odd surroundings. They actually had a pretty solid foundation. The sisters had seen using their will to achieve a desired outcome as something so natural that it had never occurred to them that they were actually doing magic! No outsider, even if they watched the pair closely, would have ever guessed that they had something to do with the end result.

Over the years, our clan had perfected this technique even more. But our progress had ground to a halt due to our teachers discouraging us from experimenting. I did understand why. Strange occurrences, things blowing up, and oddly colored smoke billowing forth from a cauldron were hard to hide in a world with access to the internet and cameras on cell phones!

Seeing an opportunity to further our knowledge and improve the lives of the clan in the sisters' time as well as mine, I shared what I had been taught with Hilda and Eldred. Since we were in a place where our experimenting would go unobserved and cause minimal damage, we worked on finding even better ways of achieving our objective. And how to do so in a manner that could not be detected.

The Magnuson Clan had always been careful to hide their powers. However, after an unwelcome visit from a group of zealots, the kin had started being even more cautious. At that point, on the orders of the girls' father, all the children's official training had ended. But Eldred and Hilda's mother had continued teaching them enchantments that she thought might help them survive in the privacy of their home.

However, they had been strictly forbidden to use their skills outside the room they practiced in. Thus, they had not progressed as far as they could have. We made up for that now! Was I interfering with history? Probably! But, as far as I was concerned, the sisters deserved some benefit from being held captive in this horrible place! And for their sacrifice of staying with me!

So, we continued to train. Even though Hilda was two years younger than Eldred, she caught on even faster than her sibling. By now, she had also mastered the tracking ability. Therefore, the girl took over when we reached a spot where her sister was unsure which way to turn. Unerringly, she led us forward. I was quite impressed.

Thus, we finally located the nexus containing Lady Emla Sutherland, who had been so kind to the sisters.

The old dame was delighted to be reunited with the girls. After introductions were made, I asked her some questions. We needed to determine how she fit into the scheme of things. We hypothesized that the enchantment had something to do with the Magnuson Clan. We were, therefore, not surprised when we discovered that Lady Emla's great-great-grandmother had been a Magnuson. Hilda believed that several others of those they had met were also kin.

This, however, left us with more unanswered questions. To start with, why was our clan the target of this curse, and who had cast this awful spell in the first place?

Chapter 17

The Rescue Begins

Lady Emla Sutherland was an interesting character. Her ties to the Magnusons gave us more clues about this vicious trap we found ourselves in. It also made Eldred, Hilda, and I more determined than ever to undo this atrocity. Left unchecked, it might eventually collect all the members of our clan, even the most distant ones! This spell, for a reason we had not yet determined, seemed to have been designed to wipe our kin from the face of the earth. This could not be allowed!

We needed to get people out of this construct to weaken the enchantment and fast! Starting with the old lady before us. However, when we asked her if she was ready to return home, she told us flat-out no. Now, this we had not expected! The girls and I looked at each other, perplexed. This place was awful! Why would someone choose to stay? That made no sense to the girls and me, but we had better figure it out! And quickly!

Gently and as tactfully as possible, we continued enquiring about Emla's life. We were trying to discover why she would rather remain in this nightmare than return to the real world. Finally, the old lady relented. Tears welled in her eyes, and she looked at us with despair. Hilda sat down next to her and held her hand to give her strength. Haltingly at first, she shared with us why she was so reluctant to return.

"I do not remember if I have told you, but I am a widow," Emla began. "My marriage was happy, and life was good. But after his death, everything changed. I am a burden to my family. They are better off if I stay!"

"But why?" Hilda asked. This was beyond her understanding. "You have been nothing but kind to Eldred and me! I bet you are a wonderful mother!"

"My daughter seems to think so, but not her husband and my son," Emla explains. "To them, I am just a nuisance."

Now it was Eldred who knelt down beside the distraught woman.

"Lady Emla, please trust us. We want to help you, to make things better, but we need to know what we are dealing with!"

Eldred's words struck a chord with the unhappy lady. But it took further encouragement and assurances from all three of us before Emla finally took heart.

"Misfortune seems to haunt my steps," Emla stated sadly.

"Please, what do you mean by that?" I asked. "Help us understand!"

Slowly, Emla began to disclose some of the details, all the time gauging our reaction to her words. She truly opened up when she realized that we actually believed her and did not judge or ridicule her. Finally, we were getting the real story! That was something the girls and I could work with!

As can be expected from someone with Magnuson blood, Emla had some minor abilities. Being completely untrained and clueless about such things, she thought she was cursed or bad luck. Her out-of-control magic seemed to have caused her a fair amount of trouble. This had landed her in an untenable situation.

Not having grown up near the clan and its resources, Emla had not realized she was gifted. Therefore, she had been terribly afraid of her powers. As far as she was concerned, they were unchristian, condemned by the church, so she had tried to suppress them. This had worked reasonably well as long as her husband had been around and she had been happy. In any case, with him to protect her, no one would have dared question her or accuse her!

What we fight, however, always gains strength! The death of her beloved partner had sent the old lady into a deep depression. Her already tenuous control had slipped. As a result, odd things had begun to happen around her. After a while, people connected these strange incidents with her. From then on, out of fear of hurting someone, Emla had confined herself to her mansion.

Our hearts went out to her. The girls and I could sense how alone and lost Lady Emla was. It had been years since the death of her husband, but we could all feel the pain still residing in her soul. She had done nothing to deserve all the additional anguish and problems! Eldred, Hilda, and I exchanged a glance. Maybe we could help?

Gently, we explained what was really going on. We told Emla about the Magnuson bloodline and the unique abilities many of us had. And that these powers were a gift from the Divine, no matter what the Church and those around her said! They were a part of us and should not be condemned as evil or feared!

The old lady was so relieved that she swooned where she sat. Eldred and Hilda immediately reached out to steady her. They decided to sit next to her, one on each side, just in case. This was a lot to digest, after all!

It took a few moments for Emla to compose herself. Then she started asking us questions. She was incredibly pleased to hear that her premonitions were just that and not a sign that she was going crazy or causing these incidents as she had feared! Our friend brightened visibly with that burden of worry removed from her shoulders.

Realizing that we took her seriously and would not make fun of her, she was ready to share the rest of her story. Thus we discovered that most of her trouble had come from one source, her own son! He was an unpleasant character to start with, and they had not gotten along well for some time. As a young man, he had been an absolute wastrel!

Eventually, his father put a stop to his debauchery by cutting him off financially. This had been a rude awakening for the youngster, but it had been effective. Emla and her husband had helped him start a business when their wayward offspring straightened up a little. But he had never forgiven them for having to work for a living! He felt this was far beneath his station and that he deserved better.

These resentments had smoldered, and to punish his parents, he had totally ignored them for years. He had not come to visit when his father fell ill, nor did he attend the funeral. Emla neither saw nor heard from this 'pleasant' individual for several years. Not that she minded. She was heartbroken enough without dealing with this cad on top of it!

Only when the son experienced money problems did he reappear. His greedy eyes then turned toward the family fortune since he needed a large sum to pay off his debts. His mother did help him, as did his sister, but he wanted more. Seeing that Emla was still in good health and not about to die anytime soon, he had plotted against her. He had started rumors in the town that she was crazy and bad luck.

Eventually, he went as far as claiming that she was responsible for his father's death. That creep had even tried to convince his own mother of that! Hearing this really upset Eldred. Her free hand was balled into a fist. Good thing that this guy was out of reach! The lady's son had seemed so sure in his beliefs that he had made Emla doubt her sanity. Especially since the nonsense he had spouted coincided with her deepest fears!

How much the possibility that all he was saying could be true had scared and bothered her! Sleep had evaded her, and her appetite had all but disappeared. The idea that she could somehow be responsible for her beloved husband's death had mortified her.

But, all that subversion had not achieved the desired result. The old lady had not taken her own life or faded away as that monster must have intended! Instead, his mother had withdrawn from everyone around her. Furious, the son had stepped up his campaign. However, Emla had been in full possession of her faculties, even if he claimed that she was not. She had known better than to trust someone like him!

The poor lady might have feared that she was losing her mind, but that did not mean she would relinquish the pursestrings to him of all people! Her husband would have turned over in his grave! But, her refusal earned her an increase in verbal onslaughts and hurtful comments. As a result, her self-doubts had grown.

The more she had panicked, the stronger her instincts and visions became. Having been raised to obey the Church, she had rejected all the warnings and premonitions, at least consciously. But some of it had stuck and had guided her actions. She had told her insolent offspring to leave her alone and get out of her house. He had not taken this well and swore he would get even with her.

No longer being able to torment his mother, the son had grown desperate enough to try having her committed to the local madhouse, an absolutely horrible place! He had almost succeeded! However, her daughter, Ayla, the Lady Satterfield, had come to her aid. The rather forceful young woman had tried reasoning with her brother. But he had his eye on the mansion and the lands around it and was done waiting to inherit it all.

To protect her, the daughter had seen herself forced to take Emla into her own household. This caused trouble from the very beginning. The young woman's husband had not been thrilled! This led to a fair amount of friction and frequent arguments between husband and wife. To minimize the unpleasantness, the old lady had stayed in her suite. She had decided to starve rather than subject herself to the man's abuse at the table.

About that time, the fairies had started visiting her. Thanks to their company, Emla had no longer felt so alone. But due to seeing them, she had feared that her faculties had slipped beyond repair. To protect the family, she had barely even opened her door. Her daughter had brought her meals when she could. Thankfully, her new friends had fetched her food from the kitchen. It had been much more fun eating with them than with that weasel who called himself lord of the manor!

The determined Ayla, however, had not given up the fight. She had always despised her brother. After what he had done, she loathed him even more. The strong-willed young woman had also grown tired of her husband siding with the scoundrel and bossing her around. Defying her spouse's orders, she had slipped into her mother's manor. There, she had managed to rescue some of Emla's favorite possessions, including the jewelry her late husband had given her.

Despite Ayla's best efforts, the beautiful mansion, the land, and most of her money, however, had fallen into the hands of the greedy son.

Emla had tears in her eyes as she told us the story. With all the ugliness waiting for her at home, she had seen the nexus as a place of peace and safety. As far as she was concerned, here she would not bring trouble to anyone else. Eldred, Hilda, and I could see her point. With her husband dead and not being welcome in her daughter's manor, what did she have to return to?

Her grandkids avoided her, having been poisoned against her by the pompous Lord Satterfield. Even with Emla staying in her suite, her son-in-law had become more hostile about her presence in his home with each week that passed. Her only friends had been the fairies. Even though she did miss those, the old lady did not see a good reason to go back. How very sad for her and those she called family!

The girls had put their arms around Emla to give her the strength to share the entire sordid tale. Needless to say, we were all three furious at the injustice this gentle and kind woman had experienced at the hands of her callous and self-centered son and the nitwit her daughter had married. No one should treat their parent like that!

This got us thinking. What could we do to even the playing field? And to help Ayla? It sounded like she might need some magic to take control of her life! Besides, she deserved our assistance for standing up for her mum! Most likely, she had some abilities as well! Could we teach her to use persuasion? But first, we needed to get Emla in a better mental space and reawaken her fighting spirit.

After a brief discussion on how best to deal with the situation, we explained to Emla what had been happening and what had caused the strange events. Seeing the light return into the poor woman's eyes did my heart good. The more we told her, the brighter she got. Knowing she was gifted and not jinxed, cursed, possessed, or crazy as her son had claimed, was huge! All of a sudden, she no longer felt so powerless!

We taught the old lady several spells to give her an advantage in her further dealings with that cretin. Once she understood the basics and could cast the enchantments, we allowed her to practice on us. This was far from pleasant, but necessary. We were just grateful that Emla caught on quickly. This shortened our agony, but Eldred, Hilda, and I felt like we had been through the wringer by the time we were done!

After several hours, when she had perfected the castings, she declared she was ready to go home.

When we reached the veil of smoke, Eldred asked Emla to recite the incantation she was to teach Ayla one more time. It was the best we could think of on such short notice. We really wanted to help that determined young woman to take charge of her life. For her, divorce was out of the question due to the times she lived in and her circumstances. But that did not mean she could not be the power steering her husband in the desired direction!

With a feral grin so foreign for one of her sweet nature, Lady Emla repeated the incantation flawlessly. That man had another thing coming! After all the misery he had caused Ayla, our friend could not wait to empower her daughter to take back her life. Especially since the estate that jerk lorded over was his wife's in the first place! As was the money! Satterfield had brought the title to the marriage but nothing else!

Shortly after, the Lady Emla Sutherland became the first of many we took home.

Once we had delivered Emla to her time and place, Eldred located the next individual. Despite all the magic the old lady had practiced on us, we had decided that we had it in us to do just one more. Once we entered the cell, we could not have left. This nexus was plain horrid! Whoever was stuck here, we were getting them out!

When we finally located the occupant of the cell, the woman seemed tired and listless. She appeared almost catatonic and barely responded to us. Eldred and I did some healing on her to bring her around, but she was desperately in need of rescue! My heart ached for her, and I was glad we had chosen to continue our mission.

The girl's dress, accent, and mannerisms identified her as someone from long, long ago. That the trap extended that far back stunned Eldred, Hilda, and me. If our guess was correct, it was taking people from a time span of over a thousand years! That was almost inconceivable! This one might be one of the first settlers to arrive in Gairloch from Norway!

After introducing ourselves to Signe, we started asking her questions. We were trying to understand how she had been drawn into this evil scheme. As we had expected, the young lady was a relative. She was one of the daughters of Finna and Bjørn, the earliest known ancestors of the Magnuson Clan here in Scotland! The girls and I looked at her with awe. She was someone from our past we never thought we would meet!

Signe had just recently made her way to the Highlands on one of the Magnuson trade vessels. As luck would have it, the spell had captured her just two days after she arrived! She spoke English rather well but with a heavy accent. This made it hard for us to understand her at first. But, being eternally curious, Eldred, Hilda, and I wanted to know everything about her.

Had she lived among the fabled Vikings before the crossing? How many people had arrived with her? Why had she left Norway? Our imaginations were fired up by all the possible scenarios running through our minds that her words had conjured up. Discarding our desire for this to be a quick job, we sat down and encouraged Signe to tell us her story.

I was so excited. This was truly incredible! What an opportunity to fill in some lesser-known areas of the Magnuson Clan's history! Once I got home, I would write down everything I could remember. I would tell the tales of all the people I had met in the construct. That way, their stories would become part of the record books of the clan. Who knew what we would learn in the process!

Then, as if to remind me of its presence, my phone poked me. Keeping it hidden, I pulled it out and turned it on. This might be a bit much for people from so long ago! Putting it in airline mode to prevent any extra battery drain, I set it to record. I was thrilled. This was an even better means to bring Signe's story back to my kin!

Chapter 18

The Spell's Response

Once she had recovered her wits a bit, Signe was so relieved to see us that she kept touching us to assure herself that we were truly real. Not that we could blame her! Everything around us was draped in thick, roiling, yellowish fog. Shapes that looked like people appeared and disappeared. It was hard to distinguish between things that were actually there and the figments created by this eerie mist! This nexus was truly something out of a nightmare!

The young woman was sitting on a raised area on the narrow, muddy path that meandered through this scary, hazy bog. It was one of the few drier spots in this wet environment. She had been lucky to find it! The trail was partly submerged for long stretches, and pools bubbling with swamp gas could be seen in several places whenever the miasma lifted a little.

This setting was much worse than the one I had ended up in! Good thing that we had decided to continue with our mission! The idea of Signe remaining here all alone much longer was abhorrent! She was rattled enough as it was! Any of us would have been! Hilda looked around and then shuddered. She obviously shared my sentiment about this awful spot!

Our new friend was only too happy to talk to us. She really did not want us to leave! We found out that she had been on her way to get water. It had been a gloomy, rainy day. Thick bands of mist had drifted across the lands and the trail before her. She had just walked into one of those ribbons of vapor when she suddenly felt dizzy. Signe had staggered on for a few more feet, not paying attention to where she was going. Finally, the lightheadedness had gotten so bad that she had to sit down.

When her head cleared, Signe realized she had no clue where she was. She did not recognize any of the landmarks around her. The girl concluded that she must have stumbled off the path before passing out. Since she had just recently arrived in the Highlands and was unfamiliar with the area, the young woman naturally assumed that the murkiness was due to time having passed.

Signe believed herself to be lost but not far from home, a perfectly rational conclusion. After all, the strange surroundings resembled the landscape near the clan's camp. Not wanting to make the situation worse, she had chosen to stay close to where she was. This would have been a prudent course of action if she had been back in the real world!

Who could blame her for staying put! This place was awful! She was lucky to have found this little knoll to rest on!

None of us were cowards, but even the idea of wandering around in this dreadful landscape all alone gave Hilda and me the shivers. Eldred was certain that this cell would unsettle even those with the bravest of hearts! The light was dim, and the meandering way between the pools was fraught with peril. One misstep and the moor would suck you down forever! The girls and I were grateful that Signe had walked as far as she had! It had already been quite challenging to reach her!

As luck would have it, the young woman had stumbled some distance beyond the smoke. How she had stayed on the trail in her stupor was beyond us! Maybe at that time, the path was still isolated from its surroundings. We were not sure how far she had come, but we could not see the haze from our location. Then again, it could have been close but hiding between the bands of fog.

All that moisture in the air, however, was concerning. None of us wanted to lose sight of the way out! Getting stuck here was not on our agenda! Still, tramping through this wavering, gross-looking vapor was what nightmares were made of! On the way to the girl, our feet had sunk into the morass up to our ankles with every laborious step. Our trek along this soggy, mist-shrouded path had seemed to take forever!

We had moved with extra care and held on to each other in case there was no bottom. The fear of that had been only too real, and we had no desire to find this out the hard way. The girls and I hoped that as long as two of us were on semi-solid ground, we might be able to pull the third out of the mire! We were greatly relieved that it did not come to that, but progress had been exceedingly slow! Traversing this by yourself would not only be foolish but also incredibly dangerous!

This place was certainly different from all the others the girls had been to! Only the knowledge that some poor, unfortunate soul was stuck in this mess kept us going. We were glad that Signe had waited and hoped that one of her brothers would find her. Besides, thanks to the dizzy spell, she had no idea from which direction she had come! Anything could have happened to her!

However, as can be expected in such a dreadful environment, the young woman had grown increasingly distressed as time passed. And she had been just about hoarse from calling for help when we arrived!

I could perfectly understand why she had not suspected foul play. Why would she? She was new to the area and did not have the reference points Eldred, Hilda, and I did. We knew something was wrong since we were familiar with the region. It was good that Signe had not moved.

The nexus she found herself in was unlike anything we had expected. It was much eerier than mine, and it was deadly!

While the girls talked to Signe, I looked around in fascination. We had been so concentrated on our steps on our challenging hike to her that we had paid little attention to what lay beyond the trail. This was the first time I had a chance to study the scenery better. I was not thrilled with what I saw! The bog the path ran through was daunting! And here, the route was not straight like in my cell but meandered!

We had been lucky to make it this far safely! Good thing that we had moved along so carefully! The path and some of its immediate area appeared to be the only solid ground near us. Here and there, where the mist was less dense, I could see deceptively calm pools next to ones with streams of bubbles. The water appeared oily and was a disgusting brown color. It could be hiding anything!

I was sure we would be sucked right under if we fell into that, never to be seen again! This place was incredibly unappealing and full of peril. I can usually find something pleasing in even the most dismal scenery but not here. This landscape was devoid of beauty. It gave me the creeps. What had it been like for Signe to be stuck here all alone? It must have been awful!

Even the plants were disgusting! Most of the vegetation around us looked slimy. It appeared to be on the verge of decay. As we had discovered, bizarrely twisted tendrils and roots were always ready to trip you up and send you sliding off the track if you stepped wrong. This was a dangerous spot, especially with the lighting so dim. The murkiness reminded me of a rainy day right before night falls.

The lack of discernibility made it challenging to gauge if it was safe where you were putting your feet! I was glad Signe had stayed put since even the trail was so treacherous! This was definitely not a place to wander around in without extreme caution! And a buddy or two! I only wished that we had some rope to tie us together!

Suddenly, the miasma parted for a minute, and I got a quick glimpse at the little house in this nexus. It was more of an utterly dilapidated hut, built out of stone with a roof made of moldy thatch. It was even more shabby than the small cabin in the spot where I had landed! Sad, really, that such a fascinating relic of days of old was in such terrible shape!

When I looked closer, I was starting to have doubts that we could even reach it! You had to cross an especially vigorously bubbling section of the moor on an almost nonexistent trail to get there. I was not sure that I wanted to brave that, not even to get a look at this piece of history! But I was tempted, for an instant! However, I talked myself out of investigating the cabin without too much trouble.

A loud pop drew my attention to a nearby pool. In fascination, I watched for a moment. Now that I had time to observe at my leisure instead of probing every step, the glaring difference between this place and my prison hit home. Unlike the spot I had landed in, the scenery here was not frozen in place! Nor was there a distinction between the path and its surroundings! And the fogbanks were actually moving, and the mud was roiling!

Was something out of the ordinary happening here, or had the construct captured enough people to power the entirety of the cells?

The girls had been to many nexuses and were keen observers. Maybe they had seen other spaces like this! I would have to ask them!

"Eldred and Hilda, have you been to other places in the hive where things moved?" I therefore enquired.

"No, not like this! One spot showed an occasional, sudden twitch, but that was it," Eldred responded thoughtfully.

"Has something changed that we now have motion? Is that what you fear?" Hilda inquired.

"I am not sure. I have not seen as many of these cells as you have, but this place discourages exploration. If it had not been for your talent, Eldred, I do not believe we would have reached Signe safely. She was smart to stay put!" I explained.

"Yes, I see what you mean," Eldred agreed, looking around. "Could the spell be reacting to us taking Emla home? It might be fighting back and finding better ways to keep us here!"

"That could very well be," I agreed.

Us depriving it of one of its prisoners was the one significant change we could think of. The enchantment had lost one of its power sources. Was it trying to make sure that the rest of us remained? That would make our mission to return everyone trapped to where they belonged so much harder! But do it, we would, no matter what that evil construct sent our way!

Eldred and Hilda did not like it here much either. This place was exceedingly hostile and wild. On occasions, the fog got so thick that we could barely see a few feet beyond where we were sitting. In contrast, Emla's cell had looked just like mine or at least very similar. But, then again, she was not that far removed from my own time, having been born a couple of hundred years after the girls.

I am not sure I would have done much experimenting had I arrived here! Moving around was not only difficult but also unsafe. These surroundings made me hypothesize that the nexuses adjusted to the era as well as the area a person came from. Also, I suspected that they could play on our deepest fears. Entering more cells in this honeycombed construct would either confirm or disprove my assumptions.

We would have to be alert for further repercussions from this monster for depriving it of its human batteries! But first, I intended to take advantage of meeting this daughter of Finna's. I wanted to learn more about the couple who so many of the clan's people were descendants of. This was, after all, a once-in-a-lifetime opportunity!

Signe had listened to our conversation, but she had not commented. For a child of a Viking, she seemed awfully meek, not at all like I had imagined one of the maidens. Were they all like this? I had assumed the women to act more like the men, to be warriors, fierce and brave. Something was wrong with this picture but what? Looking her over closely, I noticed how awkward she sat. Was she injured?

"Signe, what is wrong? Are you hurt?" I asked her, full of concern.

Instead of an answer, the young woman pulled back her skirt, giving us a glimpse at her upper leg. Hilda gasped and averted her eyes.

This looked terrible! No wonder Signe had no fighting spirit! She had to be in awful pain! It was surprising that she could even walk! The dreadful wound was puckered and angry looking, not very old.

The poor girl! Her thigh had been mangled beyond repair, most likely by some sort of an animal! It was nowhere near healed. Magic must have saved her life, but it had not undone the damage. It would take a skilled healer several sessions to fix this now. And, even then, the chances of restoring the leg back to full health were slim!

But from what I remembered, Finna should have been able to do just that! There was definitely a story here, and I hoped Signe would share it.

Chapter 19

A Difficult Healing

Eldred, Hilda, and I knew it was rude to stare, but none of us had ever seen an injury as ugly as this.

"What happened?" Hilda asked gently.

"I got surprised by a boar out in the woods. My mother did her best, but she did not have much time. If our clan was going to escape, we had to leave that night. A few people, including my parents, remained behind to make it look like we were still there," Signe explained.

"Could you have stayed behind?" I asked curiously.

The young woman's mother, Finna, was known for being an incredibly talented healer. She could have minimized the damage, given a chance.

"No, I would have just been a liability," Signe said sadly.

"Your situation was that dire?" Eldred inquired.

"Yes. My mother worked on me until they carried me to the boat. Unfortunately, the ship's healer was not strong enough to do more than keep it from getting infected."

"I am so sorry! That must hurt terribly! You are lucky to be alive with an injury like that!" Hilda stated, moving forward to hug the girl.

"If not for my mother, I would have died. She healed me as much as possible in the little time we had." Signe stated.

My heart went out to this brave young woman. To begin a sea journey with such a severe injury had taken a lot of guts. But what had made their situation so desperate that they had loaded a severely wounded person into a boat?

"Just curious, but what was going on that you had to leave?" I wanted to know.

"Raiders were lurking not far from the village. From our observations, we felt they were getting ready to attack any day," Signe said matter-of-factly.

"So those who remained behind gave the rest a chance to get away?" Hilda enquired.

"Yes, and they would have to move fast to escape themselves when the time came," Signe affirmed.

"They had a place to hide from the raiders?" Eldred questioned, caught up in the story.

"Yes, in the nearby caves."

"Why could they not take you there?" Hilda quizzed our new friend.

I was wondering the same thing. We were trying to understand why the severely hurt Signe had been shipped off in the first place instead of remaining with her mother, who could have worked miracles on her leg.

"For a couple of reasons," Signe explained patiently. "The caves are dark and dank, not at all conducive to healing. And everyone had their assigned jobs. I would have been there alone with no one to care for me. Besides, my mother's magic was needed to keep up the illusion that we were still in the village."

"Getting on the boat really was your only option then," Eldred declared.

"It was."

"How brave of you! And walking on your injured leg to get water despite the pain? You are a true warrior, Signe!" I praised her.

Signe's face lit up at my words. Having her accomplishments acknowledged meant much to her. I had a good idea of the thoughts that had gone through her mind when no one came looking for her. She must have felt totally abandoned and feared they had had enough of taking care of her. From what I had read about the family and her brother Leiv who was in charge of the settlement, I doubted this very much.

Not knowing she had been caught up in an enchantment, the young woman had come to the most logical conclusion. My praise, however, demolished the last few remnants of Signe's laboriously maintained composure. Her calm and reserved demeanor vanished in an instant.

"When no one came, I started thinking that I had been cast out or that I had been killed and ended up here as a punishment," she mumbled with a sob, sounding completely heartbroken.

All three of us reached out to hug her. After a moment's hesitation, Signe moved into our arms. She started crying bitterly. Who could blame her! Her nerves had to be totally frazzled from the pain and the last few hours in this awful place! I was so glad that we had found her and were in a position to help!

From the look on Eldred's face, I knew immediately what she was thinking, and I agreed. We needed to get Signe out of here and locate someone capable of helping us give this young woman her life back! Besides, since our arrival, the fog had thickened. It would be impossible to find the plume of smoke now. The hut and parts of the trail were also shrouded in mist! I realized that we would not be able to get her home from here even if we tried!

"Signe, do you trust us enough to come with us?" I asked.

"Yes! I do not want to stay here by myself! This place is awful! It reminds me of the Land of Death!"

The Land of Death? Interesting! I could see how she could assume that. The never-changing twilight, the bubbling moor, the dense fog weaving about - this place was enough to creep anyone out! Our new friend had not hesitated with her answer, and I was glad. This meant that she still had the will to fight and live.

The three of us got to our feet, careful not to step off the little knoll. Then, we proceeded to help Signe up. We had to be very careful since every movement caused her tremendous pain. And still, this courageous young woman had gone to fetch water! My esteem for this determined lady rose in spades. She truly had the grit of the Magnusons! Not surprising her family's descendants were so tough!

"Alright, Eldred, can you lead us back to the in-between and find us a healer?" I inquired.

"Yes, but we need to move slowly and carefully, just as we did getting here. Hold onto each other! I do not trust this place! I fear that it will separate us if it can!" Eldred said, orienting herself.

Getting out of here would be even more of a challenge than reaching Signe in the first place! With her leg so weak, the young woman was not that steady on her feet. We would have to watch out that all four of us did not end up in one of those bottomless pools!

The fog had gotten so thick that it was hard to see more than a couple of feet in any direction. This made the narrow, perilous path even more dangerous. However, staying put did not seem like a good option to any of us. If we waited much longer, we might end up trapped in this dank, cold, mist-shrouded place! That option held little appeal for any of us! Therefore we decided that Eldred would use her instincts to guide us through this morass.

Quickly, we lined up single-file. Hilda and I put Signe between us. This way, she could hold onto my shoulders to steady herself. And, when she needed to rest, leaning against me would allow her to take some weight off her injured leg. In this manner, we hoped to traverse this treacherous terrain without any significant mishaps. Hilda would grip Signe around the waist and give her what help she could from behind.

Once we were ready, Eldred firmly took hold of one of my hands and started pulling us along. Without hesitation, she wove between puddles and dark, steaming pools, never wavering. Watching her was really astounding. Her instincts allowed her to navigate this horrible place with astonishing ease, even when the path was completely submerged!

Slowly but surely, we made our way along the sodden, slippery trail. After a few minutes, the fog started to get even denser. It seemed almost like it was responding to our actions and trying to keep us in this prison! The visibility was soon so limited that we could barely see each other. Also, due to Signe's injury, we had to rest every few feet. Still, we continued to make steady progress, but it took us a long time to traverse this nightmare setting.

When we finally reached the barrier, we let out a sigh of relief. Eldred stepped close, and an orifice opened before us, allowing us to push into the adjacent tunnel. We were back in the in-between space! I had not liked it much in there before, but it was spades better than that bog we had just escaped from! Had it not been for Eldred's talents, we would not have! The miasma had continued to get thicker until we were virtually blind!

At least here, there were no bottomless pits to disappear into! And walking was much easier for Signe. However, she was exhausted from our slog through that deep, sticky mud! But she refused all offers of further support and limped along on her own. Hilda stayed beside her, and soon the two were involved in an animated discussion. Seeing them together like that, you could not miss the family resemblance. These two could have been sisters!

Following her gut, Eldred led us around other spaces in this evil enchantment toward the one where she believed help could be found. We briefly considered going through the cells to save time, but the walls felt like a living membrane, very weird and distinctly repulsive.

Pushing through them was an odd sensation, one reason we had not gone in a straight line but had skirted the other nexuses.

Also, we had no clue what to expect from any of these places. They were all different. After the dreadful setting we had rescued Signe from, none of us wanted to take chances. That spot had done its best to keep us imprisoned! By the time we had reached the barrier, the fog had gotten so thick that Eldred was moving on instinct alone! We did not need another adventure like that, not anytime soon!

Plus, there were the occupants of those prisons. How could we leave them? At the moment, we had our hands full with our new friend. Also, for some reason, the in-between space felt safer, as if the spell's power was limited here. Since we suspected it was out to get us, it was better to be cautious.

For a while, Eldred and I walked together in silence. When I glanced back, I noticed that Signe looked done in for. Her strength was rapidly failing. Despite her earlier refusal of help, she started leaning on Hilda. I rushed over and supported her from the other side.

We moved on slowly but had not gotten much further when Signe got worse. She looked barely conscious. The girl had reached the limit of her endurance. All she could do was keep her injured leg up, nothing more. A few minutes later, the pain became too much. She passed out completely. Now Hilda and I were carrying her between us while Eldred saw to her legs. Even though she was a slender girl, she started to feel heavier with every minute. We were rapidly getting tired.

Finally, we arrived at our destination. Once we had pushed our way through that creepy membrane, we took stock of our new surroundings. The girls and I were happy that this nexus was reasonably bright, almost like the real world, and had no fog! That alone made it a sort of haven for us. Eldred and I carefully looked over the path and scenery to ensure it was as safe as it appeared.

Thankfully, the landscape here was frozen. Nothing moved. The only sound we heard was a lively song that a lady's sweet voice intonated perfectly. Eldred led us to her without hesitation.

"Hello there! How lovely to see you!" a pleasantly rotund woman greeted us as soon as she caught sight of us.

I liked her immediately and knew instinctively that Signe would be in good hands with her. This one was obviously just the healer we needed! Hilda agreed, and so we moved as quickly as possible toward this friendly person.

"Well done, Eldred!" I whispered to the girl, who blushed at my praise.

"I am Revna, and it is a pleasure to have your company!" the wise one informed us when we reached her.

Revna had been studying us carefully as we approached. Trying not to be too obvious, I watched her as she talked to the girls. Everything about her reminded me of happiness and sunshine, and the power emanating from this lady was impressive. Like many with such an intimate connection to the Divine, she had a timeless quality. Shiny, bouncy, brown curls framed a sweet, unlined face with skin so smooth and youthful that it made her appear much younger than my senses told me she was.

When I met her knowing, almost violet eyes, I saw so much kindness and understanding in their depths that I was instantly drawn to her. Her competence was such that I knew she would help me shoulder the responsibility of all those caught in the trap. Relieved, I felt myself relax for the first time since I had decided to remain and help the other victims.

Until that moment, I had not been aware of how much of a burden my own sense of duty had placed on me! Revna made me wish my mother had looked at me this way and had been more like her. This lady gave off a feeling of comfort, of unconditional support! I loved it! What would it have felt like to grow up with that? I sighed. My parents were who they were; that did not make them bad people.

However, the distance between us had always left me longing for more closeness. I was grateful to have found this with Phillipe and his family.

Revna returned our smiles with one of her own. A wave of love washed over us. She had read us perfectly and understood our need not just for the healing of Signe but also for a spot where we could feel relatively safe. We required a base to operate from, and her support would make the task ahead of us so much easier! She obviously did not mind mothering the four of us, and of that, I was glad.

Eldred began the introductions. The healer nodded at each of us in acknowledgment. It turned out that she also was a Magnuson. With formalities out of the way, it was time to deal with the problem at hand. Signe was still unconscious, hanging between Hilda and me. Revna stepped closer and gently touched our friend's feverish brow. She took in the lines of pain on the young woman's face. They made her appear much older than she was.

"You need my skills, my poor girl!" she muttered, examining her further. "Where have you children been to be so covered in mud?"

"The nexus where we found her was not pleasant like yours," I explained. "It was wet, cold, and deadly!"

"The worst kind of place for such an injury! We need to get her clean and keep her warm. Good thing that you got her out of there!" Revna praised us.

"We did not know what else to do. Even if we had been able to find the smoke in all that fog, we could not take her home in this condition!" Hilda put in.

"You did right bringing her to me. No one should suffer like she has!" Revna said with much indignation.

I could not agree with her more!

"I need her lying down so I can get a better look at her injury!" Revna instructed Hilda and me.

We obeyed immediately and gently slid Signe to the ground. Revna was right. With magic at our disposal, healing even severe injuries was possible. No one should have to live with pain like this!

"We are happy to lend you some of our power," Eldred told Revna. "And, we would like to learn, if you do not mind!"

"Mind? Not even a little! I am happy to teach you what I can. There are never enough healers to go around. Even a basic spell can make the difference between life and death in times of need," Revna informed us.

Once everything was arranged to her liking, the wise one examined Signe's scarred leg. Then, she checked the rest of her. Eldred, Hilda, and I crowded around and observed. Revna explained what she was looking for and shared her findings.

The severe pain and lingering infection had taken a considerable toll on the young woman's body and psyche! The dreadful nexus and slogging through that sticky, slimy, disgusting mud had not helped. At this point, Signe was running a high fever. The wound, which had already appeared pretty ugly before our trek through that morass, was now incredibly hot and angry red. I knew enough about injuries to realize that this was not good.

Once the examination was complete, Revna got down to business. She singled Hilda out to assist her while Eldred and I watched. First, the wise woman placed her hand on Signe's forehead. Even though she was unconscious, the wise one sent her into a deep sleep that would allow the girl's body to start restoring itself. Only then did she start working on the thigh.

With a wave of her hand, Revna banished all the mud caking Signe's clothing and footwear. Then she gently removed the shoe and slid up the skirt. Now that the leg was clean, the redness appeared even darker against her pale skin! The wound had scabbed over in some spots but was oozing in others. Where it had been mended by Finna, thick scaring had fused together tissue and muscle, making motion extremely painful. This looked bad!

Much had to be undone! The deep-seated infection had to be attacked at the roots to ensure clean healing. Eldred and I watched with absolute fascination. When Revna moved her hands just above Signe's skin, we could almost see the energy flowing from her fingers! This was incredible! We had truly lucked out to find such a strong and talented healer for our friend!

Since the damage was so severe, it was slow going and took tremendous power. When Hilda grew too fatigued to continue, Eldred took her place. She and Revna were making good progress. Soon, all the infection had been drawn out. It was time to work on the scar tissue. Once enough of it had been softened in just the right places, the adhesions that trapped muscles and ligaments could be detached. How Signe had walked was beyond us! The pain she must have felt with every step! It had to have been extreme!

Finally, it was my turn to assist. I closed my eyes and, with my mind, followed along as Revna began to reknit some of the severed muscles, veins, and arteries. The damage was so extensive! Bit by bit, she restored some of the tissue. But there was so much left that needed addressing! I realized that we would not be able to complete this in one day. More than one session would be necessary to set this right!

Since the clan did not have an energy worker who had the skill to handle this, Signe would not be going home anytime soon!

When we had done all we could for the day, Revna and I sat back and rested. The healer decided to wait a while before waking the young woman. This would give her body time to recover from all the trauma it had endured over the last weeks. The rest of us got comfortable. To pass the time, we shared our stories. Our new acquaintance turned out to be not only incredibly powerful, but she was also a warm, gentle, and loving person!

Revna agreed to let us stay with her in her nexus. She offered to help us heal the young Viking maiden, thus giving her a shot at a normal life. Hilda went over to hug her and ended up sitting next to her, cuddled up in the wise one's arms. The sisters had lost their parents not long ago, and the girl obviously still missed her mother immensely. Our new friend's soothing presence did her good.

Finally, it was time to wake the patient. All of us got up and crowded around her. With a slight touch on the forehead, Revna brought Signe around. At first, she looked disoriented. She had been unconscious when we arrived, so she had no idea how she had gotten here. But once she saw Eldred, Hilda, and me, she relaxed. Then, suddenly, she remembered what we were here for. Quickly, she checked her leg.

Signe's eyes teared up when she saw the reduction in redness and healthy pink color in many of those places that had been severely inflamed. This healing was just the beginning, but the thigh looked better already. The young woman's face was a picture of total disbelief as well as incredible gratefulness. She used her fingers to examine every inch of the ugly wound. The ridges of the scar tissue were there but not as pronounced nor as hot as before.

The maiden could barely believe she could touch and move the leg without causing severe pain. When the reality of this welcome change finally set in, a look of such delight crossed Signe's weary features that she looked years younger. With immense gratitude, she threw her arms around the healer's neck. She kept thanking her and us for making this possible. Then, from one moment to the next, she broke into tears.

Revna, having that motherly air that drew Eldred, Hilda, and me to her so strongly, held Signe and let her cry. This was a release of sorts. It would help wash away some of the hurt and pain this terrible injury had caused the young woman. The sharp tusks of the large boar had dug in deep. They had ripped tissue, tendons, and muscle. Both the tibia and fibula had been broken as the animal rammed her against a tree. Had help not arrived, it might have torn off the leg!

Within just a few minutes, the attack had made Signe a cripple. That she had been unable to care for herself on the boat had been hard enough, but facing a lifetime of being unable to hunt and provide for herself had been worse. As far as she had been concerned, she was nothing but a burden to the clan, someone who no longer contributed anything of value. Having been a warrior, being utterly dependent on her family's charity was a devastating turn of events.

Had I been in her shoes, I would have hated that too, and I was not a proud descendant of a fierce Viking father!

Between sobs, Signe shared how she had felt. Our hearts went out to her for what she had endured. I could tell that Revna was more determined than ever to return the young woman to her home healthy and hale. Having had time to relax, I remembered Signe's role in our history. She was too important to our clan to be allowed to continue suffering like this!

As it was, we were her only option. It could be months before her mother arrived. By then, the healing would have been even more involved. Possibly, it would have been too late to affect much positive change. Providence had brought us together! At least something good would come of us running afoul of this evil enchantment! After a few more minutes, Signe composed herself. She wiped her eyes, smiled at us, and thanked us for the blessing we had bestowed on her.

Her spirit was much restored. For the first time, a sparkle had returned to her eyes that had been missing. Signe once again had hope and felt much more optimistic about her future. She was ready to repay us in the one way she could. From our expectant faces, she had gathered that all of us, including Revna, were extremely curious about her and her family. We wanted to know what their lives had been like!

Who would not be! How often do you get to meet or hear an actual account of the people at the root of your family tree? Signe, her parents, and her siblings were the founders of our clan! They were the original Magnusons! Taking our cue from her, we made ourselves more comfortable. It was story time! I decided to record her tale and reached into my pocket.

However, I was not careful enough when I brought out my phone to record Signe's account. Eldred caught a glimpse of it! Immediately, she wanted to see what I was trying to hide. That is all it took. They all had to examine it closely! Since the technology went beyond anything they had ever seen, I had to explain what this strange gadget was and what it did. Naturally, everyone wanted to touch it, look at it, and see some pictures of my home.

I opened the folder with the images of my pets. Bear, our male German Shepherd, with his big, soulful eyes, was a huge hit with the ladies. They felt my sweet boy was beyond handsome, and his younger sister Hella Rose was just adorable! They loved her antics and thought her highly entertaining. Hella was brilliant as well as mischievous, a dangerous combination! Little Micha, our dachshund/corgi mix, was pronounced absolutely the cutest thing ever, and Arianna, our older German Shepherd, regal and stunning.

Not unexpectedly, Hilda fell totally in love with the two guinea pigs. They appealed to the little girl in her just as they did to mine. She asked lots of questions about the difference in their looks. Orion's hair was smooth and silky, while Teddy's was short and wiry. She then insisted on seeing the pictures of other ones I had owned, and I showed her Pacino and Pepper, who had long since passed on. And Sammy and Marie, who had been my familiar. However, tiny Theo, who lived to be almost seven years old, was her absolute favorite.

That these small creatures came in a variety of types delighted Hilda to no end. She decided that once she got home, she would find a way to get some of her own!

Poor Cedric! That young man had no idea what he was in for!

Chapter 20

A Daring Escape

My phone turned out to be a huge distraction, but since it helped to further perk up Signe, I indulged our group. The only problem was that they wanted to see everything! How much of my life, of a future none of them would ever see, was safe to share? I was still considering possible implications when Eldred took the decision out of my hands by snatching the thing! Having watched me closely, that brilliant young lady had no problem swiping her way through the files!

However, when she spotted a picture of Phillipe, she came to a dead stop and stared. Then, she showed the image to Hilda. Her sister was just as surprised.

"He looks just like our Cedric, just in strange clothes!" Eldred finally managed to squeeze out.

"He does, doesn't he?" I agreed.

"How did you know?" Eldred enquired immediately.

"I saw a painting of Cedric in one of our books."

"You have books with pictures of us?" Hilda wondered.

"Yes, we do. Of some of you. Strangely, the history started getting more detailed with you two!"

"With us?" Hilda gasped. "But why?"

"I do not know," I told her with a shrug. "But from your time on, the accounts in the clan's private history are very detailed."

"Could it be because of us meeting you?" Eldred speculated.

You could almost see the gears turning in that pretty head! Maybe she was onto something! I had to think about that for a moment, but then I saw her point. We had already spent a while together, and they had gained an understanding of times to come that few of their era would ever have.

"That is very possible," I finally had to admit.

"I am certain," Eldred stated decisively. "Until now, I always thought recording events was such a boring and useless task! Knowing that folks will read and treasure all we pass on puts keeping the clan's history up to date in a whole new light! When we get home, I will copy anything I can lay my hands on about our people. That way, it will come to you!"

"What a wonderful idea! And thank you!" I exclaimed.

"We should encourage any Magnusons we meet to do the same!" Hilda added.

"Yes, we should!"

On this, we were all in agreement!

"Back to your Phillipe and our Cedric. Is it not strange that they look so alike?" Eldred wanted to know.

"Phillipe and I are distant cousins through his mother, but his father is a Mackay," I explained. "You two are his ancestors as well as mine."

"When the time comes for us to go home, you will have to meet our Cedric," Hilda declared firmly.

One look at her told me that any objections would fall on deaf ears. Her face was set in the same mulish look that Eldred's got when she dug in on something!

"I have to admit that I am curious and had already intended to deliver you to him personally," I informed her with a grin.

Hilda smiled back at me. "Good! You better!"

There would be no arguing with her; that much was sure! Not that I minded meeting another of my ancestors! Especially not one who looked so very much like my beloved Phillipe! After all, how many people ever got the chance to get to know those who had come before them? As much as I disliked the enchantment, this one aspect of it genuinely intrigued me.

Meeting people who I had only read about was incredibly fascinating! And for the others, seeing what the world would look like in the future was a real treat. When the girls finally returned the phone to me, Signe was sufficiently recovered to tell us her story.

The beginning of the Magnuson Clan can be traced back to one Viking couple and their descendants. I was hoping that Signe could fill in the gaps and increase our understanding of those times long past! Finna Breckingsdottir, her mother, besides being an exceptional healer, was a vølva, a seeress. A very, very good one at that. Where she had come from or what had happened to bring her to Norway and then Scotland had only been hinted at. Not much was known about her husband's origin either. To have a record of this would be priceless!

Naturally, Signe was curious about the process of recording. After I showed her how it worked and let her hear what it sounded like, the young woman agreed to let me use my phone to capture her every word. But, being a little intimidated by the importance of our project, she had a hard time getting started. I decided to help her.

"Let us begin with your mother. Would you please tell us about her?" I prompted the young woman.

Signe smiled at me gratefully and began.

"My parents have not shared much with us children about their history, but here is what I do know. My mother started having visions at a very young age. Her father, the advisor and best friend to the chieftain, realized quickly that what she was foreseeing came true. He had magic himself and had some training, something he kept well hidden. Therefore he knew how rare and precious his daughter's talent was and what could happen if anyone found out.

"Since my grandfather did not want his child taken from him, he and the clan's jarl devised a plan. They used my mother's predictions of impending disasters, but they concealed the source by finding ways to keep everyone safe without raising the alarm. This worked until my mamma had a vision during a ceremony, what kind I do not know, only that the whole clan was there. They had to act immediately to save everyone.

"People were grateful, but word got around that my mother's vision had saved them. Before long, it reached a rival jarl's ear. Being a true raider, he decided he wanted this oracle. Having her would give him an advantage over the other clans. He tried buying my mother first, but her father refused. As did the chieftain."

"Buying her? How awful!" Hilda whispered.

The rest of us nodded in agreement. The idea of being treated like a mere possession did not sit well with any of us!

"That man, however, was determined to have her. Therefore, one dark night, he and his men caused a diversion. In the resulting chaos, they kidnapped my mother and whisked her away to his stronghold. From then on, he kept her hidden, confined to his home. He had her watched by a few trusted guards at all times. Not only did this prevent news of her whereabouts from getting out, but the jarl was informed when she had a vision," Signe continued.

"My mother hated the man and his cruel ways. He kept her isolated except for the guards and the healer who taught her. Over time, she learned to sense when a foretelling was coming. She found ways to hide it and give the jarl as little information as possible. Usually, she only shared visions that would save lives. She was not about to further her captor's ambitions more than she had to!"

"Good for her!" Eldred cut it.

Signe smiled proudly and then continued with her tale.

"At first, she was also suspicious of the man's son. He often volunteered to watch her. Once they started talking, she soon realized he despised his father even more than she did. And he was prepared to help her!"

"How brave of him!" Revna added.

All of us were caught up in this story and hanging on Signe's every word. I was sure Eldred would record everything she remembered when she got home!

"Eventually, the two formed an alliance to keep as much from the jarl as possible. But, as time went by, my mother fell in love with him, and he with her. Realizing that they would never have a life together while she was a prisoner there, he devised a plan to get her out of the house and away from the village," Signe went on.

The rest of us were now leaning toward her. None of us wanted to miss what happened next.

"The two snuck out during a snowstorm. It was the middle of the night, and most people were asleep. Disguising themselves, they crept through the village like they were heading north, toward her home. Then, wading up a creek to hide their scent from the dogs, they circled back to the small boat the young man had hidden. He had been preparing for this day for months and had ample food on board, gold, and several changes of clothes.

"The blizzard caused them some trepidations, but they decided to head out anyway. First, they made their way along the fjord. Both were terrified to be caught since the punishment for their escape would be swift and cruel. Thankfully, the dense snow provided cover. On the other hand, visibility was significantly reduced, and the strong winds tended to do odd things in the fjord. This made sailing extremely hazardous.

"Under those conditions, rowing was not an option. Therefore, they put up the smallest sail they had. My mother hooked a shuttered lamp to the bow and acted as their lookout. She could only see a few feet ahead and had the extra oar up there with her just in case she had to prevent them from crashing into something. Or fend off one of the many logs!"

I could only imagine what that trip must have been like! Out in that kind of weather, working their way along the fjord in the pitch black, afraid of discovery the entire time. Even with the light, they had been practically blind! Their pursuers could have appeared out of the blizzard at any moment! How brave of them to make such a daring escape!

"Since calling out might get them discovered, and it was impossible to see hand signals, they thought of an alternative. They used ropes tied to his legs to direct him which way to turn."

"How very clever," interjected Hilda admiringly. "The man, he is your father?"

"Yes," Signe confirmed with a smile. Then her face grew serious again, and she continued.

"Somehow, my father seemed to steer around any obstacle. He was guiding their boat mostly by feel. It was truly miraculous that they did not run into something. Since they were moving rather slowly, it took my parents many, many hours to get to the mouth of the fjord. Both were exhausted and freezing by that time. Once out in the open sea, they decided to continue with just the storm sail and to let the fierce winds push them along.

"They made their way in an easterly direction as best as they could. From their description, it was a rough crossing. The seas were huge, but at least they were going with them. Still, they frequently had to bail out the freezing water and scoop out the snow. The rest of the time, they huddled together for warmth.

"When my parents finally spotted land days later, they worked their way along the coast. They were careful not to get too close and kept an eye out for other ships so that they could avoid them. My father had dyed the sails a stormy blue in preparation for their escape. In addition, he had painted the hull a similar shade. This made them almost invisible since their little boat blended in perfectly with the winter sea."

"Your father is a very clever man," Revna praised.

Signe nodded. Her eyes shone with love and pride for her folks. And with good reason! How courageous and resourceful they had been!

"Having accompanied the clan on several raids, my father knew these waters. He was wise to the tricks the sea liked to play in those areas and steered them clear of the worst of it. My folks headed north along the coast, always staying just out of sight until they spotted the tell-tale group of islands announcing the entrance to a huge fjord. From there, they sailed west.

"The more distance they put between themselves and their home, the better they liked it. But my parents remained cautious. The jarl had larger ships that could easily do what they had not dared - cross the large stretch of sea heading northwest! My mother was too much of a prize to let her get away! My father knew the clan was out looking for them, and his instincts kept telling him they would be safer on land. My folks decided to heed his gut feeling.

"Not wanting to be seen, they made landfall in a hidden cove. They had felt drawn to this particular one. Here they discovered a cave that allowed them to hide their trusty vessel. The Gods had guided them there for that reason! Leaving my mother behind, my father walked back to the town they had seen in passing. There, he acquired a sled and dog team. By himself, he attracted far less attention than with my mother. It was hard to hide her beauty, and his kin was looking for them together.

"Once he returned to the inlet, my parents decided to move the boat to a more isolated location further up the coast. There, they loaded all their possessions on the sleigh. Then, with a heavy heart, they smashed in the bottom of the boat from underneath. If it was found, this made it look like it had run afoul of the rocks. Next, they raised the sails and pointed it toward the open sea."

I cringed. The idea of scuttling a perfectly good boat was abhorrent to me! I loved sailing vessels and firmly believed ships had souls. Signe's parents seemed to have felt the same way but had seen no other option. They could not afford to leave a trail.

"My father had calculated the size of the breach correctly. The boat did exactly what my parents intended it to do. It sank a little way offshore, thus removing all evidence of their landing and having set out from this particular spot. Both donned plain garb and hid anything that could have betrayed their origin or identities.

"From there, they worked their way inland, then turned west, and eventually north. My father had been told that crossing the mountains during that time of year was not wise, so they stayed near the coast. As a precaution, they changed their names several times on the way. Also, they continued to switch clothing and appeared either as poor farmers, tradesfolk, or traveling nobles. They kept this up until they got close to where they were heading. Then, they started to introduce themselves as Inga and Gorm, a couple on the way to visit relatives in some city on the coast.

"Somewhere along their trek, they crossed paths with Olaf. He befriended them and eventually brought them to the sanctuary. Here, he introduced them to the rest as Finna and Bjørn Magnuson," Signe concluded the tale of her parents' daring escape.

"What were their real names? And do you know where they started out from?" Hilda asked curiously.

"They never even told us, their own children, where they came from!" Signe sniffed with indignation. "Nor what their names were before they fled! We were lucky to find out this much!"

This was obviously a sore spot for the young lady! But she was in luck. That mystery had bothered my father and had therefore been examined to a great extent!

Chapter 21

The Sanctuary

Having parents who also liked keeping secrets, I understood Signe's frustration only too well. Should I keep the information I had on Finna and Bjørn to myself? I considered possible implications for a moment, but then I concluded there was no harm in sharing what I knew.

"My father had your parents extensively researched," I began.

"He did?" Signe said instantly, sudden interest lighting up her eyes. "What did he find out? Please tell me!"

"We did not find much, but from what we discovered, your folks came from a place near Aalborg in what we now call Denmark. You might know it as Danmork. We narrowed down the jarls to three possible men. Any one of those could have been that nasty grandfather of yours who imprisoned her. But, since he kept her hidden, we could not determine exactly which one," I told her.

"Thank you! That is at least something! Not that I ever want to meet that man, but he is my grandfather!" Signe declared indignantly.

"Why will your parents not tell you who he is?" Hilda questioned.

"I think they are afraid my brothers will pay him a visit!" Signe laughed.

"Oh no! I can see why your folks would not want that!" Eldred exclaimed.

"Me too," Signe had to admit.

"With the information you have given me, I will be able to find out more about them once I get home," I declared confidently.

"Too bad you cannot share it with us!" Eldred stated drily.

I had to agree! If only there was a way to stay in contact! I genuinely liked all these ladies and hated the thought of never seeing or talking to them again once we made it out of the enchantment!

"Can you tell us more about your family?" I asked to distract myself from the sad thoughts crowding in.

Signe smiled her assent.

"During their flight, my father discovered that he had the gift. For obvious reasons, my parents decided to keep their abilities hidden. They had done everything possible to avoid leaving a trail and were not about to get themselves into a situation like that again. Olaf sensed they had powers and understood their need for secrecy. He and his group were dedicated to helping people like them."

"We did come across some information on them. Many of the men were powerful warriors with magic powers. They had experienced the same persecution and challenges as those they were helping!" I added.

"They were knights of sorts?" Eldred questioned.

"Yes, and they have their own code of conduct. Their lives are dedicated to assisting all those with magic. They still exist in my time," I explained.

"So Olaf was not the first?" Signe inquired.

"No, he was not. There were others before him and since. The knights have saved many over the years. Unfortunately, to this day, folk fear the unusual and those they do not understand," I stated wistfully.

"Yes, sad, is it not?" Hilda commented.

"It is," Signe agreed. "As a result, our village wanted little to do with outsiders, but we did welcome others like us. We were a haven for all those who did not belong and will be so again in our new home."

"I love the idea of a place people can go to avoid persecution!" Hilda exclaimed.

"Some of your folk were hunted by someone?" Eldred inquired curiously.

"Yes, many, my parents among them. Most were fugitives. Some were worth large sums of gold if handed over. A few weeks before my mother and father arrived, the people were betrayed by someone wanting that prize. A short while later, the settlement was attacked. Thankfully they were warned by one of the seers. This allowed them to make preparations. When the raiders sneaked up on the village, they did not catch them unawares. Instead, folk fought back with all their might.

"When the battle was over, many of the invaders lay dead, and the devastation to the village was terrible. Most of the huts had been burned to the ground. Olaf decided it was no longer safe there, so they moved to a different location. They used the boats they captured during the battle for transport. Fearing this could happen again, they found a spot even more secluded. However, Olaf's dream was to create a safe haven far from Norway for all those like them.

"To filter out all those who could not be trusted, they maintained some presence at the original settlement. When my parents arrived, they were questioned very thoroughly. Olaf turned out to be the leader of the village. Realizing that only the truth would earn them shelter, my folks shared their entire history with him. They even told him who they were on the run from," Signe stated with a frown.

She was clearly annoyed that her folks had not shared this information with her!

"Maybe they did not want their children's lives overshadowed by the stigma of that man?" I suggested gently.

"Maybe," Signe agreed with bad grace.

"From what I have read about your parents, they loved you and were very protective of you," I tried to soothe her.

"They do love us and do their best to keep us safe," the young woman acknowledged, somewhat mollified. "But, back to the story. Since they had been honest and desperately needed shelter, my parents were welcomed into the community. They were taken to a secret, well-defended location called Trygg Havn shortly after. That means Safe Harbor," Signe finished with a wistful smile.

"How long did you live there?" I asked curiously.

"It was our home until we came here," Signe responded. "The sanctuary was hard to find. To keep us secure, no outsiders were ever allowed there. When my parents arrived, my father built a sturdy cabin with the help of the neighbors. My brother Leiv was born before it was even finished, then Erik, me, Auga, Torsten, Svend, Hilda, Sten, Rune, Njal, and the last one was Yrsa. I believe that my mother had enough at that point and has been using her magic to prevent any more of us from coming along."

"Eleven? Who can blame her?" Eldred added with a shudder.

Signe laughed. "I have no intention of having that many myself!"

"Me neither!" Hilda agreed. "How about you, Cara? Want to add some more little darlings to the Magnuson Clan?"

"No way! Phillipe and I are not sure if we want any at all!" I confessed. "My brother has enough heirs to carry on our line!"

"What happened next?" asked Eldred, having grown tired of discussing children.

"Preparations for the eventual move began after Yrsa was born. About then, Olaf decided we needed to learn to blend in better with the folks around us. He asked several of the knights to teach the rest of us how to hide our abilities. Their motto was that nothing gives you away faster than out-of-control magic! We all took this to heart, having seen the scars on some of our neighbors!"

"Those who do not understand us can be so cruel," Revna added regretfully.

It seemed she had had her own experiences with the ignorance of fearful people!

"The planned relocation would grant us a second chance at a normal life, but only as long as no outsider knew we were different. Therefore, Olaf drilled into us to never use our powers in a flashy manner or where we could be observed. Instead, we devised new ways of doing things," Signe explained.

"We still use many of those techniques in my time. People are a little more open-minded, but if they knew what we can do …" I had to say no more; they all understood.

"With both of our parents being gifted, my siblings and I have stronger powers than most. Around us Magnusons, things just happen. To really confuse things, often long after we are gone. Now that is fun!" Signe pronounced.

I totally agreed. The time delay was something that I had developed into an art form, much to Phillipe's amusement.

"Those abilities will be just as strong in some of those coming after you!" I informed her. "We Magnusons are encouraged to marry within the large extended family or to others like us. My parents are scarily powerful, and so is my brother. My gifts are different; they lend magic to my words, and I can see timelines. We are taught to control our powers early on, even those who choose not to use them."

"How can anyone deny their abilities?" Signe asked without comprehension for such silliness. "They are part of who we are!"

Secretly, I agreed with her, but those of the clan did have free will.

"Where do you teach your people?" Eldred inquired.

"The clan has its own school now, the Magnuson Academy. It was opened in 1809. Initially, it was meant only for the kin. However, eventually, they started admitting other children who needed its teachings," I informed them.

"We have our own school? That is something!" Hilda stated.

Eldred nodded her agreement. Even she was impressed.

"Tell us more about your life at the sanctuary, please! What was it like for you before you came to the Highlands?" Revna piped in.

The healer had mostly been quiet thus far but had paid close attention.

"When my parents arrived, life was hard, especially since folks had just settled there. After their recent experience, the villagers were afraid to reestablish their trading connection. Having been betrayed once was enough. The community relied heavily on fishing and the few things the knights brought, but it was not enough. Too often, everyone went hungry.

"So, once my father completed the house, he decided something needed to be done. He and a few others were not content to just exist and wait for the day we would move to the Highlands. He wanted more for his family than such poverty. As it was, discontent was rampant, and several others happily joined the group he formed.

"After some discussion, the rest decided to sanction my father's plan. Disguising himself, he traveled around. He watched and listened carefully. His magic helped him to identify just what their hearts desired! When he returned home, he and the group started making or procuring those things for their neighbors. The business was an incredible success. As soon as the boys were old enough, they got to help.

"When he was ten, Leiv came up with the idea of employing our people to make nets imbued with a slight bit of magic. The rest of the traders wanted nothing to do with this, so it became a family enterprise. The first few attempts were a disaster! But eventually, we got it just right and started sending them out to be sold.

They were quickly in high demand once word spread of how easy it was to catch fish with those special nets. This allowed us to employ more folks from the sanctuary.

"Olaf, still the chieftain of our tribe of refugees, was thrilled with this venture by our family. He preferred it to the trade we had been plying since it brought in goods and gold with minimal exposure to the outside world. And it gave the villagers something productive to do. They were very proud of their handiwork and well paid for their efforts. Making nets became a community affair.

"Soon, those working with or for my family were building up substantial nest eggs. Each person also contributed to a fund for land in far-off Scotland. The gold from the trade and the nets allowed my father to purchase several ships within the next few years. First Leiv, then Erik, went with him and the captains to learn all they could."

"Your ships traveled with some of the Viking raiders, did they not?" I asked, intrigued.

"Yes, my father had befriended some of them. He felt there was safety in numbers when you are out there on the sea. If you run into trouble, the others can help! In return for their protection, the raiders got nets. They loved them since they never went hungry again on a voyage," Signe explained.

"I would have thought that those fierce Vikings would rather steal the nets if given a chance!" Hilda interrupted! "Was your father not taking a chance of drawing attention to your village?"

"Oh, he had that covered! Business was always done away from the sanctuary. Also, there was a rumor going around that if the makers or sellers of these miracles were harmed, the magic would fade in all the nets. I am certain my father had something to do with starting that tale! It made the raiders feel rather protective about us and ours!" Signe laughed.

"How very clever!" Hilda applauded, clapping her hands.

"Thank you," Signe responded with a smile. "Our trade really took off about that time. More and more gold kept coming in. It made us, as well as the rest of the village, very wealthy. We could suddenly afford luxuries many had only dreamt of. Some gave in to temptation. They did not want to wait until we relocated to have fine things.

"But, buying all these items could not be hidden forever. It drew attention to us we did not need. Olaf and my parents grew very concerned and decided that the time had come to relocate somewhere safer. Shortly after, my father left for Caledonia. I believe that you call it Scotland. Secretly, he met with several lairds of the Mackay. He was determined to negotiate a safe haven among the clan for our people before we got attacked again.

"At first, he was making little progress. But then he met the right laird. After some back and forth, my father managed to purchase a forested section outright. In return, he would supply the Mackays with reasonably priced goods, a win-win for all."

"That was well done!" Hilda exclaimed.

Signe smiled proudly at this praise of her father.

"Were the Vikings that had settled in that area aware of his dealings?" I wanted to know.

"No, those were kept a secret. That lot is more prone to taking than negotiating. Should they find out, they would see this as a weakness. They would be full of contempt and would no longer provide safe passage for our people. But theirs and our grandfather's brutal ways are not to my father's liking and never have been. Besides, there are clear signs in the stars that their influence is waning.

"Our mother, and some other seers, have foretold the invaders would be driven from the Highland shores by the fierce clans before too much longer, so some separation is in our best interest. We considered warning them, but our Viking friends tend to scoff at such things. Besides, if we threw our lot in with them, we might also be forced to leave.

"My father plans to stay apart from either group for the time being but be useful to both. He needs the goodwill of the Vikings, or his ships would become prey, but also that of the local laird so that our people can live in peace."

"I can see where he found himself in a difficult position being a friend to both!" I added thoughtfully.

"Yes, and playing one side against the other greatly bothers him. But, the time of the Vikings is coming to an end. So, to cement the alliance with the laird, my father promised him my hand in marriage. He is supposed to be a stripping man, tall, dark-haired, and fair of feature," Signe told us with a sigh.

She looked down for a moment, visibly saddened.

"I am much better after the healing you did but still disfigured. My sister Auga will most likely take my place once she arrives."

"Oh no!" Hilda commiserated with her. "There has to be something we can do!"

"Can we mend her leg all the way, Cara? Revna?" Eldred asked me.

"I know about healing, but this is beyond me …" I began.

"We will get you healed as good as new, Signe. Just you watch!" Revna interrupted me.

Her confidence made all of us feel better, and Signe smiled at Revna gratefully. If the lady said we could restore Signe to full health, then it was only a matter of time!

Chapter 22

A Rapid Departure

Hearing that we were determined to help her, Signe brightened visibly. As intelligent and resilient as she was, the young woman would make a fine wife to the local laird! All we had to do was make it possible. The girls and I were determined that she would fulfill that destiny. Then something occurred to me. Or was it to be Auga's? Were we about to change history? What of the consequences? That thought bothered me greatly but had not yet occurred to anyone else. Hilda and Eldred were only too happy to assist our new friend.

Centering myself, I ignored all the others for a moment. I can sense connections and just know things. In addition, I can slightly manipulate the threads of fate in an emergency. But, this far back, that could have unforeseen consequences!

"Cara, what is it?" Revna, who had watched my face go blank, asked me with concern.

"We might be about to change history! I need to send my mind back through time to examine the threads. If we mess up, none of us might ever be born!"

"Oh!" Hilda said, stunned.

"I did not consider that," admitted Eldred.

"Neither did I," added Signe.

"Doing the healing feels right to me, but this is complicated. Is there a way you can show us what you are about to do, Cara?" Revna requested.

I considered this for a moment, then decided to go ahead and share my consciousness with the others.

"Yes, please, form a circle and take my hands!" I instructed.

We were ready shortly after, and I began. Moving back through time, I located Signe and the event that had caused her severe injury. The vibrations of the incident were all wrong. Her altercation with the boar was never meant to happen in the first place! The young woman had stepped in front of another and had protected someone else! She took the fate meant for her sister Auga! How brave she had been!

I realized that if she was not healed, history would be distorted, not the other way around. Some of the threads of fate were already starting to twist! We had to set things right and fast!

"We need to heal Signe and soon!" I declared firmly.

I explained exactly what they were perceiving to the others and pointed out the trouble spots. After that, we were all in agreement.

"Could she finish the story first, please? While we continue to recover from the last healing? I really want to know what happens next!" Hilda begged.

The child in her hated a tale left hanging, but I must admit I was also curious.

"I do believe that we have that much time, especially since it seems to stand still here in the nexus," Revna assured her with a smile.

"Please, Signe, what happened next?" Eldred asked, eager to hear more of the narrative. The young woman smiled and obliged her.

"Once everything was in place for our arrival from Norway and a few houses had been built, my father sailed back to the sanctuary. While he was gone, the rumors of a planned invasion of our settlement grew louder every day. Just the night before, we discovered that we were being watched. An attack was certain, and we could not wait much longer! Each day was taking us closer to our doom. Anxiously, we waited for him to bring word that the way forward was ready."

Hilda's eyes grew big, and Eldred hung on Signe's every word. I was sure they would write down much of what they heard here, thus passing it on to their descendants. How wonderful that our history books would be much more complete after this!

"We were lucky we still had the boats from the last raid. By the time my father arrived, we had already packed everything that we could take on such short notice. We had been careful not to give ourselves away and had done as much as we could behind closed doors and at night. Leiv, on the orders of Olaf, had made sure that everything looked as normal as possible during the day.

"Unfortunately, Olaf had fallen ill while my father was away. He knew he was dying and would never see our new home in Caledonia. Unable to keep up his duties, he passed the leadership role on to my father, who was his advisor and best friend. Most had expected this and were pleased. Only Lars Anderson was not. Craving power, he had been vying for the position for years.

"Olaf told my father to watch him, and it was a good thing that he did. Lars was so angry that he was going to sell us out! He and his father-in-law were caught sneaking out of the village toward the raiders! My father was saddened that his first official act as jarl was to sentence the two men to exile. He gave Estrid, Lars' wife, and Inga, their daughter, a choice. They could go with him or remain with us. Aware of their situation, he offered them a place in our household.

"The two looked at each other, then glanced at Lars. They started smiling, walked over, and spit at his feet. Without hesitation, they declared that they wished to go to Caledonia with the rest of us. Then,

Estrid went back over to her husband and relieved him of the pouch of coins he had with him. No one objected, not even her father, Lars' only friend, who was just like him - lazy, mean, and dishonest. It was her by rights anyway. All the gold had come from labor the two women had done!

"Can you believe that Lars made them give him all they were paid for the nets they made while he spent his time lying about and drinking? And her own father was in on it?" Signe told us, outraged. "And to top it all off, they kept Estrid compliant with threats to Inga! Olaf had suspected something, but Estrid had begged him to leave it alone. Where would she go if her husband cast her out? Not back to her parents!

"My father, with her agreement, had paid her less for the nets and had saved the remainder for her and Inga. Those two worked so hard! As a result, she had a pretty tidy sum built up already! And she knew where Lars had hidden all the coin he had taken from her over the years! She now retrieved it all.

"Estrid suddenly realized that she was a wealthy woman. This gave her power she had never had before! Having the new jarl's protection and the desire to start fresh in our future home gave her the courage to right then and there request a divorce. My father granted it gladly.

"You should have seen the smile on Ingrid's face, Estrid's mother, when she realized that both men would be banned. Then she kept hugging her daughter and granddaughter. She was so relieved that they would finally be safe. None of us had known their lives were that bad until that moment. Not wanting trouble, they had hidden it well. My father offered Ingrid the same terms as he had Estrid and Inga, and she joined our household as well."

"How sad their husbands treated them so badly," Hilda commented. "Our Cedric would never do such a thing!"

Eldred agreed with her sister. I have to admit, I was secretly amused. These two were a force of nature! Only a fool would tangle with either of them but together? No way! Revna, sitting next to me, must have read my thoughts. She caught my gaze, and the laughter in those violet orbs spoke volumes.

"To keep an eye on the horde watching us, we had scouts all around the settlement. I was one of them, and that is how I got hurt. Over the next few days, several more ships joined the first. This was bad! We suspected that they would attack soon, maybe even by morning! Leiv, Auga, and I were in such a hurry to get back and warn our people that we did not notice the herd of pigs until it was too late." Signe grew pale as the memory washed over her, but then she continued on bravely.

"Once the worst of the bleeding had been dealt with, my brother threw me over his shoulder and ran for home. We could only hope that nobody else would meet up with that vicious boar, but we had no way to warn them. Since we looked like we had been out hunting, none of the watchers seemed to think much of a single man arriving in a hurry carrying someone obviously needing help. Accidents happen. The rest of the scouts and Auga slipped in later unseen.

"While the healers tended to me, my brother informed my father what we had seen. We were out of time and had to go. My mother did the best she could for me, but she was exhausted and needed elsewhere. Since it was a moonless night, she led our people in calling up a fog as thick as they could make it. As soon as there was enough cover, the longships were brought in. They hauled all the previously packed things and me on board as quietly as possible.

"There was no time for long goodbyes. As soon as a boat was full, it made room for the next. They were all tied together to make sure that we would not lose each other in that dense mist. We kept listening for shouts that our frantic activities had been discovered, but none came. I was so relieved when our ships silently slipped away into the night. Thankfully, the fog stayed with us until we were far from land.

"The hardest thing was leaving some of my family behind. My parents, two of my siblings, and a few friends stayed in the village. They would make it look like nothing had changed and that our sanctuary was still occupied. My father tasked Leiv, since he is the oldest, with looking after everyone until he and the rest arrived in Caledonia.

"I do not remember much of the voyage. My injury was hurting terribly. The healer my mother sent with me did her best to keep me comfortable, but she got seasick and became too weak to continue the mending. Out of desperation, I tried doing it myself. But that wore me out very quickly. I think I slept most of the way. I never even got to catch that first glimpse of our new home that I had dreamt of for years!

"Once we arrived, Leiv called everyone together. He had the entire group work on me under the guidance of the healers. After that, I could move around a little, but not without pain. Still, I tried to be useful. That is how I ended up here. With all of you!" Signe finished with a laugh.

This young woman had been a warrior, a competent scout, healthy and superbly fit. Even after several weeks of enforced inactivity, she was still well-muscled and slender as a reed. Signe must have been truly formidable before her run-in with that boar! She probably could teach me a thing or two about swordplay! Her story had touched all of us deeply, and we were determined to find a way to give her back the life she had lost.

Revna suggested that we rest for a bit longer before we do any more healing. Hilda looked around questioningly. There were not many comfortable places along the path, but this nexus was far nicer than mine! Maybe the dark thoughts I was having had something to do with that? I was not sure but suspected as much. Signe had given up, and her space had been awful! Did our emotional states affect our surroundings? Only further exploration would tell!

When nothing else looked even remotely usable, we finally settled on a large section of moss. Sleep, however, eluded me. It seemed that it, along with food and drink, was not something we needed in this strange place!

Chapter 23

An Unexpected Encounter

Even after just one session, Signe's leg looked better, and the young woman's face was no longer as pinched from the pain as it had been. Once we had rested quietly for a while, we did another round of healing on her. Afterward, she and Revna settled down on the bed of moss for a chat while Eldred, Hilda, and I got ready to set out. We had work to do if we were to deprive this enchantment of some of its power!

Since Signe was not going anywhere, we needed to find someone else to take home. Determinedly, we made our way to the in-between space.

"Try to locate the person with the most need," I suggested to Eldred.

After finding Signe in such a state, that seemed to be the most prudent approach. The young woman concentrated for a few moments.

Then, without a word, she took off at a fast trot. Hilda and I exchanged a perplexed look and followed behind her.

We wove around several of the cells until we reached the one that had drawn her. The minute we pushed through the membrane, we heard the little one's heartbroken cries. Now all of us were running toward the sound.

To our surprise, Hilda put on such a burst of speed that she outpaced Eldred and me. She got to the baby first and picked it up. When we reached them, she was holding it tightly against her. This poor little one! The three of us exchanged furious glances. This child was not even two years old! How cruel of the enchantment to draw in such a helpless being! Once again, I really wanted to get my hands on the person responsible for this malicious construct!

"Where is the smoke," Eldred asked, searching the surrounding area with her eyes. She sounded worried. This immediately alarmed Hilda and me.

All three of us looked around us, perplexed. Finally, we spotted a trail of haze hanging in the distance, well hidden among some dead-looking conifer trees. This tiny girl had toddled a long way to get this far away from where she had entered the nexus! For someone so young, she was quite the explorer! If she did this frequently, she must be driving her parents crazy! From their thoughtful faces, it was obvious that Hilda and Eldred had similar thoughts.

"Rethinking that mother thing?" I teased them. "Just remember, Phillipe and I are your descendants! I am sure they are not all as precocious as this one!"

All my comments earned me were mock dirty looks. The sisters continued to fawn over the infant who was in Hilda's arms, clinging to her. When the child calmed down a little, she raised her head off the girl's shoulder and wiggled around so that she could see me.

"Mama!" she cried, stretching her little chubby arms longingly toward me.

Mama? Me? Eldred, Hilda, and I exchanged puzzled looks. Was this little one from the future? Phillipe and I had no intention of having a child! But could it have happened anyhow? Curiously, I stepped closer. When I did not take her from Hilda immediately, the toddler started to wail. Loudly! No matter how I felt about it, this one would not be denied! Seeing no other option, we indulged her. Thus, I ended up with her in my arms.

"Cara! You two have the same eyes!" Eldred exclaimed.

Both the baby and I had turned toward her at the sound of her voice. Hilda, seeing us that close together, caught on that instant.

"Is your name Cara?" she asked the child.

The little one nodded.

"Cara! She is you!" Eldred chortled. "You were that handful! No wonder you do not want children!"

Eldred and Hilda laughed so hard that tears streamed down their faces. The joke was definitely on me! I kept looking at the equally curious infant in my arms with wonder. It was understandable that she had mistaken me for my mother. We looked alike but had very different personalities. My parent was much more reserved, and business came before everything else.

I had always wondered why she had bothered having children at all. She most certainly did not like spending time with Oliver and me! For a moment, I was tempted to protect this child and bring her up with the love and attention she deserved.

"I know what you are thinking," Hilda said quietly beside me. "You cannot keep her. Nor can you spare her what is to come."

"And despite everything, you turned out amazing!" Eldred added reassuringly.

By now, we knew each other well enough that they could guess how I felt. We had been very curious about each other's lives. The girls had been blessed with loving parents who had just adored them. They had thought it sad that mine were more interested in the clan's business than their children. In their defense, my folks had a lot of responsibility and often worked late.

Oliver and I were practically raised by the staff. We were moved into the dorms of the Magnuson Boarding School once we were old enough. In some ways, we might have been better off. My mother had no patience for children!

"You are right," I finally sighed. "But, can you think of a way to armor her against all the destructive criticism and the rejection she will endure?"

"I can," Hilda stated after giving it some thought.

Determinedly, she moved closer.

"Both of you, look at me," she ordered.

Little Cara and I regarded her curiously. Then, Hilda began to speak, and her voice took on a hypnotic quality that mesmerized the child and me.

"You are loved, always. Never forget this. Sometimes people will say mean things because they are unhappy with themselves. Do not let it touch you but forgive them. You are perfect just the way you are and beautiful, inside and out. May sunshine reside in your heart and soul always, may any bad vibrations bounce off you and back onto its sender, and may you be protected all days of your life! For I so will it so mote it is!"

The power in her voice washed through me and released some of the bitterness I was still holding onto regarding my parents. I could feel my heart expand, free itself of those bands of pain that had been tightly wrapped around it. I started to cry, letting the last of the hurt flow away. The baby in my arms also had tears rolling down her face. Our eyes locked, and the bond of love that formed between us at that moment took my breath away.

Part of me would always be with her, and she would always be with me. Hilda had given us a gift that would allow this little one to grow up without all the self-doubt and feelings of rejection I had endured. She would remember that she was immensely loved and would not have to try so hard to earn this feeling or acknowledgment from parents who could not give her the assurance and comfort she needed.

"Thank you," I breathed.

By armoring the child, she had healed me. With much of the resentment gone, I could look more objectively at my parents' behavior and understand them better. They were who they were. That they had been unable to give Oliver and me what we needed was no defect in us as they had us believe. Sadly, being products of their environment, the flaw was in them. This did not make them bad people, just damaged ones.

Little Cara could feel my gratefulness. She reached for Hilda, who took her and hugged her close.

We spent a little more time showering this child with affection. We wanted to ensure that she would remember that she was immensely loved no matter what. I held her for a long time, rocking her gently. Through the bond we shared, I could feel both of us heal. How much damage had already been inflicted on one so young was stunning! This made me so sad for our parents.

I realized that they wanted the best for my brother and me. However, they lacked the emotional capacity to understand children and to give warmth. An entirely new understanding blossomed within me. I realized that my parents were not intentionally cruel but products of their upbringing. Growing up, I had gotten along well with my grandfather, but he and my mum had been pretty adversarial.

Those two had a complicated relationship since he had expected unquestioning obedience from her and my grandmother. He had pushed her to excel at the company. Therefore, my mother was remarkable at her job but felt lost when it came to raising her offspring. She had never learned how to nurture and was trying to be as different from my grandmother, who she saw as weak, as she could be.

My father's parents had also been heavily involved with the clan's businesses. They had left the raising of their children to the hired help. When one of the teachers discovered that my father was being abused by the nanny, instead of firing her, he was sent to a boarding school in Gairloch. He could not stay in Ny Havn since the dorms were just being built. My grandmother just did not have the time or patience to deal with him herself.

My parents truly loved each other and us. However, how to be affectionate with their children was something they had never learned. At times, they did try; I had to give them that. But lacking the emotional aptitude, they often handled us in a heavy-handed, authoritarian way, always assuming that they knew best.

Right then and there, I forgave them. Completely. The little one, back in my arms, was curled up tightly against me and had fallen asleep. With some of those old wounds finally healed, a new feeling emerged, a kind of longing. Maybe it would be nice to have a child of my own? To raise it with all the love and affection I had never experienced?

At that moment, I realized that Phillipe, who had a very happy childhood, would make an amazing father. I adored his parents and family. They were so warm and caring! I always felt welcome in their house. The love that pervaded the home when we spent holidays with them was almost tangible. They made me feel like I belonged, but being around them sometimes made me sad.

Oliver and I had missed out on such closeness growing up. We had usually been left at the boarding school over the holidays. If we were lucky, our parents might drop by for a few minutes, but more often than not, they were dealing with one emergency or another. I would insist my brother and his family celebrate Christmas with us this year. He needed to experience Phillipe's kin for himself! Besides, it would be wonderful for all of us to be together!

Having been raised so lovingly, Phillipe would have a much better idea than me on how to raise a child properly. All I knew was what not to do and how I would have liked to have been treated!

"You look like a natural with that little one in your arms," Eldred teased. "But, you have to give her back! Are you sure you do not want one of your own?"

"I could get used to this," I answered musingly, fondly looking down on the baby.

"Cara," Hilda insisted gently. "We need to take her home! I bet your parents are looking for her! Let me assure you that whenever

someone is unkind to her, a shield of love will surround her and shelter her. She will be alright, I promise!"

Her words reminded me that somewhere out there, my mother was looking for her lost child. She did love my brother and me in her own way and as much as she could. Unfortunately, she tended to show that by being controlling and fiercely protective of us, sometimes overly so. Naturally, I had resented this. After all, there was a whole world out there to explore, adventures to be had, and kids to be played with!

Instead, my brother and I were often confined to the house to do homework. Even before officially starting school, we had been forced to learn all about the clan and its history. We had lessons most days. It got even worse once Oliver moved into the dorms, and I was all alone. Being bored with studying, I had created opportunities to slip out and explore with Phillipe.

Learning to read at such an early age did have some advantages. I was fascinated with the books on herbology, especially sleeping potions. When I knew my parents would be late, my strict and oh-so-efficient au pair would mysteriously fall asleep after drinking the tea I had served her. I would make sure she was comfortable, change clothes, slam a hat on my head to hide my long hair, and then head out the door.

Phillipe had a perfect sense of timing. Somehow, he managed to show up shortly after I escaped from the house. On those rare occasions of liberty, he and I rode our bikes down the steep hill behind the house, something that had been strictly forbidden! We played in the brook, climbed onto the roof of the hotel, and ran through the woods like two wild things.

Every time, I was thrilled and delighted to be unsupervised and free for just a few moments!

Knowing the consequences, I was careful never to get caught or seen by anyone other than Phillipe. My instinct usually told me when it was time to return. Racing to my room, I would pull off the pants and shirt I had swiped from Oliver's closet. Most of the time, I managed to be clean and properly put back together before the au pair woke up.

However, on a couple occasions, when I misjudged the dose, she came to before I entered the room. I usually had an excuse handy, and she was not about to raise a fuss with my parents since she had been asleep and, therefore, derelict in her duties. To buy my silence, she would even help me finish the assignments before my parents got home if I was not far enough along. Neither one of us wanted to get in trouble!

Thanks to Phillipe teaching me useful abilities whenever we spent time together, I learned to be very proficient in sneaking about. I got really good at sensing and avoiding the staff while slipping out and back in. The stakes were high, and getting caught was not an option. Those times when I ran happy and free with Phillipe, without a care in the world, had been magical.

They had been so much fun and helped me through the years at home alone. By the time I got to boarding school, I was highly proficient at moving about unseen using a combination of magic and skills. There, however, I had more freedom than I had ever known! Now I understood why Oliver liked it so much!

Being away from home and all that supervision was incredible, but I must admit that, at first, this change felt strange. I was allowed to go play outside when the weather was good! The other girls and I did things together, and I made new friends. We were only seven but were given an astonishing amount of trust. We did have chores, but I loved those. Working in the herb garden and the greenhouses were my favorites, as was helping in the kitchen. Our house mother was kind and treated us as if we were her own children. Needless to say, I thrived!

Life improved drastically once I got out from under my mother's iron control. My days were no longer regimented down to the last minute, and I actually had fun. Realizing this made it easier to return little Cara. But, to ensure I would not change my mind, I let Hilda carry her on our way to the smoke. Now came the hard part. Where had she come from? Try as I might, I could not recall this incident!

We lived in Ny Havn at the time, but my parents did travel. Sometimes they would even take Oliver and me with them. Mini-me could have made her escape anywhere! The baby was too young to tell us where she had come from. But she did long for her mother. That would have to do for us to guide her back home.

At first, the spell fought us, but finally, we dialed in a location that felt right. It sure looked like the woods outside Ny Havn, so this had to be the place! As expected, nothing moved, but we could see several people in the forest frozen in the act of coming our way. My parents would have mobilized the entire village the moment they realized the baby was missing; of that, I was sure.

Hilda dashed toward them without even thinking and laid the little one at the feet of a frazzled-looking woman. I could not help it; my heart went out to my mother. She looked terribly distressed and utterly scared. She did love me; that much was evident! Maybe tiny me had decided to go on an adventure out in the woods all alone! Or was that the day some of my abilities manifested themselves?

After little Cara's experience in the nexus, I hoped she would stay put for a while and give our parents a break!

"Hilda, come on!" Eldred shouted. "We need to go!"

Her younger sister was still fussing over the baby. She seemed to have difficulty saying goodbye. Precisely for that reason, I had stayed near the smoke! Plus, we needed to anchor the portal. Also, none of us knew what would happen if I walked out there. The toddler and I were the same person, and the portal might just close behind me!

Thus, Eldred and I kept one foot and part of our body within the smoke. It would not do to have it disappear on us and strand us in a place where no one could see, hear, or interact with us! All three of us wanted to return to our homes eventually!

When Hilda continued to stay with the infant, Eldred finally ran out of patience with her sister.

"Hilda! Now!" she shouted, exasperated.

That did produce a result. Hilda gave the little one a last pat on her shining curls and headed our way.

"Do you think there is a way that we can keep an eye on her until she is safe?" she asked us, full of concern.

"Maybe. We could try moving a little way into the smoke and see if we can watch from there," Eldred suggested.

"Good idea, Eldred!" I agreed. "That might just work!"

Hilda held out her hands to us, and we grasped them. Then, carefully, we entered the plume, backwards this time. We worked our way in step by step until the world before us finally came alive. Then, we stood there silently as my distraught mother spotted her child. She picked up mini-me and held her tightly against her. Tears of joy and relief were streaming down her face.

How had she become so cold and detached in later years? Or was that loving parent still there under the mask? The baby was just as happy to see her, but she did take one last look over our mother's shoulder. She met first my eyes, then Hilda's and Eldred's. I was stunned. Little Cara could see us, but none of the adults could!

That was one fact I would file away in the drawers of my mind and remember the next time I had to deal with the clan's offspring! Never underestimate the little ones! Their stories might just be true!

Hilda let out a longing sigh as the group of jubilant villagers disappeared in the distance carrying the tiny version of me along. They were happy that their search had been successful and the child had been found alive and well. Things did not always turn out this way! Knowing my people, I suspected this would become an occasion for a boisterous celebration.

"Little Cara saw us, but no one else did," Eldred said thoughtfully.

"Yes, she did. Did we avoid their notice because we stood perfectly still? Or are we just invisible to all those over a certain age?" Hilda responded quietly.

"I am not sure, but let's keep that in mind and not take chances!" I whispered.

Therefore, we remained as we were until the successful and joyful search party was out of sight. Only then did we turn and reenter the nexus. To our surprise, it seemed to be wavering just a bit! Was it about to fade away and take us with it? That possibility was all the incentive the girls and I needed to run for the membrane and pass back into the in-between!

At least this time, there had been no complications, unlike with Signe! Her leg was much better, but she was nowhere near ready to be sent home!

"Are you up for another one?" I asked the girls.

"Yes, I am. Did you notice that dialing in the right place was not as hard this time?" Eldred asked us.

"Now that you mention it, yes," Hilda replied.

She had been too busy pining for the baby to notice much of anything!

"And it was faster!" I recalled.

"Yes, it was," Eldred agreed. "Maybe the next one will be even easier?"

"We can hope so! Only one way to find out!" Hilda laughed. "Lead the way, sister of mine!"

Chapter 24

Finna

Once again, we traveled through the space between the nexuses. Eldred seemed to have a specific target in mind, leading us there unerringly. We pushed through the membrane one after another when we reached our destination. I cringed as I started working my way through. The process reminded me of what it must feel like to be born, but it was unpleasant. The texture of the barrier was warm and leathery but also somewhat slimy. Amazingly, this was a living thing, as was the entire construct created by the enchantment.

After our experience in Signe's cell and what we were now seeing, we stopped right next to the wall. We were going to evaluate the situation before proceeding. Neither Hilda, Eldred, nor I were thrilled that the path was only a few inches higher than the churning water that enclosed it on both sides! We were still trying to get our bearings when we were suddenly soaked to the skin by spray from the pounding surf. Now it made sense why the dirt of the trail was all wet!

Rotten algae and other marine plants dotted the pathway and the narrow strips of beach that ran alongside it. The air smelled awful, reminiscent of the sea but with a disgusting undertone of decay! The clean scent that I associated with the ocean was definitely missing! Also, no dilapidated house or gnarled trees were to be seen anywhere. Instead, slimy icebergs floated here and there among the oily-looking, restless waves.

And it was cold, as was evident from the dirty white, dimly sparkling patches of frost on the trail! The girls and I, damp as we were, were shivering already. Could this be near Norway? In any case, this was very different from the other spaces we had seen! I was curious who we would find and where they had been snatched from!

Suddenly, something registered that I had missed until then. Little Cara's nexus had resembled the forest she had come from. The cabin had been like those you would expect to find in the woods around Ny Havn! I would know since my family still owned one! Signe must have wandered into a boggy place on her way to fetch water! Her dilapidated hut, similar to those her father had built, had been overgrown with some disgusting slime and weird moss, just like you would expect in a swamp.

Did the enchantment tailor our environments according to where we came from? It most certainly seemed so! On Arran, once you passed the houses, an orchard and horses were right next to the path. Since I had been oblivious to my surroundings, I could only assume I had crossed through the smoke there. The cell the sisters came from I had never actually seen. But I would bet that it resembled their environs! Fascinating! Yet another piece of information to add to the rest!

"Hello? Anyone here? We are friends, here to help you!" Eldred called out when we did not spot the inhabitant of this wet prison.

Slowly and carefully, we headed down the path. Since we assumed this resembled the sea around Norway, we could be dealing with a raider. So far, all those we had met were women but still! Viking maidens were nothing to mess with! That much we knew after meeting Signe! Even injured, that young lady was a force to reckon with!

We had gone just a little further when a fierce-looking woman suddenly jumped out from her hiding spot on the beach. How clever! She had buried herself in the sand to avoid detection! However, the long sword she obviously knew how to use expertly glistened and looked mightily sharp! Instinctively, we raised our arms. The last thing we wanted was for her to attack us!

"We are not here to hurt you but to help you get home," Hilda stated soothingly.

I was watching the tall blonde closely. She distinctly reminded me of somebody! For a few seconds, the answer eluded me, but then it hit me! She was an older version of Signe! Could this be a sister or maybe her mother? The story we had been told gave me the clue I needed.

"Finna? You are Finna Magnuson, are you not?" I addressed her.

"How do you know my name?" the warrior maiden growled.

Her answer was heavily accented but understandable. Was that part of the enchantment? Did it allow us to communicate with each other? If that was true, it had to be unintentional! The person who had created this malicious construct had been too angry to do something nice for his or her prisoners! He or she must have assumed that we would never meet or we would be unable to talk to each other!

"We rescued Signe! Would you like us to take you to her?" I offered.

"Signe got caught in this? Are there others?" Finna asked curtly.

She still did not trust us and had yet to lower that intimidating blade.

"Yes, unfortunately. We have managed to take home a couple, but there are so many more to go!" Eldred answered regretfully.

"How many?" Finna queried, suddenly all business.

She was still regarding us through squinted eyes, ready to go on the offensive at a moment's notice. What an amazing person! Finna was magnificent! So confident, wild, and free! Signe must have been like this before she got injured! No wonder she was so tough! My respect for the young woman rose even further.

"Hilda and I met 29 others, but we suspect there are more," Eldred informed her.

"So many!" Finna seemed momentarily stunned.

Then she jumped into action, threateningly pointing that deadly sword our way.

"Move! Take me to my daughter!" she demanded with a growl.

The movement of that weapon ensured that we responded promptly and moved with alacrity.

Single file, we started back toward the membrane. We were walking fast, more than ready to escape the frequent drenchings of ice-cold seawater we had to endure as we went. Hilda was shivering uncontrollably by now, and all of us, even the fierce Finna, were close to getting hypothermic. The vigorous movement helped warm us somewhat, but we would have to deal with this problem just as soon as we got to the in-between.

When we reached the barrier, Finna regarded it suspiciously. She stretched out to slice it open. To our surprise, it quickly moved back from us to avoid the sharp blade. The lady eyed it full of annoyance and swung again with the same result. So she stepped closer, determined to hack her way through. This time, the nexus went on the offensive. It bulged up beneath her feet, causing her to lose her footing. Had we not stood behind her, she would have ended up in the sea!

Finna was spitting mad, but she knew when she was beaten. She was starting to see that we were not the enemy and was finally ready to listen. Eldred patiently explained to her what the wall was and, using her hands, made it part before her. Being a warrior, Finna allowed us to pass through only after she had assured herself that no one was waiting for us on the other side. I watched with admiration as she continued to adapt to these totally new and out-of-the-ordinary circumstances.

Eldred went first, then Finna. She did not like the process any more than we did but managed to suppress the revolted shudder that escaped the rest of us.

Once we had used a spell to banish the freezing cold from our bodies, we used another to dry our clothes. Then, Eldred led the way. Finna kept all three of us in front of her so she could keep an eye on us. Obviously, she still did not fully trust us. The girls and I were too tired to argue. Silently, we made our way toward the space where we had left Signe and Revna. We pushed our way through the membrane and remained in front of our captor as we headed down the path to the spot where we had last seen the two women.

When we neared the large bed of moss, Signe did not notice us. She had her back to us. However, when Revna caught sight of our group, her face alerted the young woman that something was happening. The girl spun around where she sat. I noticed that she was turning with considerably more ease. Our healings were working!

"Mother!" she shouted as soon as she caught sight of the figure behind us.

Getting to her feet, Signe made her way toward us. I was glad she was walking with much less of a limp than before! Our mending of her injured leg had made a significant difference already! Only once she moved around the girls and me did she notice the blade Finna was still pointing at us.

"MOTHER!!! These are my friends! Please, sheath your sword at once!" she admonished her parent.

To our relief, Finna complied. Once the weapon was safely stowed, she rushed forward to hug her daughter.

"You can walk!" she exclaimed with wonder. "The healer I sent with you could not have done this!"

"No, my friends here did," Signe explained. "Let me introduce you!"

"This is Eldred, her little sister Hilda, Revna, who has directed the mending of my leg, and Cara. She comes from a time far into the future, even further than the rest of them. These are our descendants! They are all Magnuson women! Can you believe that?" Signe asked her.

The young woman could not keep the wonder she felt from her voice. She was an adult, but still, having her mother with her had turned her back into the girl she had been not too long ago.

"Our descendants? What do you mean?" Finna inquired, perplexed.

She obviously had a hard time wrapping her mind around the possibility that we were the children of those who would come after her. Who could blame her? All this was rather unusual!

"Eldred and Hilda are closest to us, only about 600 years into the future from what we can guess. Revna lives in a time after them, and Cara is from the year 2023! Can you believe that? Just look at her clothes!" Signe spouted excitedly.

Finna eyed each one of us carefully, taking our measure. She was not sure just what to think of her daughter's declaration, but when I finally showed her my cellphone and some of the images, she was almost convinced. She even consented to me taking a picture of her and Signe. I promised to use it to have a painting done that would hang in a place of honor among the rest of the Magnuson ancestors in our mead hall.

Once she truly comprehended the implications of what we had been telling her, her only regret was that her husband was not here with us. Getting his likeness as well would have been nice! But at least we had finally managed to break the ice!

"Are they not wonderful?" Signe exclaimed. "We can be so proud that we have started such an amazing lineage of people!"

Finna smiled at her daughter's enthusiasm. After talking to us for a while longer, she finally started to warm up to us. But then, her curiosity got the better of her. Boy, did she have a lot of questions! Revna, Eldred, Hilda, and I took turns answering her.

Sometime later, with all the tension dissolved, we got tired of standing around. Also, Signe's leg was starting to pain her. So we sat down on the soft moss for a long talk. I suspected Finna knew something about this enchantment, and I was dying to find out what it was! Eldred seemed just as eager. Now that we had somewhat sated the fierce lady's curiosity, we felt it was our turn to ask her a few things.

"Finna, what do you know about this spell we find ourselves in?" I finally queried her.

"It is an ancient enchantment from dark times when people used such evil magic to achieve their goals. From what I remember, the more people it imprisons, the more power it has. I had really hoped to be the only one here! Do I assume correctly that this spell is aimed at our clan?"

"Yes, it seems to be," I answered evenly.

"Whoever cast this had a serious grudge against us! We just took home a tiny Cara! Can you believe that? A baby? What kind of monster would do that?" Hilda added, full of indignation.

"You met your past self?" Revna asked me, clearly fascinated but also horrified since she feared this might cause a time paradox.

"Yes. She had gotten lost in the woods and stumbled into the trap," I explained.

"That is just awful! The poor little one must have been terrified!" Finna stated, appalled.

"She was, until we got there. We calmed her down and then took her home. We even figured out how to watch her being found to ensure she was fine!" Hilda explained.

"To draw in a baby! You do intend to find that person? And punish them?" Signe addressed me.

"I would love to, Signe, but I suspect that whoever did this might be out of our reach," I informed her.

"I agree with Cara," Finna stated, to my surprise. "From what you have told me, I believe that the one who cast this is a she. Maybe a woman scorned who hates the Magnuson Clan."

"That would make sense," Revna agreed. "Hurt people hurt other people."

"They do," Finna concurred. "If I understand this evil construct correctly, once the enchantment was completed and captured the first person, any connection to the witch was severed. However, this spell came with a steep price. It used the life force it drained from the caster to create itself. It would have killed her had she allowed it to continue to draw on her energy."

"That is horrible!" Hilda gasped. "She sacrificed years of her life just to get even?"

"Whoever wronged her must have pushed her over the edge!" Eldred mused. "I wonder what he did for her to hate him so!"

"To drive someone to such an evil, desperate act, it had to be significant," Finna declared. "Once the enchantment was separate from the witch, it continued on. Unless stopped, it will do what it was created for forever."

"Exactly! I sense that per its design, it has taken on a life of its own, using all of us to power itself." I added.

"Where does one even learn to do such a thing?" Hilda wondered.

"I suspect from ancient grimoires dealing with the dark arts," Revna added. "I, for one, had never even heard of such a thing!"

"I read a reference to a similar spell in one of our history books. The intended victims, several women, were captured by it. Once it grew, however, it even drew in a few men!" I explained.

"Could it have been talking about us?" Eldred wondered.

"Very possibly so!" I had to agree. "And you and Hilda did mention that you met some men during your exploration!"

"Do you remember who was responsible for it?" Signe inquired.

I had to think about that for a few minutes. Somewhere in my mind, that pertinent information was stored. I just needed to locate and access it. Determinedly, I searched for the correct reference and finally found it.

"The person who cast the spell was a young woman. She was associated with a guy who bought his way into one of the families of the Magnuson Clan. Blinded by jealousy, she saw the new wife as someone who stole her lover from her, never realizing that the lady was also a victim. Then something happened with the witch's child, and she must have felt she had nothing left to lose, so she cast the enchantment." I began.

“Do you know what happened to her afterward?” Hilda, always compassionate, wanted to know.

“The book did not go into a lot of detail. The tale was meant more as a warning. It seemed that in her misguided anger, she must have decided that the bride and her family had to pay for the injury done to her,” I slowly stated, remembering the particulars as I spoke.

“How sad!” Hilda whispered. “Does it say what happened to the guy who caused all this?”

“The reference was vague on that point, but I believe he disappeared while hunting,” I told her.

“Serves him right!” Eldred stated firmly.

“All this misery because of one man?” Revna scoffed, shaking her head. "You got to be kidding me!”

“Yes, and he was not much of a prize to start with, I think,” I told her.

“We need to send everyone home and undo this awful spell!” Eldred said, her voice full of determination.

I could only nod my agreement, and so did Finna. For a few moments, we were all deep in thought. Then Revna suggested doing another round of healing on Signe. The sooner we could return her to her own time, the better, and not only to weaken the enchantment!

That clever young lady had already picked up too much information from the rest of us. It was inevitable that this would change her!

How would this affect history? Beyond more detailed records being passed down? I was not sure, but we could be in dangerous territory! That, however, was not the only reason we were glad to restore Signe’s leg to perfect health. We loved seeing how much she had improved already and how happy this made her. And, this time, we would have Finna to help us. Her well-deserved reputation as a skilled and innovative healer had been passed down through the ages.

I could not wait to see Finna in action and hoped to learn some of her techniques. Between all of us, Signe’s limb should be mended before too much longer! Then, we could return her and her mother to

where they had been snatched from. Being hale would allow the young woman to marry that laird she had so longingly spoken of!

Judging from the dour expression on her face when she spoke of this, the idea that her sister Auga would get him did not appeal to her. Not that I could blame her. From the description of the man, he was rather dashing. I truly hoped that Signe could recapture the destiny that had almost escaped her.

The warrior maiden was so brave and admirable. She did not deserve the fate she had taken on! Even crippled, Signe had done her best! I hoped fervently that she would get her heart's desire!

Chapter 25

A Difficult Decision

The subsequent healing we did on Signe's leg took a lot out of all of us. Revna and Finna worked together this time while Eldred, Hilda, and I lent them our strength. We stopped when we were so exhausted we could barely move. But we had made tremendous progress. The severed muscles and tendons had all been re-knitted, and only the scarring remained. Tired but thrilled with the end result, we curled up together on the moss to rest.

Finna, a master of finding loopholes and getting around a spell, even one as complicated as this one, showed us how to regain power from the construct. Using the method she taught us, we slowly recharged. But, since the evil enchantment was draining the life force out of other people caught in its trap, we did not take much, just enough to restore us a little.

I was glad to have such an option available to us. We could use it in an emergency or if we found someone who had been here a long time and was severely depleted. We could keep them from fading away more and even reverse some of the damage. Then, something else occurred to me. Once all the people had been returned to their time and place, I might even be able to use this technique to revive the poor horses!

The thought cheered me immensely, especially since it would further weaken the enchantment!

Once Eldred, Hilda, and I were recovered enough, we set out to take more of our captured clan members home. This time, however, we dealt only with cells adjacent to Revna's. This sped things up a little. To be able to add to our history books, we intended to talk to each person for a few minutes. The first lady we encountered was stunningly beautiful but had a very delicate disposition.

As we were trying to find out who she was, she fainted on us several times! The only things we managed to get out of her were that her name was Lilah, that she lived in Ny Havn in 1885, and that she was the mother of two boys. We were lucky she told us that much! The three of us were made of sterner stuff and had a hard time relating with someone so fragile. Eldred, Hilda, and I were only too happy to deliver her home!

The frail woman was immensely grateful once she was back in familiar surroundings. She thanked us several times before slowly walking toward the large manor we saw in the distance. It only dawned on me later that she must have been a direct ancestor since she lived in the same house my parents now called home. I suspected that she was my great-grandmother, Delilah Magnuson.

The person we dealt with after her was very different. She pretended to be sweet and innocent but could not fool the girls and me. We realized very quickly that she was anything but. I pitied any man who had to deal with her! That vixen even tried to manipulate us with some of her wiles! Eldred dealt with this very efficiently. She just crossed her arms and stared her down.

That one, who introduced herself as Elanora Dickinson, was a distant Magnuson cousin by birth. She lived a little outside Ny Havn and, judging from her clothes, most likely on one of the farms. Elanora was captured in 1739. The woman tried to make herself out as someone rather important to impress us, but none of us believed her. We could sense a lie when we heard it! And most of what this one spouted was just that!

Eldred, Hilda, and I were happy to see the last of Elanora. The next person, Genevieve Magnuson, was exceedingly gracious and genuine. It took us no time at all to warm up to her. It turned out that she was someone with real power, not a pretender like the last one! She was calm, self-assured, and competent. I watched her closely and decided that I liked her mannerism. Her very presence made you feel at ease.

Genevieve was used to taking charge of any situation, including our conversation. She said she would gladly share her history with us but only in return for hearing ours. This made things a little more complicated, but she deserved to know the truth about the situation she had landed in. The lady was also very interested in hearing about our adventures since we had arrived in the time trap.

Before we knew it, we were talking like old friends. With amusement, I noted how one-sided the chat was. The woman cleverly elicited the information from us she desired without giving any in return. Genevieve was a force to be reckoned with! She would have made a great spy! Or maybe she was one? She sure acted the part! When the lady realized I was onto her, she gave me a conspiratorial wink.

I almost started laughing and had to hide it behind a hiccup. Since I was worried about Genevieve acquiring too much information, I started asking our new acquaintance some questions. I hoped to steer her away from delving too deeply into the girls' and my history. The clever Genevieve, however, knew exactly what I was up to and how to deflect my probing inquiries. Instead of answering, she assured us that she had no intention of sharing what she had learned.

For one, the people around her would think her mad if she told anyone she had been caught in a spell and met people from other times!

She did have a point there! But still! I noticed how evasive the brilliant lady became when I queried her. She appeared very reluctant to reveal anything about herself. This made me wonder. Maybe our suave friend was much more than she seemed?

When I explained why we wanted to know, she finally relented. I could tell the moment she decided to trust us. As it turned out, Genevieve was a Mackay by birth, just like Phillipe. She had married into the Magnuson Clan. Since the lady hated sitting at home, she assisted her husband with his business by collecting information about their clients and everyone else they met. My instinct had been right! She was a spy of sorts!

Genevieve ended up here while walking in her garden on a foggy morning. She had never even noticed the smoke. The year she came from was 1737. Interestingly enough, she had been snatched just a couple of years before the last person we had taken home! This led to the mention of Elanore. The lady knew of her and had even met her a couple of times.

In her estimation, the vixen was harmless enough, just manipulative and a terrible flirt. When we looked doubtful, Genevieve gave us some background on her. Elanore had once been married to an actual laird, but he had died and had left her penniless. After selling the house and most of the land to cover his debt, all she had left was the little farm. No wonder the woman had tried so hard to make herself seem important! She missed the life she had once had!

Eventually, it was time to return Genevieve to her location. We wished each other well, and the girls and I quickly returned to the in-between. I was deep in thought on our way back to Revna's. The spell seemed to have collected several ladies from around that time! Could this be significant? We would have to ask Finna; she might know.

Taking three home in a row was the most we had ever done in one session. Eldred, Hilda, and I were pretty tired when we returned to the others. Revna took one look at us and ordered us onto the bed of moss. I fell into an exhausted stupor almost immediately. After some rest, we did yet another healing on Signe's thigh. When we were done, she could move the leg freely and without any pain. Most of the muscle had been filled in, and only the scars were still visible.

But they were ugly! Red and angry looking and still raised above the rest of her skin. It was sad to see such a well-shaped limb so disfigured! Finna assured us she had it from here and that we could concentrate on taking more individuals home. She wanted this enchantment shut down just as much as we did and before it could collect even more people!

It felt strange to not need food, drink, or sleep. Even weirder was having no bodily functions despite being awake. The best we could figure was that we were in some sort of stasis that allowed us to function but kept us from aging or burning calories. This condition felt very unnatural to all of us, but, on the other hand, it was a relief.

We had yet to spot something that we cared to ingest! Everything in this trap looked rotten, moldy, or just plain gross! We were truly grateful that the patch of moss we had been using to sit and sleep on was not quite as disgusting as the rest! Once Eldred, Hilda, and I felt up to it, we left the others in that semi-pleasant spot and went to a neighboring cell.

Our destination was the same location Elanore had been imprisoned in. As we had suspected, the nexus had changed. We were learning more about this construct all the time. Together with Finna and Revna, we had come up with the theory that once a cell lost its captive, it vanished. Once out of the way, one from further out slid into its place. Our previous hypothesis that each environment reflected the surroundings of its inmate had also been confirmed.

What new revelations would this excursion bring?

Pushing through the membrane, the girls and I came to a stop. We could not help staring. The inhabitant was a man! A rather attractive, well-dressed, and extraordinarily charming one at that, at least superficially so! I had met his type before and was instantly on guard. True to form, the guy attempted to flirt with me. When he realized I was not interested, he moved on to Eldred.

I could not believe my ears. That cad was using the same outrageous lines on her that he had just tried on me! She had been right there and had heard them all! Did this guy have no imagination? His repertoire was most certainly on the limited side! Eldred, no dummy and in love with Cedric, just gave him one of her best signature glares. When I got home, I would have to practice those in front of the mirror! They were undoubtedly very effective!

My, she was good! The guy stepped back a couple of feet in surprise and seemed to wilt before that steely-eyed stare! I loved it! I would have to take lessons from her! What an incredible wife she was going to make to the chieftain! This young lady did not need a sword! The power of her mind was plenty to intimidate anyone who dared earn her ire!

Being the youngest and least experienced among us, Hilda finally became the recipient of all his nauseating attention. She was the most impressionable and least weary of us three, and he soon had her giggling and blushing. Eldred and I exchanged a worried glance. It was best to put a stop to this quickly! That young woman could be rather headstrong, and it would upset history something fiercely if she fell in love with this con man!

For one, my Phillipe might never be! That realization was enough for immediate action! Eldred felt just as strongly about separating these two. Her sister was not going to fall prey to a scoundrel like this, not on her watch! Together, we herded the two toward the smoke. Hilda, realizing our intention, started to pout, but one look from her older sibling put her in her place.

Seeing the dynamic between these two girls in action was rather interesting. They were both very strong-willed and exceedingly stubborn. Hilda's magic abilities were different and more powerful than Eldred's. Still, the younger girl deferred to her sibling, and the loving bond between them was something I envied. My brother and I had become so distant over the years! We barely saw each other these days. Maybe it was time to work on that when I returned home!

Naturally, the cad pretended to truly like Hilda. He was flirting outrageously. Eldred and I rolled our eyes when we heard some of his over-the-top declarations. On several occasions, we bust out laughing. Hilda, however, seemed to be eating it up. No one had ever complimented her like this, and even if he was somewhat repetitive, the guy was good! This schemer knew just what to say and how to do so!

When he wanted to hold Hilda's hand, Eldred had enough.

"You, keep your hands off my sister!" she barked.

Her sudden interference caught the man, entirely focused on his prospective victim, very much by surprise. He jumped away from Hilda like he had been stung. The girl gave us a dirty look. But, even she appeared to have realized something was up, for she was now moving toward the smoke without further prompting from Eldred and me.

The rogue happily flounced along beside her, unaware that the game was up. He would not have been so cooperative had he realized what was about to happen. Grabbing his hand, I pulled him around to face me.

"Dear sir, before we can allow any more flirting, please tell us who you are and where you come from," I addressed him sweetly.

He promptly fell for my saccharine tone and turned his attention to me. I maintained a firm hold on his hand to keep him distracted from Hilda. Not to be outdone in this charade, Eldred grabbed the other one.

"I am Harald Magnuson, the laird of Ny Havn and the Magnuson Clan, dear ladies," he declared proudly.

Seriously? He wanted us to believe that?

Hilda just suppressed a snigger. She was an expert at detecting a lie when she heard one. Since the man, whoever he was, had his back turned to her, he could not see her expression. Even if Eldred and I had not felt the false vibration of his statement, the outraged expression on the girl's face was telling.

"It is our pleasure to meet you, Sir Harald. Please, tell us more about your home! Do you live in a castle?" Eldred prompted him.

What followed was a grand description of a magnificent mansion with a broad staircase, plenty of servants, and beautiful, well-manicured gardens. But, still holding onto his hands, she and I picked up the facts of the matter. The place we sensed him living in was anything but and made us feel sad for the man. He obviously took much liberty with the truth!

His home was a shabby cabin on the outside of the village. It was dirty and run down, and sadly enough, not too different from the one in the nexus! This guy talked a good game but was too lazy to pick up a hammer or do some cleaning! His house was not where we would want to spend our lives! What did this rogue think to gain with all his lies? A noble bride? To better his station without putting in the work? Most likely!

That image, however, was all that we needed. Hilda joined us, and together, it did not take us long to dial in his home. Once it solidified, Eldred gave him a sudden, strong push into his own world that had him stumble a few feet before catching his balance. Grabbing Hilda's hands, we rushed in the opposite direction as fast as we could. We kept right on running until we reached the in-between. Here we collapsed. We were laughing so hard that we cried!

"Do you think he followed us?" Hilda gasped out between chortles.

Eldred and I looked at each other, horrified. That possibility had not occurred to us until just then! Quickly, we opened just the tiniest of windows back into the cell. We were greatly relieved when we watched it fade away and a new one moved into its space. The portal was closed, barring Harald, or whoever he was, from entering the time trap forever. We were out of his reach, a thought that pleased us immensely!

"I was almost tempted to leave him in the nexus where he could do no harm to any innocent ladies!" Eldred confessed. "What a liar!"

"He was no Magnuson chieftain, that is for sure!" Hilda giggled. "Did you two really think that I was falling for him?"

At the look on our faces, she roared with laughter.

"Seriously? You should give me more credit!" she admonished us sternly before succumbing to merriment once again.

What a relief to have gotten rid of that unimaginative gigolo! He was a disgrace to the Magnuson name!

On we went to the next one! At least this one was a woman! The petite redhead was terribly distraught when we found her. The lady was very pampered and fragile, with hands that had never seen a day's work. Her tear-stained, heart-shaped face was stunning, and her blue eyes reminded me vividly of cornflowers. Her dress was covered in jewels and so expensive that all three of us stared at it in wonder.

The young woman looked up at us helplessly from where she sat in the dirt, trying to portray a picture of total innocence. However, her carelessness with the fabulous, priceless gown did not sit well with us. The person she was trying to portray would have valued this treasure and not treated it so cavalierly! Something did not ring true here!

Eldred took an immediate dislike and moved away from her. Even the usually more outgoing and gregarious Hilda was not rushing forward to assist this delicate damsel in distress. To my surprise, she was hanging back. Maybe this female was too foreign a creature for them? Since nobody else volunteered, dealing with this spoiled society dame fell to me.

"Hello there! I am Cara. Who might you be?"

"Never mind who I am! I demand that you help me up and get me out of here immediately!" the woman snapped at us.

Involuntarily, I took a step back, as did the girls. I looked down at this vision of loveliness in disbelief. Her behavior was a great indication that her beauty was only skin deep! What a nasty creature!

"We are not your servants! So mind your manners, or we will leave you here!" Eldred retorted haughtily.

She and the woman promptly glared at each other. I could sense the antipathy they felt toward one another intensify by the second. They looked like they were about to start fighting!

"Eldred is right," Hilda piped in, to my astonishment. "Who are you to treat us in such a way?"

"How dare you speak to me like that? Do you not know your betters?" that viper in human clothes screeched back at her.

Her face was distorted from the outrage and disgust she was feeling, and now she was anything but beautiful!

"We are leaving," I decided. "We will come back eventually to see if you have remembered your manners!"

The cusswords that followed us were definitely not becoming a lady! Some made my ears burn, and others I had never even heard! This tirade would have done a sailor proud!

"That woman is evil to the core! She was in the middle of doing something awful when she ended up here. I just know it! We should not take her back to where she came from!" Hilda told us very quietly but with conviction once we reached the in-between. "The people there are better off without her!"

Such a comment from such a sweet person stopped both Eldred and me in our tracks. We searched our own feelings and saw the truth of her words. Wherever this one went, she would cause trouble. That gave me an idea.

"Remember the place I told you about, the one that promised peace and oblivion?" I asked them.

"Yes!" Hilda agreed instantly. "It is perfect! She cannot harm anyone there, and she will be happy. A perfect solution!"

Eldred looked very thoughtful.

"Do we have the right to interfere like that?" she questioned eventually.

But for once, Hilda, who was usually kind, gentle, and always ready to forgive and see the best in everyone, was not budging on her opinion. She was determined to see this one safely stowed away in a place where she could not inflict her nasty temper and malicious designs on anyone else. I was utterly amazed at the strength of her conviction.

We discussed what to do. Soon, however, the sisters were dug in on opposite sides, and neither was prepared to budge.

"I want to know more about her, and if she is as bad as you think, then I will happily help you take her to that place," Eldred finally agreed.

Hilda and I nodded. That seemed to be the perfect compromise to this disagreement.

After dealing with two such vile creatures, we almost stopped for the day but then decided to take one more home. We could sense that the enchantment was already shrinking, which was good. Dialing in the right location was no longer as difficult as it had been at first. Eldred went within for a couple of moments. Hilda and I looked at each other. We had no idea what she was up to. We waited patiently for her to finish what she was doing.

Suddenly, Eldred opened her eyes and raised her head. Then, she determinedly led us to a nexus a few cells away. Following her lead, Hilda and I pushed our way in and gazed around. This one had to also be from Ny Havn! The surroundings looked somewhat similar to several other ones we had entered.

After walking down the uneven path for a bit, we came upon the resident of this space. Another man! But this one was quite old and turned out to be very different from the scoundrel we had sent back a little while ago! To our pleasure, he was delighted to see us and very friendly. What a contrast to the last person we tried to help!

"Ladies, you have no idea how happy I am to see you! I am Cletus Magnuson from Ny Havn. I am a teacher there at the school."

Eldred, Hilda, and I instantly warmed up to him, and we introduced ourselves. Within minutes of talking to him, we realized that this man was very perceptive and exceptionally knowledgeable about clan history. We figured that he had some interesting tidbits to share. Therefore, we happily accepted his invitation to sit and chat for a while. It seemed that he had been very lonely since his arrival in the time trap!

Cletus was immensely curious about the enchantment and what had brought all of us here. We told him as much as we could. The old man was especially interested in the people we had met in the nexuses. Hilda shared with him our encounter with Harald, or whatever his name was.

"That one was a real scalawag! His real name was Sten Coffers, and he was not even a Magnuson by blood! He was adopted into the clan because he had magic. Persuasion, I believe! He finally got caught impersonating our chieftain one too many times. Harald himself put him on a ship to some far-off land," Cletus told us with much amusement.

"What about life in the village? How are things in Ny Havn in your time?" I interjected.

Cletus had a way with words. I realized that his subtle inquiries were exceedingly clever. Just like Genevieve, he was gaining much information about us and our times, but he had given us little so far. The girls joined me, and we started asking questions. Soon, we had a fairly detailed picture of life in 1901. That gave me an idea. The woman we had left in her nexus had to be from somewhere close to that time! Maybe he knew her or had heard about her?

Hilda seemed to read my thoughts because she started sharing more details about our run-in with that foul-mouthed harpy when there was a lull in the conversation. Cletus looked thoughtful for a minute, then brightened.

"That must be Victoria de Monde, as she called herself. Her sudden disappearance raised some eyebrows, but mostly, everyone was happy she was gone!" Cletus told us.

"Do you know any more about her?" Eldred enquired.

"Let me think. The woman showed up one day acting like a fine lady, at least whenever anyone of means was around. I did not count among those! Anyone not of the nobility got to see some of her 'real' personality, and it was not pretty. She treated us with total disdain and like we were her servants. And, she enjoyed getting us into trouble," Cletus began. He paused for a moment.

"Her ending up here explains her disappearance, but I do not understand. You are taking people home, are you not?"

"We are," Hilda replied. "She is the only one we have come across so far that I feel very uneasy about. I believe taking her back where she came from would be a terrible mistake!"

"And it would be!" Cletus agreed vehemently. "At that time, Harald was not yet our laird. His father was still ruling. The boy was engaged to a lovely young lady, Liv Magnuson. That snake Victoria was making eyes at him. One day, she had almost managed to seduce him when they had to evacuate the manor due to a fire alarm. A small blaze had 'mysteriously' broken out in the room next to Harald and her! The staff was prepared to do anything to stop her!"

"Is she really that wicked?" Eldred wanted to know.

"Child, you have no idea! That one will use any trick in the book to get what she wants, and she does not care who she hurts in the process! There was even an attempt on Liv's life! As it was, the girl survived but was confined to bed for several weeks. I am certain Victoria was behind it! She would have tried again had she not vanished!"

Eldred looked at Hilda and me searchingly.

"She really is evil, Eldred," Hilda told her gently.

"And she never returned, which confirms that we did not take her back to Ny Havn," Eldred stated the obvious. "I still do not like it, but I am starting to see why the two of you feel so strongly."

"Miss Eldred," Cletus addressed her taking her hands and looking at her imploringly. "If you bring her back, you doom us all, but especially poor Liv! She and Harald are happy together, and their children are sweet and well-mannered."

The old man paused for a moment, then continued. "That Victoria, she is the meanest, cruelest person I have ever met, and I have been teaching school for many, many years! Talk to her, girl, if you must. You will see what I mean!"

Cletus had most certainly left us with much to think about. After a few more minutes of chatting, we took him to his home. Once he stepped out of the smoke, the old man turned and met each of our eyes.

"Thank you, my ladies, for returning me to Ny Havn! Is there a way that you can wait here?"

"There is if we stay right at the border of the smoke," Hilda informed him.

"Then I will go fetch you the account of the devastation Victoria caused our village!"

"We will wait," I agreed immediately, now even more curious than ever.

The three of us sat down right on the edge of the haze. We made sure to be half in and half out, thus anchoring the location into place. Cletus returned faster than we had expected, with a bag and a thick book in his hand. He opened the tome to the chapter that showed a picture of the stunning beauty we had met earlier that day. Eldred decided to read the account out loud. The further she got, the paler she grew. Finally, she handed me the book and became violently ill.

Silently, Hilda and I finished the story. Victoria had not been at the settlement very long, but accidents happened wherever she went, and people got hurt. And not just in Ny Havn! The horrid woman seemed to enjoy seeing others in pain and would laugh at their misfortune. Naturally, if any from the nobility were around, she behaved like a perfect, angelic being who could not harm a fly.

After a while, the rumors of her treatment of those less fortunate reached the laird's ears. He was not pleased and had a long talk with his son, who started avoiding the lady. But, shortly after, Liv had her accident and was confined to bed. Using the opportunity, Victoria did everything she could to seduce Herald. The servants, in turn, tried their best to prevent Victoria from becoming their new mistress without her knowing who the culprits were.

The entire staff at the manor was terrified of her, and not only because of her vicious tongue. Anyone who crossed that evil woman somehow ended up hurt or dead. How brave they had been to devise ways to undermine that wicked female's campaign to marry Herald! However, mishaps kept happening wherever Victoria went. Finally, the Mackays forbid her to set foot on any of their grounds.

Behind her back, Victoria was referred to as the devil's spawn. Folk made the sign to ward off evil or crossed themselves whenever she walked by, always careful that she did not notice. She was spreading terror all around her. Then, when the laird of the Mackays, who had banned Victoria from his lands, fell off his horse and broke his neck, people grew even more afraid.

After that, no one dared to deny her anything she wanted, and the shrew took full advantage of that. The entire region lived in fear of her. To say that she was hated was putting it mildly. When she had come up missing in 1861 on the way to an assignment with Harald, hope had arisen that she was gone for good. Suddenly, smiles were seen again around the manor and the village. Even the air all around them seemed to have cleared.

Harald had been immensely relieved that the she-devil, who had been blackmailing him to get him to meet with her, had disappeared. He loved Liv and wanted to wed her. Fearing that Victoria might reappear, the young man decided not to wait for his bride to recover. He dragged the priest to her bedside to perform the ceremony. This way, even if that harpy did show up again, he would be a married man.

However, the relief he felt to be free of that fiend made him a prime suspect in her disappearance until one of the servants came forward. The well-respected man testified that he had been watching the young master in case he needed an interruption if Victoria got too amorous. He stated firmly that Herald could not have done it. He had had him in his sight all day long.

The constabulary could not find any evidence to the contrary nor of foul play. Personally, I suspect that the officers did not look all that hard. According to the accounts, several of them had had run-ins with Victoria themselves that were none too pleasant. The one witness they did find reported that she seemed to step into a cloud and then vanished, never to be seen again. Or so they hoped!

Some of the less educated ones from the area decided that Victoria had been some sort of a demon. They believed she had been called back to hell, where she belonged. It was as good an explanation as any! Life went on, and the region slowly recovered from all the fear and chaos the evil enchantress had sown in the few months she had been there.

Victoria having magic and abusing it was another explanation for all the accidents that had occurred around her! And one that made sense!

When we reached the end of the chapter, I closed the book and handed it back to Cletus.

"Thank you for showing us this. Using her gift for the purposes she did is beyond despicable! It appears that Victoria has used her powers to kill. For that, there is no redemption," I said sadly.

"No, there is not," Eldred agreed. "Still, I want her to be comfortable where she is going. She needs a different dress."

"You are right; the one she is wearing is not made for comfort. Besides, it would be a shame to waste such a beautiful gown on someone who obviously does not appreciate it!" Hilda agreed, smiling downright evilly.

Wow! Victoria sure had a way of bringing out the worst in people! And she did not even need to be present to do so! I could not wait to see her safely stashed away in those lovely hills!

"It is not hers to start with but Liv's. She stole it," Cletus told us indignantly. "I grabbed a simple dress from my wife, hoping you would see it this way."

"Well, we are getting it back! She does not deserve it!" Hilda declared firmly, taking the offered dress from Cletus.

This piece of clothing was nothing like what that hellcat was wearing at the moment. It was rather plain but perfectly serviceable. It would allow Victoria to move around comfortably. And, she could sit in the dirt and pout in this all she wanted for what we cared! But I was sure the dress would not be to the spoiled woman's liking!

The way I saw it, and Eldred and Hilda agreed, Victoria was lucky that we were decent human beings and very unlike her. Had her fate been left up to someone less kind, she might have found herself in that landscape with no clothing at all!

Chapter 26

A Dangerous Place

It was time to say goodbye to Cletus and return to the nexus. The old man wished us good luck and warned us to be careful when approaching Victoria. He believed her to be a powerful witch. The accounts of her exploits showed that she was a master at getting the drop on people and that she had no scruples or morals of any kind. She would not like what we had planned for her and would not fight fairly. Therefore, we needed to be prepared. As I had learned from battling with a sword, a good offensive was often the best defense!

Once we reached the in-between, we came up with a plan. Hilda suggested a shield that would bounce any spell or curse back onto the caster. Usually, this would have been returned threefold, but Eldred balked at that. Eventually, we settled on double. If she was trying to hurt us, getting a taste of her own vile magic was no more than Victoria deserved!

To my absolute surprise as well as her sister's, for once, the gentle, kind, caring Hilda was the most radical. Her dislike of Victoria was intense! That, by itself, said much. Eldred and I better take notice if someone as compassionate as this girl proposed such measures. What was she sensing that we were not? It had to be extremely bad for her to suggest such drastic methods!

Finally, we had taken all the precautions we could. Each of us was well shielded, and our magic was at the ready. We had woven an enchantment in the form of a net and had imbued it with special properties. The moment that woman attacked us, the spell would home in on her and surround her. It would drain her powers away. In this manner, her fate was in her own hands, and Eldred's conscience was somewhat appeased.

Carefully, we slipped back into the nexus where Victoria was imprisoned. We tried to sneak down the path, but the lack of cover made this tricky, so we stayed as low as possible. This was not easy for the girls in their long dresses, but they managed. As soon as she spotted us, the malicious woman raised her hands. Victoria glared at us while she wove her spell!

As expected, she had used the time we spent with Cletus to prepare for our return. That hellcat was not about to play nice! Since she could not fool us by acting sweetly and we had not fallen for her other guiles, she intended to overcome us so she could force us to do her bidding. Her malevolent nature made her believe nothing else would work after our last encounter!

Victoria was far from stupid but limited in her vision of the world. As most of us do, she saw things through the biases of her own experiences. But, even worse, she assumed that all others would do the same thing she would do in a situation. Since the shrew was evil to the core, she expected the worst from everyone else. Therefore, she figured we would attack her, so she intended to get us first!

To present less of a target, we threw ourselves flat on the ground behind any cover we could find. This made Victoria, who had expected us to return much sooner to start with, even more furious. She hated to be kept waiting and not getting her way. Cusswords were flooding in our direction. We hoped her anger would break her concentration, but she hurled that incantation at us before we could do anything else.

The instant it left her hand, the girls and I got a sense of its potency. Quickly, we rolled closer together and overlapped our shields. This would make them even stronger. Not a second too soon! We felt the curse strike, activate the net spell, and rebound right back at the irate witch!

Not expecting such an outcome, the she-devil was unprepared for what hit her. She had no protection in place. As a result, her own magic knocked her out for a moment! As we had intended, the enchantment we had prepared wrapped itself tightly around her, thus preventing any further attempts to harm us. Once she was secured, Eldred, Hilda, and I got to our feet and approached her carefully.

When Victoria woke up, she tried to yell. However, since we had grown tired of her cussing, we had added a gag. The situation was looking up, but our net was not taking her power fast enough! We realized that there was a good chance that she might free herself. What would we do then? None of us were trained in black magic!

While the girls and I were trying to decide how best to deal with this, we received help from an unexpected source. For once, even the construct we found ourselves in was happy to help. We could sense it the second its tendrils reached the witch. It drained Victoria of every bit of her power within a short time! But, to our surprise, it did not touch her life force. Now that was different!

Interesting! Had the presence of someone as evil as her somehow affected the enchantment imprisoning us all? Had it taken her magic to help us, or because it tasted like sweet nectar? The girls and I discussed this while we carefully stripped the furious Victoria of the magnificent gown she had been treating with such disregard. We had

no way of returning it to its owner, Liv, at least not right now, so we would hang on to it for the moment.

The loss of her abilities finally made her pass out. Putting clothes on a limp person was much more challenging than stripping her and took us a bit. Gently, we redressed the now unconscious enchantress. We knew that Victoria would not have hesitated for even a second to hurt us, but we were not like that. We were careful not to inflict any injury while putting her in the new garment.

The plain, brown dress would hang loosely on her slender frame, but she would be comfortable. In this, she would be able to roam those beautiful hills to her heart's content!

Once Victoria was ready, Eldred and I tried to pull her up. This turned out to be a real chore. She was much heavier than such a slight woman had any right to be! Finally, with Hilda's help, we got her up. Eldred had one of her arms over her shoulder, I the other. Slowly, we dragged her toward the smoke. The girl and I were panting by the time we got halfway and sweating when we reached our destination.

Remembering the magnificent hills, the grasses, the tall, majestic oaks, Eldred, Hilda, and I called in that destination. To our surprise, a location appeared almost as soon as we started, but it was not the one we had been aiming for. We tried again, but the portal was not cooperating in the slightest. Giving it all we got, we tried once more.

"It is really fighting us," Hilda exclaimed when nothing happened. "Almost like it has a mind of its own!"

"Look, the grass is moving in this one!" Eldred pointed out.

We looked at each other. Was this the place we were supposed to leave Victoria? Was this the spot that matched her vibrations? It was certainly dark and somber enough! We could hear wolves howling and other creatures calling to each other in the distance. This was not a pleasant location, not like the welcoming one that had been offered to me!

"We have a choice. We can take Victoria back with us or leave her here. I vote for waiting until she comes to and then pushing her in there," Hilda stated firmly.

Eldred and I shrugged. Neither of us liked this place, but the sooner we were rid of this malicious woman, the better. Not having magic after using and abusing it to such an extreme extent for many years would be challenging for Victoria. I almost felt sorry for her, but she had brought this on herself! At least she could not curse any more people or cause any more deaths!

The three of us sat down to wait. And waited. And waited. Victoria was not waking up!

"Wouldn't you know it! Now we have to rescue her from her own curse!" I spat, anything but thrilled.

But, there was no help for it. With all those predatory creatures we heard in that world, we could not bring ourselves to dump Victoria in there and just leave her. She was deeply unconscious and unable to defend herself. That would not have been very kind. Nor fair. As far as we were concerned, even she deserved a fighting chance!

Carefully, we placed our hands on her chest and nullified some of the effects of the spell that had hit her. A few minutes later, the long, lush eyelashes shivered, and finally, the gorgeous eyes popped open. Victoria sat up with our help and looked around. She seemed to have no memory of what had happened and was obviously confused why we were wide awake while she had been out. I could sense it the moment she reached for her magic.

"What have you done to me!" she screeched when she realized she was blocked from her powers. And completely drained!

"Actually, we did not do that. The enchantment siphoned off your magic but did not block you. You did that with the curse you threw at us!" Hilda told her without mercy. "You had intended to separate us from our powers so that you could kill us at your leisure! But, instead, it hit you. I, for one, call that justice!"

Furiously, Victoria struggled up and lunged for Hilda. However, Eldred had been waiting for that! As the woman moved past her, she landed a well-placed kick to that hellcat's hip. The force of that thrust pushed that she-devil right into the landscape on the other side of the smoke! We heard a distinct click like a door had just shut, but we could still see the homicidal shrew through a thin veil of smoke.

Victoria stumbled for a few feet, but once she caught her balance, she turned to come back at us. Her squinted eyes were threatening murder. Even without her magic, she was going to be a dangerous foe! The three of us got ready to do battle. Then, to all our surprise, including our would-be attacker's, she ran into an invisible wall. Now that was new! It must have slid in place when we heard that sound!

Ferociously, the incensed Victoria started beating on it. Her face was a mask of hatred and anything but beautiful. I felt sad for her. The path she had chosen was a dark one, and she was now paying the price.

A loud rumble told us it was time to go. Victoria was still violently banging her fists on that invisible barrier, trying to force her way through. We were uncertain how long it would hold, but once we exited and the cell vanished, that pathway would be closed. Quickly, we made our way across the nexus, picking up the dress on the way.

"We should have taken her shoes as well," Eldred grumbled. "They matched the gown."

"Now, Eldred, what happened to all your compassion for the lady?" Hilda teased.

"Lady? That one was no lady!" Eldred scoffed.

"No, she was not," I agreed. "Sad, really, when the world is better off without you! I do not ever want to be like that!"

"Me neither," Hilda agreed, and Eldred nodded wistfully.

"Have we had enough for the day?" I asked the girls.

I, for one, needed some rest. This incident with the evil Victoria and my recent meeting with mini-me had been emotionally draining.

"Let us go back and check on Signe," Eldred agreed.

Chapter 27

The Naming

Signe was happy to see us. She had been rather bored since Revna and Finna were deep in a spirited discussion that she was not included in. We spotted the two ladies sitting further down the road. From the looks of it, they had been talking for a while. After exchanging hugs with our friend and sharing a little about our encounters, we curled up on the moss. This time, I actually fell asleep, but with that came dreams.

In my nightmare, Phillipe was frantically looking for me. He knew something terrible had happened and could sense it through our connection, but he was unsure exactly what. I initially felt rather helpless as I watched him, but then I decided to act. Who said that you cannot affect things in this realm? Determinedly, I kept sending my husband the message that I was ok and that I would be home before too much longer.

At first, he did not hear me. He was too frantic and not in a receptive state. But our beautiful, sweet Bear received my sending loud and clear. He eventually forced my husband to sit down and relax just a little. It was then that his senses were able to pick up my words. The love flooding back through our connection was so immense that it made me feel like he was holding me tight.

I let that delightful sensation warm me all the way through. Our immense affection for each other flowed back and forth between Phillipe and me, calming us both. Finally, I drifted off into deep, restoring slumber and woke sometime later, completely refreshed. Silently, I sent my thanks to the construct, and to my total surprise, it answered back.

Naturally, being curious, I took the opportunity to get to know it better. Soon, we were in the middle of an intense dialogue.

After talking with it for a while, I had a better sense of the spirit of the enchantment we were trapped in. It seemed that the longer it was disconnected from the witch who had cast it, the more conscious and independent it was becoming! It could now communicate with those of us willing to listen! It was also getting increasing control over the situation within the time trap. To my surprise, it wanted to improve conditions for all its prisoners! But, being basically new-born, it was not sure how. It needed our help.

Even more unexpected was the revelation that it did not like what it was designed to do. It did not want to feed on those of us within its cells to sustain itself and was looking for another source of power. At the moment, it was not yet capable of fighting all of its purposes, but it was working on that. At least it had managed to stop collecting more people from the Magnuson clan and was no longer growing! That was a huge first step, and welcome news!

My sense of this emerging being was that it resembled a sensitive child. It was learning, growing, and evolving. All of us captured inside it were its teachers. During our conversation, it confided to me that it could feel all our emotions and read most of our thoughts. Now that I found very disturbing! The idea of someone browsing through my mind was not a pleasant one!

With every passing hour, the entity was developing a more distinct personality with likes and dislikes. Some of us, it enjoyed having around, but others not so much. For one, Victoria's presence had greatly disturbed it. It claimed that not even the woman who had created it had been that evil! I had to think about that for a moment, but then I had to agree.

The one who had cast this enchantment had done so out of hurt, not maliciousness! Victoria's mind must have been pure poison! That one enjoyed hurting people! The awakening spirit was genuinely grateful that she was gone. It had been looking for a way to get rid of her and had even considered somehow dumping her back into her time. I imagined she must have felt similar to a terrible toothache or something!

Most of the people in the construct seemed to be decent souls. Their goodness was heavily influencing the evolving spirit. It was learning from our thoughts and wanted nothing to do with those who harmed others. What must it feel like to have all these minds within? Rather strange, I would guess! What astonished me most was its assertiveness where magic was concerned. It had chosen a side and wanted to progress along those lines. Therefore, it had a request.

Within the construct was another person who was angry and bitter and cried all the time. Could we please take that one home next? Her vibrations were very irritating to the innocent being. I happily agreed, realizing that removing any dark influences would shift the power of balance even more toward the light. It might make life in the cells easier for all of the enchantment's prisoners!

The longer we talked, the more the being seemed to evolve. It was learning and growing in wisdom and understanding. This was really quite astonishing to observe! After a while, I felt like I was conversing with an actual person! Since I was unsure what to call it, I asked if it wanted a name. The wave of pleasure radiating through me was answer enough. So I started going through several possibilities until I found one I liked.

'May I call you Bo? It means resident in Viking," I asked. This time, the warmth was not only in my mind, and I opened my eyes in surprise.

Our entire nexus had brightened visibly! The others had also sensed the change and were looking around in wonder. The moss was greener and softer, and the air felt cleaner and clearer. It had lost much of the damp feeling that had made it far from comfortable.

"What happened?" Finna wanted to know.

"I named it."

"You did what?" Revna asked, growing pale.

"I named it Bo. It has feelings and desires, just like a real person, so I thought it needed a name," I answered somewhat defensively.

"Bo! I like it, and it did save us yesterday," Eldred came to my assistance.

"Oh, child! Do you know what you have done?" Revna groaned. "By naming it, you have given it life!"

"Oh," was all I could say.

Hilda, however, was delighted. Lovingly, she patted the moss, and in response, it gained even more color and became even softer!

"See," she stated happily. "It likes us and is being rather sweet!"

For a second, Eldred looked around. Then her face took on a blank expression. Not to be outdone, she had decided to communicate with Bo herself.

"There is a person he really, really wants gone," she stated after a few moments.

"Yes," I affirmed. "That will be the next one we are taking home. With Bo's help, it will be much easier to dial in the destinations from now on!"

"Does it have influence over that now?" Finna wanted to know.

"He seems to," I answered thoughtfully. "The location we took Victoria to showed up just as soon as we tried calling in the one we had decided to drop her in. We tried to change it, but it would not budge."

"You mean it decided where she should be sent?" Revna asked with concern.

"It seemed to," I affirmed.

"If it has that kind of power, we need to stay on its good side!" Revna informed us. "You guys better hurry up! Go and remove that person it sees as a thorn in its side!"

"Cara, does he identify with being male?" Finna questioned.

"Yes, now that you mention it, " I answered thoughtfully. "I got that distinct impression just as soon as I made contact."

"I did too," Eldred confirmed.

"It makes sense. Most of the prisoners are women, so he is the balance to us," Finna declared.

"Well, I guess we better start calling it him then," Revna decided.

"I guess," Finna agreed with a resigned sigh.

"Hello there, young man! I am happy to meet you!" Revna called into the nexus.

Her words had a positive effect on our environment. It brightened even further! I was thrilled with the changes, and Eldred, Hilda, and Signe were smiling. Our surroundings were starting to look downright sunny and pleasant! That made all of us happy!

"Thank you, Bo!" we shouted together.

Chapter 28

The Bond Grows

Since we had agreed to free Bo of the person whose emotions bothered him so, Eldred, Hilda, and I quickly said goodbye to the others and went on our way. When we reached the membrane, we were in for a welcome surprise. It opened up on its own accord! We were able to walk right through! The girls and I were absolutely delighted. None of us liked squeezing through that slimy, leathery barrier! Bo was helping us!

Then, he was guiding us to the cell where his unwelcome prisoner resided. All we had to do was stay within the large bubble the mist formed around us. On its own, it traveled in the direction we needed to go. This was incredibly easy, but we felt distinctly herded along. Every time we slowed even a little, the rear of our capsule approached rather quickly to move us along! I had not pegged Bo for being so impatient!

When we reached our destination, the wall opened up before us. We heard the wailing just as soon as we entered. Now it all made sense! No wonder Bo had rushed us along! This was just plain awful! The voice was shrill and grating, like fingernails on a chalkboard! Hilda instinctively covered her ears. She adamantly refused to go any closer to that dreadful sound. Therefore, dealing with this person fell to Eldred and me.

Hilda retreated back to the in-between, and Bo promptly closed the membrane sealing us in. Great! Eldred and I were on our own! Resolutely, we made our way down the path.

The closer we got, the more disturbing the noise grew. It took tremendous willpower for me not to retreat. The loud sobs and shrieks were so piercing that they hurt our ears. This woman was obviously hysterical and affected by her imprisonment in the worst way. When we finally laid eyes on her, we noticed that the smoke was right next to her. Had Bo been trying to take her home himself? It sure seemed so!

"Hello," I shouted as loud as possible, trying to make myself heard over the yowling. I had to repeat myself several times before we caught the woman's attention.

"Do not come any closer," she wailed once she took notice of us. "Why have you brought me here? What is this place? What have I ever done to you, you wretches!"

The encounter went downhill from there. Next thing we knew, the very stout woman was up and threatening us with the umbrella she carried. We tried to explain to her that we were here to help, but she swung her weapon at us and almost hit us!

"Liars," she shrieked. "Keep away from me, or you will regret it!"

Neither Eldred nor I were making any headway with this person! It was evident that we would not be getting any information from her. We stepped back and evaluated the situation. As we watched, the smoke was moving imperceptibly closer now that this loud individual was distracted. Thank you, Bo!

"Everything bad always happens to me!" the woman started to wail. "Why did it not take my sister? No, naturally, I am the one who ends up in this nightmare while she is comfortably at home with her husband! I bet she is happy that I am gone!"

If that was the way she usually behaved, most people would be! A momentary pause made us hope she was finished complaining, but the tirade continued.

"Did she send you to get rid of me? That would be just like her! It is not my fault that her husband fancies me!"

Eldred and I looked at each other and shuddered. How anyone could be attracted to this was beyond us! Not only was she grossly overweight, but her personality was even worse! Yuck, yuck, and just yuck!

"The room she makes me live in! I deserve the master bedroom, not the best guestroom! And do not even get me started on the food! Fit for the swine, I say!" the most unpleasant woman screeched in her shrill, irritating voice.

At this point, I tuned her out. We needed to devise a way to get her home without approaching her and fast! Eldred and I were no angels; we might lose our tempers and use our magic to knock her out!

Seriously, who could blame the sister if she wanted to be rid of this self-centered, nasty, ungrateful sibling she was obviously taking care of? Not me! My tolerance for her theatrics was just about gone. That umbrella was a formidable weapon! I bet she used it on people all the time! Both Eldred and I already had several welts where this awful being had managed to hit us. And she had kicked dirt in our faces! My eyes were still tearing up, trying to get rid of the grit!

We could not do this on our own. We needed assistance. Getting in touch with the spirit of the construct, I laid out my plan while keeping a wary eye on the threatening parasol. Bo then shared my idea with Eldred, who gave me an appreciative grin. At this point, neither of us cared much about where this awful person ended up as long as she was far away from us! Anyway, if she did not make it home, her sister would have a much more peaceful life!

Taking turns feigning attacks, we distracted the wretch enough for the smoke to enclose all three of us. We kept the belligerent woman occupied and on the retreat, at least for a bit. However, suddenly, she lunged toward me, swinging her weapon for all she was worth. I quickly evaded her by backing out of the haze into the place beyond. At least we had her on the right side of the veil, but now I was afraid this harpy would block my way back. Or that the gate closed!

Eldred had anticipated my need and was anchoring the location. I shot her a grateful look over my shoulder as I ran across the field at an angle. My pursuer was right behind me. For one of such girth, this female was awfully fleet on her feet! Huffing and puffing, she was determinedly chasing after me. I could only imagine what she would do to me if she caught up with me!

Once the rotund person was far enough away from the portal, I changed course once, then again. The maneuver gave me the extra space required to safely get around her. Now, I picked up speed. With everything I had, I barreled for the hazel cloud. Grabbing Eldred's outstretched hand, I disappeared into the smoke. She ran alongside me, and we kept going until we were through the veil and back in the cell. But even there, we did not rest. Slowing only a little, we raced toward the in-between.

Bo opened the membrane for us as we approached, and we rushed through. He closed it behind us so quickly that we felt the wind of the movement on our necks. Both Eldred and I stopped within a foot of the barrier. We were trying to catch our breath. Each of us had several large welts from the encounter with this horrid woman. These were sure to become good-sized bruises! Our hair was in complete disarray, and we had dirt on our faces.

Hilda, who had been waiting for us, regarded us with an incredulous look.

"What happened to you?" she asked us, aghast.

"We had a run-in with a large woman and her deadly umbrella!" Eldred finally managed to squeeze out between gasps. "You could have warned us, Bo!"

We could sense his contriteness but also that he had not foreseen that the situation could get out of hand to such a degree. Being so new to this world, he did not have much experience with human interactions.

"Did you see where she ended up?" Eldred asked me.

"No," I managed to get out between breaths. "I was too busy running for my life!"

"Bo took her to the same place as Victoria!" Eldred informed us.

The three of us looked at each other, stunned. Then, a grin spread over Hilda's face.

"I can just see those two meeting up!" she chortled.

Hilda turned out to be superb at spinning a yarn. She described the encounter between these two unpleasant people and the resulting battle in such a hilarious way and in such detail that she had all three of us roaring with laughter. Even the in-between was starting to shake as Bo, who had been listening in, joined in on our merriment.

Finally, after we had let go of the last of the tension that had resulted from our confrontation with the umbrella-swinging woman, we decided to return to the nexus that had become our home base. None of us were up to facing another person for a while, we needed time to regroup, and we wanted to check on our friends.

Bo was very accommodating as we moved along. We chatted with him as we walked, hearing his voice clearly in our minds. Our bubble opened up the membrane when we arrived at our destination, creating a large entrance. I was so grateful that he was saving us from having to push through! I, for one, had had enough unpleasantness for the day, and I hurt rather badly in several spots where the umbrella had hit me.

That, however, was not the only change Bo made to please us. The instant we entered the cell, we came to a dead stop. What was going on here? The place was so bright that Eldred, Hilda, and I were almost blinded for a moment. Our eyes had grown accustomed to our dark and dreary surroundings and had to adjust to the transformation. We had to blink a few times before they would focus.

Once we could see, we realized that the light level was not the only difference. Revna's nexus had taken on an entirely different look! The air smelled sweet and was clear, all the mold and nasty-looking fog were gone, and the walkway was now in good repair. The scenery was much more pleasant and resembled the world we had been stolen from! How had this happened?

This space was downright nice! Eldred, Hilda, and I could barely believe our eyes. Were those sunflowers along the path? We had to touch one and examine it closely to make sure it was real. Bo finally got our attention. We had been so focused on our immediate surroundings that we had not even noticed what had been done to the house! We could only stare in wonder!

The cabin was no longer in ruins! The roof was intact, the windows straight and shiny, the porch roof was solidly held up by stout columns, and the door was back on the hinges! The place even had paint now, a soft doe-grey with cream-colored trim around the windows and along the roof. It was really quite pretty! A narrow but well-kept path led right up to the entrance.

Obviously, we were meant to follow it. Cautiously, Eldred, Hilda, and I moved along it, still not trusting that all this was real. Somehow, we expected it to revert to its former self at any moment!

Signe must have spotted us because suddenly, the door was thrown open, and she rushed out to greet us.

"What do you think? Is this not so much better?" she gushed when she reached us, excited like a little child.

"It is! How did this come about?" Eldred asked curiously.

"My mother had a chat with Bo and told him very firmly that the surroundings were completely unsuitable for her daughter and would slow down the healing," she explained with a laugh.

"At first, having no experience with such things, he was not sure what she meant," Revna, who came to join us, added, grinning. "So, Finna described the place she had grown up in."

"Bo just needed a bit of instruction," Finna declared, downplaying her part in this remarkable transformation. "Once he decided that he wanted control over the environments of the nexuses, he took it. Did he not do a marvelous job?"

"He most certainly did!" exclaimed Hilda. "We almost did not recognize the place!"

"Well done, Bo!" Eldred and I told him in unison. The praise was not lost on the newly awakened consciousness, and the light around us took on a slight reddish tinge as if he was blushing with pleasure.

"Come! You have to see the inside!" Signe stated, herding us along toward the door.

The alterations to the outside of the house had been incredible, but we were in for even more of a surprise!

Chapter 29

An Unexpected Sacrifice

The girls and I were stunned. The house now had an upstairs with several small rooms! Hilda fell in love with one with cornflowers on the wall and on her comforter, and Eldred's was decorated with yellow lilies. The one I claimed had a delicate pink rose pattern. Since roses are my favorite flowers, the space appealed to me instantly. It was quite lovely and had a large, amazingly comfortable bed covered in soft blankets. A cotton nightie was waiting for me on the pillow. What a change from sleeping on the moss! This had almost all the comforts of home!

After cleaning up, I decided to lie down for a bit. Slipping between the sheets, I pulled the covers over me, relishing the feeling of being in a real bed. But after a few moments, I started to feel very lonely and a little lost. It seemed so strange not to have Phillipe next to me. I missed his arms around me, the feel of his warm body next to mine. A deep longing shot through me, and silent tears rolled down my cheeks.

Suddenly, I heard footsteps in the hallway, and then the knob of my door turned. Two tussled heads poked through the crack, one fair and one dark.

"We are having a hard time sleeping. Can we join you?" Eldred asked.

I nodded. My heart warmed with affection for these two beautiful girls. I knew only too well that they had felt my distress and that this was why they were coming to my room. Quickly, they slipped into bed next to me, one on each side. We curled up together, taking comfort from each other's presence. Once we closed our eyes, we were out almost instantly.

When I awoke several hours later, the girls were still asleep. Their closeness was not a perfect substitute for Phillipe, but it helped. The longing for my husband grew more intense the longer I stayed here. I had not married the man I could live with but the one I could not live without! Being apart left a hole in my heart and soul. From the dream, I knew he felt the same about me and missed me just as badly.

Not wanting to wake Eldred and Hilda by getting up, I let my mind wander. Eventually, I reached out to Bo and roamed through the chambers in this honeycomb-like trap. He allowed me full access and supplied me with any information I requested. I thanked him profusely since this gave me a clearer picture of the hive's construction.

As we had already discovered, in between each cell was a narrow corridor filled with dense mist. Each chamber was separated from its surroundings by a thick membrane. We had not known that it was organized around one large space in the center, which we had not yet located because it was well-protected. It was ringed solidly by nexuses! That must be where the spell operated from! It would be the final place we would need to visit to implode the enchantment!

Every time we sent a person home, the vacated cell disappeared. With those around the outside perimeter, it just left a hole. The ones further in, however, were replaced by another cell that slid in its place.

This kept the entire spell nice and tight. The design reminded me vividly of a beehive with its queen in the middle. What would we find in that central chamber? We would have to wait to find out since neither Bo nor I could gain entry.

Since we had taken several people back to where they belonged, the entire construct already felt slightly smaller. It would continue shrinking with each additional person we took home until only the spot in the middle remained. Once it was dealt with, the enchantment was down. But that brought up a different concern. What about Bo? He was starting to get more and more conscious and independent of his original purpose. Was it fair to punish him for what he had been designed to do?

I could feel his affection for me, for all of our group here in Revna's nexus. He had come such a long way in such a short time! His understanding of us and willingness to meet our needs was really quite astonishing. Bo persistently displayed empathy, compassion, and kindness, all human traits. Realizing that Baby Cara needed to be returned quickly took understanding and awareness. I felt strongly that Bo did not deserve to be undone along with the spell.

How could we separate him from the enchantment? Also, it would greatly benefit us all if he found an alternate power source that was not human. But wait! He was no longer drawing strength from any of us in this prison! So, where was he getting the energy for his continued existence? And for all the nice things he was doing for us? Only one way to find out!

'Bo, how are you maintaining yourself?' I asked him gently.

'Oh, you realized,' came the immediate response.

He sounded rather weak. At that instant, it dawned on me that he was cannibalizing his own reserves! That would not do! Since first making contact, I had grown rather fond of him and had started to regard Bo as a friend. I knew that the girls felt the same way. Letting him just fade away was not on our agenda. Something had to be done!

In addition, sending people home and moving around this hive was so much easier with his help! And, if this construct collapsed prematurely due to Bo's demise, it was a good possibility that all those still within it could be forever trapped in some sort of void outside of time and space! Not a pleasant thought! Not that losing our new friend would not be bad enough, but never returning home? Unthinkable!

I lay there for a few minutes, stunned by the horror of such an unpleasant possibility. Then, determination kicked in. This could not be allowed! But how could we save Bo and disarm this trap at the same time? I did not have a clue at that moment, but I was determined to come up with a solution. Maybe the others would be willing to help, especially now that he was seeing to our needs so admirably!

If we came up empty and could not find a way, we would have to get as many people home as quickly as possible. Not having to maintain so many cells would reduce the energy expenditure necessary to maintain the construct. This would prolong Bo's life. But we would not be able to save him! Nor all of us! That was an unacceptable outcome! Where could we direct him for some much-needed power? I needed more information!

Once more, I let my mind sweep through the entire complex. I was hoping to get a better understanding of how many more people were trapped here and how extensive this construct was. I was not happy with what I discovered. We still had a way to go to clear it out! I fixed its size in my mind to compare it to a later assessment once we had taken more folks home. As I swept through the magical prison again, I noticed a sparkle underneath one of the cells.

What was that? I dove that way to investigate.

As I reached that faint glimmer, I discovered a ley line running right beneath the hive. It came close to the surface at that spot and had been used to anchor the construct. I moved closer to check it out. This was not a major line, but it carried enough power to sustain Bo indefinitely. How perfect! He was so weak already and did not want to hurt anyone or anything that it took some convincing before he tapped into that readily available energy source.

Within minutes, I could feel him strengthening, but I also noticed that Bo was being very prudent in how much he siphoned off. My respect for this thoughtful being grew even more, as did my determination to not let him die. He sensed this and sent a wave of gratitude in my direction that warmed me from the inside out. Since the immediate problem of keeping him from fading away had been solved, I went back to sleep for a while.

Sometime later, Hilda started to stir. When she turned around to face me, I smiled at her. Quietly, we slipped out of bed and then out of the room, leaving Eldred in a peaceful slumber. Still in our nighties, we went to join the others. We found Revna, Finna, and Signe comfortably ensconced before the fireplace in the kitchen, each with a steaming mug in her hands. They had tea! And there was an actual fire!

Hilda and I relished our own beverages a few minutes later. It felt a little odd since neither of us was hungry or thirsty. However, the steaming liquid was exceedingly satisfying and welcome, even without milk or sugar. Another comfort of home! The entire house blushed when we sent Bo our exuberant thanks. While we sipped the hot treat, I shared with the others what I had discovered and how things had changed in the last few hours.

Hilda was terribly upset when she heard that Bo had chosen death over draining our life force. She was such a sensitive person, and the idea had her in tears, which greatly upset Bo. Finally, the girl went over to hug a corner of the house. In as stern a tone as I have ever heard her use, she strictly forbade him to ever do such a thing again. Still, it took a while for her to calm down, even after he promised.

Eventually, we moved on to other subjects. To our delight, Signe's leg was looking so much better. Finna had done an incredible job dealing with that terrible scarring. By now, only faint red areas remained of the severe injuries! Hilda and I were duly impressed and very happy for the young woman.

Another good thing to come of this whole debacle! Thanks to ending up in this time trap, Signe would have a shot at a normal life. However, our friend was tired from all the hard work her body was doing healing itself. Not unexpectantly so, but at least she was almost ready to go home. She and Finna were anxious to return to their own time, but at Hilda's and my request, they agreed to stay and teach the sisters and me for a while longer.

Once that was settled, there was work to be done. We decided Hilda and I would set out with Revna to take more people home. We would let Eldred sleep since she obviously needed the rest. All her nervous energy and the anxiety she had been feeling had taken a toll.

With Bo's aid, two of us would be enough to dial in any required destination. But, if we did run into trouble, having a third person present would be helpful. Besides, now that she was no longer needed to heal Signe, Revna was curious about the in-between and the other cells. And she wanted to meet some of the people caught in this time trap. She was so excited by the prospect of exploration that she could hardly wait to get going. She started rushing Hilda and me to finish our tea so we could get ready.

We were just about to sneak upstairs to retrieve our clothes when they appeared on the kitchen table. It was nice to have one's needs anticipated! Hilda and I quickly dressed, and the three of us set out to take care of business. Bo was only too happy to assist us in any way he could. He opened the membrane and created a bubble for us to walk in.

Bo was so grateful to be feeling better that he allowed Revna to examine the thick mist-like substance that filled the in-between. With his approval, she even stuffed some in her pocket. The white stuff turned out to be much more substantial than I had thought. It reminded me a little of airy cotton. Hilda and I ended up getting our own samples. Who knew when something like this would come in handy!

Hilda and I agreed that it was such a relief to get around the construct so easily. Until Bo started helping us, Eldred had been the only one of all the people caught in the hive who could make her way through this material and the membranes. It just kind of retreated from her, and an open space would form around her, allowing her to go wherever she wished! Revna believed that her magic must directly oppose the construct's vibrations to have such an effect.

Was that the reason that she was so tired? Had Bo's loss of energy affected her somehow? I sent my mind out to ask him about this, and he instantly reached out and checked on the sleeping girl.

As it turned out, they were connected! Bo immediately fed Eldred some energy from the leyline. Then he reported back to us that she was now awake and fully recovered. Revna and I exchanged a concerned glance. This was an additional complication that we had not considered. My two young friends would have to be taken home long before we were ready to deal with the last remnants of this enchantment to prevent Eldred from being harmed!

At least for now, Bo sustaining himself from the leyline would alleviate some of this problem. It was vital for him to keep his strength up since that was the only way to maintain Eldred's. He agreed. Since it was not just for himself, he did allow himself to draw a little extra power. Once again, I was impressed by his care and consideration for the world around him.

Bo was more thoughtful than most people, which was very surprising for someone born from such malicious intent and the desire to entrap and harm others! I was so glad his survival no longer depended on us as his power source! It made it easier for me to take more people home, and quickly, since it was not hurting him. The more I got to know this unique being, the more attached I was growing.

The others felt the same way, even Revna and Finna, who had been less than thrilled when I had initially named him. Bo had become our friend and benefactor. We would do our utmost to save him and find a way to allow him to live independently of the rest of the spell!

Chapter 30

Arthur and Bess

We continued to move through the in-between until we reached the cell Bo was taking us to. The three of us entered and looked around. To our surprise, we saw no one! This cell appeared to be empty, but we knew it would neither exist nor would Bo have brought us here if it had been. So, we started searching. Eventually, we located a very dispirited middle-aged lady. She was curled into a ball behind a mossy stack of wood. Once we managed to coax her into unrolling herself and coming out, she introduced herself as Bess Delande.

At first, she had not believed we were real. She thought that we were just a figment of her imagination. The poor thing must have been here a long time! No wonder Bo had guided us here! It took us a while to get through to her. Finally, she grasped that we were there to take her back home. Once that fact sank in, Bess was pleased to see us. Her relief was so great that her knees gave way. She would have slumped to the ground had we not rushed to support her!

When the joyful tears had stopped, and the woman was once more somewhat composed, Hilda and I tried encouraging her to talk about herself and her family. It was like pulling teeth! We ended up asking her questions which Bess would answer in a monotone voice. She was still deeply depressed and had not yet fully comprehended the change in her situation. She did not even comment on the difference in dress between her and us!

But we were determined to get her out of her funk! We needed her to remember that things had been different before her lonely time in the hive. Not knowing what else to do, we queried her about her home, children, and husband. Then, we moved on to pets. That was when we finally succeeded in bringing a bit of life into Bess. Hilda, Revna, and I were greatly relieved. We were making progress!

Bess started talking about her dog. We got to hear all about how smart he was and all the remarkable things he did. Naturally, we added 'ohs' and 'ahs' at just the right moments to keep her going.

When we thought Bess sufficiently restored and we had collected enough of her history, we took her over to the smoke. At first, she absolutely refused to enter. We could tell that the lady was terribly afraid. Hilda and I had to explain several times why it was necessary to walk through it before she consented to set foot in that mist. But she did so only under the condition that she could hold onto us. Clutching Revna's and my hands with a death grip that hurt the bones in our fingers, she tentatively made her way in.

From her description, we dialed in her location. With Revna, Hilda, and I working together, it was easy and took only a few seconds. I suspected that Bo was helping as well. Having someone as depressed as her within his consciousness upset him greatly. Once she saw the familiar surroundings, Bess broke into tears. Impulsively, she hugged us several times. She had been in the time trap so long that she had given up hope of returning to her loved ones!

Bess was immensely grateful. After thanking us numerous times, she rushed off toward the house in the distance. Hilda, Revna, and I watched her go, then went back to the nexus and the in-between. We were thrilled by our successful rescue and ready to tackle another. This one had been relatively easy compared to some. We moved along with the bubble talking excitedly.

It turned out to be a rather lengthy walk. Bo definitely had an agenda! Bess had been close to catatonic. I suspected that he was choosing those people who were the worst off, the ones who had been here the longest. With no night and day, it was hard to tell how much time passed in the hive, but I suspected some individuals had been here for weeks or even months, all alone in their nexuses. The thought made me shudder.

Being confined in such a dark and depressing environment by themselves had not been healthy for their mental states. That I could totally understand. Initially, Bess had tried crossing the smoke several times but had eventually decided that it was the source of all evil and to be avoided at all costs.

After that, she had just sort of vegetated in her cell. I doubted that the brightening of the entire hive in the last few days had made much of an impression on her. If she had noticed at all!

Intimately tied to the construct, Bo was in touch with them all. This allowed him to gauge perfectly who needed to be seen to next.

Once we walked through the membrane and spotted the inhabitant, I understood. An old, frail man was sitting in the middle of the path. Like some do to comfort themselves, he was rocking back and forth. His eyes were glazed, and he was drooling. His face was utterly expressionless, his hair disheveled, and his clothes covered in dust.

This guy was in a bad way! He was so far gone that we could barely get his attention! He cringed when Hilda or I got near him but tolerated Revna. While we stayed back, she crouched down beside him. After several attempts, she finally managed to get him to focus a little. Had he been like this when he arrived here, or was this state the result of his confinement? We had no way of knowing!

Revna called us over when she had calmed him enough to tolerate our presence. This was an excellent opportunity to teach us about healing. Ever so gently, we evaluated the damage to the guy's mind and body. Then, we fixed what we could. This made him slightly more conscious, but he was still far from lucid. However, there was not much else we could do for him at the moment.

How would we ever return him to where he came from? Since he could barely talk, and when he did, it was gibberish, or at least that is what it sounded like to us, we had a conundrum. How would we call in his location when we had no idea where he had come from? The situation did not look very promising!

It took all three of us to get the elderly gent up and over to the smoke. Searching through his jumbled and confused memories, we finally got a glimpse of a place that seemed to be home. However, we had no way to be sure. Bo decided to come to our rescue at this point. He helped us dial in the time and space from which the old chap seemed to have come. Since it felt like he belonged there, we stepped out of the smoke.

Except, now we had another problem. We could not just leave this feeble person out there in the lane where he had entered the portal! Anything could happen to him! Being so senile and confused, he must have wandered away from home and ended up in the mist. Who knew what other mischief he would get himself into if we just left him right there!

After a brief discussion, we decided that Hilda would anchor the portal while Revna and I took the old gent back to his home. Now it was just a matter of finding it. From where we stood, no dwellings could be seen. We did not even have the slightest idea where to start looking! We needed more information, but for that, we had to clear the man's mind a little more. But how? After a brief discussion, we decided to experiment.

Placing her hands on each side of the ancient man's face, Revna bid me to put mine over hers. Taking our time, we started a much more in-depth scan. Since we could not find any apparent physical damage, we checked his blood. We got lucky. The chemicals and hormones in the old man's body were completely out of whack! Carefully, we encouraged his organs to adjust the levels. We moved them in the right direction in tiny increments. The rebalancing could not be rushed!

What luck! This seemed to help more than our previous attempt. Finally, Revna located the source of some of this chaos, and we managed to set it right. I watched with wonder as the poor chap's eyes cleared. Then, his face lost most of its vague impression. He suddenly sat up straighter and seemed more robust, more with it! Revna and I smiled at each other. This was a good start!

We continued restoring him. Now that we had a better idea of what we were dealing with, Revna investigated everything in his body that could affect his brain. Much of it seemed to be in good order, but some glands and organs were secreting things that were just slightly off. Those we nudged in the right direction. But what had caused all this in the first place? That we had not yet determined.

As we kept adjusting his body chemistry, his memories started to reorder themselves. They were now making sense. Revna and I were thrilled. What a privilege to be able to give such a precious gift!

"Thank you, dear ladies! I feel so much better! I am Arthur Pickerton. Who do I have the honor of addressing?" the gent suddenly inquired.

Revna and I quickly removed our hands and introduced ourselves. As was befitting this man's obvious rank, we curtsied, and he bowed to each of us.

"Dear ladies, I seem to be rather confused and have no idea how I got here. Where are we?"

"We are not sure," I explained. "We were going to take you home, but we do not know where you live!"

Looking around, recognition showed on his features.

"We are not far from my cottage," he stated, taking a tottering step.

"It seems that I am in much worse shape than I remember. I do not wish to impose, but would you ladies mind very much helping me get there?" he inquired rather abashedly.

I felt for him. What must it be like to come to and find that one has deteriorated so? This had to be terrible for him! Gently, I took one of his arms to support him. Revna took the other a moment later, and we steadied Arthur between us as he stumbled along. At least at first! We were practically carrying him a few steps later!

"Just curious, why is nothing except us moving?" Arthur asked, somewhat puzzled.

He might be incredibly frail, but he was aware enough to notice that something was off! That was a good sign! Revna explained what was going on as we went down the lane.

With our new friend directing us, we made our way through the woods. We had to stop multiple times for Arthur to catch his breath. He thought these great opportunities to ask questions just as soon as he could gasp one out. He would listen avidly as we told him more about the place he had been caught in. Finally, we reached his abode. We took a few more minutes to get additional information about his life.

Arthur was very matter-of-fact as he gave us a short account of himself. Revna and I could not help feeling impressed. He must have really been quite something before his decline! This had both of us curious about what had caused it, but we did not have to ask. The old gentleman confided in us, with tears in his eyes, the events of that fateful day that had ended his happiness and stolen his will to live.

One day, on their daily walk, his wife, who had been slightly rotund, had grabbed for her chest. She had let out a moan, and her eyes had met his one last time. Then, she had crumbled to the ground lifelessly. She had been dead before help could arrive. The shock of seeing her perishing so unexpectedly right before his eyes had been too much. He had pulled her into his arms and had sat there holding her when his son arrived.

What a blow that must have been for him! The old laird could not remember much after that. Grief had stolen his senses. His mind, unable to deal with the horror of that sudden loss, had retreated from the world. The hurt was still there, but Arthur was grateful to us for restoring him. He had grandchildren that he dearly loved and was looking forward to watching them grow up.

Revna told him very sternly how he needed to eat and what herbs he should add to his tea if he intended to keep his faculties about him. She also encouraged him to have someone assist him so that he could go for a walk every day. To rebuild his weakened muscles, she also prescribed some light weight-lifting exercises. Arthur happily promised to do it all. He had more confidence in this healer than in any of the doctors of his time!

Not that I could blame him! Some of those still thought the letting of blood would cure just about any disease! Revna told him about our clan and that there might be someone in Gairloch better equipped to help him than around his home. I could tell she really liked the old gent and that her soft heart would have loved to stay here and aid him.

However, we were still unclear about one thing, even after all the data we had collected about our new friend. How had he ended up in the trap, and why? We finally figured it out after a few more questions. Arthur was distantly related to our clan, and his deceased wife had been a Magnuson! And we were not that far from Gairloch! This was great news since not even his son could complain about his father visiting his mother's family! It might actually bring them all closer together!

Reluctantly, we said our goodbyes. We wished Arthur well and a speedy recovery. He agreed with us that it was best not to tell anyone about our meeting. After all, who would believe him? Our clan, perhaps, but outsiders? Not so much! The old man understood that quite clearly. He was getting sharper by the minute, and was not about to provide anyone with the opportunity to call him crazy!

Now that he knew about the Magnuson Clan and more people like Revna and me, he looked forward to new adventures. He could not wait to travel to Havn and meet the rest of our people.

We left Arthur sitting at his table with food and drink. He waved to us through the window as we made our way down the lane and back into the woods. We almost got lost, but then I was able to connect to Bo. Always happy to be helpful, he guided us in the direction of the plume of smoke, still being anchored by Hilda. The woods here were lovely, but one trail looked just like the next, and I am not sure if we would have found our way back without his assistance.

Once we were on the right track, I examined a thought that had been niggling at me. Somehow, this encounter felt very significant. How would it affect all of us who were born after Arthur? Would it bring about changes that would cause trouble? Using my senses, I tried looking into the future. What I received was dim, but one thing became apparent very quickly. Somehow our rescue of Arthur would bring about something beautiful!

I was thrilled to discover this and shared my insights with Revna. She was just as curious and excited as I was but also somewhat sad that she would never learn of all the good that would come of this fateful encounter. We discussed this as we made our way back to Hilda, who was patiently waiting for us.

Always curious, Hilda demanded a complete account of our recent interactions with Arthur. She was delighted to hear that we had been able to heal him and promised to relay the story to Eldred when we had time. For some reason, all three of us were reluctant to leave here, but we had no clue why. Maybe we felt that the old gent still needed us? But there was nothing else we could do for him. His servants would look after him just fine!

Finally, when we could postpone our departure no longer, we made our way through the smoke back to the nexus and from there to the in-between. We moved along with the bubble Bo created for us without paying much attention, each preoccupied with her own thoughts. Arthur had touched all our hearts, and we hoped he would make a full recovery.

To appease my curiosity, I would look up Arthur in the history books when I got home. It would have been fun sharing what I found with the others! If only there was a way to stay in contact with my friends here! Having grown to love them, I hated the idea of never seeing or talking to Eldred, Hilda, Signe, Revna, and Finna again!

Maybe because our shared experience in the hive had bound us together, I felt very close to them. They had become like family to me. Even Oliver and I had grown apart these last few years. The distance and my brother's spoiled children had not been conducive to spending much time together.

In light of my recent adventures, I found this rather sad.

Chapter 31

Finna's Story

The three of us moved along with the bubble without saying a word. Each of us was lost in her own thoughts. In my mind, I was mapping out the locations of the folk we had taken home. Except for a few outliers like Arthur, the rest were clustered closely around Havn and Gairloch. This led me to conclude that the one who had cast the spell had lived around there somewhere. Timewise, most of the relatives who had been captured were from 1550 to about 1901, with a few like Finna, Signe, and me far outside of that.

The one source I had read that spoke of a construct like this had been purposely vague. It had not revealed names or where the people lived. Therefore, it could have been referring to us or not! Try as I might, I could not recall any more than that brief mention. This was really annoying! Knowing more about the individual responsible for this abomination would be helpful!

The center was well protected and should contain the initial part of this enchantment. But did it also include magical traps that we could run afoul of? It was all within the realm of the possible! The more we knew, the better our chance to defeat it! Whoever cast this had possessed tremendous power! And a vast amount of righteous anger! But who was this person? It could have been that sorceress, but it could have also been a man who felt rejected by a Magnuson lady!

I asked Bo, but he was unable to answer my questions. The spell would not allow him to divulge that information.

When I could not come up with any way to figure this out, I finally shared my thoughts with Revna and Hilda. A man being responsible for this awful construct just did not feel right to us. However, we could not discard it outright! Too much depended on that. Women could be devious, but we assumed that a female would be less likely to devise some hidden pitfalls that would prevent us from shutting down the spell.

But just to be sure, we decided to check with Bo. As we had almost expected, he was not all that communicative on that subject. This was not surprising. Revna believed he was compelled to withhold pertinent information from us. How could we get around this constraint? After a moment's contemplation, I had an idea.

"Bo, can you make a light to our right?" I asked him.

Instead of answering, the bubble lit up on the indicated side.

"Let us assume that the right side is for a male enchanter and the left for a female. Is that agreeable with everyone?"

Revna and Hilda looked at me, puzzled, but they nodded their agreement. Bo signaled his approval by brightening our surroundings.

"Bo, if I asked a question about the spell would you be able to signal the truth?" I asked him.

"No," came his reply.

Just as I thought!

"But you would be able to lie, correct?"

"Yes!" he declared, delighted we had found a way around his restrictions.

"Now, hypothetically, if I looked hard enough in the history books for the person who created you and knew just what to search for, which one would I find? A woman or man?" I inquired, feeling rather sly.

Bo only hesitated for an instant before briefly lighting up the right. He had lied and selected the male side, thus giving us our answer!

"Yes, hypothetically, this does seem like something a woman would do," Revna added thoughtfully.

Bo brightened in agreement. Since this was not a question about his origin, he was able to do so. We were much closer to when, where, and who was behind this malevolent trap than ever!

After that, we changed the subject. Revna eventually brought up that Signe needed to be returned to her home. Neither Hilda nor I liked this idea. We had grown fond of the warrior maiden and hated being parted from her. But we also realized that she was just about fully recovered. The last bit would take care of itself over time.

Finna had been growing more restless with each passing hour. We figured that she was more than ready to leave. The girls and I benefitted tremendously from her teachings, but Revna was equally as competent. For the mutual benefit of both their people, she and Finna had been exchanging recipes and techniques. Revna was willing to pass those on to Eldred, Hilda, and me.

Revna and Finna had worked well together to eradicate the last remnants of the injury and to minimize the scars on Signe's leg. Keeping the two warrior maidens here longer than necessary just to keep us company served no real purpose! One healer was enough to further Eldred's, Hilda's, and my education. By now, all three of us were solid in our basic knowledge, but there was always more to learn! After all, the human body is very complex!

To divert Hilda and me from our sadness over the upcoming parting with our friend, Revna started quizzing us on healing methods and the use of various herbs. This kept us occupied until we arrived wherever Bo had decided to take us.

When the membrane parted before us, we instantly recognized the place we had started to think of as home. Since the rescue of Arthur had taken such a long time, Bo had decided to take us back! All three of us were relieved to not deal with another captured person for a bit. Revna had poured a lot of her power into helping the old man. She was tired, and Hilda and I wanted to spend some more time with Signe before she had to leave.

Once we reached the house, we were greeted by Eldred, who had awoken a while ago. Naturally, she wanted a detailed account of each person. She was determined to chronicle everything that had happened to us in this trap once she returned home. Writing it all down and passing it on to her descendants had become extremely important to her. It would help preserve a record of these events and might serve as a warning to those coming after her, including Phillipe and me.

A few minutes later, Signe joined us. She seemed sad, and we soon found out why. Finna wanted us to take her and Signe home the next time we set out! Hilda, trying to cheer everyone up, proposed having a farewell party. Even Bo seemed to like this fun idea. Since food was neither needed nor available to us, we settled on tea and music.

Soon, we were all sitting outside the cottage with a cup in hand.

Finna, getting into the spirit of the occasion, started telling us stories. She had a real knack for this and quickly had us spellbound. I had read some of the Viking lore, but to hear it firsthand? I could not help myself; I just had to record her! Good thing that batteries did not seem to drain in this strange place, or I would have been sitting on empty long ago!

When Finna had concluded yet another tale, Revna spoke up.

"Finna, would you please share a little bit more about yourself? Where you grew up, and how you came to the sanctuary in Norway?"

"Oh yes! Please!" Eldred and Hilda pleaded.

Finna was initially reluctant but finally relented due to the girls' continued begging.

"My parents lived in a small village in a place called Danmork. I was born there. We were somewhat isolated since we were near the tip of a long, narrow peninsula in the far north. My people liked it that way, and we had our own manner of doing things. I loved the area and the closeness to the sea. It was a wonderful place to grow up, but life was hard and full of peril.

"As a small child, I started having visions of things to come. My papa realized very quickly that what I saw usually came true. To this day, I remember how much this frightened him! But at the time, I did not understand why. He told me that he would use my premonitions to keep our people safe but that no one besides him and my mother, not even my aunts and uncles, could know about my gift.

"Thus, my abilities remained hidden for many years. But then, I had a vision at a funeral. I could not control it; I went into a trance right in front of everyone! It was a warning of imminent danger and required us to act immediately. A severe storm was about to hit, and we had only minutes to get to safety. My father started yelling orders once I relayed what I had seen. He scooped me up and carried me as everyone raced to safety. Most made it in time.

"As can be expected, people talked. Word got out and, unfortunately, reached the wrong ears. We would have taken precautions had we known, but I was still a kid, and my gift was erratic. I had no indication of what was to come. A few weeks after the funeral, one of the houses on the village's far side caught fire. It was late at night, and I was asleep.

"While my father and most of the other adults were busy trying to save the home, strange men broke down our door. They knocked out my mother and grabbed me right out of bed. We were long gone before anyone noticed."

Hilda looked at Finna in horror. Her sensitive nature was deeply affected by this tale. How horrible must it have been for a young girl to be ripped away from everything she knew and loved in such a dreadful way!

"How old were you?" Eldred asked. She was just as moved by this story as her sister and the rest of us.

"I was eleven," Finna told us matter-of-factly. "They blindfolded me and tied me up! My captors wanted to make sure that I would not escape or be able to find my way back. But I knew anyway that we were going south. They traveled really fast and on foot to avoid detection. Me, they carried over their shoulders like a sack. It was awful. By the time we reached our destination, I was weak and sick from the rough treatment.

"The ruthless jarl behind my abduction was furious when he laid eyes on me. My abductors had sneaked me into his home unnoticed, but by then, I was in such bad shape that he had to call a healer if he wanted me to live. Not having much choice, he presented me as his niece to this woman. Her name was Gudrun. He claimed his men had stolen me back from the raiders who kidnapped me and that we had barely escaped with our lives.

"He was cunning, that one. He told the wise one I had to stay hidden to keep me safe. No one could know I was there, or it would endanger the entire village. I am not sure that the old woman believed him. She was much too shrewd to buy such a story. She insisted on visiting several times a week and trained me in healing, surprisingly, with the jarl's approval.

"Had it not been for her, things would have gone so much worse for me! Gudrun taught me to recognize when a vision was coming on and how to hide the fact I was having one. And she made sure that none of the jarl's men touched me. She told him my predictions would lose their accuracy if they deflowered or molested me. Naturally, he did not want that. It would have made stealing me for nothing.

"I owe her so much. She became like a mother to me. For a long time, Gudrun was my only companion. Besides her, I was not allowed to talk to anyone, and no one else in the household besides my guards were permitted near me. At rare times, they let me go outside, but only in the enclosed courtyard the jarl had built for that purpose. I could hear people walk by sometimes but never dared to call out.

"My captor was a cruel man who liked to inflict pain. My punishment would have been swift and severe had I been caught trying to talk to one of the villagers. Thanks to Gudrun, I was able to hide some of my visions from him, but not all. For years, that awful man exploited my predictions to further his ambitions. He used the knowledge he gained to amass more land and gold at the expense of those less fortunate.

"One of the men guarding me was his youngest son. He was just a little older than me. I remembered his voice from that awful trek to that village. He had been one of my abductors! For a long time, I hated him. I would pointedly ignore him when he spoke to me. His father trusted Bjørn, more than the rest of his men. Since the jarl did not want his precious prize damaged in any way, the boy was often sent to keep an eye on me.

"Even though I despised him, he was always kind to me. He would sneak me special treats, and once he found out the day of my birth, he brought me a present each year. He was the one who made sure that the rest of the men assigned to me were respectful and kept their hands to themselves, especially once my body became that of a woman. Eventually, Bjørn wore down my defenses, and I started talking to him."

Finna shuddered at the memory. She was beautiful, tall and slender, with fair hair down to her waist and piercing blue eyes. I could only imagine the kind of attention she would have gotten from a bunch of savage Vikings without some protection! Her captivity sounded absolutely awful! She must have been so lonely and scared!

"From then on, any who dared touch me ended up having some sort of mishap once Bjørn found out. It was only much later that we realized this was his magic. Due to those incidents, most of the guards thought that I was putting a curse on them. They started to fear me, which made them even crueler.

"The jarl, however, did not want to lose his advantage. He needed the information I gave him. So, after a few occurrences came to his attention, he moved his youngest son into my rooms to protect me. Due to us sharing my quarters and spending so much time together, we became good friends.

"To my surprise, Bjørn was just as unhappy as I was! He hated his father's brutality and greed. From then on, we were careful no one overheard us talking or discovered that we liked each other. It was the only advantage we had. Things went well for a while, and I was almost happy. But then, the jarl became more interested in my body.

"This terrified me. I started locking my bedroom at night, but the door was not that strong," Finna continued, a far-away look in her eyes. "One day, he sent Bjørn away on a mission. That night, the vile man got drunk and forced his way in."

What had happened after that was obvious to us all. Finna had grown pale at the memory. To have someone force themselves on her like that must have been dreadful! My heart went out to her, especially since I had had a similar experience. She and I were survivors, that was for sure! After a moment of silence, she continued her story.

All of us were hanging on her every word but especially Signe. It seemed her mother was sharing more of her early life with us than she had ever before!

"When Bjørn got back, he saw the door. He knew instantly who had done this. He was so furious that he wanted to kill his own father. That I did not want on his conscience. Nor mine! Standing there shaking with anger, he kept telling me how sorry he was and that he had failed to protect me. But, this was not his but the jarl's fault. Several times, I had to remind him that he would give us away and make things even worse for me if he continued raging like that.

"Eventually, I had to wrap my arms around him and hold him before he finally calmed enough to pull himself together. We were deeply in love by then, and he was not about to let this happen again. This left us with one option - we had to get away. Bjørn was done with that place and its cruel people, had been for a long time. He was too gentle a soul to fit in with that bunch of savages.

"Having to participate in their raids turned his stomach, but he could not let on if he wanted to keep his place among my guards. Many times, he cried in my arms after one of those outings."

"I never knew," Signe said quietly, almost to herself. "He is so good at fighting!"

"He is also extremely good at building things!" her mother reminded her. "Bjørn had secretly acquired a small boat and had been preparing it for our departure. Since the rest of the villagers were very superstitious, he had found a spot that was supposed to be frequented by spirits. Most were too terrified to go near it. He had hidden the small vessel in a cave. Unless you knew where to look, you would never find it!

"Initially, he had intended for us to leave in the spring. But as it turned out, we could not wait that long. When his father forced himself on me again, it took Bjørn only a day to get the boat fully stocked for a sea voyage. I was safe enough until his father sent him on the next mission. We used that time to prepare. Once all was in readiness, we waited for the right moment. Getting out of there would not be easy.

"Then, my weather sense warned us of an incoming storm. For some reason, the jarl had been keeping to his quarters, so this was perfect. Once the blizzard hit, we dressed warmly, which also helped to conceal my identity. We walked right through the village. As planned, no one noticed until we wanted them to. We pretended to be fleeing to the north. Being on foot was not ideal in that weather, but the falling snow made it difficult to determine if we had continued on or not.

"There was a creek just out of sight from the settlement. Once we reached it, we made our way around the houses and to the boat. So that the dogs could not track us, we walked in the stream for part of the way. The sides were iced over, but the middle was still clear. The water was so cold! I was grateful to Bjørn for waterproofing our boots. To stay upright, we were holding onto each. Keeping our footing was really tricky. The rocks were so slippery, and we had to be careful not to fall in!

"I remember how chilly it was that evening. Our hike through the deepening snow seemed to take forever. I was so relieved when we reached the cave. Bjørn lit a lamp and showed me the boat. He was so proud of it and for a good reason! He had done an incredible job painting it in shades of blue and grey. The hull, and even the sails, looked just like the sea! With that coloring, it would blend in beautifully, even during the day.

"By the time we got the boat in the water, the winds had really picked up. The windchill would have sapped all the heat from our bodies had we not had the oiled skins. It was freezing! We both knew we could die out there, but going back was not an option. To be honest, I preferred death to continuing on in my present situation. Also, Bjørn's father would have killed him for helping me escape. So we pushed off and let the wind shove the boat into deeper water.

"Bjørn raised our smallest sail, and still, we moved rather quickly. But at least we did not have to row. The sound of the oars might have given us away if anyone was out there looking for us. However, with this strong a gale, most people were hunkered down in their houses. But if the alarm was raised, this would change. Getting down that long fjord was absolutely nerve-wracking. The snow was really coming down hard, and night had fallen shortly after we set out. I feared the whole time that someone would appear out of the dark and discover us sneaking away.

"Visibility was just about nonexistent, so we would have no warning that a boat was approaching. And, to avoid hitting floating objects, we were forced to light a small shuttered lantern. There was so much snow in the air! I hooked the light in at the bow so I could watch the water ahead of us. I needed to be able to see obstacles before we reached them. Still, several times, we came close to ramming something. I stayed in the front and fended things off with an oar.

"Thankfully, after a while, Bjørn seemed to develop a sixth sense about these obstacles and managed to steer us around most of them. Once we got out of the shelter of the land and hit open water, we were both greatly relieved. But now we were dealing with a different kind of threat. The wind was so much more powerful out there than in the sheltered fjord! The sea raged around our small boat. I was actually glad I could not make out the height of the waves in the little light we had.

"Bjørn tied a rope around us and attached us to the boat just in case we went overboard. A rescue would be impossible without this. We had no choice but to run with the wind and had to be careful not to put too much stress on the rudder. Had we lost steering and turned broadside, we would have sunk within minutes. All we could do was hang on and let the storm take us where it wanted until it blew itself out."

The picture she painted of the dark night, the violent upheaval around them, and the helplessness she and Bjørn must have felt faced with the raging elements were not lost on any of us. We were hanging on her every word, and even Bo listened intently.

"We were lucky. Coming from the southwest, the gale was taking us in the general direction we wanted to go. Bjørn would have preferred heading further west, but this would have to do. No stars were visible due to all the clouds. To our surprise, I seemed to know which way we needed to travel. We did our best to maintain that heading. Together, we fought against the elements all night long. We were determined to survive.

"The waves kept swamping the boat, and the snow was also a problem since it weighed us down. This caused us to ride lower in the water. Not a good thing with those breakers! My job was to keep bailing and shoveling no matter what. Several times, I feared we would sink or fail to righten ourselves when a sudden wind shift laid us almost flat on the water! Being out there in the dark of night in the midst of a blizzard was terrifying! But at least we were reasonably safe from pursuit!

"Still, I had never been so scared in my life as I was out there on the sea during that storm! Had we not been so desperate, we would not have risked it. Bjørn was amazing. He stayed calm and kept us on course! And, thanks to his foresight, we did not lose any of our provisions! He had secured them all expertly. I was so proud of him! And so grateful that he had gotten me away from his father!

"It was around noon a few days later when we spotted land. By then, the gale had let up enough for us to be able to sail in the direction of our choosing. We worked our way along the coast for a while, but Bjørn was worried. He knew his father only too well. Eventually, if we remained on the sea, the jarl's ships or one of his fellow raiders would find us. The substantial reward he most likely offered for my return would see to that.

"So, with a heavy heart, we scuttled the poor boat and set out on dogsled. We kept going west until we found a remote farm. It was the perfect hiding place for the rest of the winter. Pretending to be husband

and wife on the way to live with family, we waited for spring. Then, we headed north. My instincts drew us toward safety. Then we met Olaf, and he took us in. Bjørn and I owe him so much!

"That wonderful man knew who we were and who was hunting us, and still, he gave us shelter! He even secretly married us that summer. My oldest son was born shortly after that."

Signe had gone very pale at this point. All of us had done the math. Finna and Bjørn had not been lovers when they had fled the jarl. This could only mean one thing!

"Leiv is the jarl's son?" Signe asked in a whisper, as if she was afraid to voice this out loud and have her fears confirmed.

"Yes, love, he is," Finna responded. "But, that makes him no less your father's son."

"Does he know?" Signe enquired.

"Yes, sweetheart, he does. But he also knows that we love him just as much as the rest of you. We told him when I realized that our leaving was not far off and that he would be the one to take our people to our new home. Your father and I made sure that he understood that we saw him as a gift to both of us. And our family. He ensured our survival during that flight. Being highly pregnant gained us shelter on many a night!"

"Why did you not tell us before?" Signe wanted to know.

"The time was not right," Finna answered simply.

For her, the subject was closed.

I almost laughed. How often had I heard a similar response myself? Typical of most seers, or parents for that matter! But, in this case, it had made sense not to tell Leiv until it was time for him to leave the sanctuary. He was young and might have felt that the injury done to his mother needed to be addressed. From what I had read about them, I was sure that his brothers would have been happy to help him.

Had that young man not been responsible for the entire clan in his dad's absence, he might have done something foolish. Such as hunting down the offender! To kill one's own father brings terrible Karma! His folks had been wise to wait until the right moment!

"Olaf knew that the jarl wanted me and that the prize for my return was substantial. He could have turned us in and fed his people for a year on the coin. Instead, he made sure we stayed safe. We could not have left him behind to die alone," Finna continued.

"Signe has told you already what happened to her and about the night they set out for Caledonia. Once they were gone, we had our hands full. We were determined to leave as little to the raiders as possible. I will tell you the rest in a bit, but first, I need another cup of tea. And I need to move around to get the blood flowing again. Sitting here is not that comfortable. Maybe we could move inside?"

Chapter 32

Left Behind

Signe was still relatively quiet as we got to our feet and entered the house. Finna noticed and fell back to talk to her for a few minutes. The rest of us moved on, giving them the privacy they deserved. This was a harsh revelation for the young warrior maiden, and I was sure she felt like the rest of us. We would have loved to get a hold of that jarl and give him his just deserts! Too bad that we could not go back in time to do exactly that! But maybe Bjørn's gift of adversely affecting those who meant him or someone he loved harm had already done its job! That despicable man had been hiding in his rooms when Finna and his son had fled!

That he had survived was evident due to the ever-increasing reward for the return of his seeress, but in what shape had he been in? That we would never know, but I did believe in Karma and people getting what they deserve. Somehow, I got the feeling that fate had not been kind to that ruthless man. Maybe I could figure out who he was by looking for the unluckiest jarl in the region? That thought cheered me immensely.

Before long, we were once again seated together. Finna and Signe sat close together. Our friend was still upset by all she had heard, and her mother kept her arm around her to provide comfort. The young warrior maiden had been curious about her parent's origin and their journey to the sanctuary, but this might have been more than she had bargained for.

When everyone had settled down, Finna continued her story.

"After everyone left, Auga and I were so busy. We were already exhausted since we had cast a glamor over the village each night. This had allowed us to move all the furnishings out of the homes into the sair, the mead hall, in the center of our small village. From there, it was taken into the caverns beneath it. Maintaining the spell to conceal all that activity had taken a lot of energy. But we were not yet done."

"You took everything out of the homes?" Eldred asked curiously.

"Yes. We did not want to leave anything for those greedy raiders! After the first attack, Olaf insisted that each home had a bolt hole. They all connected to the shaft leading to the caves. Most of the smaller items had been removed that way and were now stored in the caverns."

"How clever! That also prevented additional drain on your magic, did it not?" Hilda exclaimed.

"It did," Finna acknowledged. "We only had to hide the men moving the furniture, which was easier because it was dark."

"How did you keep those watching you from suspecting that something was going on?" Revna inquired.

"We made everything seem as normal as possible," Finna explained. "We kept up our usual routine but did just a little less each day. Thus, by the time the rest left, just a few of us could keep up the pretense that nothing had changed. And we used glamours to make it appear that we were more than one person."

"You were very well organized from the sound of it," I praised her.

"We had been preparing for such an eventuality for years and had a plan. Due to Olaf's illness, we had to modify it slightly. But that worked in favor of those getting away." Finna explained. "Those watching us had no idea most of us were gone. Therefore, they did not pursue the boats."

"We made sure that little was left for those greedy raiders! All they were going to get were empty houses with nothing of value!" Signe added angrily.

"Bjorn and our sons took advantage of the thick fog we had called in. They checked each house and removed the few items left behind, mostly bedding. Then, along with the five strapping men my husband had kept with us, they hauled what remained of the furnishings in the sair down the tunnel leading to the cave system. Needless to say, it was a busy night for them!

"One of these caverns has a direct connection to the sea. The entrance is well hidden by our magic. Thankfully, it is large enough to hold several longships. However, coming and going is only possible at low tide. The rest of the time, there is not enough clearance for the masts. Another passage allows us to row in when it is not flooded. Therefore, as soon as it is safe, we can slip in unseen and retrieve all these things at our leisure."

"No wonder our clan did so well with you as ancestors!" Hilda interrupted. Finna smiled at her praise and then continued.

"It was hard to abandon the sanctuary that had been Bjørn's and my home for over 22 years. Feeling that Olaf would be safer in the damp caves than up above, we took him to the sair and then down below. We kept up the pretense that all was as it had been that day and the next, but then we had to give it up. Auga and I were utterly exhausted."

"Not surprising! You did a healing on me, kept up the glamour, called up the fog, and tended to Olaf!" Signe cut in.

"That we did," Finna smiled.

"I am glad you made sure that the raiders found little of value! Good for you!" Eldred added.

"One of the men suggested burning the place to the ground, but the rest of us vetoed his suggestion. Those homes were built with love! I hope that others like us will move in someday!" Signe exclaimed.

"I am sure they will, my daughter," Finna said soothingly before continuing her tale. "Olaf, who Bjørn loved like a father, died just a day later. His deepest regret was that he would never see the people he had so lovingly and wisely led to their new home. Creating the sanctuary had been his idea. He wanted a safe place for others like himself and his men, somewhere they could live in peace and have children of their own."

"He always considered us his family! Olaf would have made a wonderful father!" Signe told us with tears in her eyes.

"Yes, he would have, but that was taken from him due to the cruelty of his once master," Finna explained.

"You mean they …," Hilda said with a shudder.

Finna just nodded.

"They treated him like an animal!" Signe stated with indignation.

Tears flooded the girl's eyes. She had obviously loved Olaf.

"First, they bred him to a number of women hoping his offspring would inherit his gift. When they did not, they …." Unable to voice such a horror, her voice broke off.

Eldred, Revna, Hilda, and I exchanged horrified glances. We were all thankful that we did not live during those times! Some of those people were just too barbaric for our taste!

"Olaf was a good man who loved our small band of misfits," Finna went on. "For years, he dreamt of the day when we would finally settle someplace where we could truly thrive. All of us were tired of having to worry about our acquisitive neighbors. His vision was to establish safe havens for all those born with magic, at home as well as in Caledonia.

"But, thanks to the greed of that tribe, our refuge is lost to us for the moment. But we still have the caves. The entrances are well concealed and also protected by glamors and magic. Those raiders will never find them! As long as we have them, we can collect the rest of our belongings and maintain at least a little of a foothold in our homeland," Finna stated wistfully.

Her face was sad. She loved the village and her homeland. Having to leave had been hard on her.

"You will have a wonderful life in Caledonia," I reassured her.

Finna gave me a grateful look, blinked back the tears flooding her eyes, and continued.

"With Olaf's death, the fulfillment of his vision fell to Bjørn. We slipped out of hiding to give him a proper funeral at sea. The following night, a horrific storm hit the region. This was our sign that it was time to get ready to leave. My visions had seen our homes invaded the morning after just such a tempest. We had no intention of being there when the raiders arrived." Finna paused, her voice chocked with emotions from the memory of that frightening time.

"The gale was terrible, and I was glad we did not have to go back outside for anything. Lightning split the sky, and thunder shook the earth. Before retreating, we had to block the entrance from the sair to the caves. All the bolt holes from the houses and the passage connecting them had already been made impassible. The same needed to be done with the main one to the caverns. Bjørn sent Auga and me ahead while he and the others took one last look around the mead hall and prepared to abandon it."

"I am curious how you kept the raiders from finding the tunnels," I stated.

It seemed that I was not the only one. Eldred and Hilda were also interested in this elaborate escape system these innovative folks had devised.

"Please, Finna, Eldred, and I would like to know more about your safety measures. From what we heard from Cara about the witch hunts, it would not hurt to have a way to escape," Hilda begged her.

"People like us are still being hunted in your time?" Finna asked, turning pale.

"Yes, but thanks to your warnings about keeping our magic hidden and Cedric's circumspection, Havn is spared," I assured her.

"And in your time, Cara, how are we treated?" Finna wanted to know.

"People are more tolerant, and we have religious freedom. We owe a lot to you, Finna. You and your family laid the groundwork for our people to not only survive but thrive. Thank you for that," I explained.

"I can still hardly believe that our family and those who settled with us became a powerful clan that lasted for so many centuries!" Signe said with awe.

"It is heartening, and I am glad to hear that things will get better," Finna declared. "That gives me hope. Hilda, I will be happy to share with you what we did. Maybe it will help you keep your people safe. To start with, Olaf had chosen the site for our new settlement with just such an emergency as we were facing in mind. Fearing a raid, he had searched for years for just the right spot for us to relocate to.

"We stayed in the main caves while constructing our homes in a small valley nearby. One of the trunks of the caverns led right underneath where we put the sair. It had multiple openings along the way and was partially filled with earth that had fallen in. We cleared it and used timbers to create trapdoors that could be triggered from below, then piled a lot of dirt over them, which also hid them. Each was supported by two stout posts from underneath.

"First, we built the sair, then the houses to the left and right of it. They were placed relatively close together, forming a circle. To give us a way to escape from our homes, we dug a main trench a few feet behind them. It was connected to a secret room adjacent to the sair's cellar. We piled the dirt up next to it to look like a defensive wall around the village and covered it with vegetation to keep the center of the soil dry.

"Once the tunnels were shored up with planks, we laid more timber over the top and covered those with earth and sod. Each home had a bolt-hole connecting to the main passage. The entire system was designed to be collapsible. Many small, sealed-off shutes led to the inside of the mound. They would allow the loose dirt to trickle into the passageway and fill it in when opened."

"It sounds like you had basements. Could you not have connected those?" Eldred inquired.

"We were afraid that this would destabilize the ground beneath the homes since, in some spots, it was mostly sand and gravel," Finna replied. "And, if one house was invaded, it would hinder those on its far side from getting away.

"That makes sense," Eldred said thoughtfully.

"So what happened next?" Revna asked.

"My husband and his men closed and locked the large hatch behind them. It was now one with the floor, invisible unless you knew just where to look. Then, they went down the steps and pushed the wooden door shut. The panel reached from floor to ceiling and completely sealed off the stairway leading down to the tunnel. Since the stairs would be filled in with earth, they hammered additional supports into place to keep the partition from budging under the weight.

"Once everything was in readiness, my husband pulled the lever. This released the sand and gravel we had stored in the walls of the building into the space, thus blocking off that entrance to the passage. Then, the men made their way down the tunnel toward the caves. Bjørn remained at the rear. Once the others were clear, he triggered the first of the trapdoors situated all along the passage. This allowed dirt to flow in and fill up the space.

"Unfortunately, the deluge from the storm raging above helped a little too much! Once the shafts were ajar, the heavy rain rapidly washed in a slurry of sand and gravel, making the water level rise much too quickly! Fearing for his life, my husband ran from one lever to the next. The others reached the cavern ahead of him, and I was starting to worry when he finally appeared, out of breath but unharmed."

"Naturally, father would do the most dangerous job himself!" Signe scoffed.

"He always does," Finna confirmed with a smile. "One of the reasons we all love and respect him so much! As planned, three of the men stayed behind to help others born with magic. They are living in the caves, and so will any refugees they find. To protect them, we could not risk the raiders finding the tunnels!"

"Thank you, Finna! What a clever system, and how noble of those men to want to help more people like us!" stated Hilda. "But are the caverns not close to the settlement?"

"Yes, they are, but they should be safe enough with the tunnel out of commission. The hideaway can only be entered from the sea. The emergency exit is near impossible to reach from the outside but will allow them to escape if needed. Anyone taken there will be blindfolded. That way, they cannot give the location away."

"Ah! Now I see!" Hilda smiled. "Thank you!"

She exchanged a telling glance with Eldred. These two learned fast. They were considering how to make their own escape system just in case the zealots came calling. The tunnel from the sair that they ended up constructing is still in good repair, and we keep it that way. You never know!

To the girls' frustration, the houses of Havn had been built too far apart to connect them. However, each of the homes was refitted with a bolthole.

Finna grinned at Hilda and Eldred. She knew exactly what was on their minds and was glad that she had been able to provide them with such valuable information. After getting more tea, she continued with her narrative.

"The storm that night was terrible. Even the enormous cavern that hid our boats was churning, tossing them all about. We were worried about the smaller ones bumping into the longships and getting damaged, so we pulled them out of the water and moved them far back on the rock ledge."

"Was the way to the sea not blocked off?" Revna inquired.

"The entrance was concealed by magic that would let only our ships in but did not keep the waves out. Even when the passage was partially flooded, we got some swell. During ebb, spray filled the air, and the two remaining longships pitched about so wildly that we decided to wait out the storm in one of the dry caves further up.

"The gale lasted for two more days. That first morning when the sun dawned bright and clear, Bjørn and I joined the watch at the emergency exit. As I had foreseen, the invaders came sneaking in with the first light. They ripped open the doors and filed into the houses only to find them empty. Seeing their disappointment was entertaining, but it was no consolation for losing our homes. My heart ached as I saw those brutes stomp through our village!"

I could only imagine how she must have felt! How terrible to watch helplessly as the raiders took over their settlement! Finna and I locked eyes for a moment. She appreciated my understanding of how difficult it had been to leave the place she had grown to love. She had born her children there and had led a good life. Now, this brave woman was heading into the unknown! That, in itself, was always a bit scary!

"The next night, hidden by a convenient downpour, we sneaked out of the cave and set sail for Caledonia. It was a foggy morning, and we were far away from land when I suddenly found myself here!" Finna finished her tale.

She had been out on the sea! That was the explanation for nothing but water alongside the path in her nexus! And the proof that each cell was tailored after the surroundings of its occupant. This hive was really quite fascinating! It had been designed to confuse its prisoners and make them despair. But, thanks to Bo, the conditions in the construct were much improved for all of us!

"Will you take me home now, please?" Finna addressed Eldred, Hilda, and me. "And Signe as well?"

"Yes, we will," I assured her. "But let me share something with you first. I am not sure I should, but it might help you. Within a few years, you, and those with you, will become known as the Magnuson Clan. Once you reach Caledonia, Bjørn might consider filing a complaint against the jarl who invaded your sanctuary. If I remember correctly, you will win. You will not only get your lands back but will also be granted those of the attackers."

"How is that possible?" Finna gasped.

"People love your nets and depend on them for their livelihood. When you left, they went hungry. All the jarls who use them are on your side!"

"That is incredible," Signe breathed.

She was just as stunned as her mother.

"It gets better! Due to the high demand for those nets, from then on, no one will dare threaten you again. The miscreant would face the wrath of all your customers! And any magic-born who reach the sanctuary will be safe and off-limits, no matter who has a claim on them! As a thank you, you could get them to help with the weaving for a few hours each week! A win-win for all!"

"All that because of magic nets? Could we produce them and do the same?" Eldred asked me.

"Not with the witch hunts going on unless you can find a way to sell them that is not associated with your village!" I told her.

"Hmmm," Eldred said thoughtfully.

You could just see the gears spinning! I was sure that she would find a way! Finna's story had given her plenty of ideas.

"Papa says that it is important for us to remain neutral. That is why we are building our homes apart from the Vikings and the local people. We intend to call it Havn," Signe informed us.

"We always loved that name!" Hilda spouted. "It means haven in your language, right Signe?"

"It sure does," our friend confirmed.

"Is there anything else you can tell us?" Finna enquired.

"Yes. Until things are settled in Norway, you will have some close calls with a group of raiders. They want those nets! Be prepared to defend yourselves! If you can gain the local clan's protection, attacking you will become very hazardous to their health! Those Caledonians are fierce! Eventually, that bunch will decide that it is easier to pay for the goods, a wise choice on their part!" I told her.

"Even the fierce Vikings feared the inhabitants of western Scotland and the Hebrides," Revna added rather proudly.

"They sure did," agreed Eldred, grinning rather wolfishly.

That young woman could be scary! I hoped I would never have to cross her and pitied those foolish enough to do so. Eldred saw herself as a Highlander through and through. Hilda and I looked at each other. We knew just how she felt. We were all proud to be part of this land that had been so good to our clan.

By the time the girls were born, our roots in Scotland ran deep. Only the continued contact with the settlement in Norway reminded us of our Viking heritage.

After a few more little tips, it was time to take our friends home. Revna insisted on coming along. Once we entered the cell that had been Finna's prison, we looked around in surprise. Light reflected off the water on each side of the path, and it did not smell quite as bad. It was almost pretty, and the shore no longer looked as disgusting! A bit further down, a small bay seemed perfect for wading. The sea in that area was clean and sparkled rather invitingly! What a change!

Signe said a tearful goodbye to her mother. Revna, usually so composed and calm, hugged Finna for a long time. We would all miss her very much. Even to me, she had been like a mother figure, and I was older than the other girls. Finally, postponing the inevitable started to feel awkward, so Eldred, Hilda, and I took her into the smoke.

Once we had dialed in the right destination, the boat appeared on the far side of the haze. What a fascinating vessel! I instantly took out my cellphone to snap a few pictures. Finna was highly amused. After embracing us, she gracefully stepped into the craft. Once securely seated, she turned and waved to us one last time. As we retreated, we kept an eye on her until the ship faded from our sight.

Without any discussion, we had chosen to move backward through the veil. It had felt wrong to turn away from Finna, especially since we missed her already. Our next task would be even more heartbreaking. We had to take Signe home! A goodbye forever was such a painful thing! If only we could somehow find a way to meet up again and stay in touch! But living hundreds of years apart truly made this difficult!

When we reached Signe and Revna, they were just as dispirited as the rest of us. Hilda, always ready to cheer everyone up, came up with the idea to play in the water of that inviting little bay. Eldred checked with Bo to see if this was even possible. To our delight, he could make it so. Having Finna's daughter with us allowed him to keep the nexus stable for a while longer.

Revna decided that she would stay on the beach. She found a pleasant spot in the sand and made herself comfortable. While she watched, the sisters, Signe, and I waded into the pleasantly warm water. At first, our play was somewhat reticent, but then Hilda 'accidentally' doused her sister with a huge splash. After that, the war was on. We were dripping wet by the time we were done, but our hearts were much lighter.

Arm in arm, we rejoined Revna. She walked behind us as we made our way to the in-between and our 'home.' Signe had decided she wanted to dry off before going to her nexus. We had used a spell to banish most of the wetness, but our garments still felt damp from their dunking in seawater. The only other clothes we had were our nighties, so we slipped into those once we arrived at the house.

When we were done changing, none of us felt like heading out again. Revna had mercy on us and agreed that our friend could stay one more night. Somehow, it turned into a slumber party of sorts. Eldred, Hilda, and Signe joined me in my bed! As can be expected, it took us a long time to get to sleep. There was so much left to talk about!

Bo, always thoughtful, managed to dry our things while we slumbered. We thanked him profusely for his help and kindness, especially once we spotted the steaming cups on the table. We were so despondent that morning that none of us felt like having tea, but we did not want to hurt his feelings.

A few minutes later, a sad procession set out toward Signe's nexus. For our taste, we reached it all too soon. This time, the moor on each side of the path was not as dreary as before, and the trail was dryer and well-defined. This allowed us to take in these wild surroundings in all their glory. They had their own beauty, and I gazed around in wonder. This must be what the swampy area east of the village had looked like!

Revna, who had come along to make sure that we went through with the task, even spotted some interesting plants. I watched as she carefully dug up a few sprouts and slid them into her pockets. The rest of us were only too happy to wait for her. It pushed off the inevitable a little bit longer! Finally, we glumly made our way into the smoke.

Once we dialed in where our friend had been snatched from, we said our goodbyes to our warrior maiden. It felt like we were losing a sister. She was definitely taking a part of our hearts with her. After Signe had recovered a little from her severe injury, she had taught us more about combat. As a woman, it was smart to know certain tricks to disable or disarm a much larger opponent quickly and efficiently!

As a result, Eldred, Hilda, and I were now even more capable of defending ourselves! My instinct told me this would come in handy somewhere down the line. However, I was not looking forward to hurting another human being. Practicing was one thing, but when it came to inflicting harm? That went so against my nature! Nonetheless, I would use whatever was at my disposal if a life was threatened! As would Hilda and Eldred!

Signe pulled the girls and me into a last group hug. We held each other tight for a long time until she suddenly stepped back and leaped into her world. She sprinted down the path so quickly that we lost sight of her within seconds. All we could do was stare with tears in our eyes. The knowledge that we would never see her again was heartbreaking.

Hand in hand, Eldred, Hilda, and I made our way back into Signe's nexus. We had to walk down the trail a bit before we found Revna, who was quite intrigued by some of the vegetation. Try as we might, we could not pry her away from all the fascinating herbs and flowers now sprouting here. We finally had to ask Bo if he could transplant a patch of the moor to Revna's cell. As usual, the helpful being was only too happy to oblige us. He even let her pick the spot she wanted!

Only once it vanished before her eyes and left a void in its place was the lady ready to head for the in-between! Bo guided us toward home since he sensed that we were too sad to deal with anyone else this day. Returning Finna and Signe to their time had been emotionally draining, especially since the girls and I knew that our own goodbyes would come one day soon.

The only one thoroughly distracted from all this unhappiness by Bo's gift was Revna. She wanted to get to her place just as quickly as possible! Impatiently, she hurried us along.

Chapter 33

Leiv's Wife

Bo continued to amaze us. He constantly gained more control over the construct and worked on making it more pleasant. We now had a time each day when it got darker outside, but he did provide a spotlight for Revna that evening. As soon as she saw the transplanted patch, she headed for this new addition. She forgot that anything else existed, including us. We watched for a few minutes as the healer examined each plant and its surroundings. Before long, she was knee-deep in mud.

Revna and Finna had become close friends, and we knew the healer bitterly missed the Viking lady. However, every person has their own way of dealing with sadness. Diving into work was Revna's. Her mind was busy imagining all the potions she could brew from this treasure trove. The lady was still examining the vegetation of her piece of the moor many hours later and did not even come in for tea nor to sleep!

That night, it was now easier to call it that since it was quite dark outside; Eldred, Hilda, and I cuddled up sadly in my large bed. All too soon, we would also be parted. We did not look forward to that. The girls and I had grown so close and genuinely loved each other. These two were the sisters that I had never had. Bo tried his best to cheer us up, and soft music started wafting through the room. How had he come up with that?

It was truly incredible what he could glean from our minds! Had he not been our friend, we would have resented the invasion. As it was, he had started asking before he rooted around in our memories. I, for one, appreciated that bit of thoughtfulness, and I was grateful for the sweet tunes that filled the room around us. They helped calm us and eased the pain of parting from Signe a smidgen.

"We have to find a way to stay in contact," Eldred mumbled, half asleep.

"Yes, we do," agreed Hilda.

For a moment, I hugged them even closer. We cuddled further under the covers, and eventually, the pleasant warmth from our bodies made us drowsy enough to drop off into a restful slumber.

When the soft light of an imitation dawn started filtering into the room, we knew it was time to get to work. We had people to take home and things to do. The hive still had a fair number of prisoners just waiting for us to free them. Who knew how long some of them had been here? Not that we felt like it that day, but none of us were so selfish that we would indulge ourselves by staying in bed while others might be suffering.

For some reason, Bo seemed to be very excited about something or someone. That made the girls and me curious and eager to discover what it was! Usually, his surprises were pleasant, and we trusted that this one would be as well. Eldred and Hilda headed off to their rooms to get dressed, and soon after, we met downstairs.

After our morning tea, we hugged Revna goodbye. Her eyes were all red. It could have been from a lack of sleep, but we suspected she had been crying. Before setting out for the in-between, Eldred asked her if she would teach us about some of the plants she had collected. As expected, that cheered the healer up significantly. She promised to have our lesson ready by the time we returned.

Once we passed through the membrane, we let Bo takes us where he felt was best. He definitely had a destination in mind! Once again, he was hurrying us along! This did not seem to be an emergency, so that was unlike him! The spirit of the construct was usually so patient with us!

Eldred, Hilda, and I exchanged a puzzled glance. We might feel rather blue, but we were getting more curious by the minute. Finally, we reached our destination, and the membrane of the cell gave way to allow us entrance.

The first thing we heard when we entered the nexus was a lively tune. This person had a beautiful voice, and the accent reminded us vividly of Signe. All three of us sped up. Who was this? One of our friend's sisters? Or maybe someone from around that same time? Once we rounded the bend in the path, we spotted the singer. She had to be in her late thirties or early forties and was sitting quite comfortably on a large log. Strangely, she seemed perfectly at ease with the situation.

The lady, and that was what she most certainly looked like, was so into her performance that it took her a moment to spot us.

"Hello!" she greeted us with a smile.

Then she looked closer, and her face lit up with pure delight.

"You are Cara," she stated, pointing. "And you are Eldred, and you Hilda?"

"Yes," we answered, rather surprised.

"Seriously?"

The three of us almost started laughing. My use of that word seemed to have spread to times long ago!

"Yes," Eldred said firmly.

"When she first told me, I thought she made it all up. But then, I ended up here! From her description, I would have recognized you anywhere!"

Judging from her clothes and demeanor, there was only one possible conclusion! We all arrived at it at about the same time.

"You know Signe!" Hilda shouted with joy.

"Yes! She is my sister-in-law! I married her brother Leiv," the woman explained.

"How is she?" Eldred and I asked almost simultaneously.

"She married that laird she had her heart set on, Christopher Mackay. He is a little older than she thought, but they are very happy together! They have seven children!" the lady informed us. "Oh, and I am Uma, Uma Magnuson!"

"Welcome, Uma, to the time trap!" Hilda laughed.

"I figured as much when my surroundings changed so suddenly! I knew there was witchcraft involved! Signe told me that you were taking people home. I have been here for a while but figured you would find me sooner or later!"

"We sure did!" Eldred confirmed with a grin.

"Do you mind staying with us for the night? We have so much we want to know about Signe!" I asked Uma.

"I would be happy to! I would love to see the place that all of you call home! I have heard so much about it! Shall we?" she said, getting up off her log.

Bo was delighted with his surprise! The girls and I made sure to praise and thank him. The more we did that, the more cooperative he became. He just loved flattery and could not get enough of it. And he more than deserved it! Born from such a malicious enchantment, he could have turned out downright evil! But instead, he had chosen to be and do good. That, in itself, said much for him and was a miracle of sorts!

Eldred, Hilda, and I felt blessed to be able to call him a friend and for the thoughtful gift he had made us. We chatted rather excitedly with Uma the whole way back to our nexus. Revna actually met us on the path. She had figured that company was coming from how things were sprucing themselves up around her place!

Uma greeted her like an old friend, and the two hit it off instantly. They started talking about potions, but then our guest remembered that she had wanted to see the house. Five cups of steaming tea were waiting for us in the living room since the kitchen table was covered in herbs and plants. But first, our new friend insisted on a tour.

She instantly recognized the room that was to be hers! Uma was beyond delighted by its decor. Something this frilly and feminine had always been her dream but was hard to come by in a village still putting down roots!

Once we were all comfortably seated, Uma started to fill us in on the events of the years since we had last seen our warrior maiden. Signe had been quite busy, it seemed! Not only had she married that laird and born him all those children, but she had also brokered a deal of protection for her clan with the fierce Highlanders! No one even thought about raiding Havn these days!

Using the money from the family business, Signe's father had legally acquired a few more stretches of land from his son-in-law. He eventually signed a covenant accepting the official hospitality of the Mackay Clan. That agreement included a clause for mutual defense and assistance in fighting off any invaders to the territory.

"What about your life?" Hilda asked when we had heard a whole lot about Signe.

"Leiv is a good husband, but he has his moments," Uma laughed.

"Like all men!" added Revna wisely.

"Yes!" Uma agreed, grinning from ear to ear. "As the oldest son, Leiv took over the clan after his father. Even more so than Bjørn, he has convinced the villagers to keep their magic use and abilities a secret. To the folk nearby, we seem just like them, maybe a little eccentric, but otherwise no different!"

"We still do that today," I informed her. "People are more tolerant, but all it takes is one religious fanatic getting it in his head that we are evil to cause trouble!"

"Exactly!" Uma agreed. "Leiv skillfully spread the suggestion around that we bring our neighbors good luck and that they benefit from our presence. Even if something out of the ordinary happens, it is easily forgiven and quickly forgotten."

"How clever!" Eldred added admiringly.

I was sure that she was taking mental notes. No wonder Cedric turned out to be such a good chieftain! He had her and Hilda to keep him straight and give him ideas!

"And how did you get them to believe this?" Hilda asked, as always perfectly in tune with her sister.

"We make sure that no one remembers where the warnings or rumors come from, start them at several spots in the region, and add just enough compulsion that they spread quickly and accurately!" Uma explained.

Eldered and Hilda exchanged a glance.

"Brilliant!" Hilda exclaimed.

"Would you teach us how to do this, please?" Eldred asked.

The rest of us added our pleas to hers. Such a skill could really come in handy and benefit us all!

"You want me to teach you?" Uma said with wonder in her voice.

The young woman had never seen this as anything special and just now realized what a gift this was! We all nodded enthusiastically.

"I would be honored!" she stated, beaming.

"Could you please explain how you started all this a little bit more?" Revna said, smiling encouragingly. "And finish your story?"

"We built a network by making friends with trustworthy and well-respected people in the community. We use them to get the word out." Uma explained.

Seeing that we needed more detail, Uma decided to get more specific.

"Let me give you an example. Let us say that the seers have a vision of a devastating storm heading our way. Several of us will head out and tell our friends that we heard from a local sorcerer that a terrible gale was on the way. Then, as soon as we leave, the compulsion has him or her call the servants to send them out to spread the word that we need to prepare for bad weather. Some are even sent to us to warn us!"

"And no one has a clue it was you who started it all in the first place!" Hilda said, delighted at such a clever way to keep the clan safe.

"What about the sorcerers?" Eldred wanted to know. "Do they not object to being the source of the warnings?"

"No, not usually. Most of these magic men are very self-important and vain. They love all the praise for saving everyone, so one usually steps up and takes credit!" Uma told us with a mischievous grin.

"I bet you have saved many a life over the years!" I said in awe of such a simple but efficient way to spread a warning.

"I get that part, but I do not understand how that makes people believe you bring them luck," Hilda piped in.

To be honest, neither did I!

"Once we have been officially informed, we really spread the word. Folks appreciate that. We also hire local people for our fields since most of us work on the nets. This has brought prosperity to the region. But it is really much simpler than that. All you have to do is start a rumor that says so, and the more people believe it, the more traction it gains!

"Also, we have several close allies who reinforce how much things have changed for the better since we arrived. Our secret warnings give people ample time to prepare. So the region has less property damage and fewer deaths, once again affirming the suggestion!" Uma told us with a smirk.

Bjørn had done an excellent job picking and ensuring a safe place for his people! And it sounded like Leiv was just as skilled as his father! No wonder the clan had done so well under their guidance!

"My husband put everyone through some additional training when he took over. He made sure that our people perfected the skill of hiding our abilities so that we fit in better with the locals." Uma went on. "Only those who pass the training can volunteer to join the peddlers. They now travel the countryside visiting farms and smaller hamlets."

"Marvelous!" Eldred exclaimed. "Why confine the clan's business to only trading by sea, at the markets, and with the local lairds?"

"Exactly!" Uma confirmed. "Leiv wants to sell to more folk inland, and that is the way to do it. He also uses the peddlers to collect information and, if need be, spread a tale. And he has them keep their ears open for what our neighbors need, want, and dream of."

"Bjørn did that too, did he not?" I asked Uma.

"Yes, back in Norway. Leiv worked with his father. When he took over, he knew just what to do, and he had a well-thought-out plan! He got the business started here in the Highlands. For the first couple of years, the peddlers and their wagons returned to the village. But after we had a few customers showing up looking for goods, Leiv decided to buy some more land and build a trading post there. Figuring that his men needed homes, several log houses followed. Soon it was a good-sized settlement that we named Bytte Hjem, trade home."

"I can see how keeping the traders separate from you would work better when you needed to spread information," Eldred interjected thoughtfully. "And having a place for people to congregate would help with the information collection, especially if you were serving drinks!"

The girl's sharp mind had immediately grasped the intricacies of Leiv's spy network. I was almost certain she would talk Cedric into using the family business for a similar scheme. With the witch hunts burning through Scotland, knowledge about what was happening and what people thought and felt was vital!

"You and Leiv would get along famously!" Uma said with a smile. "The traders range all over the region, buying and selling things. They pick up goods from far-off places. We mix our products, except the nets, in with those. That way, no one is any wiser where they come from! This allows us to use our magic to the benefit of our neighbors.

"The store at Bytte Hjem flourishes. It appears to be independent and does business with everyone, including the Mackays and the raiders. It and the traveling merchants buy and sell the goods we bring in by ship from the many places we trade with. Due to all the offerings, more help was needed within just a few months! We have no shortage of volunteers from the clan and have added more homes to accommodate everyone who wants to work there."

"I remember reading in the clan's journals that you know just what people want," I prompted Uma when she paused. "Do you use magic for that?"

"Yes, to make folks feel comfortable around the guys so that they will confide in them. Sometimes they do not even know they need an item until the peddlers show up! We usually concentrate on those things that benefit the greatest amount of people and that everyone will want, something that makes their life better. But also things that are fun and fashionable!" Uma laughed.

"Where do you get those things? We do a fair bit of trading, but sometimes popular items are hard to find," Eldred stated.

"Each peddler has a budget to acquire items. They are then delivered to the trading post. Some goods go on the shelves while the rest are distributed to the other wagons. Also, a good amount comes in by ship, and we hide the things we copy or design among the wares. This way, we avoid drawing attention to Havn."

"That makes good sense," Eldred said thoughtfully.

"Exactly," Uma agreed. "Leiv constantly reminds our people to remain cautious, even in Havn when we are among ourselves. My husband is a good leader and does his best to keep us safe. The Highlanders are more accepting, but why let our guard down? Many of us still remember fleeing in the middle of the night. Trust comes hard to us."

"You must be making a fair bit of gold and are probably richer than your neighbors. How do you deal with that?" Revna wanted to know.

"We are careful not to appear better off than those around us. We still remember what happened the last time our neighbors got resentful. That did not work out well for us! It is in some humans' nature to envy the success of others. If we look too wealthy, we might get raided by some laird's fierce warriors or by the Vikings who still live nearby."

"And everyone cooperates?" Hilda wanted to know.

"Yes, we have agreed to not display our wealth openly," Uma replied. "Only if you look closely will you see that some of our clothes are of finer quality and our furnishings more exquisite. We make sure that outwardly our village resembles the others in the region. We improve our living conditions only slowly and in step with our neighbors."

"Leiv sounds like a great leader, extremely cautious, and he is a brilliant tactician," I praised.

"He is, is he not?" Uma said, smiling with pride. "His peddlers keep their ears open and warn us of any rumors regarding Havn circulating in the region. That way, we can address issues before trouble brews. Leiv wants better conditions for us, but the only safe way to do this is to improve the lives of all those around us before or right along with our own!"

"You can be very proud of him," I told her. "His wisdom is still being passed on in the clan's stories that all of us children grow up with. From very little on, I was told how important it is to hide my abilities. 'No one must ever know' remains the motto!"

"Eldred, appearing just like our non-magical neighbors is essential, especially in your time. Witch trials will take place in many parts of Scotland. Cedric, as ruler, will have to make sure that the Magnuson settlement at Gairloch appears so normal and above suspicion that no one will ever look twice!" I warned her.

I could see Eldred swallow when she grasped the importance of this message.

"Thank you for your warning. Hilda and I will do what we can. We have learned much here today!" Eldred assured me.

"In your history, did Cedric succeed in keeping us safe?" Hilda wanted to know. I could tell that she was scared.

"Yes, love, he did," I assured her. "He has the two of you to advise him! How could he not?"

"Thank you, but we will be extra careful anyhow!" Hilda promised.

"It is so unfair that having powers makes us a target!" Revna threw in.

We all agreed. Unfortunately, many in the world around us were afraid of that which they did not understand! Sad, really, that prejudice and rash judgments can do so much damage!

"That is why Bjørn continued Olaf's practice of searching for individuals born with powers," Uma told us. "The peddlers make great scouts in Caledonia and back home. Leiv has a few working there as well. They approach those in less-than-ideal situations, and they offer them sanctuary. Those free to do so join them gladly, but for many others, we can do nothing except inform the knights."

Hilda and I looked at each other and shuddered. Finna's story was still fresh in our minds, and we had heard several gruesome tales from Signe. The treatment some of these poor souls received was anything but kind! No wonder some of them had used their powers to get even with their oppressors! Unfortunately, that had made life harder for all others with magic because they were now feared even more!

We were truly blessed to have escaped such a fate, even if we were stuck in this enchantment!

Chapter 34

Uma's News

Revna, Eldred, Hilda, Uma, and I spent a couple more hours talking. Since I had been fascinated by the history of our clan, I had spent a lot of time in the archives. My friends now used the opportunity to ask me questions. I answered them carefully since we could not afford to alter the past. But how could I withhold something that might save one of their lives? Using my ability to check timelines, I was relieved to discover no major changes had occurred so far.

That alone seriously puzzled me. As it did the others when I mentioned it. Being from such different eras, just our meeting should have altered our fates, at least some! Then, something occurred to me. What if all this was already part of our lives? It was the only thing that made sense! After some discussion, the others agreed. From then on, no longer fearing the consequences, our sharing reached a whole new level!

Since its official creation, the Magnuson Clan has prospered in Scotland. That it has faced relatively little adversity was an enigma. Some of this can be explained by us having the advantage of foresight but not all. Knowing what might happen unless action is taken or who to beware of is an incredible gift. The greatest danger to any of the clairvoyants was being captured. Their abilities were priceless, and in Norway, many a jarl dreamt of having their own seer, seeress, or magician at their disposal.

During Uma's time, folk with arcane abilities were feared by many but also in high demand by others. Some of those who did not offer their services willingly were taken and forced to do their new master's bidding. They were entirely at the mercy of their captor, just as Finna had been. It was really a paradox. On the one hand, they were highly prized, and on the other, they were treated like slaves.

"Please, tell us how things are for your people now that you have found your haven!" Hilda begged.

"Things are better in Caledonia, but even here, some magic users who have been captured are treated as commodities. They are bought, sold, and traded without regard for their feelings. Some have been property since childhood and have developed an attachment to their owners despite being maltreated. Olaf's knights have expanded their range to include the Highland but only rescue those who want help."

"How do they keep the owners from finding them again?" Eldred wanted to know.

"They usually buy the person, but they are extra careful in those rare cases when they have to free one. Those individuals are taken far away, usually across the sea."

"Do any of them live with you in Havn?" Hilda inquired.

"No, not usually. Leiv does not want to take the risk," Uma explained.

"Do you teach them about their magic?" Revna questioned.

"Only after there is no doubt about their loyalty and affiliation," Uma answered.

"Now that makes perfect sense," Revna commented with a grin. "One has to beware of those who speak falsely!"

"Exactly!" Uma agreed. "Cara, do you know anything about the trading post you could share with us?"

"Sure," I said with a smile. "As the number of those who freely join the peddlers grow, more houses are built around the store. Eventually, it becomes a second village, a refuge where people can hide in plain sight. Glamours are terrific for that! Also, the settlement has no apparent ties to the clan except for selling some of their nets and other items. It becomes a sanctuary for magic users. Any newcomers are given the option to train and join the traveling wagons, or they can help with the running of the business."

"What about Havn?" Uma asked urgently.

"Most thought it a sleepy backwater with little to offer, a community of artisans and craftsmen. Leiv came up with this great story that the miraculous fishing nets were made from some magical thread you import from elsewhere. Naturally, the peddlers were instrumental in spreading that rumor," I began.

"Ok, someone, please explain to me what is up with those nets!" Revna complained.

"They were imbued with just enough magic to attract fish. If you threw one in the water, you would likely catch something. People did not go hungry as often. Bjørn was really smart and, despite the high demand, he priced them just a little higher than the regular ones! All the fishermen wanted one and would save up to buy them," I informed her.

"Depending on where they are going, the traders usually carry a few," Uma interposed.

"Those nets were highly prized in Scandinavia as well as the Highlands. Due to the cleverness of Bjørn and his sons, they kept the manufacturing costs low. Most people could afford one of the smaller ones, and those who could not usually made a bargain of sorts. The fishing nets were a great source of income and gained Havn the protection of all those who relied on this gear.

"This, alone, helped to stave off raids by some of the more ambitious fellows around the area. If any even contemplated such actions, their neighbors, including the trading post, would turn against them. Suddenly, they would find themselves without the supplies they had come to depend on. That usually gave them pause and drove home the point that it was best to leave Havn alone," I explained with a smile.

"It took a couple of years after we arrived, but eventually, even the remaining Vikings figured out that any goods they might acquire by force would not make up for what they would lose in the long run!" Uma added with a laugh.

"Fascinating!" Revna admitted. "Who would have believed that they could see sense?"

"Please tell us more!" Hilda added.

Leiv's wife was happy to oblige us. She loved having such an attentive audience and really rose to the occasion. Since much of our history then was passed on verbally, she was a great storyteller. That evening, she shared with us many entertaining snippets that gave us a better picture of what life was like for her in Norway and Havn.

It turned out that Uma and Signe were still the best of friends even now that they were married. They visited each other as often as they could. The girls and I were glad to hear that our warrior maiden was still just as fierce as she had been. The laird she had married just loved it and encouraged her to continue training. She and the other women of the keep regularly practiced with their weapons and were ready to back up the men if need be.

Eldred looked very thoughtful when she heard that, and Hilda was absolutely delighted. Did they intend to follow in Signe's footsteps? As if reading my mind, the siblings grinned at me. The older girl's smirk looked pretty feral. If she continued to hone her fighting skills, she would be a force to reckon with! I could envision her backing down an enemy without hesitation, especially if it meant protecting those she loved! Woe be to the fool who crossed her!

The sisters were extraordinary in many ways! Their magic was strong, they were adaptable and intelligent, they learned quickly, and they had good hearts. Cedric could not have asked for better wives!

"Who did the rest of Signe's siblings marry?" Hilda inquired, subtly changing the subject.

"Yrsa and Rune wed Highlanders; the rest married within the clan, someone with magic or accepting of it," Uma told us.

"That makes good sense. After all, who wants to hide their true nature in the comfort of their own home?" Revna put in, immediately grasping the crux of the situation.

"Not me!" Eldred uttered vehemently.

We all agreed with her sentiment!

"I am so glad that Signe is happy with her laird! She hated the idea of Auga marrying him!" Hilda said with a laugh.

"She sure did!" Eldred agreed. "That was what upset her most about being crippled! You know, I always wondered why our clan is so closely related! Now it makes perfect sense! Marrying someone else with magic makes it stronger in our children as well!"

"Good thing then that Cedric has some abilities, or you might decide to throw him over for someone more powerful now that you know that!" Hilda roared.

Eldred's face grew red. She was in no mood to be teased.

"I would not! I love him!" she objected haughtily.

She was, however, protesting a little too loudly, and Hilda, realizing that, was not about to pass up an opportunity to tease her sister. I just knew that these two were about to get into a fight! Time for a diversion!

"I am exhausted," I therefore voiced. "I am going to bed! Do you need anything, Uma?"

"Hilda, could I please have another cup of tea?" Uma asked, cleverly catching on to what I was trying to do.

Having been married 19 years and having five children of her own, she was well versed in subtly but effectively separating two combatants before things got out of hand. Uma's request successfully diverted the girls' attention. A few minutes later, they had made up and joined me in bed.

The morning seemed to come all too quickly. Bo enjoyed waking us gently by brightening the light little by little, almost like a real dawn. He did so much to help us feel at home. Once again, I thanked him for all his thoughtfulness. This imprisonment could have been so much worse! It was difficult enough as it was, especially on Hilda. She had pushed up so tightly against me in her sleep that I felt the need to stretch to unkink my body.

Getting to know all these amazing kin and then having to say goodbye forever was hard on her. I could feel her body shaking and realized that she was crying. Without hesitation, I wrapped my arms around her. I hugged her close for a few minutes, giving her what comfort I could. Gently stroking her hair, I waited for her sobs to grow further apart and for her to calm down. When Eldred woke up, she slid on the other side of her.

Between the two of us, we finally managed to stop the flow of tears. No wonder Hilda had picked a fight with her sister! It was much easier to be angry than carry this much sadness!

"I want to find a way for all of us to stay in contact, but I have no idea how," I said gently. "Do you?"

Eldred immediately started devising ways, some more ridiculous than others. Finally, Hilda joined in. When her older sister came up with an especially uproarious suggestion, even she started laughing. But, after that, the three of us got serious. We pulled Bo into our conversation and, eventually, came up with a viable plan. However, we would need both Uma's and Revna's assistance, but we were sure they would not mind helping.

Bouncing out of bed, we raced downstairs. We found the two ladies sitting companionably together, having a cup of tea. Carefully we explained our idea.

"Signe will love it!" Uma exclaimed. "I will be happy to aid you!"

Shortly after, we congregated in the living room. We sat down in a circle and, to make it easier to connect with each other, we clasped hands. Once we had a good understanding of the construction of the spell, we busily separated out parts of the enchantment. Then we remade those pieces to serve our purpose.

Bo could now assist us by creating a second bubble outside of space and time. Once this was accomplished, we added details. Thus we crafted a beautiful place that reminded us of home.

Our house there was much like the one we were staying in now but much grander and with a beautiful garden. And it had a view of the water with mountains in the background! Sunny meadows and forests stretched down to the loch. The air was crisp and clean, and walkways led down to the shore and into the hills. The landscape was truly stunning! Using the images he saw in our minds, Bo helped us get the details just right.

We gave our meeting place as much substance and definition as we could. A small part of our souls was bound into it, allowing us to meet there whenever we wanted. Not physically, naturally, once we left the time trap, but in spirit. But that was far better than never seeing each other again! And as magnificent as we had made the landscape, it would definitely do for some great outings and a lot of fun!

Bo was instrumental in shifting substance from the construct to the small world we had created. All of us present were tied to it, and we could invite others. Uma would take an object with her that would allow Signe and Finna to join us. In addition, this space would serve another purpose. Since we had grown genuinely fond of Bo and he of us, we did not want him to fade into nothingness. Therefore, we connected his consciousness to our creation.

Bo could retreat there and survive when we destroyed the time trap if nothing else had occurred to us by then. As far as we were concerned, this was not ideal, but better than losing him altogether. That way, we would see him every time we came to visit! We had no clue what else to do. Unlike the rest of us, Bo had no physical body. We could not create a vessel for him from nothing!

But then Eldred, sly as always, proposed using part of the construct to give Bo form just as we had done for the Meeting Place.

That would make him solid in the hive and in our pocket dimension! Revna agreed that this might work and that we might even be able to give him a semblance of life.

The only other thing we came up with was not to our group's liking. Putting Bo inside of someone else's body was not an acceptable option! Depriving another man of his vessel to host our friend was neither fair nor ethical.

Chapter 35

A Whole New Bo

While we were sifting through the enchantment's tangled threads to find some extraneous substance, Hilda suggested that we might be able to free Bo from more of the constraints the spell put on him. He had gained increasing autonomy the longer he existed but had to fight the construct for every improvement he made for us and his continued independence. Having him help us was against the original design of the time trap, and it did not like it.

Eldred took over from here. With her as the lead, we looked through all the different strands. Carefully, we changed things here and there. To our surprise, we discovered that a tentative connection remained to the person responsible for this nightmare. That was not good news as far as we were concerned. What if she used it to change everything back to how she had set it up?

After some discussion, we cut that link and walled off that area. We made sure that the almost non-existent filament could not reattach. None of us wanted to take a chance. The powerful witch might discover that things here were not going according to plan! She had intended to punish the Magnuson Clan, to do us harm, but we had managed to turn this to our advantage. To keep it this way, we ensured that no outside force could wrest control of the hive from Bo.

He was delighted that we trusted him enough to put our lives in his hands. With our alterations, he could now affect most things in the construct without it working against him! We could feel Bo's relief, and for the first time, we realized how hard it had been for him and how much energy had been required to make and maintain the changes in the cells. He had hidden it well.

As we found out later, with his new power came an unexpected bonus for us! For the first time, Bo was able to provide us with something to eat! We had wondered how he managed the tea, but water was everywhere and easy to access. He gathered what it should taste like from our minds, and reproducing the flavor had been no problem. Food, though, was a different story.

Bo could not bring in substance from the outside. However, now that he was in total control of our environment, he could make the orchard in my cell bloom and accelerate its crop production! Suddenly, several shiny, red apples appeared right where we were sitting! Their arrival was greeted with cries of delight. The crisp fruits were an incredible treat after not having anything edible the entire time we had been here! You have no idea how much we savored each and every bite!

After relishing our snack, we returned to work on our bubble. We decided to celebrate our success once everything had been arranged to our liking. Now that his actions were no longer constrained by the enchantment, Bo asked if he could join us. In physical form! He was tired of being everything but also nothing at all! And he wanted a better way to interact with us.

We were going to do this anyhow, so why not right then? Since Bo could use the substance of the hive to create things such as the houses and the tea, we saw no reason why he could not make his avatar. He could use some of the material from the hive we had separated out. Besides, having a body would allow him to communicate with some of those left in the construct without frightening them. As far as we were concerned, getting to work on it was an excellent idea!

Since we were all in agreement and would genuinely enjoy his company, we asked Bo how we could help. He considered this for a few seconds. The trap did hold some younger men, but he did not want to look similar to any of them. I got the distinct impression that he detested these guys for some reason. Not knowing anyone else, he asked us for an image of someone whose likeness he could take.

This led to some discussion among us ladies. My husband's image was out. Seeing Phillipe and him not being the real thing would have been incredibly hard. And painful! I already missed him so much every waking moment that it made my heart hurt. Bo resembling him would have made my longing even worse! Eldred felt the same way about Cedric; Hilda could not think of anyone, and the man Revna loved was also unsuitable.

Finally, Uma volunteered the image of her oldest son, Ulf. We helped her project a picture of Ulf within our circle and watched with fascination as the body took form. With a wave of his hand, Bo created a mirror so that he could take a look at himself. To our surprise, he frowned at his reflection.

"Bo, what is it?" Hilda asked curiously.

"He is very handsome, but I do not care for these clothes. They feel wrong, like they are not from my time somehow. Eldred, may I share your memories so that I can see Cedric and how he dresses?"

Eldred was only too happy to oblige him. She allowed the rest of us to witness what she was showing him. Patiently, she presented him with several different outfits, anything from work clothes to what she suspected he would wear at the wedding. Bo liked the kilt. He decided to reshape the trousers into one but did not care much for it on himself. After thanking her politely, he turned to me.

"Cara, would you allow me to see into your mind? Would you please share some pictures of Phillipe?"

I could do better than that. Whipping out my phone, I pulled up the file I had made just for my husband. First was a shot from that fateful morning when I had last seen him. He had looked so dashing in his black jeans and a nice shirt that I had snapped a picture of him. Then I showed Bo Phillipe in his suits, how he wore the kilt with a uniform-like jacket, his exercise outfits, and more casual wear.

Finally, we reached the image of Phillipe in his black tuxedo. My husband was so incredibly handsome in that getup that every time he wore it, I could not wait to get him home and all to myself! That look was such a turn-on! To my surprise, Bo seemed to be aware of this as well. Had he read my mind?

"Thank you! That is much more my style!" Bo stated with obvious delight.

He copied the tux down to the last detail and then consulted the mirror. But, he was not yet happy with his appearance. When had he become so dapper? Was this new, or had he always been like this? There was no way of telling since he had not had a body before. Or was there? Anything Bo had created had been perfect, down to the last detail! Not surprising then that he took such pains now!

After a moment's consideration, the tousled hair Ulf would have sported became neatly parted and combed. Next, the small beard disappeared. It seemed that Bo preferred being clean-shaven like Phillipe! Once he had everything just right, he smiled at us with happiness.

"What do you think?" he asked, turning around to allow us to admire him from all sides.

"I never realized that my son could be so polished!" Uma said, very impressed and a little breathless.

The tux Bo wore was unlike anything Ulf would have had available to him. It looked stunning and set off his physique in a way that was not lost on us ladies. Hilda was speechless, and Revna and I clapped to show our approval. Eldred, however, looked thoughtful. What was going on in that sharp mind of hers?

"Ok, Eldred, what is it?" I finally asked her.

"We were here much longer than you, and Bo never made contact with us. Remember when you first arrived? Did you sense a consciousness then?" she asked me.

I thought back to the day I was captured and realized that she had a point. The construct had been this unfeeling, treacherous mechanism designed to make its prisoners' lives as uncomfortable as possible, to keep them confined, and to use them to power itself. Bo was nothing like that. After some deliberation, I was confident that he had not yet come into existence when I arrived.

"No, there was only the time trap," I began, then remembered. "But there were a few seconds when everything wavered and felt odd!"

"We felt that too!" Hilda affirmed.

"We sure did!" Eldred agreed. "We wondered what was going on!"

"I thought that moment was significant!" Revna stated with a sense of wonder. "That was the instant of conception!"

"But nothing came of it at first!" I objected.

"I believe something else had to happen first!" Revna told us.

"So what was the catalyst for Bo's creation?" I wondered.

"Our meeting!" Hilda stated with certainty. "When you found Eldred and me, something changed!"

"The power of three," Revna added thoughtfully. "But timewise, he seems the most closely linked to you, Cara."

"Bo? Is that true?" I inquired.

"My affinity for clothes from your era does point in that direction," he answered after some thought.

"A simple yes might have sufficed," Eldred laughed.

"Yes, but would it have been as precise?" he teased her.

This quickly led to a discussion between these two that the rest of us listened to with amusement.

Now that Bo had an actual body, we had more to celebrate. Since he was already impeccably attired, something that reminded me very much of Phillipe, the rest of us went upstairs to get dressed up as well.

To our amazement, our closets now held several magnificent gowns, the styles designed to please the taste of each of us ladies.

Mine were all floor-length, tight at the waist, and had flaring skirts in a style I adore! They were very reminiscent of the gorgeous clothes Eldred and Hilda were wearing. Cries of delight were coming from all the rooms as we discovered this bounty. Next thing I knew, the girls raced into my chamber with an armload of dresses.

Together, we picked the ones we thought would look the best. The rest we returned to the cupboards. However, getting in and out of these magnificent creations was not easy! Therefore, we helped each other get ready. Down the hall, we could hear Uma and Revna chatting. They were doing the same.

By the time they knocked on the door, Eldred, Hilda, and I were beautifully attired and made up. We all wanted to look our best as a thank you to Bo.

The gowns were not the only surprise awaiting us. The entire cabin seemed more festive as we made our way down the stairs! When we entered the living room, we noticed an ornate entry that had not been there a few minutes ago. The house had expanded even further! Bo greeted us with compliments for each lady. He was thrilled that we appreciated his gifts and genuinely enjoyed no longer being constrained by the original design of the construct.

Once we were all ready, Bo threw open the elaborately decorated doors. When Hilda got a closer look at them, she squealed with delight.

"These are just like the ones to the great hall!"

Eldred, who was ahead of her, turned and examined the intricately carved panels herself.

"They sure are!" she agreed. "Bo, did you get these from my memories?"

"I did!" he confessed. "I hope that you do not mind! I just thought them so beautiful that I could not help myself using the design here!"

"No, I do not mind," Eldred stated. "I am just amazed that you remembered all the details!"

Bo blushed with pleasure, then continued to lead us into the space beyond.

The chamber was dark until he clapped his hands. Then, candelabras burst into light all around the room. We could not believe our eyes! We were in one of the most magnificent ballrooms I had ever seen. Mirrors covered some of the walls, reflecting the light and creating the illusion of a much larger space. The hardwood floor was polished to a high sheen, and the columns supporting the glass dome were decorated with flowers and ivy. In one corner was a long table holding glasses of what looked like champagne!

Several French doors led to a well-tended garden, and we could smell the heady aroma of flowers. Bo was really expanding his repertoire! This was truly incredible! He was immensely pleased when we told him. Everywhere we looked, we saw some sort of wonder. While we ladies stood there, staring in awe, taking it all in, Bo waved his hand. On his signal, music began to fill the room. He bowed before Revna, asking her to dance.

The rest of us watched this for a moment, but the music was calling us, so we also paired up. Our biggest problem was trying to figure out who should lead, but soon we were all swirling around the room. I was dancing with Uma. Once we worked out the steps, we had a lot of fun. Throwing back my head with pure delight, I looked up. Only then did I notice that I could see the evening sky through the crystal dome!

We switched partners for the next song and for the one following. After that, we were thirsty. It was time to try out the champagne! At first, I took a careful sip, tasting the bubbly liquid tentatively. It was delicious! And definitely alcoholic! I was genuinely impressed. Hilda was rather surprised by the effect. After the second helping, she was giggling and weaving. Uma, on the other hand, had several glasses and still walked a straight line! She was used to drinking mead, so this did not faze her!

Dancing with Bo was very pleasant. He had done an incredible job creating his form. His hands felt warm, and his body was solid and exceedingly male, which did not escape any of us ladies. Some of us might have a partner, but this did not mean we were blind or immune to his charm! Hilda, however, soon started monopolizing him. Bo did not seem to mind.

When I joined Uma, standing by the champagne table, I noticed her watching the two.

"Does Ulf have this kind of sex appeal?" I asked her curiously.

I had to explain the meaning of the expression, but eventually, she understood.

"He wished," she laughed. "Bo took this several steps further! May I see the pictures of Phillipe?"

We noticed the similarities in movement and expression as we went through the images. Bo had clearly fashioned himself to be as like my husband as he could without actually looking exactly like him! Incredible! Also, he had used and combined several places Phillipe and I had been to for this extraordinary room's design and creation! How clever of him! He was so much like a real person in some ways, but here in the construct, he also had the powers of a god!

Would he be happy and content with living only in the bubble we had just made? Or did we need to find another option? Was there a way to bring him into our world?

Chapter 36

Hope

Bo felt it would benefit us to maintain our natural rhythm and had adjusted the construct accordingly. As we danced and enjoyed ourselves, the lights dimmed outside. Stars twinkled, and the moon shone through the glass dome. The six of us were having a wonderful time and often switched partners. Being the only male present, Bo made sure to give each of us some attention. But, to our amusement, Hilda somehow managed to get many more dances with him than the rest of us did.

Not that we minded. Uma, Revna, Eldred, and I had developed our very own style of dancing. We whirled and swirled together or apart, whatever we fancied at that moment. The room was filled with lighthearted laughter, and we had such fun. This was just what we needed! It helped relieve some of the tension that had built up during our time as prisoners of this time trap.

Eventually, we all started yawning. Only Hilda, being the youngest of us, wanted to keep dancing. However, Eldred was not about to leave her alone with Bo. Those two were getting entirely too cozy for her liking. She loved Cedric but knew Hilda saw him more like an older brother. The younger girl was glad to marry him because this would allow her to stay with her sister. Or at least she had been. Had she changed her mind? Did she want a man of her own to love?

If she did, Bo was not it. He did not exist outside the construct. Eldred and I exchanged a worried glance as we watched the two. There was definitely something developing between them! Sadly, we saw no possibility for it to flourish and endure. Hilda would be going home soon. She would only be able to see him in our Meeting Place. This was heartbreak in the making!

Therefore, we took the girl by the hand, said goodnight to everyone, and dragged her to bed with us.

The morning dawned even sunnier than usual. Bo greeted us in the kitchen. He had hot tea and apples for all of us and seemed to be in an excellent mood. He brightened even further when he spotted Hilda. She came down a few minutes after us and had taken great pains to look her best and to make quite an entrance. This was not lost on the young man; all his attention focused on her.

He brought her tea, served her the apple, and sat down beside her. Soon, their heads were close together, and they started a whispered conversation. To my surprise, neither Bo nor Hilda hid their attraction for each other any longer. Before we were even finished with our beverage, the two were openly flirting! They did make a cute couple, but what hope was there for them?

Eldred, on the chair beside me, let out a sigh. She gave me a helpless look. I could not blame her; she was not sure what to do. She and Hilda would be married just as soon as they returned to their own life. This was the one chance the girl had to experience falling in love with an attractive young man. Was it fair to deprive her of this opportunity?

"You two, could you please stop that for a bit?" Revna finally intervened, seeing how glum Eldred was getting. "Hilda, Bo, you do know that …."

"We are aware that this has no future," Bo interrupted her. "Hilda and I have talked about it. We just want to enjoy the moment."

"Eldred, please! Bo and I just want to experience what falling in love feels like," Hilda added. "Can you let us do so without frowning quite so much?"

"What about Cedric? Have you changed your mind about the wedding?" Eldred asked her straight out.

"No, I have not. But you and Cedric, you love each other. He is just marrying me to make you happy. I want to know what it feels like to be in love and have my feelings returned! And so does Bo! Even if it is only for a short while! Please, Eldred!" Hilda pleaded with tears in her eyes.

Eldred looked at me, not sure how to respond. We both turned to Uma and Revna for help. None of us thought this was a good idea, but how could we deny them? They did have a point and were aware of the limitations and consequences. Besides, if we did forbid them, they would most likely find a way to carry on behind our backs!

"I just do not want to see you hurt, neither of you!" Eldred finally relented.

Hilda got up from her chair to give her sister a big hug. Her face was aglow with happiness. With a sinking feeling in my stomach, I watched her return to her banter with Bo. The way they looked at each other said everything. How were we ever going to pry them apart when the time came?

Since we would take Uma home on this day, Eldred and I started asking her more questions about her life. This helped to distract us but also managed to draw in Hilda and Bo, a win-win all the way around! Our new friend shared more details about her husband, children, and Havn. Her description of the village during its construction fascinated all of us. It was so different from the place we knew!

During Eldred and Hilda's time, most of the houses were log cabins built on the rock foundations of the previous generations. By my time, Ny Havn had become the main settlement. The remnants of the original village were now a heritage site that people came from near and afar to visit. Only the mead hall was still in use. Most of the other buildings were in ruins, but the oldest surviving intact stone structure was still covered in thatch, just like it had been during Uma's time!

Seeing our interest, Bo volunteered to project the image of what Havn looked like in those days into the room. Uma thought this a great idea. To make it easier, he stepped up behind her and placed his hands on her temples. Having a body and being concentrated in one spot did seem to have some drawbacks, but I do not believe that he minded!

Thus we soon saw pictures of Uma's children and Signe, Finna, and Bjørn. She showed us the real Ulf. As attractive as the young man was, Bo had taken his good looks to an entirely new level! He was not just a copy of Uma's son; he had a personality and style all of his own that reflected the individual he had grown into.

Seeing the remarkable difference between them drove home how far Bo had come in such a short time! He had well-developed likes and dislikes and knew precisely what he wanted. In our eyes, he was no different from the rest of us now that he had a body. He even had a soul. Where it originated from or how this had happened defied explanation. But there was no doubt that he had one! We could all sense it!

For all intents and purposes, this and some other attributes he had acquired over the days made him human. Bo had consciousness. He abhorred seeing anyone in pain; he could think and feel. He had compassion and empathy, more than many individuals I had met in my lifetime. Where had this all come from? How was it possible that a part of an enchantment gained life? Especially one that was cast with such ill will!

We had no idea! In the time trap, now that we had freed him from the spell's restraints, he was almost omnipotent. Using its matrix, he was able to create many things. He could affect the environment of the cells in the entire hive and change it as he saw fit. Had he wished it, he could have made our lives utterly miserable! That he did not abuse his power said much about who he had become!

Had the situation been different, he would have made a great husband for our Hilda. Too bad that this was not to be!

With a shake of my head, I brought my thoughts back to what was going on. Now that we could actually see the place, Uma took us all around the village. She showed us how it developed by letting us witness its expansion from the first houses Bjørn had built and how it grew into the thriving settlement it had been when she ran afoul of the trap. Living hundreds of years later, we had many questions that she patiently answered.

Once we had exhausted our exploration of Havn in time and space, Uma switched to sharing some of her adventures with us. She really got into that. Having them appear in vivid pictures delighted her to no end. As we soon discovered, in her time back in Norway, she had faced many dangers. And she had overcome much. As a small child, she had witnessed the brutal killing of her family. She had been the only one to survive.

Olaf had come upon the destroyed farmstead and, by pure chance, or maybe fate, had found the little girl in her hiding place. He had brought her back to the village with him. Finna had immediately volunteered to take her in. She had raised Uma with much love and understanding. It had taken many months for the child's nightmares to fade and for her to stop being afraid of her own shadow.

Uma had often awoken the entire house in the first few weeks with her screaming. Finna had finally decided to include her in the combat training her kids were participating in. She had hoped that learning to defend herself would make the girl feel more empowered. It had worked and had given her much-needed confidence.

Very soon, the little girl had excelled in the classes. Uma had developed a passion for swordplay and could outshoot most of her peers within a few weeks. Thus, at a relatively young age, she had been invited to join the guards who patrolled the hills and woods around the settlement. Being admired for her abilities and knowing she could take down most attackers quickly and efficiently had helped her feel more in control.

After a couple of years in Caledonia, she had married Leiv. Ulf had been their first child. She had been the perfect spouse for the leader of Havn and had even taken part in a few battles at sea! She and Signe had been just as good with a sword, knife, and bow as the men! What an incredible life she had led!

Eldred was deeply impressed with Uma's prowess in combat. She asked if we could see a practice bout. Both she and Hilda leaned forward and watched every move. Sometimes, they requested to see a specific maneuver again and wanted explanations for why one used a particular movement in defense or offense. I could just see the writing on the wall and chuckled at the thought of what Cedric was in for.

After their time in the time trap, his wives would be even more of a handful than ever! They had grown so much more confident and were learning more magic by the day! I was sure that we would be adding additional combat classes to that! Signe had taught us some interesting and rather unconventional moves, and I could help them improve further. But I was not yet an expert with the sword. After all, I am a writer, not a fighter!

Watching Hilda and Eldred coming into their own filled me with happiness and pride. Their abilities were growing with each day. This made them a force to be reckoned with! I intended to suggest to them to hold combat classes for the women inside the mead hall. Teaching them how to deal with intruders would not hurt, but it was best if these activities were not broadcast to their neighbors. For one, it provided an element of surprise in case of an attack and could turn the tide in their favor!

My young friends would truly be the power behind their husband. If they decided something, Cedric would be hard-pressed to deny them! Not that he was prone to, since he loved Eldred and was prepared to do just about anything to please her!

As I knew from our history, all this would greatly benefit the clan in the end! We would get through those perilous days of the witch hunts almost unscathed. Only one woman ran afoul of those horrid fanatics who killed hundreds of innocent people. The unfortunate lady married an outsider. She moved away from Havn with her husband to the south of Scotland. There, she was arrested as a witch.

Her husband knew nothing about our abilities or those of his wife. She had hidden them well and, as far as the records showed, had done nothing to warrant the unwanted attention. She was incredibly brave during the entire ordeal. Instead of giving away the family's secret, she stilled her own heart when she could no longer withstand the torture. Her picture still hangs in the mead hall to this day, and she is greatly honored for protecting the clan from the evil of those religious zealots.

I was glad that people had grown more tolerant of us in my time, but I had also seen evidence that they still feared what they did not understand. Therefore, we did not flaunt our powers.

Uma's vivid pictures of an outing she had gone on with Signe and all their children drew my attention back to the conversation. Some of the kids' antics soon had us roaring with laughter. Her recall of the incidents was so detailed and vivid that it held everyone's attention. Our friend's love for her family shone through loud and clear and almost made me wish for a child of my own.

One such event was just beyond funny. Uma's youngest boy had decided to bathe in a nearby mud puddle while the older ones, who were supposed to look after him, were not watching. By the time they had noticed, he had been covered in dirt and slime from head to toe. Knowing their mother would be greatly displeased, the others had tried to wash him off in the creek.

The little guy had not suffered this peacefully. He fought his siblings with all he had. Who could blame him for not wanting any part of this! The water was cold, even in the summer! Eventually, the two oldest had picked him up by the arms and drug him in. But they could not get him to dunk under so he would get clean! So the rest of the children came to help. The rocks were slippery. As can be expected, in the end, the whole lot of them had returned to their mother dripping wet!

They had been quite perturbed when Uma had not believed their excuses. The kids had not known she had been watching them the entire time! This now allowed her to share this misadventure with us in colorful images. My side hurt, and tears ran down my face from laughing so hard by the time she was done. Several more stories like that had us begging for mercy. Bo, unfamiliar with family life, enjoyed himself immensely!

Eventually, after another cup of tea and several more but less hilariously presented tales, we could no longer postpone the inevitable. It was time to take our friend home. Bo came with us as we guided Uma back to her nexus. She hugged him goodbye right along with the rest of us before she, Eldred, Hilda, and I stepped into the smoke. With a heavy heart, we dialed in her destination. After one last round of embraces, the girls and I watched with much sadness as she walked away.

Uma turned every few feet to wave to us. Despite our eyes being so blurry, we could see the tears on her face. The parting was as hard on her as it was on us! Good thing that we had created the Meeting Place!

Chapter 37

The Time Has Come

Eldred, Hilda, and I felt deep sadness to see Uma return to her own time and place. Revna was even more upset. After just taking Finna home, this had been too much. She was crying in Bo's arms when we reentered the nexus. The two ladies had really hit it off and had become fast friends in the short time Uma had been with us. They would truly miss each other and had already scheduled a get-together in the Meeting Place. The girls and I decided to add a bit to our enchantment to make it easier for them. It worked like an alarm and would let us know when someone arrived.

Uma had agreed to bring Signe and Finna on one of her future visits, but that first one would be just for her and Revna. The two were working on something they were not yet ready to share with the rest of us. We were more than happy to grant them some privacy. In any case, even if we had to wait a little longer, seeing the warrior maiden again was something Hilda, Eldred, and I were looking forward to.

Bo had kept his arm around the sobbing Revna as we made our way to the in-between but handed her off to me there. He and Hilda exchanged a conspiratorial glance. Oh oh! They were up to something!

"Since the Meeting Place is going to be my home, we are going to work on it some more. Hilda is helping me decorate," Bo informed us.

Taking each other by the hand, those two took off running before any of us could object. We watched Bo and Hilda go with some trepidation, but none of us had the heart to stop them. Revna listlessly shrugged her shoulders, but she did come along with Eldred and me to find someone else to take home. That was probably better than her returning to the house and crying all day!

Eldred used her instincts to guide us to the next person to deal with. Bo appeared to be otherwise occupied, so we had to push through the membrane. None of us were pleased with that! We spotted the house once we walked down the path a little way. It looked awfully much like the one in my cell, just much more welcoming. And it was in better repair than that place had been before Bo took charge and upgraded the nexuses!

We were glad he had bettered life for all the captives of the time trap and not just us. At least now, these people had a house to shelter in and beds to sleep in! What an improvement over when I first arrived! We made our way up the walkway and knocked on the door. It took a moment before the person living there opened it. To my surprise, she was a young woman I knew!

"Brigit!" I exclaimed.

"Cara!" the young woman sobbed and threw herself in my arms. "I have been so alone! Where are we? What is going on?"

After introducing my companions, I explained to her what had happened. Brigit had tried to return home through the smoke several times but had finally given up and taken refuge in the cabin. Bo had been kind enough to provide her with tea and books, and she had been reading when we arrived. Since I already knew enough about this young lady, there was no reason to delay taking her home.

However, we could not let her return to her time as upset as she was. Revna set her sorrow over losing her friend aside and stepped in. Her spell eased much of Brigit's distress and would continue healing her frazzled nerves over the next few days. The young woman had not handled this adventure and her solitary confinement well, so we spent a few more minutes with her.

I watched Brigit with concern. Eldred and Revna were obviously from a time different than hers, but she showed no interest. All she wanted was to return to the world she was used to and forget her imprisonment in the hive had ever happened. When she seemed composed enough, we took her into the smoke and dialed in her home. Soon, the familiar landscape of Ny Havn flickered into place.

Brigit could not wait to leave. She barely even said goodbye, nor did she thank us. The young woman was in such a hurry that she ran off the second we told her it was safe. She did not look back even once! How very different from the parting we had gone through just a short time ago!

Eldred, Revna, and I left the smoke and returned to the nexus. To our surprise, the light had dimmed in the cell. With everything going on, we had lost track of time! Thanks to Bo setting up a 24-hour cycle, our life had taken on a much more natural rhythm. But having done without that for so long, we were still adjusting. The day had passed, and it was now evening. Therefore, we returned to our home.

Of Hilda and her compatriot, there was no sign. We finally gave up waiting for those two when it grew very late and headed upstairs. I was so tired by then that I fell into bed. Eldred crawled in beside me. Since she was upset with her sister, we curled up together. The warmth of each other's bodies gave us the comfort we needed, and we were asleep within minutes.

Almost immediately, I began dreaming of Phillipe. I watched him desperately looking for me. He was determined to find me, but his instincts kept telling him I was not in our realm. My husband does not give up easily. He figured there had to be a clue somewhere that would lead him to me, and he was going to find it.

I hated seeing him so upset, but especially since I could not find a way to interact with him directly. Still, I wanted to give him some sort of a sign that I was well. We could usually pick up on each other's emotions even when separated by large distances. Would that work from here as well? It just had to! Maybe it even had before? I could not remember, but I could not leave Phillipe in the state he was in!

Concentrating on my husband, I reached for his mind. At first, nothing happened. I continued sending him all the love I felt for him. It flowed out of me in waves and seemed to finally reach him. I watched as he stopped his frantic searching and stood perfectly still. After a moment, a smile curved his well-shaped lips, and he calmed. He had gotten my message and knew that I was alright!

Was this real? It sure seemed so! I missed Phillipe just as much as he did me. My whole body ached with the pain of being separated from him. I so badly wanted to reach out and touch him, hold him, kiss him, feel his arms around me, and have the feeling of utter and complete safety and belonging. He, more so than any place, was my home!

That dream faded away only to be replaced by others I forgot just about as soon as they happened. Sometime during the night, Hilda slipped into bed with Eldred and me. We barely moved. We were emotionally tired from all the magic we were using and the goodbyes from those we had grown to love.

When the girls and I awoke in the morning, we dressed and headed downstairs. Revna greeted us warmly as we entered the dining room. We could tell she had not slept well and had been crying since her eyes were all red. Our friend got up from the table where she was sitting with Bo. She gave each of us a long hug. Then, she asked us to join her. She had a proposition for us.

Revna realized how much we admired her healing abilities and loved learning from her. She had decided to intensify our classes. The girls and I were happy to hear that. From then on, we split our time between learning and taking people home. With all this training and doing, we fell into bed each night, utterly exhausted from all the energy we had spent that day.

Still, Bo and Hilda found time to spend with each other. Eldred was not overly happy with this but did not complain.

The dialing-in of destinations became more manageable with each person safely delivered back to their time and place. Soon, we no longer needed all three of us to bring about the shift. But it was still impossible for me to do it on my own. Therefore, the girls stayed with me. Revna spent some part of her day at the house but at least a couple of hours each morning conferring with Uma at the Meeting Place. We still had no idea what those two were up to but figured they would enlighten the rest of us when the time was right.

After a while, Eldred and I were the ones who did most of the returning of people to their homes. We traveled throughout the nexus, looking for the next persons to rescue. Hilda came along on occasion, but more often than not, she spent time with Bo. Those two were definitely in love but tuned things down around the rest of us. For one, they did not want to upset or frighten her sister. What they were up to in private was anyone's guess!

Eldred and I asked Bo if bringing people to us would work instead of us searching them out. But we were informed we needed to be in their nexus to dial in their home. At least for now, it was too hard to do from the one we were in. However, he promised to give this some consideration and work on it. Maybe he could set up a neutral cell next to ours to serve as a transport chamber.

The entire time, the sisters and I continued to learn and grow. Eldred and Hilda were quite incredible. Getting in touch with their gift and realizing they could influence the world around them gave them such confidence! Both stood up taller and walked with a self-assurance that had been missing before. Having Bo just adore her also had a positive effect on Hilda. She was even bubblier than before and so happy! Her joyful laughter was a pleasure to hear and lightened all our hearts.

Even without her sister, Eldred and I had fun meeting and saving people! It felt good to be able to help them return to their home! As a result, she and Hilda smiled much more often. This alleviated some of the sadness that had taken root in their hearts. Confinement in this dreadful place had been brutal on them until we met. Since then, we had taken an awful situation and turned it to our benefit. I was very proud of all of us for making this possible.

Eventually, Bo set up the nexus adjacent to ours for guiding people home. His motivation was clear to Eldred, Revna, and me. Not having to locate people and travel through the in-between allowed Hilda to spend even more time with him. We thanked him profusely and asked him to assist us in sending out instructions to all those left in the hive to travel to us and how to do it.

One of the first to arrive was Mæva MacClair, another Magnuson descendant. She had heard our summons and led a whole group of people our way and into the transport cell. They had picked up a couple others on their way, and their number had grown to eleven by the time they reached us. Being faced with so many, we set up a system to deal with them most efficiently.

Bo provided Hilda with paper and helped her get each person's name, place, year, and brief history. Revna saw to any healing that needed to be done and handed out tea. Most of the worst cases had already been dealt with, but some new arrivals were severely depressed. They needed to be reassured and talked to. The healer had this well in hand and, using a combination of magic and just being herself, had them feeling better in no time.

Needless to say, it took us hours to take them all home. Usually, we did three, maybe four, in a day, so this was utterly exhausting. Bo had to help us with the last few. But I could sense that the nexus was shrinking fast now. We had discovered a while ago that the 29 folks the girls had met had been less than a quarter of all those imprisoned in the hive! However, after freeing so many from the time trap, it now lost a significant bit more size and power with each individual leaving!

At first, we had been worried about how this would affect Bo, but if anything, he seemed to be getting stronger! Hilda was greatly relieved to see this. She had been watching him like a hawk all day and would have probably stopped us from returning people to their homes had he come to any harm! The ley line seemed to sustain and protect him.

After realizing what we were up to, Mæva decided to remain behind and assist us. I loved her mane of wild auburn hair that obviously resisted any attempt of taming. It reminded me of a halo of coppery fire. As luck would have it, our new companion turned out to be far more powerful than even Revna, and we welcomed her with open arms. We now had a second teacher for the girls and me! Learning from her was a once-in-a-lifetime opportunity as far as I was concerned. Eldred and Hilda felt the same way.

We were thrilled she was willing to share her knowledge with us and kept asking her to tell us more. Since the transport cell was empty and no others had arrived, we put taking people back on hold for the next few days to study with her. We felt that this was more important. On our request, Bo subtly encouraged all the remaining prisoners to stay in their nexuses for a while longer.

As a result, we had lessons from sunup to long after it set. Physically, we did not really need sleep here in the hive. But our brains needed the rest after all the knowledge we crammed into them. Going to bed at a specific time helped maintain our natural pattern and restored some of our energy. It also enabled us to absorb more of the priceless information Mæva and Revna were passing on to the girls and me.

All three of us were greedy for more. We finally got them to agree to continue our lessons in the Meeting Place once we had all gone home. That took off some of the pressure to learn everything they had to offer all at once!

After six days of nothing but classes, three people arrived who wanted to leave. Once they had been taken care of, our teachers declared that the time had come for Eldred and Hilda to return home.

Naturally, we protested at first. There was so much left the sisters and I wanted to learn from Revna and Mæva! Only their assurance that the girls would be joined by a witch equal to them finally swayed us.

That afternoon, Mæva gave the three of us one last lesson. Gently, she prepared the sisters for returning to their own time. Eldred was looking forward to reuniting with Cedric and becoming his wife. Hilda, however, did not like the idea of leaving Bo and me behind, but especially Bo. The two of them disappeared at the first opportunity. Who could blame them? They would be parted all too soon!

Later that day, Mæva took me aside.

"Revna and I have been talking. We think that it would be a good idea if you stayed with the girls for a bit. Share with them things from your time that will help them survive."

"Even more than I already have? Will that not upset history?" I asked immediately.

"We do not believe so," Revna, who had joined us, assured me. "Knowledge is power. We think you can safely tell them about healing and hygiene practices in your days and everything you remember about what is to come."

"It would help them a lot," I had to admit.

"Yes, it would," Mæva agreed. "This spell was directed against our clan, so I do not feel guilty about giving our kin as much advantage as possible. Use our history to guide you. Be as open as you can be; just be careful what you tell them. Agreed?"

"Agreed," I stated gladly.

Once I saw their home, I would know what information would serve them best. Also, staying with them for a few days was a welcome holiday from the time trap. Besides, it was going to be hard to part with the girls I had grown to love. They had become more like little sisters than far-off ancestors!

"And another thing," Revna began. "Hilda loves Bo. She will need you. We are so proud of her for taking this as well as she has, but once you get there, try to distract her and give her what comfort you can!"

"I will," I promised the two concerned ladies.

The following morning, when all was ready, and the three of us were appropriately dressed, we made our way toward the cell that had been the girls'. We had chosen to depart from there instead of next door since it would give the lovers a few more minutes together. Both had looked unhappy but resigned when they had come downstairs. Only the redness of Hilda's eyes had given away the fact that she had been crying all night.

Now, Bo and Hilda walked some distance behind us, hand in hand. I could hear them whispering urgently to each other and felt for these two. Bo could not go with her. Until we thought of some way to fully bring him into the world, his physical form only existed in the hive and the Meeting Place we had created. Everywhere else, he was a disembodied spirit.

Revna had been afraid that if the sisters stayed much longer, Hilda might balk at leaving. The girl could have remained in the Meeting Place with Bo, but what kind of life would this have been for a young woman? How long would it have taken before she would have regretted the separation from her older sister and all that she had ever known? It was bad enough that one of the lovers was stuck here!

Each of us was preoccupied with his or her thoughts as we made our way to our destination. The lighthearted, cheerful chatter that usually accompanied our excursions was noticeably absent today. As we entered the nexus and walked toward the cloud, nobody talked, not even the lovers. Even from a distance, I could feel Hilda's and Bo's sadness at the upcoming parting. Occasionally, I could hear her sobs.

Abject misery came of these two in waves and brought tears to my eyes. Mæva, Revna, and Eldred were equally as affected. We exchanged concerned glances. Would Hilda go through with the departure? She loved him so much! They might never be able to be together again like this! But what would happen if she did not? My Phillipe was one of her descendants! Would he just disappear? The idea alone was terrifying!

If she decided to stay, there was not much we could do. Would I be able to force the young woman to leave out of pure self-interest? I considered this for a moment. The answer I came up with was no. I was not selfish enough to put my happiness before Hilda's, even if losing Phillipe would break my heart.

The tenseness I felt as we approached the cloud of smoke was indescribable. So much hinged on the next few minutes! If Hilda decided to remain with Bo, the clan's entire future would be affected. All those descendants of hers would never be born. History was hanging in the balance at this very instant, and all that weight was on the slender shoulders of a sixteen-year-old girl! And she was only too aware of this! It had to be crushing her about now!

Since the very beginning of the Magnuson Clan, all of us had been raised to put its interest first! I truly felt for her and was glad I was not in her shoes. What must it be like to have to make such a monumental decision? To have to give up one's own happiness for the greater good? Would I have chosen Phillipe over my people, and the consequences be damned? I loved my husband with all my heart and soul, but knowingly doing something that would cause harm to others? That was not only bad Karma but also not in my makeup.

When we reached the smoke, Hilda hugged the man she loved as if her life depended on it. I could hear her heartbroken sobs. Her entire body shook from crying so hard. Eldred went over to say her goodbyes and comfort her distraught sibling. Hilda desperately clung to Bo for another moment. Then, she visibly composed herself, stepped back, and turned toward the barrier. Hot tears were streaming down her face as she approached Mæva and me.

Bo followed more slowly with Eldred. The two seemed to be discussing something important. The young man finally lifted his lowered head and looked at her sharply. Hope mingled with disbelief played over his handsome features. What had she just told him? Knowing Eldred, she had found a way to allow her sister to continue seeing the man she adored. She might love Cedric, but her first loyalty was always toward her younger sibling.

Once we were ready, Mæva, Revna, and Bo entered the cloud with the girls and me. With all of us working together and all the practice we had gotten in of late, it took very little time for the right place to appear. Eldred and Hilda embraced the three who would be staying behind. Bo held his love's hand as she stepped toward the edge of the smoke. Their eyes met one last time, and the message that passed between them needed no words.

I moved along with them, which was not unexpected. The three of us being so close, Hilda had wanted me to accompany them as far as I could. Eldred knew I was coming with them, but her sister had been absent when I told her. Therefore, she was happily surprised as well as relieved. One more parting might have been too much for the girl to handle. Her heart was already breaking!

Eldred and I knew that Hilda had mixed feelings about the upcoming wedding. She would be marrying one man while being in love with another. This was not really fair to any of them. Eldred gave me a grateful look. She was glad to have me there when the procession delivered her and her younger sister to their future husband. In this painful situation, Hilda could use all the support she could get.

As an empath, I understood only too well how she was feeling. We would see how things developed once we met up with Cedric. If possible, I intended to stay with the girls for several days.

After the huge sacrifice Hilda had just made for the clan and her descendants, she deserved some recompense. I had every intention of sharing everything I possibly could with them that would make their life easier but not alter history. As agreed, Mæva, Revna, and Bo would wait for me on the other side of the smoke or in the house in that nexus. They would take turns anchoring the portal to make sure it stayed intact and open.

Since time ran so differently in the two places, I might be gone for only a few minutes or months. To be honest, I had no idea.

Chapter 38

The Return

Together, the three of us moved out of the smoke. Everything around us was frozen due to my presence. Bo had promised to adjust this, but he could only affect things outside the hive to a minor degree. Also, it took a great amount of energy. As long as I was in contact with the girls, we could see each other and interact, but I would be invisible to everyone else. He was waiting for my signal to set the spell in motion, making it possible for me to spend a few extra days with my friends. Once it took effect, the world around us would come to life.

However, finding out I was staying with them had an unexpected effect. Hilda threw herself in my arms and absolutely lost it. Her sobs shook her slender frame. All I could do was hold her, make soothing sounds, and stroke her hair to calm her. Over her shoulder, I saw how hard it was for Bo to see her so unhappy and not rush to her side.

Mæva, fearing that he would do just that, had a firm grip on his arm to prevent him from leaving the smoke! Who knew what would happen if he set foot outside the hive?

Finally, Hilda started to quiet down. Gently, I wiped the tears from her face and tried to undo some of the damage all this crying had done. I finally used a spell to reduce the redness and swelling of her eyes and nose. Once we felt ready, we grasped hands with me in the middle. I nodded to Bo, and the scene around us came to life.

To our surprise, turmoil raged around us. We had expected to reappear within seconds of the girls' abduction by the enchantment, but that was obviously not the case. Time had passed, and the sisters' sudden and unexpected disappearance had caused quite a commotion! Everyone was looking for them, and the people in the wedding procession had scattered all over the place!

Once Eldred and Hilda were noticed, shouts of astonishment, as well as a few of fear, erupted from those near us. The girls' sudden reappearance in their middle had scared some. Good thing these folks belonged to the clan and were used to magic and strange things happening! Otherwise, panic would have broken out! Still, even this bunch wanted it confirmed that Eldred and Hilda were not ghosts or wraiths of some sort. One brave man finally dared touch them and confirmed their existence.

Now that they knew that she was real, Eldred immediately took charge. First, she calmed everyone down and stopped the frantic running around. Then, she sent people out to bring the searchers back to the path so they could form up for the procession once more. But instead, the crowd gathered around us. Everyone wanted to know where the siblings had been and what had happened to them.

Since Cedric and the rest of the clan also needed to be informed, Eldred promised to explain what had transpired once they reached the gathering place. She did not feel like repeating the same story several times, even if those around us grumbled a little. Hilda finally backed up her sister. Together, they were soon firmly in control. Within minutes, they managed to get everyone lined back up. Word to proceed was quickly passed up and down the long queue of people.

If anyone thought it odd that the girls walked apart and appeared to be holding hands with an unseen person, they did not voice this. Obviously, with all that disappearing and reappearing, magic was at play here!

The pace set by those leading the march was solemn and measured, giving me plenty of time to look around. The scenery we had entered was quite different from my home on the Isle of Arran. Still, since this was the Havn of long ago, it felt familiar. I looked around in wonder. What a privilege to get a look into the Magnuson Clan's past! It was one thing to hear about it but yet another to walk among the village as it had been in 1616!

The path we were on had several houses built on the slope to our right. Around these was a well-maintained forest. This settlement was magnificent and not what I had expected. To my astonishment, each log of the houses had been smoothed and polished to a high sheen. How, I had no idea, but I intended to find out! The homes shone with an orange glow from the last rays of the setting sun and the golden light of the torches placed all around for this joyful occasion.

Each dwelling was lit up brightly by this combination. The effect was magical! Everything looked festive, perfect for such an important day as the chief taking a wife. Eldred, Hilda, and I walked along in the center of a line of singing people. It was very peaceful now that everyone had calmed back down. I gathered that the girls had been missing for just a few minutes. The searchers had not gotten far and had been easily recalled.

We had expected to reenter just where and when the girls had disappeared! No one should have missed them! With all the other people we had taken home, the time they had spent in the hive had meant nothing in the real world! Something had shifted; that much was clear. What would that mean for me when my turn came to go home? I would have to talk to Bo about that when I returned!

I had hoped to exit the time trap at the exact moment I had wandered into the smoke. But that seemed less likely now. For all the others, all those many days they had spent in the construct lived on only in their memory. They had lost no time at all in the real world. Uma had confirmed this and that she remembered it all perfectly. For that, I was glad. I would have hated forgetting all my new friends!

"Can we keep holding hands?" Hilda suddenly asked tentatively. "I need the reassurance that all this will not just disappear!"

"Yes," Eldred breathed with a sob. "I can barely believe that we are home! Thank you, Cara! And also for teaching us about our powers!"

"Yes, thank you! Now that we are back here, I suddenly just know things. We need to get going. Cedric is waiting for us!" Hilda added much too brightly.

She was putting on a brave face, hiding that her heart was breaking. Eldred and I exchanged a knowing glance. We had woken when Hilda had slipped into bed with us. She had spent the next hour sobbing in our arms. Leaving Bo behind was incredibly hard for her. The two were really in love, and I had the suspicion that things had gone much further than the girl wanted us to know.

To be honest, I was surprised that she had agreed to return at all! I am not sure what I would have done if I had been in her shoes.

I had not missed the effect Hilda was having on Bo. She was only sixteen but had to grow up fast after losing her parents. The girl had chosen to marry Cedric because she wanted to stay with her sister. I understood her reasons but felt that she was just a bit young. At least she was not forced to wed some man much older than herself! That would have been awful! This was still going on in places, even in my time. Some countries had just never made it out of the middle ages. Or they had returned to them for some unfathomable reason!

In March, Phillipe had to fly to Seattle, one of my favorite cities, for business. Naturally, I had gone along! My wonderful husband had taken time out of his busy schedule to take me to the opera. We saw an incredible performance of "A Thousand Splendid Suns." The plight of these brave women in Afghanistan had me in tears. Forced into marriage to a middle-aged man at 14? How awful! And he turned out to be an absolute brute who treated her terribly!

One of Mariam's neighbors had a very different kind of marriage. She wore western clothes instead of being made to wear a burqa! Her husband loved and cherished her. Their daughter, Laila, grew up to be a strong and resilient young woman who did what was necessary to survive. Many years later, she ends up married to the same old man as Mariam when her parents are killed before they can flee from the Taliban. The older wife resents her initially but then grows to love her. They see each other as family. It helps them to endure the abuse.

Eventually, Mariam kills their husband while he is strangling Laila. She sacrifices her life so her beloved 'daughter' and her children can escape Afghanistan. The image of her outlined in bright light, looking like a madonna, with all those dark men in the background ready to execute her, still sticks with me to this day. Purity and self-sacrifice, someone who finally loved and was loved in return in a world gone mad.

It was so well done, so well acted, that it touched my heart and soul. In a way, it was really haunting. It made me wish that there was something we could do to make things better. For everyone, everywhere! What would it be like to lose all your rights? I loved my independence and could hardly imagine depending on my husband for everything! As a result, Phillipe and I found several charities that we now donate to.

Since I was initially surprised by Hilda's upcoming nuptials, I shared that story with Eldred and her to better understand their situation. And knowing our history helped me see that this was different. My young friends would prosper and be happy with their husband.

But what about Hilda's relationship with Bo? How far had this gone?

Bo was definitely male and had created himself with all the right parts. From the bulge in his pants when the girl got near him, I suspected those were also in good working order. Had he and Hilda tried them out? They had often stayed out very late, so they would have had plenty of opportunity. Could he father a child? That was an interesting question I did not have an answer to. Maybe I would ask him next time I had an opportunity.

None of this, however, mattered right now. Eldred and Hilda were about to be married, and Cedric would claim them as his this night. No one would ever be any wiser if a child born nine months later was not his. I suspected that Bo and Hilda would continue to interact and that his house in the Meeting Place was their home, not just his. Her consciousness could easily slip away each night to spend time with him while her body rested.

Being there in spirit would feel as real as being physically in the time trap, with one exception. I doubted that she could get pregnant that way! As it was, I was very proud of Hilda for coming back with us and leaving the man she so obviously adored behind. As if sensing my thoughts, she met my eyes. For a moment, she let me see the deep sadness she felt in her heart that she was trying to hide from her sister.

With a reassuring smile and a nod, I let her know I understood and would not give her secret away. For just a second, she dropped her barriers even further. Now that she allowed it, I could sense the life growing within her. My question had been answered. Hilda was smart. She would make sure to be the first one Cedric spilled his seed into. Babies were often born early, and her being so young made this even more of a likelihood.

Eldred, on the other side of me, gave me a questioning glance. She had not missed our silent exchange. Hilda and I gave her a reassuring smile. Solemnly, still holding hands, we walked along the winding path between the hills adorned here and there with well-lit up homes.

Chapter 39

Havn

After we had gone a little further, I knew exactly where we were. How could I not recognize the location? I had been here with my parents many a time. I had played in these hills of the Magnuson lands near Gairloch! What a treat to see the Havn from long ago! The first to settle here had been our Viking ancestors Finna and Bjørn, their family, and all those who had come to Scotland with them. Over the years, the dwellings had continually been upgraded or replaced. Eventually, these magnificent log homes I was now seeing had been built.

In the 1800s, these handsome residences would be replaced by the charming stone houses of Ny Havn. Some of these are still semi-habitable to this day. No one lives in the old Havn anymore since the village has become a treasured heritage site. Our clan works together to preserve it, and we still use the mead hall and the lodge.

Once a year, around the winter solstice, we allow people to join us in the celebration that follows the tours. Those parties tended to get pretty wild but maybe not as boisterous as those we hold in private!

Delighted to see such a slice of our history firsthand, I kept looking around. I was trying to take it all in. This was such a treat! Letting go of Eldred for a moment, I took out my cell phone and took pictures of the place in all its past glory. I wanted to remember every little detail of the Havn of old! And I felt incredibly blessed to have the opportunity to visit with the girls some more!

Even if Cedric did not allow me to stay for a few days, I hoped to at least be able to share some of my recommendations with them. My observations of the village then and Ny Havn in 2023 put me in the position to suggest vital improvements. We would have a lot to talk about! Now that I better understood their living conditions, I knew what information would benefit the girls the most. For one, we needed to discuss how to improve the sanitation of this place!

Wells and outhouses were too close together! This was a great way to spread disease into the water supply! In some spots, both would need to be relocated! The privies should be downslope, and the wells above! And they should be further apart. Maybe this was something I needed to talk to Uma, Finna, and Signe about the next time I saw them! Why not pass this knowledge down through the ages?

This settlement was obviously very prosperous! The cabins themselves were set some distance from each other. They were all lit up brightly, decorated tastefully, and well-tended. I could not get over the shine of those logs! It was incredible, and the effect was just beautiful! They looked highly polished and very smooth and reflected the light to an astonishing degree. I had no idea how they achieved this. Maybe oil after sanding the wood down?

Phillipe would know! He was into all kinds of things and a fount of information. I intended to talk to him about this when I got back. I am sure he would be intrigued by all this! How much I missed him! He would have loved seeing this place! Sharing things with him somehow heightened my own enjoyment. Maybe I could take more pictures to show him when I finally returned home!

For the upcoming wedding, torches were stuck in the ground every few feet. They outlined and lit up the path. Everything pointed to this clan being affluent and conscious of their surroundings. They had worked with nature instead of against it. How clever to use pitch instead of whale oil! Having magic, these people respected life and were not about to get in on the slaughter of those remarkable creatures! What a pleasant change from some of the places in my own time!

Everywhere I looked, I saw evidence that the clan was thriving. It was hard to believe that the two young women with me were about to take this to the next level! According to our secret history, Cedric, Eldred, and Hilda would usher in a new era for our people. They would introduce many more advanced ways of doing things. But, in light of the ongoing witch hunt, they would do this carefully.

The clan would not draw attention to Havn by taking credit for the innovations. Having heard the tale of Finna's enslavement had left a lasting impression on Eldred and Hilda. They would counsel Cedric wisely and develop new ways of conducting business. The three would do their very best to keep unwanted attention from the village. In those days, it was best not to flaunt one's talents or riches!

A jealous heart is full of poison that can affect all around it and bring misery to countless souls. How many of those poor people accused of being witches ran afoul of one of their neighbors? It was so easy back then to invent some story and get someone in trouble! The religious fanatics did not need much to go after a person! If anyone had been evil, it had been them, not their poor victims!

As a wise precaution, the girls would keep their abilities well hidden. Only a few they trusted in the clan would know how powerful they truly were. Back in Norway, Olaf had taught all his charges to do magic in such a manner that it could not be observed or connected to the caster. This had become our way. Few from the outside would ever suspect that the Magnusons had magic.

Those few who accidentally did figure it out often ended up 'forgetting' that we were different. We are very careful to this day. Covertly, whenever possible, we use our abilities for the betterment of all those around us. We never flaunt our capabilities openly. Why tempt fate? You never know when things will take a turn to the dark side! All that is needed are a few fanatics gaining charge of the country!

The truly dark days for folk like us started in 1563 with the passing of the Witchcraft Act. It outlawed witchcraft or consulting with anyone seen as a witch and made these offenses a capital crime. The first major trials, the North Berwick Witch Trials, began in 1590, nine years before Eldred was born. Lucky for her, her parents and grandparents had seen this coming. They had drilled it into everyone's heads that all their lives depended on keeping their abilities a secret from the outside world.

Once the persecutions started, the clan hunkered down even more than ever before. Any lessons for their magical offspring were conducted indoors and away from prying eyes. Then, news reached them about the fate of the lady who had moved south with her husband. Realizing the danger her revealing their secret could have presented to the villagers, Eldred and Hilda's parents devised a solution.

Before setting out on that fateful journey, one of their last acts had been placing every person in Havn, even the children, under a spell. This enchantment served dual purposes. The first part prevented the revealing of anything about the magic abilities of the villagers to anyone. That way, they could neither betray nor accuse another. The second added a switch that could be triggered if they were arrested or tortured. It would help with the pain and allow for a peaceful passing from this life at will.

What a brilliant solution! The individual could die at a time of his or her choosing, thus depriving their tormentor of the ability to extract information and the pleasure of executing them. But, how terribly sad to be forced to go to such length! I could not imagine what it must be like to be afraid of one's neighbors! How careful one would have to be if someone having a grudge for some minor reason could accuse one of witchcraft! The power this gave to cruel and ruthless persons was frightening!

Thankfully, I was living in an age that was much more forgiving. I could only imagine the fear that some of these folk must have experienced. How terrible when you could never be sure whom to trust! And how sad for all those around them! The witch hunts effectively sent wise women into hiding. How many lives in the general population could have been saved had they been able to call on one of our competent healers or herbalists?

Some of the bravest ones decided to pursue their calling despite the risks, but they did so far away from Havn and the clan. The local lairds, more enlightened than most, usually had one of us working for them. In secret, naturally. No one, besides them, ever knew where this person had come from. All magic and healings were done covertly. Not even they were brave enough to openly flaunt that ridiculous law and bring those rabid zealots down on their people!

Since 75% of those accused of witchcraft in Scotland were women, the clever lairds had a well-paid doctor. But he was not the one doing the actual healing. He served just as the front and ran the hospital ward. Even the treatment room looked just like any other; it had all the usual nightmare medical equipment of the time. But it had a hidden door leading to a well-stocked pantry. Many of the remedies it contained are still used by my people today.

What might have aroused some suspicion had it not been so cleverly accomplished was that no one was ever allowed to witness what was being done, not even the patients. A sleeping draught or a touch on the forehead sent them into a deep slumber, allowing the 'nurse' to do her job. The results spoke for themselves, and the clan members trusted the medical staff. But what lengths the local lairds had to go to just to take care of their people until the ridiculous persecutions of those believed to possess powers finally ended!

In Scotland alone, estimates put the number of those executed for witchcraft by strangling or burning to over 2,500! That awful law was finally repealed in 1736. But even then, our clan did not change its modus operandi. Anything magic for outsiders continued to be kept strictly separate from Havn. For many years, traveling wagons were used to distribute some of our potions and goods among our neighbors without them ever knowing where they had come from.

Today, we sell these items in quaint stores. Those are a treasure trove for the enlightened! However, just as a precaution, they appear unrelated to the Magnuson Clan. Old habits die hard!

During our lessons, Mæva, who had traveled extensively throughout Scotland, shared the heartbreak she had seen that resulted from the witch trials. We grieved for all the innocents who ran afoul of this atrocity. After hearing the tales, I appreciated that we still hid most of our powers to this very day. The only abilities we displayed on special occasions could easily be explained away as tricks or sleight of hand.

Even after hundreds of years, trusting those who were different from us was still hard for my people. Understandably so! On several occasions, Mæva had impressed upon Eldred and Hilda the importance of hiding their abilities. From the very beginning, it had been our way. Finna had seen to that, but the precautions had gotten lax over the centuries.

Mæva herself had seen too much death of people like the girls at the hands of the zealots. To reinforce this, she had me tell them what I had read about the witch trials. To hear the full horror of those events had made quite an impression, even on Revna, who had joined us for the occasion.

Once Mæva had driven home her point, she showed us more ways to cast a spell without anyone realizing what we were doing. I was familiar with many of them but did learn a few new tricks that had not been passed down through the family. When I finally returned home, I would share all this knowledge with the clan historians. They were always happy to get more information about the past!

However, all of us, even Mæva, were a bit baffled. The time trap had been created to hurt our clan! Instead, so much good was coming out of our meeting each other! Never before had we had such detailed accounts of the lives of Finna, Bjørn, and their children! Or of Eldred,

Hilda, and Cedric! This was not what the caster had intended. Was Bo the one responsible for all the benefits we were gaining? I was not sure, but I suspected as much!

That was another thing I might want to ask him about when I saw him. I filed that thought away for later and resolutely brought my mind back to the present.

Our procession was moving along at a sedate pace. This gave me plenty of time to observe our surroundings. And to listen. The songs the kin were singing were beautiful. They were old friends of sorts and reminded me of Ny Havn. Over the years, I had heard them many times. Therefore, I knew them word for word. A few decades ago, the decision was made to share them. So, during every public solstice celebration, those from the outside world get to enjoy them as well!

Being this far from home and from the man I loved with all my heart and soul, the melodies brought me comfort. I lost myself in the music and quietly sang along. Hilda squeezed my hand. She instinctively understood what I was feeling and how much I missed Phillipe. I, in return, sensed the same pain in her. My heart went out to her. She loved one man but was about to wed another! What must that feel like?

I admired her for being so brave and going through with her and Eldred's original plan. Much had changed for her since she had agreed to become Cedric's wife, and still, she did what needed to be done. My respect for this young lady increased even further. Would I have been able to leave Phillipe behind? I truly hoped that I would never be forced to find out!

Suddenly, I realized that we were just about to reach our destination. A large loop of the wide trail led to the bottom of the flattened hill where the mead hall and the chieftain's house were located. The wedding was to take place on its broad top. As we got closer, more and more people lined the sides of the path. The smiles of gladness for the sisters' good fortune were genuine.

It was obvious that the girls were well-loved by their clan! The camaraderie and closeness that I sensed in these folk warmed my heart. No wonder they would not just survive the coming years but thrive! The bond between the kin ran deep, and they worked together for the good of all. I felt genuinely proud to be a Magnuson and a descendant of these remarkable people!

Finally, after winding our way up and up, we reached the top. As was customary then, Eldred, Hilda, and I would stop in a circle made of spruce. It had been laid out just where the path flattened out. The second we entered, I could sense the magic. I knew that the girls were now safe. They felt it as well, and we exchanged relieved glances. With some reluctance, we let go of each other's hands. I missed the contact almost immediately, as did they.

For a few minutes, we waited patiently. Finally, the cheers from the crowd told us that Eldred's and Hilda's future husband, dressed in his finest, was on his way to greet them. I was almost filled with as much anticipation as they were, even if Hilda's was tinged with sadness. She and Bo had intended to have a lighthearted flirtation, but it had become so much more! She had fallen deeply in love with Bo, and he with her, something they had not anticipated.

For a moment, I wished we could have found a way for them to be together outside the Meeting Place we had created. To be honest, I admired Hilda for going through with this wedding. Her word was her bond. She had been well raised and knew what was expected of her, even if it cost her the love of her life!

The girls' father had been the previous ruler of the Magnuson Clan. Just a few weeks ago, on a sea voyage, he and his wife had perished during a gale. With one fell swoop, these remarkable young women had become orphans. The rest of the clan had rallied around them and seen to their needs while they grieved. But life had to go on. Fortunately, the marriage between Eldred and Cedric had been arranged long ago, and her father had named him the successor.

The young man loved his wife-to-be and genuinely liked her younger sister. The three had grown up together and knew each other well. He was kind and attentive and would do just about anything to please his bride. Having a compassionate nature, Cedric genuinely understood Eldred's sorrow. He was prepared to do whatever was necessary to make her feel better.

No arrangements had been made for Hilda's future. Her parents wanted to let her choose the man she would spend her life with. Now, this was to her disadvantage. Since she was not yet of age, the decision of who she would marry suddenly involved her future brother-in-law. Being nobility, the choices were few, and none she found acceptable. Most were too old or too young. Or lived too far away!

The sisters had dreaded the idea that Hilda would have to wed one of them. Also, they had not wanted to be separated so soon after losing their folks. Sharing a household had sounded much better to them. It was a little unusual, but the inhabitants of Havn were isolated and willful enough to make their own rules, especially where their chieftain was concerned.

Therefore, on the girls' request and with the approval of the Magnuson Council, Cedric had agreed to marry both Eldred and Hilda. In addition, being the husband to two of the previous chieftain's daughters would further solidify his position as the new ruler. It had been a win-win for all three of them until Hilda fell in love with Bo.

Chapter 40

Cedric

While we had walked down the path hand in hand, I had sensed Eldred's excitement about the upcoming wedding as well as Hilda's trepidations. She knew that she had conceived. Would she tell Cedric? Before she had met Bo, I had been greatly impressed by their attitude toward their future together. The groom, Hilda, and Eldred had a lot of respect and admiration for each other. They had regarded their forthcoming nuptials as a great honor and a blessing for them all.

Being extremely close, much more than most sisters, the girls liked the idea of spending their lives together, even if this meant sharing their new husband. Cedric would not treat them as property as so many other lairds would. The men of Havn had not been like that since Finna's time. Having been a prisoner of Bjørn's father and forced to flee, she had made sure of that! Thanks to Finna, none of her female descendants had to fight for their rights!

Besides, with so many of us having exceptional magic abilities, we just had to stick together! We had some truly unique talents show up occasionally. Treating each other with respect is vital among our people since you never knew what latent capabilities a person had until they felt challenged!

Our clan firmly believed that when one party oppresses another for any reason, it breeds anger and resentment. Nothing good ever came of such an imbalance, and that we did not want, nor could we afford it. Someone who felt abused or powerless might not care about the consequences and be tempted to betray their people. On the other hand, being able to stand up for oneself gave one confidence. Therefore, it was written in our private clan charter that every girl and boy should know how to use a weapon and have equal standing.

This has served the kin well during confrontations and seemed to keep the peace in the households. Knowing that your wife can defend herself is a great discouragement of violence in a marriage! Just like the men, our women have the right to make their own decisions. And they tend to help each other. Woe to the guy who mistreated his lady! He better sleep with one eye open until he has made amends!

Finna had been instrumental in making gender equality part of the original charter. And she had made sure that those without magic were not discriminated against either. Everyone was equal, and their voices were heard. Men and women received the same education, partook in battle training, and were taught how to run a household. They worked side by side for the betterment of all.

From their stories, I knew that Eldred and Hilda had been pampered by their parents but had also been well-educated. Their father had hired the best tutors he could find for the clan. All the youngsters had learned everything a man or woman might need to know, including swordcraft. The girls, however, had practiced in the mead hall, out of sight of any prying eyes since their neighbors were not as progressive as they were. This had limited them.

Hilda was much more feminine in some ways than Eldred, who had loved practice bouts. Being very intelligent and eager to do exceptionally well, the sisters had worked hard at it all. And they had learned more in the time trap! This made them valuable allies for Cedric. He, in turn, provided them with an additional measure of protection and security. Few outsiders would dare offend the wife of the chieftain! The situation was a win-win for all three.

From our history, I knew that Eldred, Hilda, and Cedric worked well together. They made a remarkable team and did a lot of good for the clan. Personally, I found their attitude rather extraordinary. They were so selfless and giving, always concerned with how something affected others. I could not imagine sharing my husband!

But then again, I did not have sisters, which has always saddened me. Especially after seeing Eldred and Hilda together and being around them! I hoped that I would be able to stay for their wedding.

Finally, after what must have been several minutes, the crowd opened up and formed an avenue leading straight to where the three of us were waiting. I watched curiously as the groom stepped into the circle to greet his brides. He did look just like Phillipe, except he seemed rather frazzled! Having both his brides vanish into thin air must have had something to do with that!

The siblings curtsied, as did I. Cedric deserved to be shown the respect due to his rank, even if he could not perceive it or me. Or so I thought! Having only eyes for the sisters, especially Eldred, it took him several seconds before he noticed that someone was there with them. Now, this we had not expected! Instinctively, he took a step back and went for his weapon.

Realizing he was aware of my presence, I raised my hands to show him I was unarmed. After a few moments and the girls' reassurances, alarm gave way to curiosity. To be honest, I was just as surprised as he was! We had not expected Cedric to be able to see me at all! No one else had this far! The young man instantly noticed that I was not one of the ladies from the clan nor a visitor. My dress was similar but still different enough from the gowns of the rest of the wedding party that it clearly marked me as an outsider!

"Who are you?" he exclaimed.

His attendants outside the circle instantly went on the alert at his words. But they, unlike him, could not see me. This left them looking around in confusion. Noticing this, Cedric waved for them to stand down. After bowing to the chieftain again to show my respect, I met his eyes. He and I regarded each other for a long moment. My heart gave a painful lurch. He and Phillipe were distantly related, and Cedric reminded me so much of my husband it hurt!

The girls had not been kidding about that! As I had suspected from the picture in the mead hall and their comments, the two men resembled each other so closely that they could have been twins! Cedric and I continued to stare at each other. The world around us had fallen away, and I was not sure what I was feeling. There was definitely a magnetic attraction between us! He sensed it as well and was slowly moving closer.

Eventually, however, I remembered why I had come in the first place. I turned my attention to the girls. Stepping between them, I took one of their hands into each of mine. We moved forward together, just as if we had practiced this part!

"I am Cara Magnuson, and I present to you the ladies Eldred and Hilda Magnuson, your brides-to-be. May your lives be long and happy!"

With this, I placed Hilda's and Eldred's hands into his. Since Cedric did not strike me as all that hospitable, and the magnetism between us was rather unnerving, I prepared to leave.

"Farewell, dear ladies, and may your wisdom shine through the ages!" I told them formally and curtsied to each.

Hilda immediately started crying, begging me to stay. That gave the groom a start, and he eyed me even more curiously. I was just about to leave when he called to me.

"Wait! You say you are a Magnuson, but I do not know you. Just who are you?"

"One who is trapped in an enchantment, just as these two were, working on making my way back home."

With this, I turned again and, with a heavy heart, walked slowly away. I hated leaving so soon and had hoped to have a little more time with the girls.

"She saved us!" Hilda exclaimed. "Please, Cedric, can she stay for the wedding and maybe a few extra days?"

Eldred added her plea to her sisters. Cedric, unable to deny his brides anything, decided that there was obviously a story here. Also, he was more than a little curious by now. Therefore, he sprinted after me and grabbed my arm just as I was about to step outside the circle of spruce.

"Please, will you stay for the festivities? I sense much wisdom in you and fear that Eldred and Hilda will never forgive me if I let you leave. I would be grateful if you forgave my suspicious behavior. Your presence was rather unexpected!"

I looked up at him and considered his request. Cedric reminded me so much of my husband that it made my heart ache. How could I refuse? Besides, his invitation had been made with such sincerity! And his comment about sensing had made me curious. There was much more to this man than just a mere warrior!

"Cedric, I would love to stay, but I am only visible inside this circle. Once I step out of it, the magic ends," I regretfully explained.

"I can only see you within the circle of spruce?" Cedric asked with some incredulity.

"Yes. That seems to be part of the enchantment. Step outside, and you will see!" I answered.

Cedric's expression went from utter disbelief to incredulity as he left the circle and came back in. Then, his face became thoughtful for a few seconds before it lit up. Something seemed to have occurred to him!

"Not a problem!" he declared with a broad grin.

A man of action, Cedric immediately gave the order to create a larger sacred space. I observed that his people obeyed him with alacrity. Once the work was well underway, he turned to me once more. With him being this close, the effect was devastating! For a moment, I felt like I was drowning! The attraction between us was undeniable. Right then and there, I knew if the situation had been different, he and I could have been lovers. But I was married, and he soon would be!

Finally, he tore his eyes away. He let them slide up and down my person instead. His gaze lingered appreciatively on my curves. The magnificent, dark blue, silver-trimmed velvet ball gown perfectly accentuated them. It had been the closest thing Bo had provided me with to what the girls were wearing.

Therefore, I had chosen it for this festive occasion. It did look amazing. But now, it felt much more confining than I remembered. I could barely breathe! Looking down in puzzlement, I realized just how tightly it suddenly hugged each curve! The effect was very alluring!

"As beautiful as that dress is ...," he finally muttered.

Words seemed to have deserted him. I could tell he liked what he saw, maybe a little too much, judging from his pants. Not being able to help myself, I gave him a wicked smile. Eldred and Hilda, who had watched our exchange, started to giggle and moved closer.

"It appears that he might not be able to keep his eyes where they should be if you wear that!" Eldred teased.

"Yes, you have quite an effect on him," Hilda giggled with a knowing glance at the front of Cedric's trousers.

The poor guy seemed used to their taunting, but he did turn a bright shade of red. This had the sisters chortling with mirth. I decided to come to his rescue.

"Maybe it is best if I wear one of the girl's dresses for the wedding!" I suggested. "Eldred, we are of similar size. May I wear one of yours?"

"If that means you get to stay, I would love it!" Eldred informed me. She thought for a moment. "Cedric, would you please have one of the women fetch my dark-green gown from the house?"

"Happily," the much put-upon bridegroom replied.

Cedric called one of the women over to just outside the circle and whispered in her ear. After nodding her understanding, she rushed toward the large house that was obviously the chieftain's residence. A short time later, she returned with a beautiful emerald-green dress. It was almost as magnificent as those Eldred and Hilda wore but not quite! I was delighted with that!

I had never intended to outshine the girls at their wedding! Therefore, I was more than happy to change into something a little less curve-hugging and revealing! This time, the woman stepped into the circle. She paused for a second when she saw me. Understanding dawned in her eyes, and she hurried over to join us.

After a brief introduction, she held the gown out for my approval. I absolutely loved it and said so. In response, Eldred, Hilda, and Cedric assured me how pleased they were that I would stay.

"Maybe it would be better to get changed before the rest of the clan can see you?" Hilda suggested with a snigger.

Leave it to her to find all this highly entertaining! I looked around to see what she meant. Only then did I notice that the larger circle of spruce boughs was almost completed!

"Please, take our honored guest by the hand and show her to the lodge so she can change. Do not lose contact with her; just lead the way and assist her!" Cedric addressed the smiling lady who was still holding up the dress.

He pointed toward a magnificent log building. It took me a moment before I recognized it as the mead hall. All I could do was stare! The logs had the same incredible reddish color and sheen as the houses! If I told my father how it looked in 1616, he would see it as a personal affront that it was so diminished under his administration! I was sure that he would not rest until it was restored to its former glory! I would have to make sure to take a picture of it!

"Oh yes, and please hurry!" the girls added, drawing me out of my contemplation of the stunning structure. "As soon as you get changed, we can get started!"

Quickly, I laid my hand on the offered arm of the woman. Staying in physical contact would ensure we did not lose each other. And it was a prudent precaution. We promptly headed for a secluded room in the sair.

It took me a bit to strip off that super formfitting dress. At first, it did not want to come off. Fortunately, my companion could assist me, but having to keep one hand on me at all times made this a challenge. I finally managed to wiggle out of it. It most certainly had not seemed that tight going on! As a matter of fact, now that I thought of it, it had been comfortable and rather loose! Did Bo have anything to do with this? Or one of the girls?

I had barely slipped into the borrowed gown when my companion let out a gasp. She could feel the magic flowing around us! Just in time! I needed help with the lacing, and that took two hands! Since I was much less endowed than Eldred, we had to snug things up a bit, but very soon, the fit was perfect. I took a glance in the looking glass and was glad to see that this dress was nowhere near as seductive as the blue one had been!

How it had turned into a sex-bomb dress was a mystery that I intended to solve! My gut told me that Hilda was the culprit. Cedric definitely had quite a reaction to me, and she had pointed that out rather boldly. Was this her way of laying the groundwork for her confession about Bo? Did she want him to understand that some attractions can be almost impossible to resist?

We all knew it. If given half a chance, Cedric would have claimed me as wife number three in an instant!

Chapter 41

The Wedding

Once the last bough had been laid down and the circle of spruce was completed, its power took effect. All of a sudden, I was visible to everyone within it. Due to its magic and Bo's spell, I could now interact with these people! That would make staying here much more pleasurable and cause much less consternation when someone noticed the girls talking to what they believed to be thin air. How delightful to no longer feel like a ghost, invisible to all but Eldred, Hilda, and Cedric!

Once some of those present noticed the stranger coming from the mead hall, they alerted the rest. The muttering grew progressively louder. Good thing that I had enough time to change! At least now I looked much more like I belonged! Hurriedly, I rejoined the girls. The whispering grew even louder. Everyone was wondering who and what I was and where I had come from.

After a moment, Eldred held up her hand for silence. Since most of those present were curious about what she had to say, the noisy babble ceased almost instantly. All those present were regarding the three of us expectantly.

Eldred gave a brief explanation of what had happened to them and how they had gone missing from the procession. All those near them had seen the smoke and could confirm its existence. She introduced me as a distant cousin they had met in the time trap. Since the girls wanted people to accept me and feel thankful for my role in their return, Eldred made me the heroine of their rescue.

To my embarrassment, she told all those assembled that without my help, they would still be stuck in that evil enchantment. My presence might have been the catalyst for some changes in the construct, but I also firmly believed that Eldred and Hilda would have eventually found their way back without me. They were just too resourceful not to! However, the way Eldred made it sound, I was some sort of a superhero who had single-handedly transformed the hive into a more welcoming place.

His arm wrapped around the girls' shoulders, Cedric shot me a grateful look, but I could sense he had questions. He was smart and clearly suspected that more had happened than Eldred was sharing. But, he was also wise enough to not bring this up in public. It would have undermined her authority. However, I was sure we would get a private interview later! As chieftain, he needed to be aware of all the details.

Once Eldred was done with her story, she answered a few questions. Some of these she responded to only in vague terms. Finally, in true Eldred style, she firmly declared that she wanted to get on with the festivities. After all, she had been waiting for this wedding for weeks and was more than ready for it to proceed! However, the kin's curiosity was not yet sated.

Thanks to Bo, the sisters looked absolutely stunning. The gowns they were wearing, his parting gifts, were just magnificent. Eldred's was made of shimmering dark green velvet. It was similar in shade and style to the one she had worn when she entered the time trap, except much more ornate. Bands of intricate silver stitching adorned the neckline, wound around her upper arm, and ran under her breasts. The effect was absolutely magnificent. In addition, small, clear gems had been sown into the decorations and sparkled all over the skirt every time she moved.

The dress was a priceless treasure. Eldred had been beyond delighted when Bo had presented it to her. She had been speechless for a moment, and tears had flooded her eyes. Since she was so choked up that she could not utter a sound, the happy bride hugged him to show her gratitude. When she could finally speak a few minutes later, she had promised to cherish the gown forever.

Eldred had every intention of passing it on to her own daughters. The dress would be so prized that it was mentioned in our private history. It would come to be called the 'Magic Frock' and loved by every woman who owned it. Each one would eventually hand it off to her own girls. During its existence, it would see plenty of weddings and balls until one day, a couple hundred years from now, it would just disappear.

The magic in the weave had preserved this glorious creation for a very long time. A picture of it still existed in the clan's private journals. Eldred would not be the only one to get married in this striking gown. As part of its enchantment, it made every woman who wore it look even more radiant than she already was. And she would feel absolutely on top of the world! What better way to start one's life with one's husband than feeling like an outright goddess?

Hilda's present was almost as splendid but had been carefully selected not to upstage her older sister. Its dark-red bodice, black sleeves, and skirt offset by ribbons with intricate gold stitching complimented the girl's pale complexion and blonde hair perfectly. The care that had gone into its making screamed of Bo's love for the young woman, and I was sorry that Cedric, instead of him, would be handfasted to her!

On Hilda's insistence, Bo had been the one to help her get dressed instead of one of us women. We all understood that these two wanted a few more minutes to themselves. No one had said a word that this took much longer than it should have, not even Eldred.

Once the people of the clan got a closer look at what the girls were wearing, any doubt about Eldred's story vanished in a flash. The gems on the green dress alone were worth a fortune and inspired the appropriate amount of awe! Also, Hilda carried their original gowns in a bag and pulled them out to show them. They had once been gorgeous, but weeks in the time trap had soiled them considerably. They would need a good cleaning or two to be restored to their former glory!

Being used to odd occurrences and magic, the kin readily accepted that Eldred and Hilda had spent several weeks in the hive. They had no problem believing all she had shared about that strange place. Most regular folk would have been much more skeptical or thought it all made up. These people, however, just wanted to know more. The malevolent enchantment was something none of them had come across before.

The account of the girls' misadventures aroused such curiosity that several individuals forgot all about the festivities! They started asking some very technical questions. Eldred grew flustered when things got more and more specific. She did not want to give anyone enough information to duplicate that spell! Cedric, picking up on her discomfort, decisively reminded everyone that this was a wedding and not the right time for all these inquiries!

After that, the subject was finally dropped. Many of the clan swarmed around us to welcome the girls home and hug them. Everyone was glad that they were back and unharmed. Those in the procession had gotten quite a scare when the two disappeared in front of their eyes! Since they were familiar with enchantments, they instinctively knew that something awful had happened and that the smoke was responsible.

Any attempts to follow them had been for naught. Several brave individuals had tried several times. In the end, even the wisest had to admit they had no clue where the girls had come off to, nor how to fetch them back! So they had given orders to do the one thing they could think of. The search of the area had been more to make people feel like they were doing something than anything else!

The most powerful among those who witnessed the vanishing felt in their gut that Eldred and Hilda were no longer in their dimension. Therefore, their safe return added additional joy to this festive occurrence. But, for a little while longer, it kept distracting the kin from the planned event - the wedding! Eventually, when no more explanations were forthcoming, all the excitement started to ebb a little. At last, the clan was ready to get on with the business at hand!

By now, the sun was no longer shining. Clouds had moved in, and it was threatening to rain. That, however, was not a problem, especially since the circle of spruce had been extended to enclose the buildings. So instead of being conducted outdoors, the ceremony was moved into the mead hall. The practice session had been held there the night before, so everyone knew just what to do.

Even the last-minute change Eldred insisted on was taken in stride. This was her and Hilda's special day, and whatever they wanted, they got! With their parents gone and no other close family members, the girls had decided I should walk them down the aisle. They had named me cousin but explained that we had grown to be more like sisters, and I was to stand in as a relative. I felt incredibly honored by their request.

Therefore, with great solemnity, I got to walk Eldred and Hilda toward the dais down the wide corridor between the assembled kin. People bowed and curtsied as we moved past. Under the beautifully decorated pergola, Cedric was waiting for us with the official. The structure had been carefully carried inside, and as I got closer, I could sense its magic. Every plant and flower that adorned this graceful structure added to its power!

And it was visually stunning as well! Cast iron rods had been twisted and welded together to form an exquisite arch that allowed for the attachment of herbs and blossoms. It was rather heavy but easily carried by several strong men. I had only a few seconds to admire this magnificent creation before we reached our destination and the smiling groom. The fragrance filling the air around us was heavenly!

With a deep curtsy, I presented Eldred and Hilda to Cedric. Then, as was the custom, I ceremoniously placed their hands in his. My task accomplished, I stepped back to stand across from his best man. A moment later, the ritual began. Fascinatedly, I watched as the clan's priest began the handfasting. I was entranced. The rite was almost the same one we used in my lifetime!

It reminded me so much of the day I married Phillipe that it hurt my heart and soul! How I wished that he could be here with me now! A history buff, he would have absolutely loved this! As it was, he was always digging up stuff on our ancient practices, but that did not compare with being present at one!

After a brief reminder of the sanctity of marriage and each person's responsibilities and duties, the priest led into the ancient ritual itself.

"We are here today to join together these three people in marriage," the official began.

"Cedric Magnuson has chosen to make Eldred Magnuson and Hilda Magnuson his wives. Please present your joined hands."

The three brought up their hands toward him.

"Cedric and Eldred, do you enter into this union out of your own free will?"

"I do," Eldred declared proudly, beaming at Cedric.

His response echoed hers, but the groom seemed lost in his adoration of the stunning vision his beautiful bride presented. Their eyes locked, and they shared a gentle smile. The love with which these two regarded each other just warmed my heart. They made such a handsome couple! That man adored Eldred and would do anything for her!

Cedric treasured her enough to bring her little sister into their communal life. Gladly, he had agreed to care for and protect them both! I was so happy for them that a tear escaped my eye. So much for not crying at weddings! Until that moment, I had never understood what that was about!

Once both had agreed to the union, the ceremony continued.

"Eldred and Cedric, let this cord represent the connection between your two lives. As your hands are bound together by this cord, so too will your lives be bound together in marriage."

The priest ran the thin ribbon over their joined hands, then tied it loosely around their wrists.

Taking their hands in his, he spoke the age-old blessing:

"These hands are the ones that will love you.
These hands are the ones that will support you and reassure you through all your years.
These hands are the ones that will catch you if you falter and provide you with encouragement.
These hands are the ones that you will work and create with.
These hands are the ones that you will use to build your life together.
Your vows form the knots of this binding.
Your promises form the knots of this binding.
Hold these in your hearts and uphold them each day through your actions.
As all those in the ages before you, so do you now hold the making or breaking of this sacred union in your own hands.
Remember and never forget!
Just as your hands are now bound together, so too are your lives."

The officiating priest then turned to Hilda and repeated the ceremony. The girl did her best to smile but could not keep tears from running down her face. This should have been Bo, not Cedric, she tied her life too.

Once Hilda had also been bound to Cedric, the age-old part of the ritual was completed. Phillipe and I had opted for rings, but some did not. It was not required for the rite to be legally binding, but many couples liked to have that reminder of their vows on their fingers. What choice had the girls made? I figured Hilda was much too fond of precious, glittering things to have passed on this opportunity!

As I had suspected, Cedric's best man stepped forward when the time came. On a dark blue velvet cushion, he had three magnificent rings. Since the groom was all tied up, it would be up to him to see them placed on the girls' fingers. Once again, the master of ceremony raised his voice.

"It not being possible to be always physically joined, you will give to each other these rings to symbolize the connection between you. May you wear them as a reminder of the sacred bond you share as husband and wives!"

The best man solemnly slid the jeweled bands he was holding onto each girl's finger and then onto his friend's. Then he stepped back to allow the newlyweds to raise their bound hands high into the fragrant air. The room erupted in happy cheers, and together, almost as one, the three stepped forward to accept the congratulations and well wishes of the clan's people.

As they walked past me, I got a better look at the rings symbolizing their unusual union. They were just plain gorgeous! The stones on Eldred's were green, the ones on Hilda's blue. When they raised their bound hands again, I noticed that the ones on Cedric's band were a dark red, probably garnets. All three must have been made by a master craftsman! Each ring sported an intricate design that most likely suited the person, a tradition we still uphold to this day!

Always curious, I could not wait to get a closer look. The band I wore had a mermaid on each side wrapped around the beautifully faceted aquamarines that offset the large moissanite in the middle. Smaller stones shone all the way around it. We had opted for moissanite rather than diamonds since those stones are much more brilliant. I just adore their sparkle and love that I am not supporting an industry I have concerns about!

Phillipe's band has two lions that look like they are holding the magnificent center stone in place. Unlike mine, the large gem was recessed into the white-gold metal, making the entire creation regal and manly.

The wedding ceremony was incredibly moving, and yes, I cried unabashedly. Eldred, Hilda, and Cedric finally slipped their hands out of the bonds without untying the knots. The cords were handed off to the best man and me. Our job was to keep them safe until they could be hung in the bed chamber later that night. But first, there would be the celebration. Having been around the Highlanders since Finna's generation, we loved parties almost as much as they did!

The revelry that followed made our solstice celebrations look relatively tame. Some sort of drink I tried very carefully flowed freely and seemed to have quite an effect. It was a bit too bitter and strong tasting for my pallet. Being around so many strangers, I did not feel comfortable losing control. I didn't believe anyone would intentionally hurt me, but still! Their customs differed from those I had grown up with!

Anyway, getting drunk is not my thing, and whatever was being passed around would most certainly get me there rather quickly! Especially since I rarely drink! When I do, it is usually champagne or wine. I can't help it; I am spoiled. Phillipe sees to that. He knows that I really, really prefer the bubbly stuff to just about any alcoholic beverage! When we celebrate something, he always produces a bottle!

People mingled while the tables were set out. Then, the delicious wedding feast was served. I was invited to share the spotlight with Cedric, Hilda, Eldred, and the best man, a delightful character named Dorian LeClaire. He and I soon discovered that we had several topics which interested us both. A most satisfying discussion resulted that was finally brought to an end when the tables were cleared and removed.

The dancing that followed the meal was such fun! The girls declared themselves my teachers for the more intricate movements. Phillipe and I love to tango, but this was very different! Several times, when I messed up royally, we collapsed onto nearby chairs with helpless laughter. After a few minutes, Cedric came to join us. The clever Eldred immediately had him take me for a spin.

From then on, I learned the steps very quickly so that I could partner with other people. It was best to not be that close to that man!

He reminded me too much of my Phillipe for comfort! One dance had been enough! The effect we had on each other was incredibly disconcerting to me. My body responded to Cedric's nearness almost as strongly as it did to my beloved husband!

The attraction we felt did not seem to bother Cedric. Or the girls, for that matter! It was not something I would act on, but still, it was there. And, it was powerful! I would have to watch myself around him!

Chapter 42

Two Very Alike

Cedric was a striking figure of a man, well-muscled, tall, and strong. It was obvious that his dark hair and strong features had been passed on to many of the males in the Magnuson line, including my Phillipe. As a matter of fact, the resemblance between the two was uncanny! Another reason to avoid any type of alcoholic beverage! I could not afford to lose control or forget that this was not my man, especially since Eldred and Hilda kept encouraging us to dance together. The siblings really wanted me to stay, even if this meant sharing their new spouse!

My presence and knowledge would benefit the clan to a considerable degree. Still, I would never truly belong here or be fully present. The enchantment had seen to that, and not even Bo could change that. Me being here at all and being able to interact with the kin had already severely stretched his abilities. Besides, I had work left to do. The time trap could not be left to regain power, and there were more people to set free.

The girls knew all that, but Hilda really wanted me with her. She loved me, and she was scared. Would Cedric realize that the child she carried was not his? Would he even care? He loved Eldred and would do anything for her, including raising a babe that was not his own. Would it be better to tell him the truth from the beginning or keep that little tidbit to ourselves?

I usually opted for honesty, but this was not my choice to make.

I was honored by Hilda's love for me. And by the trust she placed in me. Eldred was so strong and independent that she would be just fine. However, her younger sibling was a bit overemotional at this time. She had a secret she had shared only with me and faced some hard decisions in the next few hours. I was glad I could be there to support her, but staying here was not a viable option.

Instead, I would ensure the clan had the necessary knowledge to thrive, including medical and sanitary. Needing a few minutes to myself and thinking that Cedric was well occupied with his new wives, I slipped outside. It was still raining, and the air smelled cool and fresh. The fragrance of the trees and wet earth was much more to my liking than the odor of food, drink, and sweaty bodies inside the hall!

I found a spot to sit and settled in, happy to have a little time away from all that commotion.

"Not slipping away, are ye?" a very male voice uttered right next to my ear.

Needless to say, I jumped. This I had not expected! Cedric! He had followed me out!

"No, I am just enjoying the rain," I replied with a smile.

"You are a strange lass. I do not care much for all this wetness!"

"It reminds me of home," I explained.

"You miss it, then?"

"Very much so. And I miss my husband."

I figured there was no better way to let him know I would return to where I belonged than that.

"I understand. Eldred says he looks just like me."

"He does."

"Enough to pass for each other?" Cedric asked curiously.

"Yes, easily," I informed him.

He and Phillipe were incredibly alike, especially in the semi-dark!

"How are we different?"

"Phillipe is a man of his time, you of yours. My husband has a liking for well-tailored suits and perfect haircuts. And he smiles more. Not having an entire clan to worry about might have something to do with that!" I told him with a laugh.

Stepping even closer, Cedric bent down so we were eye to eye.

"I love Eldred. She is an amazing young woman. But you? You spark something in me that I do not understand. My soul recognizes yours. I feel drawn to you," he confessed, to my surprise.

"We call that soul mates," I began.

Then, deciding to be as honest as he had been, I added.

"I feel the same about you. Like I know you and always have, always will."

"Yes! Exactly!" Cedric agreed.

"I believe that we are part of a soul tribe that reincarnates together time after time. We are not meant to be together in your current lifetime, but in mine, we are."

"That, at least, is some consolation," he responded, chuckling drily.

"Two wives are not enough for you?" I teased.

"I am sure I could handle a third, but you, you deserve to be the only one. That I cannot offer," Cedric stated with a tone of regret in his voice.

How well he understood me! Yes, I could share with the girls, but it would not be my bliss. I loved the one-on-one connection I had with Phillipe! We had no walls up and no need for any since we were each other's 'Safe Haven.' There really wasn't room for anyone else in that exclusive, intimate connection. We were there for each other, the main priority in each other's lives. Best friends, lovers, as well as adventure and activity companions.

"I would never want to share you," Cedric mused quietly. "How then could I expect this of you?"

Silence fell between us as we continued to regard each other. The attraction between us was intense but also tinged with the sadness of knowing this possibility could never be explored. Not surprising! We were never even meant to meet in this lifetime! With a sigh of regret, Cedric finally turned his gaze away.

"I better go see what the girls are up to. Will you join me?"

"I will come in in a bit, I promise."

Cedric whistled. One of his men appeared out of the shadows.

"He will watch over you but not intrude," he declared firmly.

When I was about to object, he held up his hand and explained.

"This is a wedding with lots to drink; things get out of hand. You are precious to me and mine. The girls would never forgive me if I did not make sure that you were safe!"

"In that case, I thank you," I told him sincerely.

With one last smile, he turned and went back into the hall. I stayed where I was, deep in thought. My silent protector took up his station a few feet away and melted into the shadows. I would not have noticed him if I had not known he was there.

As I sat there looking out into the rain, my mind flashed back to my life. Cedric was extremely handsome, a competent warrior, and a very perceptive and understanding man. He was exceptionally well-built. That I had not missed! To top it off, from what I had observed, the guy was as good as gold. His gaze never lingered on the other attractive women of the clan, only on the girls and, occasionally, on me. He was a genuine treasure, just like Phillipe.

The two were very similar, and not only in looks and mannerisms. Their personalities were not that far apart either. Both were strong and good leaders but also gentle and kind. If I had not already believed in reincarnation, I did now. I realized that Eldred, Hilda, and Cedric were all part of my soul tribe, traveling through time together. Except, I did not appear to exist in this timeline! Or did I? After contemplating this for a moment, I decided that I did not.

Our immediate closeness started to make more sense now. Our souls had recognized each other instantly. I had always felt that Phillipe and I had known each other through time and had been together in one way or another before. Cedric was one of those reincarnations, but he was not my Phillipe. That one waited for me at home, and once I got back there, I would do everything in my power to undo the damage that nasty spell had done!

It was interesting to note that the two men's behavior differed in some ways and was similar in others. Phillipe saw me as exceptionally capable and someone he could depend on just as much as I relied on him. He knew very well that I could protect myself if I had to, especially since he had helped me to further hone those skills. If someone made the mistake of assaulting me, they would regret it!

Cedric, on the other hand, was much more protective. He regarded us females as something that needed to be looked after, indulged, and cherished. Both were very respectful and loving and made excellent mates. As much as I appreciated Cedric assigning me a guard, it had been unnecessary. But he could not have known that, and I was his honored guest.

But then, when I considered this a bit more, I realized it was probably for the best! Me, a stranger, beating up one of their own might not go over well! And getting into a fight in this beautiful dress was less than desirable. Having someone watch over me avoided unnecessary unpleasantness. The smart man had seen that all along! No wonder he turned out to be such a successful chieftain! Still, things were different here, as was Cedric's relationship with the girls.

I genuinely liked the equality I had in my marriage, especially since Phillipe knew precisely when I needed to lean on him. According to Eldred, women here had the same rights as men. However, from my observations, I concluded that the division of labor was more defined than I would have been comfortable with.

Therefore, I very much preferred my own love, time, and place. I liked the freedoms I had, my car, and my ability to travel. And, to be honest, I missed having any and all information I wanted at my fingertips! But most of all, I longed for Phillipe.

My mind wandered back to the fateful night of the summer solstice so long ago.

The first thing I noticed when I spotted Phillipe at the solstice celebration was the elegance and style he had developed. He was hard to miss. Curious, I kept watching him from my spot on the balcony. He had changed, but I liked what I saw. He was so calm and competent as he moved through the room! Knowing instinctively where to find me, he soon joined me. It did not take long for me to be thoroughly impressed with who he had become.

Phillipe was confident and self-assured but without appearing arrogant, which served him well in his profession. After our rather electric greeting, we started talking. Or had tried to. We had not seen each other in a while, so there was much catching up to do. The mead hall had been so noisy! Having to shout to be heard had not made for good conversation, and we were each curious about the other.

Therefore, we soon wandered off to a quieter spot. The little grove we hid in was a much better spot for talking! Surprisingly, I was instantly incredibly attracted to him, even more so than I had been as a teenager. After a few minutes in his presence, I made a stunning discovery. Around him, I felt safe and totally relaxed!

That was my first clue that what we shared was something special. I was intrigued enough to want to explore the possibility and start courting. We had always gotten along beautifully, but now an indescribable magnetism existed between us. I am not the kind of girl who kisses a guy on the first date, but with Phillipe, I was more than prepared to make an exception!

If I am honest, it might have gone even further than that all on its own, the chemistry was definitely there, and the night was pure magic! However, thanks to my parents, we never got the chance to let things develop naturally. Instead, our romance commenced at hyper-speed! But all worked out beautifully in the end, so maybe it was time to finally completely forgive my folks for their interference!

My husband and I live in different worlds, but we understand each other and make it work. He is a talented lawyer who would have made a capable diplomat. I am a successful author with my head in the clouds. Even when we were children, Phillipe accepted me as I was, which has never changed. I felt so blessed to share my life with him. He did not seem to mind that my way of dressing was unique and not quite as sophisticated as his.

As an eccentric artist, I picked whatever pleased me at the moment. It was usually tasteful, classy, and elegant but often very different from what everyone else was wearing. This had driven my mother to distraction! Phillipe, however, loved me for me. He was more than prepared to support and encourage my expression of self even when it differed from what he would have chosen.

Shortly after we got together, we discovered that we enjoyed shopping together. Therefore, we usually combined those trips to London with a few nights spent in a nice hotel, an opera performance or the ballet, and some leisurely bumbles through town. I introduced my husband to some of my favorite places to acquire clothes, there, in Ny Havn, and in Gairloch, and he me to his.

Phillipe actually made some incredible finds at the second-hand stores I preferred. I, in turn, ended up with some gorgeous outfits at the high-end stores he frequented that cost nearly as much as his suits! Our marriage was a blending of two worlds that worked well for the two of us!

Due to our differences, Phillipe and I are seen as a rather unusual but very happy couple; the artist and the lawyer. And, because we were pleasant and intelligent, we were considered good company. This opened many doors for us, including some important ones. Ultimately, this greatly benefitted the sale of my books and games. Eventually, it led to the production of a movie based on one of my novels.

My husband was as supportive of my writing as I was of his career, and we complemented each other well in most areas. He educated me about the intricacies of law and marketing, and I encouraged him to relax more, including when it came to his clothes. After all, Phillipe was just as hot in camping gear as in the tailored, black suits he usually wore! Keeping my hands off him was difficult, no matter what!

My attraction to him had not waned over the years, and I loved Phillipe's expressive face. He was incredibly handsome. To me, he was the most attractive man I had ever laid eyes on! After he and his family moved away from Ny Havn, I kept up with him and his career through the clan's newspaper. However, that summer solstice celebration, seeing him in person? I was stunned! He no longer looked like the gangly young man he had been as a teenager!

The last time we had been together before that magical evening, Phillipe had been rather shy. He had acted very self-consciously around me, and it had taken a lot to draw him out, but I had been determined. And, I had succeeded. That incredible night of the solstice, he was nothing like that! I was pleasantly surprised by how much he had changed! The confidence oozing off him was beyond sexy!

Once we started talking, we 'clicked' almost instantly, something that did not escape my parents' attention. Somehow, we were elected as the summer king and queen. The attraction between us was already intense, and the drugged wine had done the rest. As a result, it turned into quite a celebration! However, even without that, we might have gone there before too much longer! The magnetism between us was too powerful to be denied!

The coronation ceremony was usually not legally binding, but due to my father's guile, it ended up so for us. Since we had been tricked, we could have fought the marriage contract once we found out. But by then, we were deeply in love. We both had homes but felt it was best to have one that was ours. Besides, mine was too close to our parents, his too far away.

Thus, we went house shopping. Before long, we ended up buying a place somewhere in the middle, on the Isle of Arran.

In some respects, Phillipe and I were polar opposites when we first met. Not only was he a classy dresser, but he was also neat and always looked immaculate. I, on the other hand, had pets. Getting out of the house without at least a few stray hairs somewhere was a challenge, even if I did get dressed in the foyer! To my surprise, maybe even to his as well, he had quickly fallen in love with every one of my furry friends!

Seeing him with my pack for the first time, how kind he was to my animals, and how much they liked him was one of the defining moments of our relationship. Right then, he totally won me over! Any reservations about us going forward together I might have had evaporated at that instant. They were replaced with a sense of belonging and trust I had not experienced before.

Since Phillipe had no pets, I had not expected him to adore mine as much as I did, but he surprised me. Within just a few weeks, he could not imagine his life without them! He was the one who insisted on including them in most of our vacations which meant much to me. Hiking with the pack was just more fun and always entertaining! Besides, having them along made both of us happy.

Time has passed, and those beloved pets have since crossed the rainbow bridge. They are still missed by us both.

These days, Phillipe and I shared our home with Arianna, Bear, Hella Rose, Micha, and the guinea pigs Teddy and Orion. My husband spoiled them even more than I did, which is saying something! However, the suits and our German Shepherds were an interesting combination, but Phillipe handled this with his usual, efficient style.

A no-stick spell kept the black fabric immaculate, even when one of the large dogs rubbed all over him just as he was heading out the door. The youngest, our Hella Rose, liked to weave between his legs to cover as much surface as possible. She is brilliantly smart and does not like it if any of 'her' family leave. Usually, our furry cohort accompanied us almost everywhere we went. With them along, life was never dull!

So, we have had to fish the dogs out of the water a time or two while sailing! That is what lifejackets with handles were for, and the hoist on the boat! Or they decided that their humans were too slow and swam ashore. That had happened to us more than once! And let's not forget those occasions when we ended up with mud all over, or soaked to the skin!

No big deal! We perfected a couple of spells to get us all dry and clean in an instant! And some others to repel water and fur-proof our clothes, cars, and furniture! That, however, did not deter Hella Rose! She was mischievous and liked to use us as a towel after a swim! This usually turned into a game that led to much laughter as Phillipe and I tried to avoid her. She thought this great fun!

Her brother, Bear, usually joins in the fun, and even Arianna and Micha like to enter the fray. By the time we were done, everyone was pleasantly tired! Life with our little family feels complete, and all of us are thriving. My husband and I work out together, play together, and support each other to ensure that everything runs smoothly. We make a fabulous team!

Having one's love returned in equal measure is the most magical thing one can ever imagine. Thinking of Phillipe made my heart sing, but it also filled me with deep longing. However, it did help to tamper down the intense attraction to Cedric! After a few more minutes of enjoying my solitude, I finally returned inside, my guard in tow. Since he was an attractive young man and physically quite imposing, I felt perfectly safe dragging him out on the dance floor!

Initially, he was a little reluctant but soon warmed up to the opportunity to relax and have some fun. He was a competent dancer, and it was easy for me to follow his lead. Thus, we had a great time. But by then, not everyone was still in possession of their faculties, and he had to remove a drunk or two who thought to push himself between us.

Things were getting even more boisterous as the evening progressed. People continued to bump into us, so my partner and I gave up on our dancing. When he escorted me back to the table, I discovered I was not the only one to take refuge there! Cedric, the girls, and the best man had all fled the melee some time ago! The newlyweds were about ready to retire before the party really got out of control! They had been waiting for me.

Once Cedric signaled that he and his wives were ready to withdraw, an impromptu procession formed to accompany them to their home, which had been lovingly decorated by the other women. The three were escorted all the way to their bedroom by this drunken mob! Since I did not care to return to the party without them, I volunteered to help the girls undress. Eldred liked the idea and promptly sent everyone else away. The servants happily returned to the mead hall.

Once the brides were ready, Cedric joined us. Wanting to give them privacy, I was about to retire to the small bedroom where I would be staying when suddenly Hilda wrapped her arms around me and started crying. Eldred and I exchanged a concerned glance over her head. I realized then that thanks to the older sibling's powers, she was aware of her sister's secret.

The only one in the room who did not know was Cedric. And I was sure he realized this was more than just mere wedding night jitters!

The three of us waited patiently for Hilda to compose herself. I gave her what comfort I could. When the hiccups finally subsided, Cedric bid us to join him at the table. He had been busy while Eldred and I tried to calm Hilda. Cups of steaming tea were waiting for us.

"Hilda, my sweet, what has you so upset?" the groom began gently once we were all seated.

Clinging to me like her life depended on that connection, she finally met his gaze but could not find the words. Instead, she buried her face against my chest and refused to look back up.

"Eldred, the story you told of that awful trap was not complete, was it?" Cedric finally asked.

"No, it was not, but some of the other things that happened were for your ears only. I shared as much as I felt everyone else should know, but no more. May I tell you now or later?"

"Since something has Hilda so upset, it is more important at the moment than me bedding you, so please do," came the dry response.

With those words, Cedric rose in my estimation even more. He could have taken both girls first, as was his right, but instead, he was more concerned with the reason that so upset Hilda! No wonder he would turn out to be such an exceptional leader! We sat quietly as

Eldred filled him in on more of the details, but she did not give away Hilda's secret. That part was not hers to tell!

"You two have been through so much! For those here, you were only gone a few minutes, but for you, it was weeks! Months even! You really do believe you would have never returned had you not met Cara?"

"I am certain of it. Our meeting with her was the catalyst that somehow changed everything and gave birth to Bo," Eldred stated with conviction.

"And this Bo, he is a real man now?"

"Yes, but he only exists inside the enchantment and in the space we created," I explained.

"How very sad! To be imprisoned like that! Is there something we can do for him?" Cedric inquired.

At his words, Hilda raised her head. The expression on her face was one of disbelief.

"You would help him if you could?" she stammered.

"Yes, I would. You love him, do you not?" Cedric replied calmly.

"How did you know? Eldred did not say!"

"No, she did not, and she did not have to. I grew up with you, and I know you!" Cedric responded.

"Please, forgive me! I wanted to tell you but did not know how!" Hilda cried.

Cedric came over and knelt down before us. Ever so gently, he raised her head so that she had to meet his eyes.

"Sweetheart, I am not angry with you. I knew that something had happened when you were shaking like a leaf and kept evading my eyes at the handfasting. You are an honest person. Keeping a secret is not something you are very good at!"

"I am so sorry," Hilda sobbed.

"No more holding back, you two!" Cedric addressed the sisters. "Now tell me the rest!"

"Eldred does not know!" Hilda exclaimed.

"Yes, I do," her sister disclosed. "I figured it out right after we got back!"

"Seriously?" Hilda uttered, truly surprised.

"Yes, and I do understand why you would not share this with me, but it did hurt me," Eldred admitted. "Have we not always confided everything else to each other?"

"I am so sorry," Hilda sobbed and opened her arms.

Eldred rushed over and hugged her. Now both were crying. Cedric, always kind and compassionate, wrapped his strong arms around them. He gave them what comfort he could.

"You are with child?" he asked quietly once they had calmed.

"Yes," Hilda sobbed.

"Cara, I know Bo is waiting for you in the nexus, but can you call him to the space you created?"

"I would not have to. The alarm on the portal would let him know someone arrived."

"Would it be possible for me to go there?" Cedric inquired.

"Yes, we can take you," I assured him.

"Please do. But just you," he commanded.

Soon, Cedric and I were comfortably lying on the bed side by side, our hands clasped. I centered myself and took him to the Meeting Place. He was pretty impressed with the magnificence of our surroundings as we made our way to Bo's house. The atmosphere was peaceful, and the landscape was quite beautiful in the bright light of the moon.

The door opened immediately when we knocked. It seemed that we had been expected.

Chapter 43

The Decision

Bo greeted us in the doorway. He was dressed very nicely and looked very handsome, but his eyes were red-rimmed. He had obviously been crying. Cedric gave him a look full of compassion. An understanding passed between the two men, and I could sense their instant liking for each other. Once we were invited in, Cedric entered the house ahead of me. The warrior in him had to ensure there was no danger here. He looked around curiously, as did I. Hilda had obviously had a hand decorating this place!

Cordial, as always, Cedric saw me seated first before broaching the subject of Hilda. The following conversation was difficult for both men. I listened quietly as they discussed the best way forward. Once again, I was deeply impressed by the young chieftain's kindness, understanding, and empathy. Unlike many would have, he held no grudge toward the man Hilda had fallen in love with but instead tried to find a way for them to be together.

We discussed this at some length but could not come up with a viable solution, so we ended up calling in Mæva and Revna. Since they were anchoring the gate, Bo made it possible for them to see and communicate with us from the nexus. Once introductions had been made, we explored possibilities.

Unfortunately, even with Cedric coming up with some clever suggestions, none of us could devise a way to allow Bo to fully enter our world.

The five of us were not ready to give up. We kept examining various options, but the suggestions were getting more outlandish by the minute. Eventually, Cedric brought up the possibility of Bo using his body on occasion. Bo was so moved that tears flooded his eyes. The gesture of trust that he had just received meant much to him. To be able to touch Hilda and to be allowed to be with her and explore our world was the greatest gift anyone could have presented to him!

Since sharing was the best alternative we could come up with, we decided to set down some ground rules. Boundaries are essential in any relationship, but especially in one like this. The agreement we finally hammered out would still need to be approved by Hilda, but I was sure she would be delighted. She would have the best of all worlds: physical closeness to the man she loved, her sister, the protection of a doting husband, as well as the opportunity to visit Bo and spend time with him in the space we had created.

Once a few more details were addressed, we were ready to return to the girls. We thanked the ladies and said our goodbyes to our host. Eldred and Hilda looked at us expectantly once we sat up. The hope that shone in their eyes said everything, and I was glad that we had found a way for the lovers to be together, even if it was not ideal.

"I can perfectly understand you falling in love with that young man," Cedric began. "He is not only very handsome but genuinely loves and adores you. We had a long talk and have come up with a way that would give you two a semblance of a life together. I am so sorry that that is the best I could do."

Cedric clearly felt like he had failed Hilda! What a remarkable man! He would do anything to make his brides happy, even if that meant giving one of them to another guy! Needless to say, I was very impressed. And he knew it! When the girls were not paying attention, he shot me a conspiratorial grin that changed to a questioning expression. A clear invitation!

I gave him a look stating very clearly that, as much as I liked him and as maturely as he had handled Hilda's situation, I was not about to become wife number three! But I did soften it with a smile. He was just too likable to do otherwise! The smolder I earned in return reminded me so much of Phillipe it took my breath away!

Once he had laid out the plan, both girls had tears in their eyes. They were so grateful they just kept hugging him. Agreeing to the proposal was easy for Hilda. Having Cedric's approval to continue her love affair with Bo meant much to her. She gladly agreed to be a wife to both men. We decided to hold another handfasting ceremony in the privacy of their bedroom while Bo temporarily inhabited Cedric's body, thus making them legally wed.

Since we could not physically enter the space we had created, she should not be able to conceive another child by Bo, but she was ok with that. As far as the clan was concerned, Cedric was her husband, and he would claim the child she was carrying as his. All he wanted in return was for her to give herself to him this night so that he would not have to live a total lie. He was, after all, an honest man!

"I want you to bed me. Right now," Hilda declared vehemently.

"As you wish," Cedric replied, lifting her onto the bed.

That was my cue to leave, even though Cedric did not seem to care that I was still present. He had just freed his member and pushed up Hilda's nightgown when I dashed out the door. I could feel his eyes on my back as he prepared to enter the girl. I knew what he wanted, but it was not something I was willing to give. I did not belong in this time nor this place, and Phillipe was my lover, not him!

Resolutely, I headed to my own bedroom. I was suddenly incredibly fatigued and missed my husband with every fiber of my being. Still, all the noises from the bridal room kept me awake for a while. Cedric seemed to know very much what he was doing since the sounds of delighted giggling were interrupted by passionate moaning and screams of release. Even Hilda seemed to be having fun, and I was sure that the inexperienced Bo would be learning a thing or two!

It did my heart good to hear those three genuinely enjoying themselves, but it did make me miss Phillipe all the more! My body screamed for his attention, and knowing that someone who looked just like him was pleasuring the girls not far away did not help. It had been weeks, and I was only human! It would have been easy to allow Cedric into my bed; he was more than willing. And, his wives were amenable to sharing since they were still hoping to entice me to stay.

But Cedric was not my husband. No matter how much I craved physical closeness, it would have felt too much like cheating to make love to him.

The festivities outside continued until the early morning, but once I finally managed to slip into slumber, I slept through it all. I woke refreshed and ready for the day. After getting dressed, I joined the others in the kitchen. As soon as I entered, the girls rushed over to hug me. Both looked happy and glowing. The frown lines on Hilda's brow were absent for the first time in days. I was glad to see that.

Eldred returned to her spot on Cedric's lap. She wiggled herself into place, eliciting a groan of frustration from her husband. The look she shot me was pure mischief. I had an excellent idea of that maneuver's result. After all, I loved doing it to Phillipe! Not that it took much, but the girl was learning to keep him wanting more fast! From what I had heard the night before, he was one virile young man!

Just like any other family in the village, we had breakfast together. Never in my life, except with Phillipe and his kin, had I felt so much like I belonged. We talked and joked and had a wonderful time.

I could easily get used to living in this household! So much love abounded within this home that no one would ever feel left out or unwanted!

As can be expected, Cedric had many, many questions for me. Once the dishes had been cleared away, we got down to business. Or tried to. Once again, my cellphone with all the pictures on it turned out to be a huge distraction! He wanted to see everything, but we had to be careful with the battery. Since it was no longer being held in stasis, it had started discharging.

Cedric, however, was not the only one interested. The cook, while placing a large pot of tea on the table, caught sight of a photo of Phillipe. She exclaimed in wonder.

"He looks just like our Cedric!" she stated, astonished.

"Yes, he does, does he not?" I agreed.

"I am much more manly," Cedric protested, flexing his arms.

This elicited laughter all the way around.

"Yes, you are," Eldred appeased him. "Want to borrow him for a night, Cara? For comparison? After last night, Hilda and I could use a break!"

The hopeful look on Cedric's face was so endearing it almost was my undoing. My traitorous body most certainly liked the idea of making love to this man! Our eyes met and held. I could see the hunger in their depth. Part of me wanted him just as bad, but I took my marriage vows seriously. I was Phillipe's and Phillipe's alone and only in our time! If not for the time trap, Cedric and I would have never even met! That growing desire needed to be denied no matter how much I wanted to give in! And how many times he was pushed my way!

"I am not sure how Phillipe would feel if I took you up on your kind offer," I stated firmly.

"Well, he is yours any time you want him. And look, he is all ready for you!" Eldred laughed, raising up for a moment to display the bulge in her husband's pants.

"He really needs seeing to," Hilda agreed. "It would be a shame to waste that! Are you sure you do not want to relieve his torment, Cara?"

"Girls! It would feel so wrong! I would be cheating on Phillipe! Please stop," I begged.

"We are sorry," the two uttered, but they did not look at all contrite!

Hilda and Eldred were very much enjoying themselves, but they did have ulterior motives. The sisters had not given up on the hope that somehow they could tempt me to stay.

"Well, we cannot leave him like that! Come along, Cedric!" Hilda ordered, dragging him off to the bedroom.

Soon after, we could hear the bed creaking all the way into the kitchen as those two had their fun!

While Cedric and Hilda were otherwise occupied, Eldred and I sipped our tea. The folks in Havn had always been different. Even to this day, many see nothing wrong with having a good time at our summer solstice celebrations. Some even exchange partners for the night! However, I was surprised that Eldred and Hilda were so unencumbered by society's rules to offer me the use of their husband!

"Relax!" Eldered told me when she saw the perplexed and a little worried expression on my face. "It seems that you are more uptight than we are! You are family, and sharing Cedric with you is our pleasure. He is a very lusty male and has been well taught how to please a woman by the same maid who serviced my father."

"Your mother approved?" I asked curiously.

"Oh yes! Since she did not want him to father more children, she wanted him so satisfied that he would never even look at another woman," Eldred explained. "She raised us to be understanding and accepting of physical needs. How about yours?"

"My mother is very different," I stated diplomatically.

Eldred just gave me a look. I guess in that aspect, I have always been more conservative. Before the night of the solstice, when I made love with Phillipe, I had not participated in the summer king and queen ceremony. I had known that the couples had sex to celebrate the occasion and had therefore avoided it. Also, none of the men from the clan had interested me enough to want to go there until Phillipe showed up again in my life!

It was common knowledge that the punch was spiked at that boisterous event, so I avoided it altogether. My parents did not, but still, my mother was always proper. She would drag my father off into the chamber reserved for them, and they would not reappear for some time. Making love out in the open or joking about it as if it was the most natural thing in the world, like we had been doing this morning, was just not her thing!

Eldred and I talked about various subjects. I could see that she was tempted to go join her sister and husband but did not want to leave me alone. But the continued sounds from the bedroom were getting to both of us, and she was growing more fidgety by the moment.

"Go!" I finally told her. "I am going to take a nap!"

"A nap?" Eldred laughed. "Is that what you call it? You could join us!"

She knew exactly what I would be doing! I had to take the edge of this sexual tension before I let Cedric do it for me!

"Enjoy!" the girl tossed over her shoulder as she was racing to join in the fun. "And if you change your mind ...."

It was sometime later before I returned to the kitchen. Eldred showed up shortly after, looking happy and satisfied. She informed me Bo was getting a turn and that the others would be out in a bit. We made tea and continued our chat. Or tried to. The sounds of pure unadulterated pleasure coming from the bedroom kept interrupting our train of thought!

After a while, it seemed that those two lovebirds were experimenting. Only one of them could be heard at a time, and there was no more creaking! This had Eldred and me so curious that we almost went and took a peek! But we decided to honor their privacy. The moans that continued to drift down to us were really something! Hilda making love to Bo sure sounded quite different than when she had been with Cedric!

Finally, Hilda and Cedric rejoined us. Eldred and I could barely suppress a snigger since they both walked a bit funny. Kind of stiff-legged! Just what had she and Bo been up to? We exchanged an amused glance. Should we ask them? Whatever they had been doing, from what we had heard all the way to the kitchen, they had clearly enjoyed it!

Seeing our puzzled expression, Cedric immediately volunteered to show us. I declined graciously, but Eldred almost agreed but then changed her mind. As she saw it, there would be plenty of time to play with her husband once I was gone! Especially since her sister seemed to be so sleepy that she was uninterested in our conversation!

Hilda was so very relaxed she ended up curling up on the bench! She was out within seconds! For a few moments, the rest of us watched her in amusement. Cedric yawned, but at least he was able to stay awake! He, Eldred, and I started discussing how to best take advantage of the time I would spend with them.

We ended up making a list and got started right after lunch. By then, Hilda was awake again.

Chapter 44

The Secret Meeting

Now that Cedric was no longer as distracted, he turned out to be just as shrewd as my husband, and Phillipe is a highly successful lawyer! Yet another thing that they had in common! His inquiries were right down to the point and extremely well thought out. The young chieftain was looking ahead and trying to find ways to better the lives of his clan members. The pictures of Phillipe and I in our time had given him ideas.

In return for sharing valuable information on various subjects, I discovered much about the lives of the folks in Havn. However, I was careful about what I told the girls and Cedric. Too many technical advances too fast might alter the course of history. Once I explained this, they all understood. None of us wanted Phillipe or me not to be born or for me to return to a world that I no longer recognized! And, I would be the only one to know the difference! That alone would make readjustment a challenge!

Therefore, we decided that all the knowledge I shared would stay between the four of us. Cedric was intelligent enough to implement any improvements he considered necessary carefully and in such a way that they could not be traced back to the clan and Havn. With the witch trials going on, a settlement full of people possessing magic could not afford to draw attention to itself!

We discovered that we had much to learn from and about each other during our discussion. The cook kept us supplied with food and tea but otherwise stayed clear. She was obviously well-trained and very respectful. Since Cedric had given the order that he did not wish to be interrupted, we talked until late in the evening and reconvened right after breakfast. Thus, the first couple of days just flew by.

It was good that I was there and not just to share knowledge. The girls were raised in the country and had been told about marital relations. Still, they had questions. I explained some of the things to Eldred and Hilda that their mother would have. As a result, we grew ever closer. At the wedding, they had introduced me as their cousin. Somehow, this felt right. We were family. Our experience in the nexus had bonded us, and we would miss each other terribly once I returned to the time trap.

Staying, however, was not an option. I missed Phillipe more than I could say. Especially since I was around someone who looked very much like him and was him in a previous life! I could not help but feel a growing attraction to Cedric, and it was getting harder not to act on it. On several occasions, I had to still my hand as I was just about to reach out and lovingly touch his face as I did with my husband!

I knew that I could not stay much longer. The more I got to know Cedric, the more I admired and liked him. And the more of a danger he became to me! Giving in and yielding to my desires would have been so easy! But how could I face Phillipe after that? We had promised each other to be exclusive, and we had meant it! Our marriage was built on trust. Even if Cedric looked just like my husband, making love to him was still a betrayal!

To make things even more challenging, the two men were very alike, and not only in looks. Cedric and Phillipe even moved similarly! They reminded me of relaxed but alert mountain cats, always ready to react if they sensed danger. They turned their heads the same way, and their voices were almost identical! For me, it was growing more difficult to keep them apart. Every time Cedric called my name, my heart sped up just like it did with my husband!

They did differ in ways, but much of this was due to the era they lived in. Phillipe, at least on the outside, was calm, cool, and collected. He was very civilized and had an air of elegance that had many a woman do a double take. Superbly healthy and fit, he walked with the easy grace of a dancer or fighter, someone supremely comfortable in his own skin. My husband was warm and helpful around others but kept his private life to himself. Joking about it like his ancestor did was not his style.

Cedric was just as competent, attractive, and kind, and he was a superb leader. He was more down to earth than my stylish Phillipe, who loved to wear black suits. When he was working, my husband was very much in control of his emotions and facial expressions. Cedric was much easier to read, at least most of the time. However, I had seen him retreat behind a mask of quiet reserve when the situation demanded it.

He had really reminded me of Phillipe then! They even smiled the same way when they were happy and relaxed. To sum it up, Cedric was a younger, more muscled, and a little rougher version of Phillipe but exceedingly likable. Both men were wonderful husbands, and Eldred, Hilda, and I agreed that we were fortunate to have them in our lives.

The four of us got along so well that no one would have guessed that we had not been together all our lives. Or that I was not wife number three. Cedric most certainly would have been up to the task! From what the girls told me, his stamina was indeed something else! They continued to make great efforts to draw me into their play, hoping

I would stay. I did my best to turn them down without hurting their feelings.

However, every day I was around the newlyweds and listened to the sounds of lovemaking coming from their bedroom, I missed my husband more. When I finally made it home, I was not going to let him out of our bed for a day! Or at least a few hours! I could not wait to get some relief from all this sexual tension! And I longed to be near him.

The sensation when Phillipe held me was incredible. It was like nothing I had experienced before! When he wrapped his strong arms around me, I felt like I was floating in a sea of bliss! It seemed like I was being filled with fire, light, peace, and happiness all at the same time! It was like becoming one not only with each other but all of creation. We usually slept close together, sat right next to each other, and walked hand in hand because we enjoyed the connection.

Even at the premiere of my first movie in Paris, we had stayed in physical contact. Phillipe had kept his arm around me, his hand on my waist. He had instinctively known how nervous I was. His solid chest against my right shoulder and his quiet, calming presence next to me had allowed me to shine my brightest while giving autographs. My husband truly was my rock, and I loved him with all my heart and soul.

But Phillipe and my pets were not the only reasons I could not stay. As I had suspected, I lacked visibility outside the circle of spruce! For now, it was being carefully maintained on Cedric's orders, but over time, that vigilance was sure to lapse. Once it was breached, I would just disappear. We had checked on that, just to be sure. Hilda had insisted on holding my hand as we stepped over the circle. Good thing that she did!

She had been the only one able to see me, probably because we were in physical contact with each other. I feared if she let go, everything around me would freeze. I would no longer be in sync with their time! I doubted that stepping back into the circle would undo the damage. My gut told me it would not. At that point, I would have one option left. I would have to return to the time trap without even being able to say goodbye. That would break the girls' hearts! And mine!

Eldred and Hilda had been terribly sad when we confirmed our suspicion. Even if I wanted to, it was impossible for me to remain with them. At least we still had the Meeting Place and could keep up with each other's lives. However, as far as Eldred and Hilda were concerned, that was a poor consolation for losing their adopted sister.

To prevent the girls from dwelling on the inevitability of my leaving, I kept them busy. One thing we did in the privacy of their home was practice the spells Mæva had taught us. Both siblings were very powerful, but especially Hilda. Cedric was very impressed with their progress. He attended as many of our sessions as possible since he liked to watch them. And learn. Being a true Magnuson and well-familiar with magic, he was thrilled that his wives had the gift!

Discovering that they had such special abilities immediately set his mind in motion. He came up with multiple ways that they could benefit the clan. And it made him cherish these talented young women even more. As far as he was concerned, they were a treasure and should be treated as such. Anything they wanted, they got! I was rather amused. Those two had their husband even more wrapped around their little fingers than I did Phillipe!

Cedric extensively talked to us about the benefits their capabilities would bring to the kin. He had grand plans for all his people, those with magic and those without. But, neither Eldred, Hilda, nor I had forgotten about the warning Mæva had drilled into our heads. If anyone from outside the clan found out about their abilities, it might bring trouble down on Havn.

Those fanatics powering the witch hunt were often tipped off by individuals motivated by greed, envy, or misguided religious fervor. I believe that they were not at all concerned if someone was innocent or guilty! If a person was in their way, or these zealots or their friends had something to gain by removing them, their victim would be found guilty.

Most of the trials were a total sham, the evidence fabricated or based on ridiculous superstitions! The best thing for our clan was if that lot stayed far away from us! We discussed these implications with

Cedric at length. Being a shrewd ruler, he decided to take preventative actions.

That night, Cedric called a secret council. He invited those people he trusted implicitly. Once all were assembled, he swore everyone present to secrecy. He had Hilda use her magic to implant a compulsion to ensure the oaths were unbreakable. Nothing that would be discussed that night would ever leave the room, especially once we made sure that no one could listen in.

To my surprise, Cedric laid it all out. I really respected him for that. Not many chieftains were as honest as he! He even revealed my true origin to ensure they knew where he had gotten the information from and that it was valid. This led to many questions that the three of us answered patiently. Naturally, once he mentioned it, everyone wanted to see my cell phone and the dress I had arrived in. I was happy to indulge them.

Once the groundwork had been laid, we shared Mæva's lecture with them, including the history of the witch hunts to come. That alone was enough to shock most of them. They had all heard the rumors but had assumed they were an exaggeration. This was Scotland, after all! People here were just not like that! Reality hit them hard, but they appreciated the intel. Forewarned is forearmed!

Most of those present had magic or were wed to someone who did. They were wise enough to see the dangers of jealous people and envious neighbors. Keeping their abilities hidden from even some of their own kin seemed best to them all. The village had a few new people who had not been there when the girls' parents had placed the enchantment. Nothing stopped them from giving Havn's secret away, especially if they or their loved ones were threatened!

But even if they did not have a clue about the magical abilities of the Magnusons, so many poor souls who ran afoul of those horrid individuals would make up all kinds of stories to save themselves! The group considered this revelation carefully and decided that each person who had joined them or would in the future be placed under the same spell as the rest of them had been with one addition. They would not remember unless they did get into trouble.

Keeping people's nature and gifts hidden was difficult. Accidents happened. And, without practice, how would budding sorceresses like Eldred and Hilda learn to control their powers? Nothing gave a person away faster than having some wild magic floating around! And, what good was any of it if they could not successfully use it in case of an emergency? In addition, Hilda, Eldred, and some of the others needed guidance if they were to fully develop their skills.

Ideas were batted around and discarded. In the end, one of the men proposed to bring in an enchantress he knew. They would do so under the guise of hiring her as an advisor for Cedric. That, after all, was an acceptable practice in this part of the Highlands, and no one would think twice about it. Once she was in residence, she could clandestinely teach all those wanting to develop their talents. A vote was called for, and the motion was passed.

Once the decision had been made to bring in the wise woman, it was time to address a painful subject. Could they trust all those in the village to keep a secret? The furtiveness of the meeting, in itself, answered that question. Most of the kin were good folks, but there usually were some bad apples in every lot, even among the Magnusons. We were especially concerned about a few individuals who had married into the clan lately. Any of them could be a danger.

Unfortunately, several people immediately came to mind. They had already attracted my attention with their churlish behavior. If anyone would cause harm to the rest, it was that lot. Since I knew about the other properties the clan had acquired around that time, I brought up the possibility to subtly, and if need be, with the use of magic, encourage those persons to settle on one of those.

Cedric, naturally, thought the idea brilliant. He decided that they would start another trading post surrounded by a few homes on one of the parcels far enough away to discourage frequent visits back to Havn. They would offer a bonus to all those 'volunteering' to build the new settlement there and give them all the help they might need to get started. One of the men immediately volunteered to oversee the project.

Hilda cleverly suggested using a subtle enchantment to keep them there. Cedric liked her idea. The only people who should be going back and forth would be those who could be unreservedly trusted. In that, we were all in agreement.

Once that issue had been dealt with, Eldred brought up the possibility of folks being questioned and tortured. She wanted some way to help these unfortunate ones withstand the pain while keeping them from making false accusations. Her parent's spell gave death as the only way out. She felt that this was too extreme. Most of the others agreed, as did I. There had to be a better solution!

After some discussion, it was decided that everyone in Havn and the trading posts would be subjected to a carefully crafted enchantment designed to aid them in case of that kind of trouble. We set down some of the basic parameters, but the details still needed work. The sorceress Cedric was going to bring in would surely help to polish it up. However, we had made good progress for one night's work.

A problem is not as overwhelming, and one does not feel as helpless if there is some action to take. Now that Cedric and his friends had a plan, they felt better about things to come.

Chapter 45

The Enchantress' Arrival

Once the decision had been made, it was amazing how quickly it was implemented. Cedric was definitely a man of action! The enchantress arrived the very next evening! Since I remembered her name from our history, I was happy to meet her. Geira Sorunsdottir was not only extremely powerful but also incredibly motherly and kind. She was just what the girls needed! She and I liked each other on sight. Knowing that she would be there to look after Eldred and Hilda once I was gone made me feel so much better!

When she heard about the spell I was still caught up in, the sorceress took me aside for a private conversation. She made sure that we were not overheard. Geira felt that the less was known about these kinds of despicable enchantments, the better. There was no need to provide anyone with the information that would allow them to use such horrid magic! The kin were good people, but even they might decide that a spell that collects the fanatics driving the witch hunt was a good thing!

Not that I could blame them! Even I might have considered it in their situation! Without those zealots, the world would be a better place, but they did have lives, parents, and families. One cruel act does not justify another! Unfortunately, anger or fear can seriously affect someone's judgment. It can even make the most gentle of souls do something that they would later regret. Therefore, the less the kin knew about the time trap, the better!

Geira felt that teaching us how to get out of such an enchantment differed from explaining its makeup in detail. But her instincts told her that if I was to succeed in shutting it down, I would need that knowledge. Therefore, we dove in, but first, she made me swear a binding oath that I would never cast it myself or share it with another. I was only too happy to oblige her since that presented an additional barrier, just in case I ever got tempted to try it!

Over the next few hours, I learned things I would have preferred to remain innocent of. That incantation was even nastier than I had thought! And the price the witch had paid! How much hatred and desperation must have driven her to do this! I was glad that I had brought the girls home and that they would not be with Revna, Mæva, and me when we confronted the inner workings of that foul construct!

Even more than before, I now understood why Bo had wanted to separate himself from that spell. It truly was an atrocity! That such a remarkable being could be born from such a vile seed was a genuine miracle. Geira was confident that such a thing had never happened before. That young man was one of a kind! However, not even she, with all her wisdom, could think of a way of fully bringing him into our world other than sharing Cedric's body.

During our talk, Geira imparted everything she knew about these kinds of traps to me. She was a true fount of helpful information! The more I learned, the more I realized that it would be best if the knowledge of how to cast such an evil enchantment faded from everyone's mind. We had been so lucky that we had managed to turn the situation in our favor! Things could have turned out very differently!

By the time we were done, my head was spinning, and my respect for Bo had grown even further. During Geira's lesson, I realized that whatever had caused him to become conscious had been an extraordinary event. The greatest miracle, however, had been him rebelling against the malevolent incantation and his intended nature! His personality could have just as easily gone the other way!

Bo could have become the undisputed evil overlord of the hive with god-like powers! As such, he could have made our lives a living hell! Instead, he had chosen to embrace the light!

The girls gave us a curious look when we joined them for a snack a while later. Geira gave them a brief explanation of what she had told me but without going into depth. She quickly turned the conversation to another subject and had us roaring with laughter before long. The distraction worked so well that the young ladies forgot all about the time trap, at least for the moment. Cedric joined us for the evening meal, and the conversation around the table grew even livelier.

Eventually, all of us made our way to our beds. Geira was now part of the household and had been assigned a room close to mine. We dropped Cedric and the girls off at their chamber and headed for ours. Once we were alone, the enchantress gave me a couple more tips to remember. There was much we would have to look out for once we reached the very center! And we might have to protect Bo!

Needless to say, all this information tumbled around in my mind. As can be expected, I had a hard time falling asleep. Once I returned to the hive, so much depended on us getting things just right! Hilda would be heartbroken if something happened to Bo! The rest of us also cared for him deeply. He was so special and had become a good friend!

To get my mind off the subject, I considered all the vital things I would share with the kin the following morning. Finally, my eyes closed of their own accord.

The new day dawned brightly. After breakfast, we assembled in one of the larger meeting rooms. This morning, not only Geira, Eldred, and Hilda would be attending, but several people from the clan would join us as well. I started with the subject that would be most helpful to them all - health. Carefully and in terms they could understand, I told them everything I knew about disease and how to prevent contagion.

This led to a lengthy discussion about ways to better living conditions in the village. Cedric, who had been there to introduce me at the beginning of my lecture, was determined to improve his people's basic hygiene. I made several suggestions that met with his approval, especially since they were easy enough to implement. Knowing how many women died during childbirth due to unsanitary conditions, that topic was dear to both of our hearts.

Hilda was already pregnant, and the way Cedric was going at it, it was only a matter of time before Eldred would get there as well. In easily understood terms, I explained the dangers of introducing bacteria into the womb or into a wound. Everyone listened intently. They had all seen the results but had not understood the cause until now. Even Geira was fascinated by all this new information. She came up with several ideas that would help the clan tremendously.

Some of the concepts I shared with those present would be cautiously taught to the rest of the clan. Unsurprisingly, a few things were initially met with skepticism. So I explained them at great length and why they were important. It was not easy to put everything in terms that those present comprehended! Some of the data I presented would not be fully understood until hundreds of years later!

Once I clarified the issues and the attendees were able to wrap their minds around them, curiosity won out. Suddenly, they decided to take full advantage of my knowledge and the benefits it would bring. More and more questions came my way, and I tried to explain the details the best I could. Good thing that tutoring at the university had prepared me for this! Some of the students needing a lot of extra help had forced me to think outside the box!

Cedric was very thoughtful throughout my lesson. His quick grasp of these totally new concepts was astounding! The questions he asked were intelligent and well thought out. Several times, he and I got into a fascinating discussion. Some of the subjects we ended up addressing went way beyond what I had initially shared with the group. The entire room would grow quiet and listen. He and I got so involved in our in-depth dialogues that everything around us ceased to exist.

As a result, we ended up delving much further into some of the topics than I had intended! Cedric was cleverly milking me for all the information he could get, and I knew it. But how could I deny these people and the girls I had grown to love a chance at a longer and healthier life? Even if it ended up subtly changing history? My heart would not allow it.

As chieftain, Cedric wanted the best for all the kin. Increasing their chances of survival was huge as far as he was concerned. Several of his scribes were taking everything down so that not an iota of all this valuable knowledge was lost. I could just see the gears spinning in his head. He was constantly thinking of what else he should ask me. No wonder our people thrived under him! This man was a natural leader and probably the shrewdest person I had ever met!

Since I was not officially here, and from the far-off future, everyone in attendance was sworn to secrecy. They had been privileged to be allowed to listen but sharing this information in a careless manner could invalidate it. No matter how much something made sense, it might be met with skepticism when presented as coming from a total stranger.

Most of the villagers just saw me as the girls' cousin, some woman none had ever met. Why would they believe anything I said? We needed a different source for the disbursement of these concepts. Luckily, Geira already had a well-established reputation as a healer. She was known for her novel approach to many a problem. Therefore, once I was done, Cedric asked her if she would be willing to claim all this information as her own and share it with the council one bit at a time.

After making sure I did not mind, Geira agreed with his plan. Once the suggestions had been presented, discussed, and approved, Cedric would have them written into law. Some might complain about the new rules, but having come from a renowned sorceress, wise woman, and herbalist, they would eventually accept them. What a slick way to deal with the problem! It effectively circumvented people's prejudice against ideas from an outsider!

I was impressed. Cedric's strategy was just plain brilliant! Grudgingly, my respect for him grew even further. Doing it in the way he proposed assured that the changes would stick! When I told him later that evening how clever this was, he turned a slight shade of pink. Then, he looked at me with such longing that my heart contracted. Why did he have to remind me so much of Phillipe!

It was so hard to resist him, and getting more difficult each day! And it was challenging not only for me! Cedric was suffering as well. The attraction we felt for each other was karmic, almost impossible to deny! The way he eyed me made me feel like I was his 'Holy Grail!' It was difficult to tear my gaze away. He should be looking at Eldred that way and not me!

Then, suddenly, he burst out.

"I wish you would stay!"

"Us too! Since he looks like your Phillipe and Cedric obviously likes you, we will happily share him with you! You know that!" Eldred added immediately. Hilda agreed with her sister.

I was speechless by this incredible honor expressed in front of everyone at the table, so I walked over and hugged them. After a moment, Cedric joined us and wrapped his strong arms around the three of us. We just stood there for a while, taking comfort in each other's presence.

"We could use your knowledge, you know," Eldred told me.

"If things were different, I would consider staying. I love you guys and will miss you so much, but I do not belong here."

"Cara is right. She needs to return to the nexus and then home. Think of all the people still stuck there, waiting for her to return!" Geira reminded them.

At this, Hilda made a face. She and Eldred were still grieving for their parents, and soon, they were about to lose me. Within seconds, she was crying bitterly, which greatly disturbed Cedric. He felt utterly helpless when confronted with such a flood of tears. Being so very male, it was in his nature to want to fix whatever was wrong just to make her happy again. How very sweet! Phillipe was just like that!

Geira and I exchanged a concerned glance. Cedric would do anything for the girls! Would that also include keeping me here against my will? I hoped not, but I was not about to give him a chance to try.

"As long as the time trap exists, none of us Magnusons are safe," I reminded them. "The enchantment is weakened, and Bo has it under control for now, but maintaining the spell for me to stay here takes a lot of power. There is still a chance that it might start ensnaring people again if I do not return. Who knows who it will snag next?"

"Cara has to shut it down from within. I believe that she is the only one who can do it." Geira stated firmly.

"But why her? Why not someone else?" Hilda sobbed.

"I do not know the answer to that, child," Geira admitted.

"She is the catalyst," Eldred stated quietly and rather sadly. "When she found us, something shifted. Geira is right, Hilda. She has to go back and soon."

Her words gave Cedric pause. I could clearly see the thoughts going on behind that furrowed brow. Keeping me here had advantages and would make the girl disconsolately sobbing against his chest very happy. But, it would also put his wives and the rest of the clan in danger. As chieftain, he was responsible for them all. But Hilda was crying ...!

It was Eldred who finally came to my rescue.

"Hilda, it is not like she is lost to us forever! We will still see her in the Meeting Place. Please consider what it would do to her if we made her stay here! Keeping Cara away from her husband would be cruel!" she said gently, wrapping her arms comfortingly around her little sister. "That is not love, sweetheart, but possession, and would make her a prisoner here, inside the circle."

"Cara could never go for a walk with you or accompany you to the village! She would always be stuck inside the ring of spruce. What kind of life would that be for her?" Geira added. "And what would happen to her if the sacred circle gets broken? She would become nothing more than a wraith in a world that is frozen unless she manages to return to the time trap! Do you really want to condemn her to that?"

Hilda was so shocked at their words that she stopped crying abruptly. She stared at me in horror. For the first time, the true extent of my situation became clear to her. Detangling herself from Cedric, she rushed over and threw her arms around my neck.

"I did not think of that! Nor how it would make you feel! I am so sorry for being so selfish!"

Then, drying her tears, Hilda resolutely turned to her husband.

"We need to let her go no matter how much we want her to stay!"

Cedric just nodded. He knew she was right. Geira, never one to pass up an opportunity to take charge and organize things, came up with a compromise that suited us all.

"How about we spend the next couple of days together, just our household? We do not need the scribes; we can record everything else Cara wants to share with us that we find important!"

"Would you be amenable to that?" Cedric asked me courteously.

"Yes, I would be, and what a great idea!"

So it came to be that the following morning found Cedric, Eldred, Hilda, Geira, and I gathered around the dining room table. We had a lively breakfast and then got down to business. Both the enchantress and Eldred were taking notes. That day, we covered a variety of subjects. Luckily, I had been able to indulge so many of my interests at university! All that knowledge sure came in handy as we tackled some of the problems facing the clan.

At some point, I wondered if my visit to the past had not contributed to the coming prosperity of the Magnuson Clan. Good thing that Cedric was such a fair and wise ruler! From our history, I knew he would end up sharing much of this information with other folks in the area. It would be done covertly and so cleverly that the point of origin would remain unknown for many decades. Eventually, long after her death, all this wisdom would be attributed to the enchantress.

Geira would be considered to be way ahead of her time. By disseminating the information to different spots in the region and not claiming it as theirs, the clan would prevent causing jealousy among the nearby people. And they would avoid drawing unwelcome attention to themselves, thus giving the fanatics no reason to come investigate. Most would think that the settlement was a sleepy and utterly unimportant backwater.

In this manner, Cedric would effectively improve the lives of not only his own people but also their neighbors. In a few years, he would be responsible for creating a network of clans that worked together for the greater good of all. All the kin would revere him and his wives for their wisdom and kindness to those in need. However, only by their immediate family and the few aware of their abilities would these three be celebrated for their magic!

It was stunning to think that all this good would come from Eldred, Hilda, and me getting caught in that malicious enchantment!

Chapter 46

Return to the Time Trap

Toward the evening of my sixth day there, I became increasingly restless. With each passing hour, it was getting harder to sit still. It was time to go; the time trap was pulling me back. I had stayed as long as I could! And I had given my kin as much information as possible to improve their lives. What they did with it was up to them. But, knowing Cedric and his determined wives, none of what I had shared would go to waste. We could only hope that we had not changed history too much and that the world I would return to was one I still fit into and recognized!

Also, being around Cedric was getting ever more difficult. It was hard not to touch, reach out, or fall into his arms since I longed for my husband more than I could say. I was careful to avoid being alone with that man but did not always succeed. As far as I was concerned, our attraction to each other took away from Eldred, and I was not ok with that, even if she was. The newlyweds could finally settle into their marriage once I was gone and no longer a distraction.

But what would await me in the construct? Had Bo managed to keep the enchantment from collecting more people? I sure hoped so! There were enough folks left for me to take home before I could return to Phillipe! My mind was already making plans and devising ways to set everyone free as quickly as possible. I was out of patience and prepared to work long hours to put an end to that spell.

The others noticed my distraction and knew that I would be departing soon. The sadness in Hilda's eyes when she realized this hit me hard. In a way, I felt that I was abandoning her just as she needed me most. Geira, who noticed my reaction, gave me a reassuring smile. Instantly, I felt a little better. The enchantress was one of the most capable women I had ever met, and she would be there for the girls. They would be well looked after!

That night, Hilda slipped into bed with me. I held her while she cried bitter tears. My leaving was the hardest on her, but she did have her sister, Cedric, Bo, and Geira to look after her. She finally fell asleep in my arms. It took me a while longer to slip into slumber. I had a lot on my mind. For one, I would miss the girls. We were family, even if we lived hundreds of years apart. And what was waiting for me at home? Would Phillipe and I be able to recapture the incredible closeness we had shared before the spell interfered in our lives? I had no idea.

Early the next morning, Eldred woke us. She and Hilda helped me dress in the gorgeous green gown I had worn to their wedding. Lovingly, they brushed out my long hair. We spoke very little. None of us had the heart to joke around as we usually did. Finally, they declared me sufficiently beautified. We went to the dining room, where Geira and Cedric were already waiting for us.

Knowing that food would not be available to me in the construct, the cook had gone to great efforts to make this last breakfast special. She had produced quite the spread! I did my best to do this bounty justice, but my stomach felt tied in knots. It was hard to get anything down! Understanding my situation, Geira told me not to worry. They would send the leftovers with me. There was enough here that they would sustain me for several days!

The girls and I dreaded the upcoming parting. Therefore, the meal was much quieter than the previous days. Even Cedric's attempts to lighten the mood fell flat. None of them was eating much either, and the cook soon appeared with a basket and packed up what remained. We had some more tea, but eventually, we could postpone the inevitable no longer. It was time for me to go.

Naturally, the girls, Cedric, and Geira, accompanied me on my way to the spot where the smoke wafted across the path. My relief upon seeing that it was still there was profound. Part of me had been terrified that my unease was due to its disappearance, which would have left me stranded here. I would have never seen Phillipe, my family, friends, and our pets again! That was something too painful to even contemplate! As much as I loved the girls, I did not belong here, no matter how much they wished for this to be different.

Our group stopped at a distance. Knowing it had collected his wives before, Cedric was not about to take a chance. He did not want them anywhere near that ominous cloud. Not that I could blame him! Actually, I really liked his protectiveness over the girls as well as his thoughtfulness toward them. Hilda and Eldred were in good hands. My presence here was wanted but not a necessity.

Their husband and Geira would support Eldred and Hilda and look after them. Not that they needed it; they had survived just fine in the time trap! Their resilience and perseverance had seen them through the weeks before they met up with me. Together, however, we had been a force to be reckoned with. I had gotten very used to having them around and dreaded the coming separation.

However, that they were so well loved and cared for was a comfort. Knowing they had such wonderful people around them made leaving just a little bit easier, but not much. How I would miss them! Our closeness had further intensified over the last few days, and we loved each other like sisters. Now that the moment of parting was at hand, the three of us clung to each other.

Cedric joined our huddle. He did not hide his sadness at seeing me go and wrapped his strong arms around all three of us and hugged us tightly.

"I would have liked having you as a wife," he sighed.

"Two wives are not enough?" I teased him back.

"It would have made my girls happy. Besides, what is one more but added joy?" the smart man retorted.

"We would not have minded sharing with you," Hilda assured me.

"We would have been happy to, Cara!" Eldred affirmed. "We have a parting gift for you. Something that will always remind you of us. Cedric?"

Smiling, her husband pulled a magnificent ring from his pocket. It reminded me of the beautiful bands he and the sisters had exchanged at their wedding. Cedric grabbed my right hand and slid it on my ring finger. It fit perfectly!

"This makes you one of us," Eldred informed me.

I was extremely touched by their gesture which resulted in yet more embraces. Finally, I broke away laughing.

"If we keep this up, we will never get this parting over with!"

"We do not want you to go, but we understand why you must," Cedric stated gravely. The girls nodded their agreement.

"Thank you for everything. I will never forget you!" I told them, my voice choked with emotions.

"Nor we you," Eldred replied tearfully. "We want to see you at least once a week in the Meeting Place and do find a way to bring Phillipe!"

"I will, I promise!"

With a heavy heart, I finally started toward the smoke. There was no sense in drawing this painful goodbye out any longer. Cedric firmly kept his arms around Eldred and Hilda to prevent them from following me. Geira was the only one who walked with me, but even she knew better than to get too close.

"Take care of yourself, and do not worry about Eldred and Hilda. I will look after them for you!" she told me. "Oh, and the ring? I placed an enchantment on it that will protect you in the nexus. Be very careful when you confront the locus of that spell!"

"Thank you, Geira! How thoughtful of you! I will be vigilant, and I am certain that I will not have to face it alone!" I assured her.

"Good! Now go before one of those girls comes running after you!" Geira commanded.

Fearing that possibility myself, I rushed toward the plume but then turned to get one last look at the people I had grown to love. I wanted to remember them and this place, so I pulled out my phone and shot several pictures.

"Farewell! May all your lives be blessed and full of joy!" I called from the edge of the smoke.

When they waved, I snapped one last photo of Geira and the little family that had become so dear to me. I could barely see since tears were blurring my vision. It was hard to leave, but at least I would have the images to remind me of our time here together. I turned and ran into the cloud before I could change my mind.

Mæva was glad to see me when I stumbled out of the other side of the barrier. I fell into her arms and let the tears flow. Much of the hurt and pain I had been suppressing ever since the time trap first affected my life was washed away in the resulting flood of emotions. As was my nature, I tended to keep a tight rein on my feelings, which was not always good. They will be expressed, inevitably, in one way or another, so letting them out was much healthier than pushing them down.

Once I was calm again, she and Bo wanted to hear all about the wedding and what I had been up to. Both full-heartedly approved of my sharing of knowledge with the clan. At least the girls would have some extra benefits from being caught by this awful enchantment! We spent a few minutes talking before leaving the nexus that collapsed in on itself just as soon as we entered the in-between. The finality sent a shiver of loss through me that just about sent me to my knees.

With that cell fading away, my physical way back to the girls was gone forever. Mæva gave my arm a comforting squeeze. She understood just how I felt. Pulling myself together, I gave her a sad smile. This was no time for grieving; there was work to be done and people to rescue. Bo had managed to keep the hive the same size, and two of us were now more than sufficient to accomplish the returns. It was time to get back to taking folks home, so we might as well get to it!

To do this systematically, we decided to start on the outer cells and work our way in. In this manner, we would know when we were reaching the end. The first nexus we entered was another woman, Heather Magnuson, from 1789. We got her information and sent her on her way. The lady we met after that was Gudrun Mackay, married to a Magnuson. She was from the year 1567. Then, we came across a man, Rodger Magnuson. All three of us took an instant dislike to him. He was just plain rude!

Kira Magnuson was as sweet as that cad had been dour. Mæva, Bo, and I spent a few minutes talking to her, and she was just a delight. Only 13, the girl was as innocent as freshly fallen snow but also as capricious as a fairy, an absolutely delightful mix! And Kira was bright! She was happy to see us and just as curious about us as we were about her. To our astonishment, her lengthy imprisonment seemed to not have affected her at all!

Suddenly, without saying a word, Bo took off. When he returned, he was not alone. With him was an elderly lady dressed very similarly to the way Eldred and Hilda had been.

Since we could use a break after dealing with that grouch and were enjoying Kira's company, we decided to head to the house in this nexus and take some time out for tea. Revna, led by some instinct, came to join us before long. Suddenly, I got this feeling that we needed to have a conference! Taking people home would have to wait. We had some figuring out to do! It just seemed vitally important right then and there!

On my phone, I had kept track of the origins of all those from our clan that had been unlucky enough to get caught in this construct. I added the dates for these ladies to that, then converted the data to a chart. Sometimes that can be helpful as a visual aid. Once it had finished processing, we looked for a pattern.

The very first occurrence had been Finna. So far, I was at the other end of the timespan. To our surprise, while talking, we discovered that Bo's companion, who he had rushed out to fetch, Norene Magnuson, had known Eldred and Hilda's parents as children. Mæva and I quizzed her extensively. The girls' folks seemed to have been just as gifted and determined as their offspring!

Then, something fell into place. Maybe we were meant not to notice this until that moment, or the spell had finally weakened enough that its control over our minds was slipping. Suddenly, out of the blue, it hit home that the enchantment was taking people from over 1000 years! That, in itself, was incredible! But who was the person who had run afoul of someone who meant to do her harm?

None of the ones we had taken home so far seemed to be that one. And it was not Mæva, Revna, nor me! From what we could tell, neither Kira nor Norene, who had been very paying close attention to our discussion, were the victimized party either! Who then? For now, we were still missing that vital piece of information. However, someone still in the construct had to know more! We just had to find them!

To speed things up, Bo volunteered to call more of the people stuck in the hive to us. Maybe if we got them all together, we could figure this out. Hopefully, someone had the tidbit we required.

We moved to the larger living room of the small cabin of Kira's nexus and waited while those that remained came to join us. We bid them to take a seat once they arrived. Before long, our number grew to 14, and introductions were made. Our little group consisted of Mæva, Revna, Bo, Norene, Kira, myself, and then the newcomers Katrín Magnuson-Delaby, Rita Lindström, Eileen Westerby, Willow Mackay, Xavier O'Rourke, Zelda Stewart, Maxwell Mackay, and Conall Sinclaire, all part of the Magnuson clan in one way or another.

With this lot, almost everyone still in one of the outer nexuses of the time trap was accounted for. That left only those in the very center. According to Geira, none of those were in any shape to move about. Naturally, explanations of what was happening were needed before we could get down to business. It was understandable that they all wanted to know how they had gotten here.

While the others were talking, on a whim, I decided to plot the years of all the new captives. Looking at the curve, we noticed an even more distinct bell shape. Finna and I were still the outliers, but a whole cluster of individuals was very close together around the year 1800! One of those had to be the person this had all started with! My guess was that it had been none of the ones we had taken home already. But several others were sitting here with us!

That meant one of the folks in this group was the poor soul this was centered on. When I shared my findings with the others, a brief discussion ensued. Many objections were voiced. Nobody wanted to be the one who had caused all this misery. However, in the end, everyone agreed that my logic was valid. Still, not a one of them volunteered any useful information!

The one who had inadvertently set the events in motion that had led to all this was either unaware or not telling. Not that I could blame them! After all the protests, they might fear that the others would get angry and hold them responsible for this mess, possibly even retaliate against them for having been ripped out of their lives and brought here!

Since no one would come forward, Mæva locked eyes with each individual. She was searching for any sign of guilt or deception.

My friend was determined to figure this out!

Chapter 47

The Spell's Origin

After a while, Bo, Mæva, and I grew frustrated. So far, our meeting had not yielded the desired information. Nobody was prepared to admit that they might be the cause for all the misery wrought by the enchantment. Understandable, but also not helpful! But there was another option. The individual in question might not even be aware that they had somehow contributed to the despair of the witch that had cast this malevolent spell!

Since even Mæva's most intimidating glare was not getting any results, I decided to try a different approach.

"Do any of you have an enemy or know of someone who might wish you ill?" I enquired, thinking some prompting would help, but I was wrong.

Once again, we got nothing!

"Did anything odd happen to any of you or your family members before you ended up here?" Mæva finally asked them after all our other questions had come up empty.

The great urgency in her voice did give our guests some pause. They looked at each other uneasily, but nobody answered. Mæva, however, was not about to admit defeat. This lot would tell her what we needed to know, or they would sit here for a long time!

By pure chance, as I was watching the group cringing under Mæva's glare, I noticed that one of the ladies, Katrín, suddenly froze. Then, a look of sheer horror crossed her face, and she turned deathly pale. Her hand flew to her heart as the implication of her sudden insight hit home. For a moment, I was afraid that she was about to get sick or pass out from the intense emotions that were clearly raging through her.

I felt for her. The realization that she might have had a part in causing enough hurt to someone for them to create this kind of spell had to be devastating! Something that had been said must have clicked! I observed Katrín more closely. This woman was an incredible beauty with green eyes, the fairest skin I had ever seen, and glossy raven hair down to her waist.

I could see why another female would see her as a threat! Her eyes, however, looked incredibly sad. Despite her good looks and rich clothes, it was obvious that her life had not been easy. Still, she was so gorgeous that Maxwell, the young man sitting next to her, was clearly smitten. Noticing that something was upsetting the object of his adoration, he reached out. Tenderly, he took her hand, trying to reassure and comfort her.

"What is it, Katrín?" I queried her gently.

The girl was upset enough already, and I did not want to make that worse. She had obviously been through a lot.

"My husband might be the reason for all this!" she eventually stammered and broke into tears.

Now she had everyone's full attention!

Maxwell, determined to make her feel better, moved even closer and put his arm around her. Seeking shelter from the storm in her heart and soul, Katrín instinctively leaned into him.

"Why do you think that?" I inquired softly once she calmed a little.

Everyone else was now watching her with bated breath. Here, finally, might be the answer to the puzzle! And relief from Mæva's inquisition!

"My marriage was arranged by my parents," the young lady explained. "My husband, Finley, is quite a bit older than me. He is not someone I would have chosen, and I fervently wish my folks had also turned him down. All the other fathers did!"

That had sounded rather bitter! Overcome by emotions, Katrín started sobbing. Feeling totally overwhelmed, she buried her face in Maxwell's broad chest. I sat down next to them and started rubbing her back. Katrín clung to the young man and continued to cry piteously. I could only imagine what things must have been like for her! How awful to be denied the freedom to choose one's own spouse!

Seeing how upset this young woman was, the others crowded around us. They all voiced their assurances that they were not angry with her. No one with a heart could have been since it was so evident that this poor soul was just as much of a victim as everyone else who had been caught by the time trap! None of this was her fault! Between all of us, we finally managed to reassure and soothe her.

That is when all her anguish, all the frustration, and helpless anger spilled forth.

"They forced me to marry him! My own parents! Can you believe that?" she finally ground out between clenched teeth. "They heard the rumors what he was like, and still they …."

Exhausted from all the turmoil inside her, she rested her head against Maxwell's chest again.

"Mine did, too," one of the other women, Rita, said quietly. "I am better off here!"

The rest of us, even the distraught Katrín, looked at the young lady in absolute horror. What must her home life be like to prefer this nightmare? Rita slid up next to us, and Katrín took the hand she offered. I could sense the emotional bond that had just formed between these two. They each gained strength from knowing that another was sharing her fate.

Katrín disengaged herself from her adorer, turned, and sat up straighter. She was now facing us but still kept her back pushed up against Maxwell, who, after a moment's hesitation, wrapped one arm comfortingly around her waist. The girl did not seem to mind. If anything, she slid even closer to this source of unexpected and unconditional support. It gave her the strength to go on.

"He is a total pig! Imagine this! On our wedding night, this woman knocked on our door. She was looking for him!" Katrín revealed with a whole lot of indignation.

She might not have wanted him but still! Having the groom's old flame show up at such a time would be extremely disturbing! I was glad to see that she was opening up more every minute now that she realized no one blamed her for the debacle we found ourselves in. Also, Maxwell's wordless encouragement seemed to help her express all the anger and hurt she had been holding inside.

"From his reputation, I knew he had been with others, but for one to come to the house that night?" Katrín was clearly still in disbelief over the audacity of that woman!

"How awful!" Rita exclaimed.

The rest of us agreed. That was a terrible way to begin a marriage!

"In a way, I was glad because it postponed the inevitable. He went down to talk to her, and the next thing I knew, I heard her yelling at him! The whole house overheard them screaming at each other! It was so embarrassing! He never did come back to bed, nor did he join me the next few nights. Several days later, he went out to get a deer. None of the hunting party ever returned."

"That does not sound like a coincidence to me!" Mæva interjected.

"He had been so nasty to me that I was so glad he was gone! To be honest, I did not care what had happened to him!" Katrín admitted. "I just hoped and prayed that he would not come back!"

"You did not think his sudden disappearance odd?" Revna asked, somewhat incredulous.

"Not until just now! The whole thing was a nightmare! If the stories they tell about him are true, then that knock on the door could not have been better timed! That man knew I did not want him! I bet he was about to make me pay for rejecting him! I was so relieved when he came up missing!" Katrín responded somewhat defensively. "I had forgotten about the woman until I heard Mæva's questions!"

"I guess I was being rather selfish and never considered her feelings at all," she added thoughtfully a second later. "And once the servants reported that the hunters had not returned, I had my hands full. Unfortunately, he was not the only one who went missing. Even if I did not, the other wives wanted their husbands found, so they came to stay with me. Who could blame them? It happened on our land! We sent out a search party every day until I ended up here!"

"You had no way of knowing anything about that young woman," I reassured Katrín. "And you did good! Despite not wanting him back, you did the right thing! That is to be commended and not selfish at all!"

"I agree," said Maxwell. "Did they find anything?"

"The servants followed the tracks that first day. They trailed the party through the woods. The men must have been chasing something. The signs of their passing were fresh and clearly visible for some distance. Then, all traces of them just vanished in a clearing near the lodge by the lake!"

"Did the searcher find anything out of the ordinary?" Mæva asked curiously.

"Now that you mention it, they did see evidence of a recent fire at the far end of the glade!"

"Ah!" Revna, Mæva, and I said as one.

"Please, ladies, would you care to explain the significance of this? Frankly, I am at a loss!" Maxwell interrupted.

I looked at the two sorceresses, and they at me. Finally, I shrugged my shoulders. Being fellow prisoners, the others did have a right to know.

"With the hunting party disappearing around there, the fire was probably used to heat a kettle. We can assume that the spell was cast right there in that clearing. The witch created a smoke portal that entrapped the men. After that, the enchantment went for Katrín, and then bit by bit collected all of us," Mæva explained.

"Do you think my husband's visitor might have had something to do with his disappearance?" Katrín wanted to know.

"Very possible! You are in the middle of the biggest cluster of people on the timeline!" I added. "How did you get here?"

"I was walking in the garden when this odd smoke drifted my way. I tried to avoid it, but it surrounded me before I could escape. I swear I heard a woman's laughter. It sounded terribly wicked! Next thing I knew, I found myself here!" Katrín explained.

"You mentioned a lodge," Rita cut in. "Is anyone staying there?"

"Not that I know off," Katrín began, but then she stopped. Her face turned thoughtful, and she looked at Rita wide-eyed. "You do not think that …."

"Mine did. For convenience, he kept his mistress nearby," Rita stated drily.

"If she was in that cabin at any time, it would make perfect sense that she would waylay him nearby," Revna stated confidently. "She would have had an affinity with the place. Being familiar with your husband's habits, she would have known exactly where to cast the spell!"

"It sounds like we have found the point of origin. The men were on horseback?" Mæva inquired.

"Yes! How did you know?" Katrín questioned.

"The horses in the pasture!" I exclaimed. "But, if the animals are here … !"

Where were the riders? I could not bring myself to finish that sentence out loud. If those poor creatures were any indication of how much life force had been taken, what shape were the men in? They, after all, had less mass!

Tuning out the others' conversation, I pondered this for a moment. Then, it hit me. I could feel the blood drain from my face and felt cold all over. Mæva gave me a curious look, but I was not about to share my insight with her in front of the others. Thus, I almost imperceptibly shook my head. I would tell her later, but not now.

I had just remembered something Geira had told me. At the time, it had been too awful to even contemplate, and my brain had refused to grasp the implication. However, hearing about the missing hunting party, I now had a good idea of who we would find at the center of this hive! The rest she had shared with me also fell into place, and the horror of their fate made me sick to my stomach.

Was Bo aware of this? I would have to ask him but not now! The atrocity at the locus of this hive was definitely not something I was prepared to share with the newcomers! The less they were aware of, the better for them! Why burden them with such awful knowledge? This was the stuff of nightmares!

"Maybe some of them found their way home on foot," Revna, who had clearly understood the interchange between Mæva and me, added placatingly.

The glance she shot me, however, told me that we would be having a private chat soon but that, for the moment, she was trusting my judgment. Her suggestion did seem to appease some of the less curious ones, but little Kira was not among those! That bright little girl had not missed the looks that had passed between Mæva, Revna, and me and knew that there was something we were not telling.

We would need to take her home quickly before she found an opportunity to make a discovery that would leave her scarred for the rest of her life!

Mæva, realizing this as well, immediately took action.

"It is time to take you back to your homes, so please split into two groups. Maxwell, Zelda, Norene, and Eileen, you will go with Bo and Revna. The rest will come with Cara and me," Mæva commanded.

She was obviously done with all this talking and ready to get on with depopulating the hive!

"Wait, please!" Willow interjected with some urgency.

She turned to Katrín. "That woman who came to your house, did she have an accent? Spanish or something?"

"Why, yes, now that you mention it!" Katrín exclaimed.

"I think that I have met her. And possibly your husband," the girl admitted.

"You are both from the same year," I stated after checking my information.

"Since you are already coming with Cara and me, we will drop you and Katrín off at Revna's place so you can chat. Try to collect as many details as possible. Maybe you will have some new information for the rest of us when we return," Mæva ordered impatiently.

My friend was clearly out of sorts for some reason.

"Are you alright?" I whispered to her once we were on our way.

"I just want to get this over with," she muttered, obviously upset.

"Do you want us to take you home?" I asked quietly.

This gave Mæva pause. She looked at me shamefacedly, realizing she was taking her irritation out on those who did not deserve it.

"No, I will see this through to the end. You will need all the help you can get if your face earlier was an indication of things to come!" she stated quickly and decisively.

I put my arm around her and gave her a squeeze. Mæva smiled back at me. She seemed to feel much better now that she had expressed her frustrations. After a minute, she started to hum. For her, this was an unconscious act that would have probably annoyed many people. I knew that only too well since I tend to do the same thing. The tune was rather cheerful, a clear indication of her improved mood.

At least she was one less thing to worry about! I was greatly relieved and gave her a broad smile. Mæva grinned back at me, then her mien turned serious once more. A nod from her toward the three women lagging behind us had me falling back to join them. Time for some information gathering and possible damage control!

Soon, I was chatting with Willow, Rita, and Katrín. They had been deep in conversation about the mystery woman. However, they did not appear to be ready to share their findings. I had caught the tail end of their discussion, but they had changed the subject just as soon as they became aware of me. This might be trouble! These three had definitely bonded. For a few moments, I felt like the odd person out, something the others noticed and quickly remedied.

To divert me from the topic they had been talking about, they mentioned how happy Bo had looked at being included in taking people home. At the time, I had been so focused on Mæva that this had escaped me, but I was glad to hear this. I immediately started asking more questions since I wondered if we had excluded him too much in the past. Belonging and being involved were important for any of us!

These young ladies thought him adorable and wanted to know all about Bo. But, I was not sure how much to reveal about my friend's origin. He hated the construct that had given birth to him and would not want the fact that he had been part of the enchantment widely known. So, I quickly changed the subject and got the ladies talking about their experiences inside the time trap.

That bit about Bo, however, I filled away for further examination. Assisting in taking these folks home must have made him feel accepted and truly one of us. He had always been helpful and kind. My friends and I had seen him so much as one of us that it had never occurred to me that he might not feel the same way. Or that he needed reassurance! He seemed so confident all the time! Was that just an act?

Without him, our experience in the hive would have been so much worse! He might not realize it, but we had much to thank him for. And Hilda loved him and carried his child. The rest of us saw him in a more brotherly way, but he was definitely part of the family. Maybe we needed to make extra sure that he knew that as well!

I would mention this to Mæva once we dropped our bunch off at their home destinations. We could surely do more if such a small gesture meant so much to him. Bo's happiness was important to us. He most certainly deserved it! Resulting from such malicious magic and choosing good could not have been easy! The temptation to fully embrace the enchantment and become like an evil god ruling over the time trap had to have been immense!

But Bo had resisted it. He had chosen a different path, one contrary to the spell's design! In more than one way, he had become his own man! He was someone I deeply respected. Still, his origin had to trouble him, especially as sensitive as he was! I really needed to find some time to talk to him!

Mæva joining us pulled me out of my contemplations, and I smiled at her. I was happy to see her return it.

"Katrín and Willow, please follow the path to Revna's place while we take the rest home," Mæva requested, addressing them much more kindly than before.

I had been so deeply in thought that I had been unaware we had reached Revna's delightful nexus. It was the perfect place for those two to wait for us. Mæva even grinned at the pair. She was trying to be friendly and to make up for her earlier grumpiness. But the young ladies were still unsure what to make of this sudden change of attitude. Not that I could blame them!

"Just make yourself at home; Revna will not mind," I assured them. "The house will even give you a cup of tea if asked nicely!"

"More tea!" bubbled Willow. "Did you hear that? I have not had tea until today in what seems like forever!"

After saying a quick goodbye to the others, she impatiently pulled Katrín through the barrier and then along toward Revna's cabin. Everything else seemed to have been forgotten now that there was a delicious hot beverage to be had!

I could not blame her; it was a true treat in this time trap!

Chapter 48

More Complications

Katrín turned again to wave to the rest of us before following the exuberant Willow, who was almost running toward the house. In a world where any nourishment was unnecessary and, therefore, a special treat, a cup of tea sounded just too delicious to resist! Mæva had already moved on with the rest of the group, but Rita had fallen behind. I hung back with her, wondering what she was up to.

After a moment's indecision, the young woman turned and rushed after her friends.

"Wait! Rita, where are you going?" I called, rather surprised.

"I am not going back," the young woman stated decisively. "You have no idea what is waiting for me!"

Mæva, who had come back to see what was keeping us, looked at me with exasperation. She threw up her hands and turned to go after the rest of our bunch, just to realize they had followed her. The frown on her face stated plainly that she was severely displeased by this whole situation. However, neither of us had the heart to send Rita home against her wishes.

We would have to consult with Bo to see what could be done. Until then, she might as well wait with the other two. Not that she was giving us an option! Oh well, some hot tea would do her some good!

"Fine! We will return in a bit!" Mæva snapped at Rita's retreating form with some irritation.

"And you lot, do not get any ideas!" she growled at the rest, who had the good grace to look somewhat guilty, especially Kira.

The girl had clearly considered staying. She hated the idea that she might be missing all the excitement! With the well-honed instincts of someone as curious as she was, she just knew that things were about to get interesting! And that there was a mystery here! Kira would have loved to see the center of the hive! But not even she was about to challenge Mæva, not with the mood that lady was in!

I sympathized with the girl on one level but was glad that Mæva had managed to keep her in line! We already had three to deal with and did not need yet another complication! But I was worried about my friend. Over the last few hours, she had been getting more and more short-tempered. The sweet-tempered healer was turning into a regular dragon lady!

Her nerves seemed to be just about shot! I was not sure she could take much more! Hopefully, this whole adventure would be over with soon! Then something else occurred to me. Could the upcoming return home be the problem? Mæva had never disclosed much about herself. Maybe it was time for me to ask her some questions!

Unfortunately, the nexus next to Revna's had collapsed. But, the time trap was much smaller now. Therefore, it did not take long for Mæva and me to take our group back to the cells they had come from. Little Kira, we saved for last. She hugged us several times and broke into tears. Then, when she could no longer push out her departure, she decided to brave my friend's anger by asking humbly if we were sure she could not stay just a little while longer. Both of us laughed.

"As much as we enjoy you, child, it is time for you to go home!" Mæva stated firmly.

But she hugged the girl once more and even gave her a gentle kiss on the cheek. "And stay out of trouble, do you hear?"

"Yes, Mæva, I will try. I promise!" Kira swore solemnly.

Turning to me, she threw her arms around my neck and hugged me.

"You are going to have all the fun! I still do not understand why I could not come with you! I could help!"

"Kira, if my suspicions are right, the center of this hive is not something I would want you to see," I told her earnestly.

Kira searched my face and eventually nodded. She was beginning to understand that this was not all fun and games! Once she disengaged herself, she reluctantly prepared to go on her way. I watched as Mæva reached into her pocket and brought out one of the enchanted items connected to the Meeting Place.

"Wait!" she called after the girl, who immediately bounced back to us.

"Yes? Can I stay?" she asked hopefully, giving us her best pleading puppy dog eyes.

"No, sweet, but I think Mæva has something for you," I told her with a smile.

Now my friend had all Kira's attention.

"Here, girl, this token will allow you to visit us in a place we created. Bo lives there, and I bet he would be happy to see you!" Mæva explained.

Kira took the gift with due reverence. She was too choked up to speak, so she hugged Mæva and me several more times instead. Finally, my friend sent her off with an insistent shooing motion. Naturally, the girl turned around every other step to check if we had not changed our minds. Laughing at her antics, we continued to gesture for her to keep moving. Both of us breathed a sigh of relief when Kira made her way out of the smoke.

But then, she whipped around. Besides me, Mæva let out a sigh. She just knew Kira would try something else! Pleadingly, the precocious teenager put her hands together and knelt to beg us to let her stay! She was really making this hard! However, my suspicions of what we were about to face helped to keep up my resolve. I shook my head sadly to convey to her that this was not going to work.

Eventually, Kira gave up and went on her way. Mæva and I watched her walk down the lane back toward Havn for a few moments longer. She would be home soon, safely away from all of this! For that, I was glad, but that girl had been such a ray of sunshine that we missed her already. She had most certainly brightened up our day!

We rushed through her cell and into the in-between to ensure Kira did not follow us. Then, Mæva and I watched the space implode and knew the portal was sealed.

The distance between far-off nexuses was getting less all the time, indicating that the hive construct continued to shrink. Therefore, I decided to slow down my steps. Now that we were alone, I was determined to discover what was bothering Mæva.

"Mæva, were you happy before you ended up here?" I carefully started the conversation, trying to avoid angering her again.

"Ah! You are trying to find out why I have been so grumpy," Mæva laughed.

I was glad she was taking my question so well, but then, she fell silent.

"Happy?" Mæva said contemplatively after some time had passed. "To be honest, I believed I was. I guess I never gave it much thought. I did my duty as was expected of me."

"You live in Havn?"

"Yes. I was born there and married our laird's younger brother. He is a good man. But once I got here and had time to reflect, I realized we had long since grown apart. I had been so busy teaching and helping with the running of the clan that I never had the time until then to consider where my life was going. Or what I want."

"Do you still love him?" I enquired curiously.

"I do believe so," Mæva answered me hesitatingly. "Life with him is comfortable, like slipping into an old shoe. But, there is no fire, no passion, no spice."

"Hmm, maybe you could add some?" I suggested.

"What do you do to keep your marriage alive?" Mæva wanted to know.

"Well, we have date nights, and …" I began, only to be interrupted.

"What is a date night?"

Ah! That was a concept new to my time but not hers!

"We set aside time just for us and do different things. Sometimes, we both get dressed up and go have dinner somewhere, or we stay in, and I put on high heels and something super sexy. Or a costume. We have a meal together, talk, make love, and give each other undivided attention."

"Hmmm," Mæva commented.

"It adds spice," I told her with a laugh.

"Do you have a picture from such a 'date night'?"

"Sure, hold on!" I told her.

We stopped, and I pulled out my phone. I opened a secret file where I kept the more risqué images. It needed my fingerprint before it would open, which had kept it safe from Eldred. Mæva's eyes lit up when she saw some of my getups.

"I can do that!" she decided. "Does it make Phillipe want you more?"

"You bet! And sometimes I just take charge and tease him until he begs for mercy," I shared with a grin.

"You wicked little girl! Who would have guessed you have that in you!" Mæva teased.

We started laughing so hard that we had tears rolling down our faces. I could feel the tension dissolve in my friend. We continued toward Revna's place, talking as we walked. Soon, Mæva had a number of ideas that she could not wait to try out on her husband!

I almost pitied the man! He was in for a huge surprise!

Since we had only three people to deal with, we were the first to be back. We found Willow, Rita, and Katrín happily ensconced in the living room, having yet another cup of tea. They were so engrossed in their conversation that it took them a minute to notice us. From the expression on Katrín's face, I figured she had come to a decision that would most likely complicate things even further.

"I do not mind helping you, but I am telling you right now that I do not wish to return to my home if you manage to find and rescue my husband!" Katrín informed us once we joined them.

The stubborn set of the young lady's mouth clearly indicated how firm she was on this point. Thanks, Rita! Now we had two on our hands refusing to return to their spouses! Mæva and I looked at each other. Just great! We would have to figure out somewhere else for them to go, but until I talked to Bo, I was unsure how to accomplish this.

We had not yet devised a way for someone to stay in a place where they did not belong, except those locations meant to keep one there permanently. Those, however, were just a trap within the enchantment and not somewhere to deposit these two! Katrín and Rita did not deserve to become a prisoner in such a destination, no matter how lovely! They had experienced enough unhappiness to last a lifetime!

The place offered to me had been very beautiful and peaceful. Its serenity had been exceedingly tempting, but it had been utterly devoid of other people. I could not see myself spending the rest of my life there, and Rita and Katrín were younger than me! There had to be another option besides that and the Meeting Place! And if not, we might just have to create one! What good was magic if you could not find a way to help others?

When our friends returned, we would present them with the problem. Maybe they had a suggestion. If not, we would have to devise some sort of a solution!

To our surprise, Revna and Bo brought back one of the young men, Maxwell. I remembered him talking to Katrín. He had seemed totally smitten by her. Upon entering the room, he immediately headed to her side. The young woman was equally as happy to see him. Her face lit up the moment she became aware of his presence. All the anger and worry that had clouded her beautiful features just melted away.

Delightedly, she reached out and hugged him. Katrín obviously felt safe with him. I could not help but let out a sigh, one that was echoed by Mæva. We had a good idea of what was to follow! Naturally, these two would refuse to be parted! Not that I could blame them. True love was a treasure! But it presented yet another hurdle we would have to deal with!

Until that instant, we had not realized just how close Katrín and Maxwell had grown in the short time they had known each other. The way they looked at each other indicated more than a passing affection. There was something real here. Who were we to deny them a chance at happiness? I just hoped that everything would fall into place once the core of this spell had been dealt with.

But, it would be a good idea to start working on that now. Leaving the others to their tea, Bo, Revna, Mæva, and I went into the kitchen. We tossed around several options before settling on one. We were not sure it would work, but it was the best idea we had so far and a definite possibility. Now, all we had to do was design the appropriate spell!

Bo laid out the perimeters. Mæva pulled out paper and pencil and started writing. If the enchantment worked as intended, people would be able to step into and become part of a place that was not their own!

Mæva continued to work on the phrasing. It had to be just right. So far, the correct wording was evading her. Maybe this would be easier once the malevolent construct had lost its power? We would have to wait to find out. As much as we dreaded it, the time had come to confront the nightmare in the center of this time trap. But first, I had a question for Bo.

"Do you know what is in the center?" I inquired.

"No," he answered honestly. "I was unaware that it even existed until you mentioned it, and I have never had access to it."

"Do you know how to get there?" Revna asked curiously.

"I have a suspicion, but that is it," Bo admitted. "I believe it is well hidden and difficult to get into."

"I am not getting anywhere with this spell," Mæva interrupted us with a sigh. "So why not go have a look?"

Getting up from the kitchen table, we returned to the living room. We were greeted with a barrage of questions which we answered as honestly as possible. Then, it was time for me to share what Geira had told me and what I suspected about the core of the time trap. The others listened attentively, but their faces reflected the revulsion and horror we all felt.

This was not going to be pleasant, far from it. But it had to be done. We were lucky since Maxwell, Katrín, Rita, and Willow were willing to help us. The consensus among our group was that we would have to do this eventually anyhow, so why not right now? On that, we were all in agreement. We might as well get this nightmare over with! When we were as prepared as possible, we went on our way.

Bo led us to the nexus in the very center. We noticed a difference from all the others as soon as we entered. Even if it looked very much like the cell I had found myself in, it felt nothing like it. Here, something in the air behaved just like static electricity! All the hairs on my arms and on my neck started rising! Then on my head! Soon, they were pointing straight up! The same was happening to everyone else.

The result was comical and led to a breakout of absolute hilarity! No comb or pin was enough to hold the women's long tresses in place. That force freed every last strand! Our heads were quickly surrounded by halos of wavering hair! Having one's locks standing at attention definitely looked pretty funny! The men were similarly afflicted, except their mops were shorter.

We tried, in vain, to smooth the offending manes back down, but that did no good. They just rose back up! We had to resign ourselves to the situation. There was nothing to be done. Once the laughter subsided, we made our way down the path. Bo figured that the entry to the locus was most likely somewhere in the decrepit house. Therefore, we resolutely headed in that direction. This was not without its challenges since it seemed to increase the static electricity in our bodies!

However, we figured we would be alright if we stopped every few feet to release some of the accumulated charges. That was not pleasant but necessary. The longer we waited, the stronger the shock! We found that out the hard way! And, we could not touch each other since that produced double the jolt! This made for slow going! Everyone was soon grumbling and getting discouraged.

The defensive mechanism was getting to us! I had just about enough of this myself. The dirt did not look inviting for going barefoot, but I decided to brave it anyhow. And it worked! My soles vibrated with every step, which tickled a bit, but beyond that, this was far more pleasant than what we had been doing! Soon, everyone was carrying their shoes in their hands, and we were making much better progress!

Once we reached the driveway, we walked along it. So far, we had not encountered any resistance beyond the static charge. However, that changed when we got closer to our destination and attempted to step into the frozen landscape around the house. A barrier, almost like the membranes to the nexuses, kept us from leaving the path! Except this one seemed impenetrable! To our frustration, not even Bo could make a hole in this! But we were determined.

Eventually, by pure chance, we discovered how to get it to yield so we could get through. It was all about the angle of approach! Before long, we had wormed our way into the space. Just to face a new challenge! If the rest of this cell had felt unpleasant, it had been nothing compared to what we were experiencing now! The sensations we were subjected to were just plain awful and almost sent several of us fleeing!

The air was so dense that it was nearly a liquid! This made it not only hard to move but especially difficult to breathe! Only Bo's reassurance that we would be alright kept the rest of us from panicking as the thick gas entered our lungs. Once we inhaled it fully, it was not so bad. We were obviously still getting enough oxygen to function. So we decided to keep moving.

Due to the enormous resistance facing us, we struggled toward the dilapidated house with tremendous effort and ever so slowly. Step for exhausting step, we fought our way onward. One thing was certain: We had to be on the right path with this much opposition! My lungs felt like they were on fire, and my head was swimming from the reduced oxygen level in my blood. Still, we pushed onward. We had not come this far to give up!

It seemed to take forever to get close to our destination. By the time we reached the structure, I was so exhausted I could have dropped. Suddenly, even the dirty porch looked like an inviting place for a nap! But, our work was not yet done. We needed to get into the house! This, however, proved to be even more challenging than crossing the membrane! But, once again, we kept at it. We were too close to our goal to turn around!

Finally, something shifted. Several of us just fell through the door we were pushing on. The rest of our group followed more slowly. As can be expected, it was much murkier inside the dwelling than outside. At first, we could see very little. It would take our eyes a few minutes to adjust. However, what we could make out surprised us. The space we had entered seemed very different from what we had expected!

Chapter 49

The Locus

We had finally made it into the house. Instead of inside a dwelling, however, we found ourselves in a large, open space. It was surrounded by shadowy shapes that could have been trees, but it was too dark to see clearly. Since the rest of the hive was structured around it, this had to be a replica of an actual place that was directly connected to the origin of the enchantment. But, unlike in the real world, there was no wind, no air movement, nothing that could have blown away the cloying smell of decay that assaulted our noses.

At first, I was as puzzled by this strange setting as my companions. Then, more of what Geira had told me suddenly clicked into place. This had to be the spell's representation of the clearing near the hunting lodge where the scouts had found evidence of a fire! Katrín's husband and his men had to be somewhere around here! But where?

Katrín slid next to me, and she and all the others crowded close. I saw their questioning glances. Everyone was ill at ease in this strange environment.

"What is this place?" Katrín finally whispered.

"I believe this is a copy of the glade where the hunting party disappeared. It was created by the spell and then overlaid over the actual scenery. Something must have lured the men there. The clearing was probably filled with smoke from the kettle, so they would not have seen the witch. Once the riders entered within, they, the replica, the person casting the spell, and all her tools were shifted to this dimension! Here, it was easy for her to overpower the disoriented men."

"Where are the hunters?" Rita asked, looking around.

"Probably somewhere further in," I responded.

"And the horses? How did they get away from here?" Bo wanted to know.

"I bet the change in scenery spooked them, they unseated their riders, and they ran," Maxwell mused.

"Most likely," I confirmed. "The witch's anger was not directed at them, so she would have let them go. She had enough to do with the men!"

"How dangerous is this place? Could it capture us too?" Willow inquired, her eyes wide with fear.

"I am not sure, but Geira said to be extremely careful," I informed her. "And we should stick together until we know what we are dealing with!"

Not wanting to run afoul of any possible traps, none of us dared to move for a moment! What was out there waiting for us?

It was dark all around us except for the light the distant fire in the middle provided. Once our eyes had fully adjusted, we could vaguely make out the trees bordering the glade and some other details. Those, however, appeared rather strange. With all my heart, I wished for more illumination. Especially once I realized what that odd thing further in resembled! Needless to say, I shuddered. Maxwell must have come to the same conclusion.

He moved closer to Katrín and wrapped his arms protectively around her. If only Phillipe had been here to do the same! My mind did not want to accept what my eyes were perceiving. It was just too bizarre to be real! And, on top of that, I am not that fond of spiders! I will not kill them but still! I usually have my husband take them outside.

Why could it not have been something else? This was making my skin crawl!

In the dim light, we could just barely make out the shadowy outline of a vast web. It hung suspended in midair, about waist-high off the ground. Talk about creepy! This was the ultimate Halloween site! I would never be able to look at that holiday the same way again after seeing this nightmare setting! My entire body was balking at walking toward that, and I stood frozen!

But we were here to do a job. Somewhere in there had to be the men from the hunting party! With Bo leading the way, we carefully moved toward it. Unfortunately, this eerie structure did not look any better from close up! Getting caught in this would be so easy! The strands were as thick as my arm and appeared exceedingly sticky! One slight brush up against any of them would be all it would take to get stuck!

Needless to say, we eyed this thing with a fair amount of misgivings and revulsion. None of us wanted to go near it, and our instincts were screaming for us to back away! However, we needed to get to the middle of this! What was our safest option? After some discussion, we decided there was only one way to reach our destination. We would have to go underneath it and stay well clear of those tacky lines! Dropping down on all fours, we started forward.

I had not moved more than a few feet when I encountered a problem. My skirt! My knees were inside it! I would never get anywhere this way! Carefully, I backed up and got to my feet. The other women followed my example. This just would not do!

"We cannot crawl in these dresses like you men can! Maxwell and Bo, you are to avert your eyes! Do you mind going ahead of us?" I asked in a low voice.

Good thing that they had not gone very far and had stopped when the rest of us retreated! Somehow, this place did not lend itself to shouting. Maybe there was a spider around here somewhere! That was well within the realm of possibilities! Keeping our voices down was a prudent precaution. Making too much noise might attract the creature's attention!

"Maxwell and I will stay ahead of you. We will not look. You have my word. Do what you must," Bo's calm voice assured us.

In short order, the other ladies and I tied our skirts up around our waists. This allowed us unhindered movement, and we could crawl now without dealing with all that fabric. Carefully, we slid underneath the web again. We were ready to proceed!

I noticed that I was not the only one who was nervous. All of us kept looking around and up anxiously. This place just screamed giant arachnid, and from the dimensions of this net, it had to be huge! Large enough to see us as tasty morsels, that was for sure! I do not mind the little ones so much, but usually, I leave it to Phillipe to take them outside! This was my worst nightmare made real!

Slowly, our weary group inched its way toward our destination. The closer we got to the center, the lower the giant spider web hung. Crawling was now too dangerous, and we were slithering along on our stomachs. That, however, was an even more torturous way to proceed, but at least it kept us clear of the sticky mess above us!

Once we were further in, the firelight allowed us to see a little better. We were so preoccupied with moving along that it took a bit before we noticed several dark blobs suspended in the web. First, thinking spiders, these scared us! But then we got a closer look. They were cocoons!

These globules were suspended at regular intervals around the middle. And, they were quite large! At first, we had no idea what we were looking at, but that changed once we reached the first one of these silk-wrapped bundles. One glance was enough for me to suspect what we were dealing with!

Maxwell reached out and carefully cut back some of the material. When he had managed to make a hole through the layers, part of a face came into view! I was utterly stunned and thought I would throw up! I had expected some terrible things due to Geira's warning, but this was over the top!

Katrín sidled up next to him. When she saw what this strange parcel contained, her eyes filled with horror and then compassion. She might have hated her husband, but not even he deserved a fate such as this!

My companions and I now had an unobstructed look at this nightmare. A bright blaze burned merrily in the center of the open area in the middle of this horrid netting. It illuminated the immediate area. A cauldron bubbled away on the flames. It was spewing out smoke that rose straight up and then spread out in all directions. And then, placed in an orderly pattern and attached to some of the closest strands were the lifeless bodies of the hunting party!

From each of these ill-fated people, flashes of greenish light issued forth. These pulses ran outward along the radial spokes of the net. They disappeared into the distance. Since we all knew how this construct functioned, our hearts filled with pity for these unfortunate souls. Their life force was being used to power this section of the evil enchantment!

The sight of all these men imprisoned inside their cocoons, systematically being drained, was deeply disturbing. It upset Bo so much he started heaving. Willow and Rita wiggled over to him to lend assistance. The true implication of what had created him had been too much for his sensitive soul. Mæva and I scooted his way ourselves and gave him what comfort we could. The young man ended up in my arms, sobbing. It took a while for Bo to finally calm down.

Not that I could blame him! Only a very sick mind could have devised an atrocity like this! From Geira, I knew that the concept had been conceived eons ago, during a time when dark magic was much more prevalent. Perhaps, it had been designed by a 'black widow.' The woman who had called this construct into life must have found the instructions in some ancient grimoire! She had adapted them to her purposes and had then deployed the spell to exact her revenge!

Katrín's philandering husband must have tangled with the wrong type of witch! It had cost him dearly, but not only him. I suspected that the one the sorceress saw as her competition was his wife, Katrín, a Magnuson. Therefore, the jealous and vindictive enchantress must have decided to make the entire clan pay, as well as the hunting party!

Only a very bitter and twisted person would do harm to so many innocents! Or a very desperate one who no longer cared about the consequences!

In my embrace, Bo was still shaking like a leaf. This was just too overwhelming for him, and I could sense that he was in the midst of a major identity crisis. Something had to be done. The words of my favorite hypnotherapist came to mind.

"Bo, this is not you. Do you understand? You are gentle and kind! You are a remarkable man we all love. This, all this, is not you!"I whispered in his ear.

I could feel him quieting. He was listening.

"You are the one Hilda loves. Do you think that she could be such a poor judge of character? She loves you for you, for all the good in you. Your origin does not matter. It is what you have done with it that does!" I continued.

Bo finally looked up, trying to reassure himself that I truly meant what I said. I held his searching gaze steadily, and when I saw the despair leave his eyes, I gave him a loving smile which he returned.

"This is not me," he stated firmly in a low voice. "I did not do this, and I chose good."

"Are you ready to get this over with?" I asked him.

"More than," came his resolute reply.

Having that problem solved, we were facing another. Mæva and I looked at each other helplessly. Where did we get started dismantling this thing? If we doused the fire, we closed the portals. This would cut off our only way home. We had too many people with us to risk that!

Quenching the flames would fall to the last person remaining in the trap, probably me. We hoped I would be spit back out at my point of origin, but that was not a given.

Unfortunately, with this kind of a complicated spell, there were no guarantees! I knew the risks and that I might never make it home. The collapse of the enchantment could lead to it taking everything and everyone remaining along with it to whatever void it was drawn into. Maybe Bo and I could create some sort of a lifeline, and he could pull me into the Meeting Place if things went wrong. That would be better than disappearing altogether! At least I would still have my friends!

We needed a plan. This part was too critical to attack without one. After consulting with Katrín and Maxwell, we decided we would cut all the hunters free one after another but leave her wayward spouse for last. Since the spell was feeding on them, the more of its energy source it lost, the more it would be drawing from those who remained. Unfortunately, there was nothing we could do about that.

Patching it into a ley line like we had done with Bo was just not an option. He had carefully supplied the rest of the construct with just enough energy to sustain it. What would this thing do with that kind of a power supply? You do not feed a monster! It could truly rev up and use the unlimited energy source to grow to gigantic proportions! That would mean the end of our clan and all those associated with us! Maybe even the end of our world!

I shuddered at the thought, as did Bo. He would have to be very careful not to get near these strands! If he was caught, connected as he was to the network of ley lines, we would all be in trouble, including his unborn child! Therefore, we asked him to hang back as much as possible and to watch himself. The rest of us would handle this part!

Our group cautiously worked their way around the first person suspended above us. As luck would have it, it was not Katrín's husband! Even now, she had no intention of facing him. With Maxwell supporting the hunter from below, Mæva and I cut the man free using the daggers she always carried. Then, Rita, Willow, Bo, and Revna pulled him toward the spot we had designated as the collection site. Nearby, the smoke was touching the floor, hopefully creating a portal. They left him there for the time being and came back for the next.

After a while, we had freed all but one guy and Finley. I could feel a significant weakening in the spell with each person we removed. But now, the construct was desperately fishing around for more sources to power itself. We had to be extra careful to avoid the loose strands whipping about. More and more of them were ripping away from the web as if sensing our presence. That, in itself, was rather scary!

By this time, it had become too dangerous for Bo to get near it, so we had him watch the rescued victims. After almost getting caught, Willow stayed with him. Rita and Katrín joined them a short while later. Only Maxwell, Revna, Mæva, and I went after the other guy. After several close calls with those tentacle-like filaments, we managed to cut him out of his cocoon.

Keeping as low as possible, we dragged him back to the others. On our way, I noticed that the movements of those irate strands were getting a bit sluggish. Mæva had observed the same thing and suggested waiting for a while before rescuing the last victim. Hopefully, it would make it much safer for us to crawl under that net! As compassionate as we were, we were not willing to risk our lives for the cad who had caused all this!

We would take the rest back, then deal with his recovery. The enchantment would be very unwilling to relinquish this last morsel, so the weaker it was, the better for us!

All those we had rescued so far were still deeply unconscious. Bo had been trying to bring them around and had channeled some of the energy from the ley line into them, but it had not helped much. They were breathing a little bit easier and less raspy, but that was about it. We decided to take them home immediately. They needed to get away from this place and out of the influence sphere of the spell. Maybe then they would have a chance to recover!

So we pulled them into the smoke. This time, calling in the right location was remarkably easy. Once it fully came into focus, we prepared to move the men into the clearing. Stepping out of the smoke was like emerging from the twilight zone into the light! But we could not stay, none of us! Our work was not yet done. Bo anchored the portal while the rest of us carried the hunters and gently laid them down in the grass.

Since only Katrín knew the place, it was up to her to get help for these unfortunate individuals. But she was not yet part of this time and place either, so she would have to leave a note at the mansion. Naturally, Maxwell, Rita, and Willow went with her. We watched the group make their way through the frozen landscape. They had some distance to go, so we settled in for a long wait.

Their absence gave Mæva, Revna, Bo, and me a chance to decide what to do next. The only one maintaining that awful web now was Katrín's husband. What was this doing to him? In the light of the sun, we had our first chance to thoroughly study the guys we had rescued. While Bo stayed within the border of the smoke and watched us, we made our way into the glade. Going from person to person, we examined each thoroughly.

The ladies and I did not like what we found. These hunters were extremely pale, their faces were deeply lined, and their hair was white. These were old, frail men! Had they started out this way? We did not believe so! None of these individuals could handle a horse! Katrín had mentioned that most of these chaps were in their thirties and forties, but they appeared to be ancient!

To our horror, we realized they had been utterly drained of their vitality. As of yet, none of them had awoken. Judging from their condition, there was no guarantee they ever would. We had a lot to thank Bo for. He had prevented the enchantment from using those it held captive in the nexuses as batteries! Had he not, the many days most of us had spent imprisoned there would have cost us years of our lives!

By the appearance of these guys, one man alone providing the energy to maintain the construct could not last long. Therefore, we were greatly relieved when Katrín and her group finally returned. They waited with us in the smoke. Shortly after their arrival, several men rode into the clearing, followed by wagons. Her note had been found and action taken!

We lingered since none of us were overly in a hurry to return to the web. We were too curious to see what would happen to these guys, so we watched the rescue party work. Katrín quietly shared with us that, having no option but to go through with the nuptials, she had convinced her parents that the groom needed to write a new will before they were married. Thanks to her foresight, if Finley did not survive, she would end up with the large home and beautiful grounds that belonged to her spouse.

Since it had been her only condition, her folks had decided to honor Katrín's wish. The document had been signed, sealed, and delivered on the morning of the wedding. As requested, Finley was leaving all his worldly possession to his wife in case of his death. This was about to benefit her greatly since I seriously doubted he would live through the ordeal. Now we just needed to figure out how to insert Maxwell into Katrín's life!

After a moment, while the others still watched the clearing, Katrín took Mæva and me aside. I was instantly curious, and so was my friend.

"Do you and Maxwell want to remain here?" Mæva asked. "The spell is almost ready but not quite."

"I will only stay if my husband does not make it back, at least not alive! But, before I can legally claim his possessions, I need your help. Please, I beg you!"

Katrín's eyes were beseeching us, and I, for one, knew that I could not turn her down. From what she had told us, I had an inkling of what was to come and what she needed our assistance with. As did Mæva.

"How can we help you?" she asked resignedly.

"Due to the interruption of our wedding night, the marriage was never consummated. As loathe as I am to do this, that needs to change. Do you have any suggestions?"

Mæva sighed. We both understood. Katrín was an honest person and not the kind of woman who would be able to lie even if her entire future depended on it. We had a quick word with Bo. He would keep the others there with him, especially Maxwell! They would continue to observe the rescue until we were done.

The three of us returned to the locus. Carefully, we wiggled our way over to Katrín's husband and cut him free from the net. He did not weigh much anymore. Gently, we lowered him to the ground. Even for one as wicked as him, we had compassion. He had suffered enough!

Just as soon as we severed Finley's connection to the strands holding him, the web started to disintegrate, and with it, the hive. Good thing that everything living was right here in the center with us and that we could dial in our homes from right here! Then, with dawning horror, my thoughts flashed to the poor steeds. I could not leave them to perish like this!

"The horses! I need to go get them! I almost forgot about them!" I gasped out loud.

"You go! We got this! But hurry! You do not have very long!" Mæva immediately commanded.

She and I exchanged a glance. In a way, it was good that I would not be here. The fewer people were present for what she and Katrín were about to do, the better. The act was distasteful enough as it was! Secretly, I was relieved. I really had not looked forward to witnessing the consummation of a marriage with someone who was mostly a corpse!

The thought alone made me shudder, and I admired the young lady for having the gumption to go through with this action!

Moving away from the locus turned out to be much easier than going toward it had been. Especially now that much of its power had been broken! I reached the horses just in time. All the other nexuses had disappeared. This was the only one left, probably maintained due to their presence. But even here, the scenery was starting to look rather diffuse! We did not have much time left!

At least these poor animals were in better shape than the last time I had seen them! I sent a silent thank you to Bo. He had made this miracle possible! They were still weak and very docile, but they could walk! Was there a way to get them home without taking them to the center? I did not think there was enough time to make it there as slowly as these guys were moving! Desperately, I searched for a remnant of the smoke that harbored the portal.

Finally, I spotted a diffuse patch between a couple of trees. I herded the animals toward it. Since the area was too small to take them through all at once, I would have to devise a way to take them through one by one. Leads would have been so handy about now, but there were none! That made me wonder what had happened to the saddles and gear they must have been wearing. It seemed to have vanished!

Knowing these were intelligent creatures, I explained what had to be done. Then, I dialed in the location and took the poor beast that appeared to be the leader through first. As I had hoped, the others followed us into the meadow beyond. Once they saw the green, clean grass, they immediately started grazing.

Hopefully, they were not too far gone and could recover. Luckily, they were much better off than their riders! I was sure Katrín would see to their welfare if I asked her.

Stopping just within the smoke, I stood there watching them. After a bit, one of the mounts, an older mare, came over and nuzzled my cheek as if to say thank you. In return, I petted her and kissed her on her velvety nose. When she insisted, I wrapped my arms around her slender neck and hugged her close. The embrace gave both of us comfort, and we stayed that way for a couple of minutes. Then, knowing I needed to go, I sent my new friend back to the herd.

The rescue party was nearby, and once the portal was closed, the horses would resync with their time. Most likely, they would drift toward the voices. But that was up to them, and I told them as much before bidding them goodbye. I do believe they got the gist of what I was saying. Animals are so much more intelligent than we humans give them credit for!

The few moments of peacefulness had done me good, but I needed to return if I did not want to get stuck here. The others were nearby, and I could have walked over. But I intended to keep Katrín's secret so

I would go back to the locus the way I had come! To my relief, since the enchantment had no power source left, it was relatively easy to return to the house. And running flat out, it did not take me very long!

Then I slowed. To be honest, I was not in that much of a hurry anymore! I really did not want to see what the two women were up to! Thankfully, when I arrived at the center of the web, Katrín and Mæva had completed their mission. The young lady now carried her husband's seed within her and was no longer a virgin. She could claim to be his wife with a clear conscience since the marriage had been consummated. Both of them were tending to Finley, who was in terrible shape.

I knelt down next to them and helped as much as possible. But there was nothing we could do for the man. All that was left of him was an ancient, dried-up shell. He would not have wanted to live like that! Shortly after I got there, Finley took his last breath. Katrín sat beside her husband and held his hand as he passed. She closed his eyes with a gentleness that spoke of unconditional forgiveness for everything he had done.

Finley's body was so desiccated and light that we had no problem carrying him into the smoke. As soon as he saw us, Maxwell rushed over to help. Together, we took the corpse through into the meadow. Just like any loving wife would have done, Katrín would have him buried in the family plot with all honors. She would not miss him, but most who knew the man would not expect her to. But, for the sake of the babe she carried, she would keep up appearances!

Our main task was accomplished, and it was time to say goodbye. Bo pulled Mæva aside, and the two had a whispered discussion. I watched as my friend hit her forehead with the palm of her hand in a gesture of exasperation.

"We got the spell," she declared shortly after. "Maxwell, you are sure that you wish to remain here? There is no undoing this once we finish!"

"I have never been so sure of anything in my life," Maxwell responded.

"Here it goes then," Mæva told him.

Together, she and Bo gave voice to the incantation. I could feel its power and instinctively moved further back into the smoke. From there, I waved a final goodbye to the young couple. I hoped that Katrín and Maxwell would be very happy together. To ensure there were no problems, we would linger. Therefore, the rest of us retreated just far enough into the plume that the pair became part of their world.

Fascinated, we watched as the rescuers came running in answer to Maxwell's shouts for help. They found the young lady kneeling beside her husband, crying bitter tears. Before long, Finley was loaded up, and, in a show of respect, Katrín and Maxwell walked behind the wagon carrying her deceased spouse. Oddly, no one thought anything of it that this stranger supported her on the way to the mansion. How was that possible? This was definitely odd!

Finley's body was proof that Katrín was now a widow. Thanks to this, she would become the legal owner of the estate within a short time. Had he remained missing, she might have had to wait years to have him declared dead. Plus, it avoided the possibility of some zealous judge deciding that she needed a guardian!

Still, it was sad that he had passed. Now Finley would never have the chance to atone for his sins! However, it was a much better outcome for Katrín! As soon as the mourning period ended, she could get on with her life! And, having money and an estate, she could do so on her own terms!

I was happy for her and hoped she and Maxwell would have a fabulous life!

Chapter 50

A Final Goodbye

Once Katrín and Maxwell were safely deposited in her time, the rest of us breathed a sigh of relief. Bo and Mæva were absolutely delighted that their enchantment had worked so well! They had finally figured out just what to add. But, our work was not yet done. We still had Rita and Willow to return before we could make it to our homes, and we did not have much time.

The passing of the man who had caused all this grief had shrunk the construct down to a small space around the fire. It was unstable and almost ready to collapse. We needed to get out of here and fast or vanish along with it forever; not a thought that appealed to any of us! After a hurried goodbye, we dropped the two girls off at Willow's origin. Bo's and Mæva's incantation would allow Rita to fully integrate into her friend's world. Everyone would believe that she had always been part of their lives.

How clever to think of including that in their enchantment! It explained the easy acceptance of Maxwell that had puzzled me so much!

Timewise, the two were only six months after Katrín. And they were in the same area! Therefore, the young ladies had already set up a meeting. Willow even knew the estate! She had been to the hunting cabin once, a while ago, with her mother. That coincidence was truly incredible! The tale of that visit had created a bond between her and Katrín.

After some hesitation, the young lady had told the rest of us the story. Years ago, her mother had felt the need for the services of a witch. She had not wanted to go alone but had been desperate enough to make the trek. So she had taken Willow along. Fearing her husband was losing interest in her, she wanted to purchase a love spell to renew their relationship.

While Willow and her mother waited for the witch to prepare the potion, the owner of the estate, Finley, had dropped by to visit his mistress. That was how the girl encountered them both. She had liked the gorgeous, sweet enchantress but had disliked the arrogant, unpleasant man from the very first moment. He had barged in and, with barely a hello, had roughly dragged the woman into the next room.

Mother and daughter could hear him having his way with her as well as the moans of pain from his victim. Once he was finished, he had stormed out without acknowledging any of them. He had left the door to the chamber open, exposing the misery he had left behind. His mistress was still helplessly sprawled over the desk where he had just brutally taken her.

Willow and her mum had helped the poor lady up and into the washroom. After what he had done to her, even walking had hurt! Groaning, the sorceress had cleaned herself up. She had needed their assistance for that and for changing her stained clothes. Tears had run down her face the entire time, and not just of sadness. To have someone witness this abuse had been highly embarrassing for the proud woman.

Nonetheless, she had been glad that they were present. Willow had assumed from some of the lady's comments that Finley had been an absolute brute before. He appeared to enjoy hurting and humiliating his paramour for some unexplainable reason. Out of gratitude for their aid and to assure their silence, she had not charged for the potion. Which, by the way, had worked admirably!

Willow had been aghast at the scene, and her heart had gone out to the abused woman. It had been beyond her understanding that she would continue to tolerate this. Why? There had been no love in Finley's heart, not a smidgen. It was not something he seemed capable of! Had she been trying to save him? Or was her behavior based on hurt from her childhood?

She appeared to be craving his respect and acceptance! But that awful man had been unable and unwilling to give it! Katrín had not been the only one moved to tears! Hearing how the powerful sorceress demeaned herself to please such a monster and win his heart, those of us who had listened to the tale had pitied the woman despite the awful spell she had cast that had imprisoned so many.

How sad for someone as remarkable and talented as this enchantress to try so desperately to win such a depraved individual's love! She had deserved so much better! Why had she been unable to walk away? Finley had just been using her! And what had happened to the witch after casting that horrid enchantment? What price had she paid for her revenge? Geira had hinted that it must have been high. That kind of dark magic took a toll on the body, mind, and soul!

I could only hope that she had found some peace. Katrín had every intention of looking into this further. After hearing what Finley had done to his mistress, the young lady had seen her wedding night in a whole new light! She had realized she had been spared a similar fate by the timely interruption!

Being sucked into the time trap had saved Katrín from a life spent in misery married to Finley! Plus, she now had Maxwell, would inherit the beautiful estate, and was expecting a child! We all knew who was to blame for the entire debacle, and it was not the sorceress! Katrín, Rita, and Willow had decided to forgive her, especially since the enchantment had also brought the three of them together. With Willow living nearby, they could visit each other whenever they pleased!

If only Eldred, Hilda, and I had been so lucky, but at least we had the Meeting Place that would allow us to get together. I suspected it would be rather busy for a while, at least in the beginning. Bo, kind as always, had invited the entire group we had collected to visit!

Now that Willow and Rita were home, Revna's was next. Her leaving was almost as hard as it had been to say goodbye to the sisters! Our friend turned a couple of times to wave to us, but I could barely see her through the veil of my tears. Then, as things continued to deteriorate around us, it was time to get Bo out of there. He needed to get to the Meeting Place before the construct took him along into oblivion. Hilda would never forgive me if I did not make sure that he was safe!

As we had planned, only Mæva and I remained. We still had one task left. One of us had to extinguish the smoldering fire, thus preventing the time trap from drawing anyone else into its sphere of influence. We did not want it to come back to life and begin to grow again! Once was quite enough! I was fully prepared to tackle this chore and douse the remaining flames with a spell, but Mæva objected.

"Cara, go home! Leave this to me!" she insisted.

"But you need to get back to your loved ones too!" I protested.

"Child, if I end up somewhere else, maybe I will find that spice that I have been missing," she said with a wink. "You have a husband waiting for you!"

"But Mæva! We have no idea what will happen! Maybe we should do this together?"

"Cara, go, return to your Phillipe!" Mæva commanded.

"But what about you? What will happen to you?"

"I will end up somewhere, most likely back at my home. It does not matter. Beyond my husband, I have no family waiting for me, and you know the state of our marriage! Wherever I end up, I will build a life for myself! I will see you soon at the Meeting Place, or if I cannot get there for some reason, I will find a way to send you a message in the clan's history books!"

"Thank you for all your help and everything you have taught me!" I told her tearfully, clinging to her for a moment.

"Let me give you one last piece of advice. I know that you are a modern woman and all that," Mæva began. "And you think you can do everything by yourself, but do find a teacher, will you? You have so much potential but much yet to learn! It is best if you know how to use it."

"I will, I promise. Goodbye, my friend, and good luck!"

With those words, I stepped into the small patch of smoke that still lingered. Calling in a destination was easy now that we had taken everyone else home, and the construct was out of power! It should only take me just a few seconds!

Grounding myself, I prepared to dial in the proper destination. To my horror, my mind went blank! After several attempts, a wave of fear crashed through me. Then, panic set in. No matter how hard I tried, I could not remember the vibration of my home! How was it possible that I could not recall the feel of my own time and space? All I got was a jumble of destinations! I could clearly recollect how to tune in to several other locations but not my own! This was ridiculous!

My heart started racing, and my breathing was shallow and fast. It seemed like a band was squeezing my ribs! I was afraid I was about to pass out and was so anxious that I could not think straight. My head was swimming, and I had no idea what to do or how to get myself home! Dark spots started appearing in my vision, and my stomach was roiling.

Realizing I needed to calm myself, I deepened and slowed my breathing, staying with each breath. Finally, the rapid drumbeat in my chest and the tightness there started to release a little. It took me a few more minutes to clear my mind enough to reestablish rationality. I remained centered like that, not focusing on anything in particular, just letting thoughts swim in and out.

Finally, the seed of an option began to crystallize. Was it possible to concentrate on a person instead of homing in on the place? I sure hoped so! There was one vibration that I could never forget. Phillipe! The love of my life! I started visualizing him, things we had done together, the loving way he touched my face or caressed my hair. As always, a smile began to curve my mouth when I thought of him. Having been away from my husband for weeks, the longing inside me grew to tremendous proportions.

I wanted to feel his arms around me and rest in the blissfulness of his embrace. That sensation was so heavenly; it was like floating in a sea of happiness, shelter, and love. I needed to hear that everything would be alright, that we could put that awful fight behind us! The more real his presence became, the stronger I could feel the pull toward a specific location. Eventually, the tension grew almost too intense to stand, like a rubber band ready to snap.

From one second to the next, I felt something give, and I found myself back on the path I had run down so long ago.

I looked around, feeling disoriented. Not surprising since I had been gone for a while! Only a few minutes should have passed here, but I had spent several weeks in the enchanted construct. So much had changed in that time, including me! My magic was much stronger now than ever before! However, the things I had seen, especially in the center of that awful hive, had left a lasting impression and provided more fodder for bad dreams!

Even before this incident, I often had nightmares. Some had been absolutely dreadful. Usually, I was called upon to be a defender of something or another. Sometimes, I tried to fly away, only to be brought down by whatever was pursuing me. Occasionally, I would wake up to a sense of danger in my home so intense that it had me cowering under the covers or in Phillipe's arms. The dogs would rush to my side whenever that happened to comfort me.

Now, my active mind had even more material for creating such horrors! How would that affect my husband and me? Only time will tell! His presence usually helped me sleep peacefully. Phillipe knew this, which was one reason he preferred to take me along whenever he needed to travel to Ny Havn. The other was that we enjoyed being together and genuinely loved each other.

As silly as this sounds, we would miss each other just as soon as one of us walked out the door! However, for me, being so in love and having it returned never ceased to be a miracle.

Hopefully, we would deal with the fallout of this exceptional adventure together. For now, all I wanted was to go home. I needed to see Phillipe and the pets! Looking around, I oriented myself. I had been going in the opposite direction when I walked into the trap! Now, the neighborhood houses stood to my right. The magical forest was to my left, where it was supposed to be. The place was correct but was the time?

I could hear birdsong and felt a gentle breeze from the nearby sea caressing my face. That alone was tremendously reassuring! I really was back! Since I was already pointed toward home, I took a few hesitant steps in that direction. Then, partly out of a sense of nostalgia since I was missing my friends but also to make sure that the portal would vanish, I turned to take one last look at the smoke that had so efficiently trapped me.

As I watched, the plume started drawing in onto itself, as if it was being sucked toward one spot! It was quite fascinating to observe since it seemed to fight against the forces reeling it in! Soon, all that remained was a dense ball of roiling mist. It hung there in midair for a moment, but then, with a sound like a pop, it completely disappeared. The way back to the time trap was gone!

Mæva had done it! The spell was finally broken! Many of us had turned it into something positive, but some of the victims would be scared for life by their experience! To think that all that misery happened because of one man! He had paid the ultimate price for his betrayal, but still, that anyone could treat others in the manner he had was incomprehensible to me. We were all human beings and deserved love and respect!

For another minute, I stood there staring thoughtfully at the spot where the portal to the time trap had been. Then, more pressing matters intruded into my contemplations. I had assumed that only a few minutes had passed here, even if it had seemed like forever in the construct. Was Phillipe still furious with me? After everything that had happened, I did not feel up to handling his anger! What was I facing? I had no clue. That was enough to fill me with apprehension!

Hesitantly, I resumed my walk toward our home. However, I had not gone far before I noticed something that had escaped me until then. I came to a dead stop. The sunlight was all wrong! Instead of coming from the east as it had been when I left our house, it was now shining from the opposite direction! It was not morning here but evening!

The sun was just about to set, and it would be dark soon! How could this be? Only minutes had passed when we had rejoined Eldred's and Hilda's wedding procession!

Chapter 51

Phillipe

Standing there frozen in place, I was feeling decidedly nauseous. Since the enchantment had been on the verge of collapse, the portal must have stopped working correctly! At least I was in the right place! That was a start. But when was this? How long had I been gone? Was this even the same day? The same year? I had no way of knowing! Or did I? I thought about it for a moment, then, all of a sudden, I remembered my cell phone. It should work now! I had totally forgotten about it since it had been little more than an expensive camera in the construct!

Whipping it out, I turned it on. Wouldn't you know it, the thing immediately started pinging. I had messages, lots of them! And they were flooding in so fast that I could barely keep track! Most were from Phillipe but also a couple from my mother. With a sinking feeling in my gut, I looked at the date. I barely caught a glimpse of it right before the battery went dead. Instead of just a few minutes or a few hours, I had been gone for over two days!

The weakening of the spell had affected things more than we had suspected! Time must have sped up in what was left of the hive once it lost its primary energy supply, the hunting party. For the moment, I had no other explanation. How had this impacted Mæva? She would have been subjected to this effect the most! Had she even made it back, and how many days or weeks had passed for her?

As soon as I got a chance to sit down and meditate, I would head to the Meeting Place and find out what had happened to her! And, naturally, to catch up with the rest! For now, I better get home, and quickly! It sounded like my mother was just about ready to head down from Ny Havn if she did not hear from me soon! That alone would result in a nightmare for Phillipe since she was not fond of our dogs! Nor they of her!

Being well-behaved, they tolerated her, but as upset as they must be by my sudden disappearance, they might not be as cooperative as usual! It was better to prevent all that chaos that would result from her visit! I needed solace and peace for a few days, and I really wanted to spend time alone with Phillipe. I had missed him so much! We would go sailing like we always did when I was stressed. Being out on the water always helped to renew my spirit!

One good thing about this time of day was that not many people were out and about. Most were home enjoying their dinner. The one person I met gave me a strange stare as I rushed past them. Only then did it dawn on me that I looked a bit out of place in my finery from days long past! But at least I looked beautiful in that magnificent dark-green gown! Using my fingers, I combed through my mane. It was wild, as usual, and beyond taming. Not much that I could do about that!

The story I had to tell was rather strange. I could barely believe it myself! However, the dress proved that I had been somewhere else and assured me that my whole adventure had not just been a dream. As soon as possible, I intended to reread our history files to see what had changed. Judging from these texts, my mother had been seriously worried. Somehow I had the feeling that she would insist on us visiting after my going missing for two days!

By spending a few days in Ny Havn, we could reassure her, and I could browse the archives. For my own peace of mind, I needed to know how and what things had been altered. We would be killing two birds with one stone. I rather liked the idea and sped up a little more; not easy in the long gown! It was meant for floating or gliding along serenely, not almost jogging!

Before I had gone too much further, I spotted a tall man with two large German Shepherds coming my way. I would have recognized that trio anywhere! When they saw me, there was no holding them back. I am not sure who ran faster! This time, the man got to greet me before the exuberant dogs. That, in itself, was a miracle! From one moment to the next, I found myself enfolded in Phillipe's loving arms. He held me so tightly that I could barely breathe while Bear and Hella bounced around us.

Something released inside of me, and I burst into tears. I clung to my husband as if my life depended on never letting him go. As usual, he understood me without words. Phillipe just held me and let me cry. Slowly but surely, the feeling of being home, of being safe, penetrated my being and warmed me through and through. Finally, I raised my face to meet his concerned gaze.

"Where have you been for the last two days, love? We have been looking everywhere for you!" he asked me, full of concern.

Fear sent a stab through me. Being a Magnuson, Phillipe could have ended up in the same trap!

"Did you go along the path?"

"No, Jensen did. Several times! I took the car down to the harbor, checked the boat, and walked the beach from there. I knew that if you were anywhere near, the dogs would find you!"

"They would have," I stated with conviction, petting Bear's head.

"I knew something had happened to you when I had this horrible sensation of emptiness a few minutes after you left! And then the dogs started howling! That really sent me into a panic!" Phillipe confided.

"I can imagine!" I knew how I would have felt had he been the one to disappear!

"What happened to you?"Phillipe asked again, his face serious. "Where were you?"

"I was so upset by our fight that, like an idiot, I walked into a cloud of hazel smoke," I admitted shamefacedly.

"You walked into an enchantment?" Phillipe was aghast and looked at me with even more concern.

"Yes, and believe me, getting back was not easy!"

Pulling me close again, my husband buried his face in my hair. I could feel him shaking now that he realized how close he had come to losing me forever.

"Shh, love, I am back now, and all is well!"

"You have no idea how happy I am to see you," he murmured into my ear.

In response, I kissed him, long and deep. I could feel our souls intertwine, rejoicing at being reunited. Slowly, we grew calmer. Finally, we drew apart a little to look at each other.

"You were definitely not wearing that when you left!" Phillipe stated admiringly, noticing the gown for the first time.

"No, I was not," I smiled back at him.

Taking a step back, Phillipe examined me from head to toe. Then, he walked around me as if to reassure himself that I was real and all of me had returned. When he found nothing amiss, he stopped in front of me. Gently, he took my face in his hands. His eyes met mine, and he searched their depths.

"Do you have any idea how worried I was? All of a sudden, I could no longer sense you! I thought I had lost you forever!" his voice was rough with emotions.

He pulled me close once more, and we clung to each other, taking comfort from the other's nearness.

"Did you feel me at times?" I finally asked curiously.

"I did, sometimes, but it seemed like you were very far away. I was so panicked when our connection just disappeared! I ran over to

Jensen's, and we went looking for you until late that night. I was going to contact the police if you were not back by morning, but then your mother called around midnight. She had sensed a disturbance in the fabric of time."

"My mother felt it when I disappeared?"

Now he really had my interest! This was definitely different!

"Yes! She immediately assembled the council, and she and the others tried to find you. They finally determined that you were alive but not on this earthly plane. The police, therefore, could not help," Phillipe explained. "Needless to say, she has summoned anyone she thought could help, and they have been working in shifts trying to locate you! We better call her and let her know that you are back!"

My phone was out of charge, so Phillipe handed me his. I was about to punch in the number when the phone rang.

"Hello, mother," I answered it.

"Are you alright?"

This was asked with an urgency that was very alien to my usually cool and composed mother. I could hear my father in the background as well. They obviously had been worried! Now, that was different! This would take some getting used to! Had the timeline changed that much?

"I just made it back, and we are on our way home," I told them.

"I know that!" my mother snapped impatiently.

Well, some things were the same! Naturally, she would know; she is, after all, clairvoyant! Trying to hide anything from her took some careful shielding and planning!

"Are you ok?" she asked, clearly upset. "What happened to you?"

"I was caught in a time trap, and yes, I am alright," I answered her calmly.

"Your father and I understand that you will need a few days to destress, but will you and Phillipe please come up to see us? We really need to talk!"

I looked at Phillipe, who nodded his approval.

"Yes, mother, we will come," I agreed.

"Good. We will see you then. Enjoy the sailing!" my parents wished me.

Since when did they know me this well? Now that was downright scary!

"We love you, sweetheart. We are so glad you are back with us!" my mother told me, her voice breaking for a second. Then she hung up.

This was definitely not the aloof, composed, and restrained woman I was used to! There had been real emotions in her voice! What else was different? So far, the changes were for the better, but they would still take some adjustment on my part. I could only hope that we had not altered the timeline too much!

"Wow! Now that was different!" I said out loud.

"She was really concerned; they both were," Phillipe confirmed.

"I am just not used to that from them," I clarified.

"They were not like that before? Wow! That explains why I kept getting this odd feeling every time I talked to them! This has been the strangest couple of days!" Phillipe exclaimed. "I was going to take the trail, but Bear and Hella Rose refused to go out the gate. Then, they started blocking me from getting near it! Next thing I know, Bear is snarling in the direction you had gone. I picked up an intense feeling of danger. Right then, I knew you were in trouble, and I just about rushed after you despite the dogs!"

"I am so glad that you did not follow me!"

"Believe me, I was going to find a way, even if I had to lock up the dogs! But your mother called and told me in no uncertain terms not to. Then she put a spell on me that rooted me to the ground the minute I got near the path! I was furious with her and asked her to undo it, but she refused."

"She must have sensed you were in danger of disappearing as well," I said thoughtfully.

"Your mother insisted that we could not afford to take action until we knew exactly what we were dealing with. But she did not stop me from taking the car and looking for you!"

"She must have known that was safe," I agreed. "Had you gone near the smoke ...."

I could not finish the sentence. The thought alone was too upsetting. In a way, having Phillipe there would have been a comfort to me. But it would have changed everything. As was my way, I would have been focused on him. We usually do things together, which somewhat limits contact with others. I would not have learned as much or spent so much time with the girls!

In addition, it would have given the construct a weapon to use against me! Had my husband been in danger, I would have done just about anything to save him!

"I could not sit at home and do nothing! I called Quinn over. He took care of our pets so I could go out looking for you. He has been helping me since."

His gaze locked onto mine.

"These have been the worst two days of my life! I do not know what I would have done had I lost you!" he ground out.

All I could do was hug him. I completely understood how he felt!

"You know, the temptation to go down that path and see what had Hella Rose and Bear so riled up was huge! But even before your mother put that spell on me, I got the strangest feeling whenever I neared the gate! I was even worried about Jensen going that way, but he insisted. Beyond a bit of smoke, he saw and felt nothing unusual."

I let out a sigh of relief. And reached out to pet my furry friends, who were crowding around us. They had decided that they had been patient long enough and that it was now their turn! Phillipe finally had to release me so that I could greet Hella Rose and Bear properly! I crouched down to hug them.

"I am glad that you did not follow me! What would have happened to the pets if you had ended up in the same place I did?" I told him over the top of Bear's head.

My big, beautiful Bear was pushed up tightly against me to give me comfort. His sister had wedged herself under my other arm. They could sense that a lot had happened while I was gone.

"Are you saying what I think you are saying? We might not have made it back had I joined you?"

"The dynamics would have been very different," I said with a shrug. "You will understand once I tell you the story!"

At my admission, Phillipe had gone pale. I immediately set out to divert him by changing the subject.

"So, how long did you stay angry with me?" I enquired teasingly.

"It was bizarre. I was so furious one minute, and then, the next, it was gone! Shortly after, I sensed that something was off! It was like waking up from one nightmare just to fall into another! Even though I could feel you were nowhere nearby, Bear, Hella Rose, and I checked the boat and the beaches. I was hoping your mother was wrong."

"She seldom is," I reminded him with a smile.

"Yes," Phillipe admitted. "But I was still going to keep looking for you! When you were not there, nor in town, we returned home to see if you were back."

Phillipe pulled me up and back into his embrace. His arms tightened around me once again.

"Sweetheart, you are squashing me!" I protested.

Reluctantly, he relaxed his grip just a little.

"We had just returned from another round when Bear raced out the pet door and toward the gate. He started dancing around and barking like crazy. A second later, Hella Rose joined him. This time, it was not a warning; they were clearly excited and happy!"

"They must have sensed that I was back!" I smiled at the dogs, patiently sitting, waiting for us to get on with the walk.

"I went out to look, and to my surprise, your mother's spell did not keep me from the gate! All four dogs were back there by then, trying to get out. I had Quinn collect Arianna and Micha and then put Hella Rose and Bear on a lead. They were in such a hurry they about pulled my arms out! And we finally found you!"

For a long moment, Phillipe and I just held each other. I could sense how upset he was, unusual for such a calm man.

"Let's go, shall we?" I finally suggested.

"Yes. I want you safe and sound in our home!" Phillipe agreed.

Keeping our arms around each other, we started walking. We had gone only a little way when his curiosity about the gown got the better of him.

"So tell me, where did you get that gorgeous dress? You did not leave in that!"

"No, I did not," I replied with a smile. "I will tell you everything but with a glass of wine or cup of cocoa in my hand!"

Gently, Phillipe squeezed my waist in acknowledgment, but he increased the pace. Curiosity was beginning to get the better of him. We reached the gate within a few minutes.

As we stepped into the garden, the sun sunk behind the horizon. The sky was magnificent, and I stopped to admire it. The hive's sunsets had been a fair imitation of all nature's glory but not like the real thing. Still, we had been grateful to Bo for making an effort. Trying to create something one has never seen before was hard. He had done a fantastic job, considering.

Maybe I could suggest to Hilda to find a way for him to see one. It was a little thing, but I had the feeling it would mean much to Bo. I was sure that Cedric would help since he knew how much all those in the time trap owed that young man. The girls' husband was usually most understanding!

I, for one, was so glad to be home. Now that it was over, the let-down from that exceptional adventure was so overwhelming that I staggered for a moment. Phillipe was immediately there to catch me. Like I weighed nothing, he picked me up and prepared to carry me inside.

Chapter 52

Home

Our pet sitter and neighbor, Quinn, pulled the door open just as Phillipe reached for the handle. The other two dogs, Arianna and Micha, had alerted him of our return. Both were ecstatic to see us, and my husband had to put me down so they could sniff me from head to toe to ascertain that I was unharmed. All four of them tagged along as we went to say hello to our guinea pig boys. Teddy and Orion sure acted like they had missed me too! I was pleased to see that Quinn had done such a marvelous job keeping them clean!

Naturally, our friend was curious as to what had happened to me. Since he had been a student at Ny Havn, he had no problems accepting my brief explanation. We promised to tell him more later after I had recovered a bit. Knowing we needed our privacy, he went on his way. But not before feeding and watering all the pets! We thanked him profusely. With the pack taken care of, Phillipe and I could concentrate on each other.

My loving husband insisted I rest on the couch while he started dinner. Since I was totally emotionally exhausted, I did not argue. Phillipe lovingly covered me up and kissed me once more for good measure before disappearing into the kitchen. To my surprise, he returned a short time later with a hot cup of delicious cocoa with whipped cream on top and some gluten-free cookies! Like I was an invalid, he helped me sit up so that I could enjoy this tasty treat.

Bear licked his chops and sat down next to me. He likes the cream almost as much as I do, and so does his little sister! Hella Rose had claimed a spot on the end of the couch, right next to Micha. She was also eyeing my mug hungrily. This time, however, I was not into sharing. I needed this pick-me-up more than they did! Even after the first few sips, I could feel the warmth coursing through my body.

Usually, I limit my sugar intake. However, my body had been burning calories with the time trap collapsing. We had been too busy to think about it then, and the food the girls had sent along was long gone. No nourishment in two days had taken its toll! My energy stores were just about depleted and needed recharging. No wonder I had started feeling weak! By the time dinner was on, I felt a little restored.

My husband and I went upstairs to change. Very carefully, Phillipe helped me out of the beautiful dress. I slipped on a pair of jeans and a pretty top in a color of blue that complimented my eyes. Like most of my shirts, it was form-fitting and set off my figure to perfection. Usually, this would have led to a fair amount of kissing and teasing. But this night, we needed comfort more than anything else.

As did the dogs! They had not left my side since I got home and stayed right next to me. And I mean, they pushed up against me! That had been ok for the snack but for dinner? We had a rule that food should be enjoyed. Therefore, we always fed the pets first! Who can relish a meal when you are looking into starving puppy dog eyes? Not me! We do not give them treats from the table either, but that has never prevented Hella Rose from trying to talk us into sharing. She is such a darling! For her, hope springs eternal!

Since Quinn had fed them, we handed out chewies. That should distract the dogs for a while! Then it was our turn. Until I sat at the table and the wonderful smell of roasted meat and vegetables reached my nose, I had not realized how hungry I was! It was tempting to wolf down everything on my plate, but that would not have done justice to this offering!

Instead, I savored each bite, especially since this meal was delicious. My husband had cooked things he knew I loved. Air-fried pork shoulder rubbed with a hint of cayenne pepper, rosemary, and parsley; asparagus; and an arugula salad. He had done an excellent job making foods that reminded me of home!

Naturally, Phillipe was burning with curiosity, but he understood that my bodily needs had to be met first. Therefore, he was being patient. Besides, talking with one's mouth full is just plain rude and does not give the meal the attention and appreciation it deserves. He smiled indulgently when I went for seconds, something I rarely do, but I am usually not as famished!

After we ate, I shared my story. Phillipe had no problem believing me. He was kin to the Magnusons, after all, even if he bears the Mackay name! We are used to the unusual and grow up being taught simple spells early on. Being aware that there is more around us than many are willing to see, we have long since come to expect that things go wrong on occasion!

Life can be unpredictable at the best of times, and even more so when you add magic to the mix! But I would not trade that for anything! That little extra sure added spice!

To preserve my report, we recorded my lengthy account. Systematically, I worked my way through all the events. I went from my entry into the time trap to my exit, careful not to forget anything important. Therefore, reaching the end took several hours and a couple more mugs of hot tea. For some reason, the wine did not taste right to me that night.

My husband asked an occasional question when clarification was called for. However, knowing I was tired, he kept interruptions to a minimum.

"So, Cedric looks just like me, eh?" Phillipe teased when I was done.

"He sure does! You guys even act alike!" I affirmed. "I really want you to meet them all!"

"I would like that!" Phillipe stated with a smile. "What an exceptional adventure you had! I now understand why my presence would have caused trouble. For one, Bo might have never come into existence!"

I looked at him, horrified. Our circle of friends in the hive saw Bo as a very special person we loved dearly. The thought that he might have never been 'born' had circumstances been different was stunning! Amazing how it had all come together to work out for the best! At least for most of us! And how the addition of one extra individual could have upset it all!

"How did Bo come into being anyhow?" Phillipe asked me curiously.

"All we have is conjecture. As far as we know, the enchantment was doing what it was designed for, except that Eldred could get out of the nexus she and her sister found themselves in! That was the first anomaly! She was the only one of all the captives who could move around! I believe her ability to visit all the others set the stage.

"Then, I came along. For some unfathomable reason, my arrival in the hive was the catalyst that created the possibility. Shortly after, Eldred and Hilda entered my cell. Our meeting and our immediate closeness were the spark for Bo's 'birth.' His consciousness was formed then. But it took a while longer for him to reach the point where he could reach out and affect his surroundings and make himself known." I explained.

"I wonder, did this happen by pure chance?" Phillipe mused. "Or maybe by the design of some Divine power?"

"From what Geira said, to have an independent agent born of such magic was a miracle to start with! That he would end up working against the purpose of the spell even more so! This was never the intention of the witch who cast it! She wanted us to suffer and be drained of our life force until we faded away into nothingness!"

"What a horrible fate!" Phillipe uttered, his voice rough with emotions.

"Her agenda was the total annihilation of the Magnuson Clan! Had we not stopped the enchantment, she might have succeeded!"

"Is it possible that a higher power had a hand in helping you?" Phillipe speculated.

We pondered his question in silence for a while.

"I think so," I finally conceded. "How else could events have developed in such an incredible manner? Whoever was looking out for us, we have much to thank him or her for!"

That, we both agreed on. Instead of robbing the clan of its members as had been the witch's intention, people had come together who would have never met otherwise! As a result, deep friendships had formed, and knowledge was shared that had improved conditions for those who lived before us.

What would the archives contain about the time trap? Phillipe was as curious as I was! He proposed to check for any messages from my new friends. Therefore, we got out my computer and logged into the restricted section. The files it contained were only for the eyes of the Magnuson Clan. The collection spanned well over a thousand years and had been lovingly assembled and uploaded by our family members.

It took us a bit, but finally, we located all the files pertaining to Eldred and Hilda. Their lives had been happy and rewarding. They and Cedric had produced a large number of offspring. I had remembered correctly; I was a descendant of Eldred, and Phillipe of Hilda. One letter, written long ago by the girls, had never made much sense to any of us until now. It was addressed to me and so full of love that it brought tears to my eyes.

Next, we looked for entries about Mæva. Sure enough, she had made a place for herself but not with her husband of long ago! Instead, she had ended up so close to my time that she was still alive! Phillipe and I looked at each other in wonder. Here was his chance to meet one of the people I had become close to in the flesh! We instantly decided we would go visit her.

For once, sailing could wait! My darling husband realized that seeing with my own eyes that this wonderful lady was safe meant more to me. Now we just had to find her!

However, locating Mæva's current address turned out to be much more difficult than we had thought. Search as we might, we kept coming up empty. It was almost as if she was hiding from us! So we kept trying different ways and sources to locate her but without any luck. This was most perplexing!

We had been at this for a while when suddenly, we realized that I would have to go before the council. Those of the Magnuson Clan with the most magic who monitored our world needed to know what had happened! The effects of those implausible meetings might still be reverberating through our reality!

Phillipe and I understood how important my information was. Sharing it could not be delayed. I was surprised that my mother had not insisted on an immediate appearance! My time to destress would have to come later. Our duty to the clan came first. Phillipe promised that he would take a week off after.

Then, we would go out on the boat, maybe even sail up the coast and explore some of the lochs. That was something to look forward to, and I was delighted. It offset my dread of defending all the meddling with history I had done in front of the council just a little!

By this point, I was so tired that I was falling asleep. Phillipe carried me upstairs and lovingly tucked me in. Bear and Hella Rose hopped up beside me, and Micha slipped under the covers down to my feet. Even Arianna got on the bed! He let them. They had missed me as much as he had! Then, that wonderful man went back downstairs. He had volunteered to call my parents and fill them in on some of the events. They would take it from there and inform the rest of the council members.

To his surprise, my folks promised to also fetch Mæva. They knew where she was! When he told me the next morning, I was thrilled! Suddenly, I could not wait to leave for Ny Havn the following day. Had I not still felt somewhat weak, we might have set out right then and there! However, when I almost lost my balance a few minutes later, Phillipe was concerned enough to call my parents.

My mother did not need to be in the same room with one to know what was wrong. She could do that long distance! After scanning me from head to toe and finding no physical explanation for my fatigue, she concluded, just as Phillipe and I had, that the two days I had lost had something to do with that. However, I got the distinct impression that she was holding something back.

My mum expertly diverted me with technical questions about the construct as soon as she sensed this. We concluded that I had been in stasis as long as the spell had been functioning correctly. Therefore, I had not needed nourishment. Most likely, all that had changed when we cut Finley free from the web. From then on, time ran very quickly. The few more minutes I had remained there were the equivalent of more than two days in the real world.

No wonder I had been so hungry! My mother told Phillipe to feed me some bone broth and lots of fluids to make up for the lack of food. And he was to let me rest as much as possible. I needed to be fit when I faced the council since they were sure to have many questions!

After we had enjoyed our breakfast, we went back to searching the internet and the archives. We were still unable to find out anything about Mæva's present location. Going back in time, however, we found a report about Katrín. It turned out that the clever young woman had done much better with her deceased husband's estates than he ever did! Finley had been too busy chasing women to pay attention to the running of his properties or the needs of his tenants! Within just a few years, she had paid off all his debt!

Katrín had given birth to a son nine months after the wedding, thus producing a legitimate heir and solidifying her position. This had shut down any attempts of her husband's distant cousin to take what was legally hers. Having the Magnuson Clan's backing also had not hurt! Once the mourning period was over, she had married Maxwell. She had born him two boys and a girl.

By all accounts, their lives had been exceedingly happy. However, the relationship with Katrín's parents had remained strained for a while. Still, she had taken them in when her father's miscalculations had cost them what money they had left. Her folks had spent the last years of their lives comfortably ensconced in a pretty little cottage not far from the manor. To everyone's surprise, they had turned out to be loving grandparents. This, more than anything, had made Katrín forgive them eventually.

The Magnuson lands, and her holdings, had been expanded due to Katrín's cleverness. She had been the one who had been instrumental in encouraging the villagers to start building stone houses, first on her property and then in Havn. The knowledge she had acquired from Mæva and I helped her take good care of the people in her charge, and they had thrived.

As a result, she had been much beloved by all those depending on her, as had Maxwell and their children. From the reports, they had forged a close-knit community that took care of their own! The oldest boy, Jameson, had eventually taken over the estates. Having been taught by his mother, he had governed them well. As could be expected, he had married a Magnuson woman.

Jameson and his spouse had a good marriage and raised seven children. One of those was an orphan boy they adopted and treated just like their own. He grew up to be a real credit to the Magnuson Clan and had expanded the trading lines further out than ever before! Some of the items he had imported were in such high demand down in London that he could set his own price!

I was thrilled to read that things turned out so well for the young woman. In a way, she owed it all to the time trap! How different her life would have been had Finley lived!

Finally, after our lunch, exhaustion got the better of me. I could no longer stay awake. Phillipe just picked me up and carried me back

to bed. I could get used to such treatment! I fell asleep right where he placed me, in my clothes. He cuddled with me for a while, then slipped out to take care of the pets. The dogs had been very patient but were not fond of missing their walks! That was unless it was raining!

Then, you might as well not even try getting them out the door! They loved the water, but not when it fell from the sky! That has never made any sense to me, but it sure did to them!

Chapter 53

A Glimpse of the Future

During my nap, my mind slipped to the Meeting Place. Once I arrived, I realized the others must have called me. The girls were waiting, as were Cedric and Katrín. We greeted each other like we had been parted forever, even though it had not been that long since we were together! Eldred, Hilda, and I clung to each other for several minutes. I really missed them and they me! Bo was equally thrilled to see me, and I was delighted that he seemed so happy.

The landscape around us was just as glorious as I remembered. I loved the purple flowers blooming on the plain to the east and how the tall grasses waved with each gust! Further on, the prairie gradually changed into woodlands that covered the flanks of the snow-covered mountains behind them. What a perfect setting to ride a horse! Maybe we could find a way to bring some here!

To the northwest, sunlight glittered like diamonds on the waters of the deep fjord winding its way inland. It streamed around a bend created by a forested peninsula, changed direction, and ended in what looked like a huge lake, perfect for sailing and kayaking! That hilly spit of land pointed almost due north. It effectively narrowed the waterway where it turned to the south and almost hid the island situated just beyond it.

Bo's house stood on a slope covered in evergreen trees that reached all the way down to the shore. It had an amazing view of all this beauty! For the first time, I noticed the horseshoe-shaped bay to the right of the hill. That looked like a perfect place to anchor a boat!

The scene was peaceful and filled with a magnificence that touched my heart deeply. A gentle breeze ruffled my hair. It brought with it the scent of the far-away ocean. Turning my face up for a moment and closing my eyes, I enjoyed the warmth of the bright sunshine on my face. This was pure bliss! It was hard to imagine that this magnificent space had not existed until recently! I was proud of us, its creators. We had done a marvelous job!

Since this might be our friend's home forever, we had wanted this sanctuary to be as large and appealing as possible. We had decided it needed plenty of room for exploration and adventuring. Therefore, we had allowed Bo full access to our minds. He had searched them for inspiration. We had cast the spell, and he had used the energy from the leylines and some of the material from the time trap to shape all this.

Expertly, he had woven several locations into something totally stunning and new. But as I looked northwest, what I saw seemed like a place I should be familiar with. The sense of recognition that hit me puzzled me enormously, but I knew that I had never been there. How could one forget a glorious spot such as this? I had no idea where this was, but I would have loved a house with a view like this!

Standing there, I felt a longing I could not explain. Something was drawing my heart toward this scene! My head started swimming, and suddenly, my knees buckled. Everything around me turned black. Then, an image flowed in with a power that stunned me. The vision unfolded, playing in my mind like a movie. I saw Phillipe and me coming back from a hike. We opened the gate to our yard and walked past the three-car garage with the upstairs apartment and storage area. We were heading toward the house.

I could not see it but knew that another dwelling that belonged to us was hidden behind the structure we were moving past. It was inhabited by a friend who cared for the pets when we could not take them. The gravel that covered the large, open space around us crunched under our feet. It extended to the main gate to our left, past the building, and to the garden area in front of the house.

Looking around, I spotted our motor home. As usual, it was parked in its shelter in the far left corner. It was big enough to accommodate four dogs and two humans and could double as a guesthouse. I just knew that, on occasion, we even took the two guinea pigs along and that we had been on several amazing trips up and down the coast and inland!

Decorative stone was used to separate the house pad from the parking area. A walkway led up to the steps in front of the doorway. To our left grew my roses. They were thriving and were sheltered from the rumbunctious dogs by a low rod iron fence. It was meant more to delineate the boundary than keep them out but smart as they were, they respected this space.

The recessed entryway to the home was breathtaking. I was immediately in love with the magnificent side panels and the transom of colored stained glass. The scenes depicted all had to do with water and were so vibrant and beautiful! I especially loved the one over the door with the sailboat! The mountains behind it were just stunning!

Once we entered, my husband and I hung up our jackets. We went into the kitchen to our left and made smoothies. Those we took past his office on the right, down the three steps to the living room, and out the French doors to the balcony. We headed for the rail and leaned against it side by side, enjoying the sunshine on our faces. Once I managed to tear my eyes away from Phillipe, I got my first glimpse of the landscape around us.

For a few seconds, I stared in wonder. Then it hit me! The view from right here was the same as from Bo's place! And there was a boat moored near the horseshoe-shaped bay that I knew had to be ours! All I could do was stand there, filled with wonder. Was this the future I was seeing? It sure seemed so!

This magnificent house was Phillipe's and my home! Of that, I had no doubt! For those few minutes, I was there, saw it all, felt it all, one with my 'self' of that time! But then, I could feel my spirit being pulled away. My friends' worried voices drew me back to the Meeting Place.

When I opened my eyes, Eldred was looking at me wide-eyed. I knew instantly why.

"You saw?" I asked her.

"Yes, and it felt like a true foreseeing!" she stated with conviction.

Then, she turned to Bo.

"Where did you get the idea and the images for this place, Bo?" she asked him urgently. "Please, try to remember! This is important!"

"Now that I think of it, these came from Cara's mind. I was not trying to snoop, but one night, while she was asleep, I was dragged into her dream. I tried to fight it, but the pull was too strong! The next thing I knew, I was standing on a balcony with the most incredible view! I was instantly captivated and decided to recreate it here. I thought it was a place you had been to, Cara!" Bo explained.

"No, I am not even sure where it is!" I responded, feeling a little sad.

"I caught glimpses of it," Hilda added. "That vision was so intense that I believe most of us did!"

She looked around, and everyone nodded.

"I bet I was drawn into it since I was in direct contact with you!" Eldred mused. "You seemed to really love it there!"

"It calls to me," I admitted. "I feel like I belong there!"

"I think you do," Bo declared firmly.

"But where is it? I do not believe that was Scotland! How am I ever going to find it?" I exclaimed.

“Do not worry! I am sure you will end up there somehow,” Bo assured me. “Leave the how to the Divine and just concentrate on the end result the vision showed you!”

At that moment, he seemed more enigmatic than ever, but his words rang true. I was still unsure what he was, but I instinctively trusted him. Bo had been the one to take our magic and weave it into this glorious pocket dimension! He had wielded the powers that rivaled a god’s then and in the construct. To his credit, he had never abused them.

If anything, Bo was the most caring and compassionate person I knew. Until he was ready to reveal more, that would have to do. I would just have to let the Divine do its thing! Sensing that I was still feeling faint, Hilda suggested we move inside. She wanted me safely on her couch until I had recovered.

Cedric took advantage of the opportunity and picked me up like I weighed nothing. He followed our host into the home. Naturally, Eldred and Hilda hovered nearby the entire way to the sofa! I would have preferred to walk in but oh well!

This was my first time in the house since I had been there with Cedric. To my amazement, it had been redecorated! Looking around, I was surprised by the furnishings. They were relatively modern and resembled those in my home! When I arched my brow and gave Bo a questioning stare, he had the good grace to turn red.

“Yes, I did get these from your thoughts the last time you were here,” he affirmed. “I hope you do not mind! Hilda and I really like your style. These sofas and chairs are much softer than the ones we had before!”

Having sat on them, I could only agree! And I was honored by their choice. Bo had been in all our heads, and that he would copy my living room was a great compliment. Soon, we were all comfortably seated and ready to catch up. The sisters wanted to know all about my homecoming and how Phillipe had reacted. While I told of my return, Cedric sat there contently with his arms around Eldred and listened. He did not seem to mind that Hilda stayed next to Bo.

I had to give Cedric a lot of credit for that. He and Bo seemed to get along famously, and the girls were happy. That, to me, was the most important thing of all! At one time, over the top of Eldred's head, he gave me a look that spoke volumes. He would have genuinely liked it had I stayed, but he was very much in love with Eldred. In my opinion, it was much better this way! I am not into sharing!

I would have to bring Phillipe next time. It would be interesting for these two to meet since they looked and acted so very much alike! Once Eldred and Hilda were finally satisfied with our catching up, we turned to Katrín. We were more than a little curious about what was happening in her life!

I had been watching her and noticed that she appeared somewhat subdued. Something was not right!

At first, the conversation with Katrín was rather superficial, but then her reserve crumpled. From then on, it took on a very different tone! Finally, she revealed what was bothering her. We all sympathized with her. Understandably, that determined young lady had been traumatized by what she and Mæva had done in the time trap to ensure her future! Any of us would have been!

It had been a challenge to get the inert body of her almost-dead husband to perform that one last function! Katrín still had nightmares about the length they had to go to for him to produce sperm and deposit it inside her. I had to agree with her. The whole thing had been pretty gruesome! However, I was able to assure her that it would yield the desired result in the end. She was happy to hear that.

Phillipe and I had read up on her. According to the reports, Katrín had genuinely loved the child she had born. Upon hearing that I had looked her up in the records, the young lady immediately wanted to know more. So the two of us went into the other room and had a long, honest chat that was very beneficial for the young mother and her unborn baby. Her biggest fear had been that any son of hers could turn out just like his father!

According to our history, he would not! Instead, he would be a great credit to the family. I could see the relief on her face when I shared this with her. Suddenly, Katrín no longer felt so apprehensive and looked forward to having the babe. Knowing he would turn out so well made her genuinely happy and encouraged her!

But then she asked a boon of me that I could not deny her. Once she was ready, I very gently took her head in my hands. Katrín opened her mind to me and allowed me in. Sorting through her recent memories, I got ready to deal with those traumatizing minutes back in the locus of the time trap.

I would do her this favor and make it easier to live with those moments that continued to haunt her.

Chapter 54

A Woman Scorned

Once I had isolated the memories of those last few minutes that Katrín had spent in the construct, I went to work. Carefully, I dialed down the emotions connected to the acts she had to perform to solidify her position. I now understood why she had felt the need. She really had no choice! Some of her husband Finley's family members were almost as unpleasant as he was and just as greedy! The young lady had not been prepared to take chances of the beautiful estate and the servants falling into their hands. Also, returning to her folks' house had not been a viable option.

I watched her entire body relax as the tension bled away along with the sting of the memories. Now that the boy's conception was no longer as traumatic for her, she would be able to raise him to be a much better man than his father. And, she had Maxwell. Since he was honest and forthright, he would be a good role model for the child!

According to the archives, magic would confirm the boy's birthright and that the marriage was legit, thus fulfilling the addendum that the nasty man had added to his will after the fact. Had she not acted to secure the legitimacy of her claim, she would have lost everything! To her credit, Katrín would never speak ill of Finley, but from another, the youngster would eventually learn just what a cad his father had been.

As fate would have it, the same witch who cast the enchantment that trapped us all would see to that a few years later!

From talking to the others, I concluded that our lives had continued on from the date we were sucked into the hive. Or, as in my case, from a couple of days after! We seemed to be going forward together, just in different times. I was genuinely happy about that. It would allow us to visit with each other at the Meeting Place for many, many years to come! Eldred, Hilda, and I would have each other and our friends going forward!

For all of us, history was still unfolding. However, the archives I had access to already included many stories about the others. From Phillipe's and my research, I now knew more about their lives. But my husband had stressed that I should be careful how much I told them until I had spoken to the council.

Therefore, I did not share many particulars with Katrín, especially not one specific story involving her son, whom she named Jameson, that was passed down in great detail. It was better if she was not aware of what was to come.

One day, when the boy was around 14, a destitute old woman showed up on their doorstep. Her long hair was stringy and lifeless, and her face was heavily lined. It still hinted at the extraordinary beauty she must have once been, but all her attractiveness had long since faded away. Time had taken its toll on her appearance and body, which was terribly frail.

Katrín, having a soft heart, had not been able to turn her away. After she had dinner with them, the stranger, who called herself Isobel DeLeón, told them who she was. She volunteered to share with Jameson, his mother, and Maxwell why she had done what she had. At first, they had been too angry at having been thus deceived to want to hear anything. However, curiosity won out, and they listened to the tale.

"I grew up in Spain, around Barcelona, as the daughter of a noble family," Isobel began haltingly. "The gift runs strong and true in our people, as it does in me. I had been trained since I was a small girl and was very powerful even as a teenager. Not long after my 17th birthday, Finley came to our village. He was charming, dashing, and so good-looking! I was instantly smitten by him. But my parents did not care for him and forbade me to see him.

"So I sneaked out to meet him, and I was not the only one. Many of the other young ladies liked him as well, and they were free to see him any time they pleased! So to win him for myself, I showed him what I could do. Shortly after, he asked my father for my hand, but my parents refused. They wanted someone better for their daughter and told Finley so in no uncertain terms!

"Since I was no longer allowed to leave the house, one of the maids carried messages back and forth. I was so happy when the letter came asking me to run away with him so that we could be married! Naturally, I agreed. He made the travel arrangments, and the next Sunday, I slipped away during church service."

"But you are a witch! Why would you go to church?" Jameson interrupted.

"Son!" Maxwell scolded him.

"The boy is just curious," Isobel soothed. "What better way to hide what we are than to act just as pious as our neighbors? My family was above suspicion as long as we gave the church plenty of money and attended services!"

"Thank you, I think I understand now," Jameson said politely. "I apologize for my rude question!"

"It is safer for people like us to hide what we are," Isobel told him.

"I can see that," Jameson responded with a smile which Isobel returned.

Then, she continued with her story.

"Finley feared that a carriage would be too slow and that my father would catch us. So he was waiting for me with a horse and the one small bag the maid had smuggled out. It and the jewelry I had hidden on me were all I took with me. We rode hard and mostly overland, trying to throw off any pursuit. He had a ship waiting for us in a deserted bay, and we set sail the minute we were on board.

"That evening, Finley proposed to me during dinner, right there in front of everyone! When I accepted, he placed a gorgeous ring on my finger. The captain volunteered to marry us, but Finley declined. He wanted a big wedding! In any case, it was quite a celebration with plenty of rum! Finley kept encouraging me to have just a little bit more until I was almost as drunk as he was!"

Isobel paused and looked at the family. She seemed to be reluctant to continue her tale.

"Some of what I am about to tell you now might not be suitable for this young man's ears," she finally stated with a sigh.

"He was my father, and I have a right to hear the truth! All of it!" Jameson protested. "I am not a child anymore, and I already know that he was not a good man!"

Katrín and Maxwell looked at each other helplessly for a moment, then shrugged. It was not like the boy had not seen the groom have at it with the maid! And he had heard the rumors regarding his father.

"Since he wishes it, please continue, Isobel," Katrín decided.

"Due to tight quarters, we had only one cabin with one bed," Isobel explained. "Neither of us was sober, and that night, Finley got very insistent. I was still floating on cloud nine and so happy, so I let him."

Isobel looked at Katrín, who nodded. She, Maxwell, and her son wanted to hear all of it.

"After that, he told me it was no big deal us making love. It was not like I was a virgin anymore! And we would be husband and wife soon enough anyhow! We finally reached Scotland, and he moved me into the hunting lodge. 'Just until we are married,' he said. And I believed him!" Isobel shook her head at her own folly.

"For one reason or another, it was just never the right time for us to wed. One year passed, then another. He continued taking me whenever he pleased. If I even tried to refuse him, Finley acted so disappointed in me! I loved him with all my heart and just could not say no! He was, after all, the man I had chosen to spend the rest of my life with! Fool that I was, I trusted him. I believed him to be a man of his word!

"My instincts kept telling me something was wrong. Unfortunately, I did not listen. I chose to turn a blind eye toward the evidence of Finley's true character. The warning signs were there! But, like so many women before me and since I had become a master at explaining them away! In my eyes, Finley could do no wrong. With empty promises, he bedded me again and again.

"In the beginning, he made me feel desired and cared for. He also gave me pleasure, but that changed as time went by. What he really liked to do was to take me in ways that demeaned me. He wanted me pliable, to be putty in his hands. Thus he systematically undermined my confidence and sense of self-worth with his abuse. I was so deeply in love that I could not admit that my relationship with Finley was one continuous downward spiral! I did not see that until many years later!"

Here she paused and asked for some more tea. Maxwell, who had caught on that she had more to tell them but would not do so in front of the boy, put his foot down and sent the youngster off to bed.

By the time she visited the estate, Isobel had no more illusions about how she had been manipulated. That night, she shared what was done to her over the years in a conversation with just the adults. Katrín saw to it that the account of this meeting and the sorceress' story was recorded almost word for word. She had wanted those who read it and any who had been in the time trap to know how this poor woman had been pushed to her limits!

According to her testament, the cruel Finley was a master at hurting others. Every whore in town cringed when they saw him coming their way. Many refused to have anything to do with him after a while. The money just was not worth it! But, he was just as vicious to his loving fiancé. For a time, his favorite way to humiliate her had been to push her against the wall, face first. He had made sure to do this hard enough to hurt her.

Then, holding her there, he would take his pleasure from her, often brutally, never giving her a chance to climax. At first, this only happened in the privacy of the hunting cabin where he kept his mistress hidden. But then, being a sadistic prig, he found ways to humiliate Isobel even more. He started taking her in public like any common prostitute, wherever he pleased but preferably where someone would walk by or could observe his lewd acts.

He would beat her and do something even worse if she tried to fight him off. He had quite the imagination and was a master at breaking a woman's spirit. Isobel learned pretty quickly that she had better submit, but the shame she felt knew no bounds. The society of the time still saw Finley as one of their own despite his depraved behavior but not so Isobel. Her good name was soon totally besmirched!

The ruthless man wanted her to feel like his whore, and for people to see her as such. He systematically set out to destroy her reputation since he had no intention of ever marrying her! Finley had decided to set his sights higher, and Isobel was a foreigner. She did not have the breeding and family connections he desired. And she was no longer a virgin!

Finley was determined to win and wed one of the daughters of a local family. As far as he was concerned, any of them would do as long as her parents were from the upper crust of society. After all, what did love have to do with it? If she was beautiful, it would be a plus. Having her on his arm would benefit his reputation as a stud!

At first, all the fathers turned him down, but Finley was not about to give up. He started collecting information on all those with eligible offspring; the dirtier, the better. As far as he was concerned, he was in no rush. After all, he was a virile man and had plenty of time left to sire children! He was sure that one day he would discover something that could be used for blackmail!

Then one of those privileged cows who turned their pointy noses up at him would be his to do with as he pleased!

Isobel had been so blinded by love that she, a powerful enchantress from an aristocratic Spanish family, had allowed all that mistreatment. She was prepared to do anything to win Finley's heart. Eventually, she ended up conceiving. But, after their daughter Cassandra was born, things only got worse. The promised wedding kept getting pushed out, and the cad continued his campaign to ruin his fiancé. He wanted to be rid of her and the child!

Unfortunately, he was not making fast enough progress for his taste. He needed Isobel so ruined that no one would have pity for her. So, he drugged his mistress and took her along to one of the low-life bars in the city. Here, he shamed her in all new ways. Having a bunch of drunk men egg him on played to his ego. It encouraged him to do things to her that not even she, as much as she loved him, would have tolerated!

His compatriots had gladly helped hold her down when she had come to and had tried to escape. They had been unmoved by her tears and cries for help. As intended, word got around. Soon, Isobel was no longer welcome in any of the better venues or in the societal circles he came from. That made her utterly unqualified as a wife and ruined any chance of the life the poor woman had still been dreaming of.

Additionally, Isobel was now more dependent on Finley than ever. She lost a good part of her income thanks to this nasty stunt. Due to the rumors, people stopped coming to her for spells and potions. Only those desperate enough to risk their peers' scorn still dropped by the cabin. This gave the depraved man even more control over her!

The things she had endured to feed her child had been truly horrendous. About that time, Isobel had gotten pregnant again, maybe even that night at the tavern. Shortly after conception, her powers started growing stronger than ever. Fearing that the sorceress might use her magic on him to make him do as he had promised, Finley started to avoid her as much as he could. He turned his full attention to buying a bride.

However, like every typical bully, the man was a coward. He was too afraid to stand up to Isobel now, and she had started insisting that he wed her and soon. He needed a sneaky way out. His mistress was running out of patience, and he could not win a direct confrontation with an enchantress such as her.

Therefore, Finley decided that he would covertly marry someone else. Anyway, once it was done, what could the witch do?

As far as that degenerate man was concerned, he was well within his rights to go elsewhere and discard his fiancé. He felt that no one could blame him. Isobel's reputation, after all, was tarnished beyond repair. How could anyone expect him to wed such a floozy? Did she not already have one child out of wedlock, and now another was on the way?

That it was his own offspring did not matter. He cared nothing for the innocent babes or the woman who loved him! Being afraid word would get back to her, he told no one what he intended. With some well-placed threats and a considerable sum of money, he finally 'convinced' Katrín's parents to give him her hand in marriage. The fiend had been absolutely thrilled and made the arrangements.

Not only did his new bride come from the powerful Magnuson Clan, but she was also unsullied. He was going to have himself another virgin! What a rare prize! Unfortunately, the deflowering of this one would have to wait for the wedding night! Knowing his reputation, the parents were not about to let him near her before then!

To Finley, it was all business. Having someone like Katrín as his wife would increase his social standing. He would have loved a huge wedding but feared Isobel would find out. With the mood she was in of late, there would have been hell to pay! Therefore, one of his conditions had been that the ceremony took place at his home and was kept hush-hush. Only a few people were to attend, most of whom were his friends.

Still, it must have been one person too many. Word got around! The rumors reached Isobel the day the nuptials took place. Furious, she came to confront her fiancé that very night. Knowing how powerful she was, he did not dare to have the servants turn her away. However, that did not stop him from gloating that he was no longer available to become her husband since he now already had a wife.

One of the many awful things that foolish man threw in her face that evening pushed Isobel over the edge. She snapped! Right then and there, she decided if she could not have him, no one would. The sorceress knew of one way she could hurt her ex-lover as well as the woman who had stolen him from her. In an instant, she had placed a wicked little spell on him that had put an end to all his sexual exploits, including the consummation of his marriage to Katrín!

But, the additional injustice and hurt that man had heaped on her were too much to bear. On her way home to the hunting lodge that Finley had ordered her to vacate, Isobel had simmered with fury. Not only had she lost him but also her home! She was in a bad situation! He was done with her and not prepared to give her another cent.

The thought that she and her child were about to become homeless filled the lady with anguish. Isobel had nowhere else to go. Even had she wanted to, she had no money to return to Spain. The sorceress was livid with herself for having been so very blind! Due to all of Finley's schemes, she could not afford a place to live, nor could she support herself and her small daughter!

Feeling utterly hopeless, she had placed the girl in the care of a trusted friend. Then, she plotted the fiend's downfall. One of the few things she had brought from home was an ancient grimoire from a long-dead ancestor. Looking through it, she had come across that awful spell. At first, she had been hesitant to use it, but then her despair and anger had won out.

A few days later, the perfect opportunity presented itself. Word had reached her that Finley would be riding out to hunt. Determinedly, she had set her plan in motion. In a clearing near the cabin, she had cast that intricate enchantment. Besides her ex-lover and his men, she had designed it to draw in anyone from or connected to the Magnuson Clan, unrestrained by time and space. Her goal had been the eradication of all of Katrín's kin!

Isobel had hoped that if enough people vanished, the one her lover had married would never be born! Not until much later did it occur to her that Katrín was also a victim. Then, she had felt bitter remorse for hurling that malevolent spell, but there had been no way to undo what she had done out of the need for revenge. The construct had taken on a life of its own!

Once Isobel heard that Finley had died, she knew instantly that, somehow, the enchantment had been shut down! She had been greatly relieved and had decided to visit the young woman someday to make amends. More than anything, Isobel craved absolution for the awful things she had done. She had not expected to receive grace, but she found it due to Katrín's good heart.

The sorceress had been greatly surprised. The weight lifted off her the moment the young woman hugged her with tears in her eyes and told her that she was forgiven was so huge that Isobel almost fainted.

Maxwell and Katrín could not help but feel pity for the woman. The spell had cost Isobel much, including her magic and the child she carried. Of all of them, she paid the highest price for Finley's betrayal! Once young Jameson found out he had a half-sister just a couple of years older, he insisted on meeting her. And then, on bringing her home!

Thus Cassandra became part of the family. She got along wonderfully with the other children, and you would have never known she had not always been with them! Isobel, who had been so wronged by the malicious Finley, ended up living in a cabin on the estate. Here, with the help of her daughter and Katrín, who became her very close friend, she slowly started to recover some of her strength and spirit.

Casting that spell had taken so much of her life force that it had nearly killed Isobel. It had aged her by several decades in just a few minutes and had rendered her unconscious for days. The happiness she found with her new family did more than anything to restore her. For the first time in many years, she felt loved and cherished. Thus her heart finally healed.

Katrín encouraged her to get in contact with her family back in Spain. Isobel's aging parents immediately invited all of them to come visit. They could not wait to see their daughter again after all these years! They had been immensely relieved to find out that she was still alive and that Finley had not killed her as they had feared. The icing on the cake had been the news that they had a grandchild!

The elderly couple had counted the days to the group's arrival! The DeLeóns had welcomed Isobel home with open arms. Her running away had long since been forgiven, and seeing what shape she was in, they showered her with love. Cassandra soon became the apple of their eye, and they could not have been prouder of this intelligent young lady. Nor of her half-brother and his siblings, which they adopted as well.

The gratefulness the family felt toward Katrín and Maxwell for taking in Isobel and Cassandra knew no bounds. On several occasions, they insisted on watching the children so that the pair could slip off together to explore and have fun. And to get away from all the commotion since the rest of the DeLeón Clan had also arrived for this joyful occasion. Naturally, with all their offspring! Thus, the large manor suddenly seemed small!

The trip to Spain turned out to be quite an adventure, but the reunion brought peace to the sorceress' heart as well as her folks. From then on, she and her family made sure to get together at least once a year, and they stayed in touch through frequent letters. Katrín and Maxwell were only too happy to host the DeLeóns at any time and did so on many occasions.

Feeling so treasured and this renewed and vital sense of belonging helped Isobel's recovery even more!

Eventually, Isobel married an older acquaintance of Maxwell's. The gentleman fell in love with this tragic figure of a woman at first sight. Patiently, he wooed her and slowly but surely taught her to trust him. Once she opened up to him and started to return his feelings, he gave her all the love, respect, admiration, and adoration she had always longed for but had never received from Finley!

The wedding was quite something! Isobel's parents insisted on hosting it, so the entire extended family set out for Spain once again. The celebration lasted for three days, and the manor resounded with laughter. The DeLeóns went all out for this very special occasion. They had feared that Isobel would never marry after everything she had been through.

Katrín, Maxwell, and the children stayed for an entire month which was great for the youngsters because they had a chance to practice the language!

This time, Isobel had chosen wisely. Her husband was truly a wonderful man. After a couple of years of wedded bliss, her heart, soul, and body healed. One day, even her powers began to return.

And with them, her beauty and youth.

Chapter 55

Change Comes on Silent Feet

Once Katrín and I were done talking, she felt better about the recent events in the time trap. However, due to all that release of tension, she was emotionally worn out and ready to return home. So she stopped by the living room just long enough to say goodbye to the others. Hilda and Eldred eyed her with concern and decided that we should accompany her to the portal. Good thing! Katrín was so exhausted she stumbled a few times and had to lean on Eldred and me the last few feet! We waved as she made her way through, then returned to the house.

A few minutes later, we were all comfortably ensconced on the sofas, chatting about whatever came to mind. The girls naturally wanted all the details of what had happened in the hive after they left. I filled them in but did not mention anything I thought was too private or hurtful for Katrín. That was her story to share! Or not! As far as I was concerned, no one else needed to know exactly what had happened in those last few minutes of her husband's life!

I had a wonderful time during my stopover at the Meeting Place. In the couple hours I visited there, we managed to exchange a lot of information. Cedric was implementing some of the hygienic measures we had discussed and needed more details. I told him what I could, but there were things I would have to research once I got home. The wells had to be the proper space from the outhouses! However, I was not sure about the minimum distance they needed to be apart.

Cedric was determined to get it right. And to make rules to pass down to his descendants. He saw no reason why his people should continue to die from drinking contaminated water now that he knew better! We agreed that I would relay those specifics to him in our next gathering. Bo stated that he was happy to have us step by any time, especially if this meant he could spend some extra time with Hilda!

As it was, I got the impression that they were seeing a lot of each other, naturally, with Cedric's approval. So far, no one else but Katrín, Eldred, Hilda, Cedric, and I had been by to visit. Therefore, Bo had devised a way to send a message to all those we had grown close to in the time trap. He would use dreams to invite them here for the party he intended to host to bring some life to the Meeting Place.

From some of his comments, I gathered that Bo was feeling somewhat isolated. Hilda could not be there with him as much as she had been. He hoped that more people would start dropping by once they had been to visit once. It had only been a few days, and he was still adjusting to the loss of the connection with everyone and everything he had maintained in the construct. His world had been so much larger then! I could only imagine how hard this change must be for him!

At times, when he thought that no one was watching, Bo looked rather melancholy. Cedric had also caught on to this and shot me a concerned glance. He genuinely liked the young man and was worried about him. Hilda loved him and would be devastated if anything happened to him! All of us would be! Maybe when we got everyone together, we could get them to help us find a solution! We all had magic! There just had to be something we could do!

I could not wait to see the others again, especially Mæva and Revna. Eldred insisted that I let them know how the council meeting went and how our friend and teacher was doing. So far, none of us had heard from Mæva, which was unlike her! Also, they really wanted to meet my husband, so we worked out a way for me to bring Phillipe along next time.

Bo, who had an intimate connection to Hilda, would inform her whenever we stopped by. If at all possible, they would then join us. Once we had worked out a few more logistics, it was time for me to return home. The others walked me to the portal. After several rounds of hugs from the girls, I was finally ready to step through, but not before taking one last look at the amazing vista of the Meeting Place.

Our creation was indeed a place of beauty, as was the portal itself. We had made our entryway into this dimension a true work of art! Remembering a picture I had used on my website, we had placed it at ground level inside the trunk of a huge old oak tree near Bo's house. It was so whimsical! The door and frame were plain magnificent! The dark, highly polished wood was intricately carved and covered in runes.

An old-fashioned copper lantern hung from a metal support above it, illuminating the portal and the wide treetrunk's immediate surroundings. A little round window beside the door was lit up from within and made the whole thing look like this was someone's home. And it was just as welcoming on the inside! We had made the interior of the oak appear like a living room. It had a reading area with a chair and a table, all basking in the warm, yellowish glow of a small lamp!

The setting reminded us of the dwelling of a gnome or dwarf out of the fables. We had taken our time and had a lot of fun making the entry to this pocket dimension as elaborate as possible! Even the step leading up to our portal was carved and had a mat bidding one welcome. We wanted people to enjoy visiting and to want to return!

The part of the landscape I could see from here was much like our beloved Scotland, with deep lochs and tall, snow-covered mountains.

The sea shimmered in the distance, and several islands floated right offshore. It was majestic but peaceful and reminded us so very much of our home. The view that had affected me so was not visible from here, but I could feel it calling to me. Maybe someday I would find out where it was!

Gazing around, my glance fell on Bo. As much as the rest of us loved this place, for him, it was also a prison. He, unlike us, did not exist in the outside world. Sharing Cedric's body occasionally was a poor substitute for having the freedom to come and go as one pleased! We just had to find a way to bring him fully into the land of the living before his depression deepened!

When I woke up, I shared all the highlights of my visit with Phillipe. I also relayed Cedric's request for more information about the placement of wells compared to outhouses. Then, I brought up the subject of Bo and his sadness. Would he and Hilda ever be a couple in our world? From what we had read, she provided Cedric with several children and was instrumental in making things better for the clan. Beyond that, she was only mentioned on occasion. That was strange!

From one point on, most of the information was on Eldred and Cedric and their role in the clan! We decided to check the archives once more. What we could find on Hilda were a few references in the first few years and several birth announcements after that. Then, she seemed to have gone traveling, and little else had been passed down! Very interesting! Especially since there was so much on Eldred!

Did Hilda and Bo end up making a life together? This was starting to look like a distinct possibility! But where? In the Meeting Place? Maybe the microfiches in the clan library would have some additional facts, but as far as we knew, everything had been scanned into the computer. After checking on the lives of several of my other friends, it was time for dinner.

Phillipe and I started the meal. I love our air fryer! While it cooked, we fed the pets. Once they were all taken care off, we set the table for a romantic candlelight dinner. But, since I was feeling much better by now, we barely made it through the meal. Not surprising! It had only been a few days for Phillipe, but for me, it had been weeks! And, there had been the temptation of Cedric! Needless to say, I was hungry and not necessarily for food!

Had we not had a long trip ahead of us in the morning, we would have played much longer than we did. As it was, our lovemaking alternated between hot, furious passion and gentle, slow tenderness and anything and everything in between.

The next morning, after a quick breakfast, we loaded the dogs into the car. We were just grateful that Hella Rose no longer got as carsick, but just in case, we gave her a pill. On occasions, she still drooled rather badly. Since this was easily avoided, there was no reason for her to be so miserable! Our friend and neighbor Quinn would see to the piggies Teddy and Orion.

As usual, I genuinely loved the ferry ride and then the drive. I could never get enough of the magnificence of the landscape we traveled through as we made our way north. Scotland is just so gorgeous! All this beauty made my heart sing, but strangely enough, the images of that other place I had seen in my vision kept coming to mind, overshadowing what I was seeing. I had looked on the internet, but so far, I had no idea where it was located!

For once, my parents insisted that we stay with them instead of in our own quarters. I did not have the heart to turn them down. To my surprise, the welcome we received was the warmest that I could ever remember. Even my brother stopped by to say hello! Had something I had done in the time trap caused this major shift? I had no idea and decided to ask my mother just as soon as we had a moment alone.

"Did something happen while I was gone?"

To my surprise, she squirmed in her seat. Imagine my always so composed and controlled mother fidgeting on her chair! I had never seen her do such a thing before, ever! That would have wrinkled her immaculately ironed outfits! How many times had she yelled at me for doing this? Now, however, she was either completely unaware or she did not care. This had me even more curious than before!

Finally, she hesitatingly spoke in a low voice.

"I felt it the instant you left this plane. Something snapped inside me. It was the most awful feeling that I have ever experienced. One minute, there was the warmth and love you emanate; the next, there was just a hole."

Slowly a tear trickled down her face. After some initial hesitation, since uninvited shows of affection had not been previously welcomed, I reached out to comfort her. To my surprise, my mother actually hugged me back! This would take some getting used to! The invasion of her personal space by any of us had never been much to her liking!

"Your father came storming in just a few minutes later, and from his ashen face, I could tell he had felt it too. Then, your brother phoned. We immediately called a council meeting. We tried to find you, but all we could establish for certain was that you were nowhere on this earth!" she broke off with a sob.

"I am back now," I assured her.

"Yes, you are. All of us sensed it the moment you returned. Your father and I, we were so relieved! We did a lot of thinking during those days. All your lives, we have been so preoccupied with clan business! We never gave you or Oliver the attention you deserved! We realize it is a bit late now, but we hope we can make it up to you somehow!"

To say that I was stunned is putting it mildly, but I was more than happy to have closer relations with my parents. Not that I needed their approval or love that much anymore! I had long since learned to give it to myself, but finally having a loving family would be nice. I had always envied Phillipe's closeness with his folks. Maybe here was my chance to have this as well?

The council meeting was set for early the next morning, so Phillipe and I spent a pleasant evening with my parents. That neither of them objected to our rambunctious dogs in their immaculate home was telling. I even caught my mother petting Hella Rose and slipping her special treats when she thought no one was watching! Our pup followed her around from then on and laid down close to her, providing the comfort this human so obviously needed.

That I had to disappear from the face of the earth to bring about this kind of change was a bit sad. But, in the end, it was one more beneficial thing that resulted from that evil enchantment! The spell, however, had been gross magical conduct and therefore had to be reported and investigated by the council. Since it had affected the Magnuson Clan for more than a thousand years, they would want to make double sure that it was gone.

The gathering was to be very official. It would be held in the lodge situated on the same hill where Hilda, Eldred, and Cedric had lived. That brought back memories of those days long past! I have to admit that I really missed them. In our short time together, I had grown to love the girls. In a way, meeting them had been a gift, not just for me but also for the clan. The warnings about the witch trials had helped save many of our people but also others in the region!

In addition, everything I taught them about hygiene made a lasting difference. The number of mothers dying in childbirth went down drastically! Most wounds and injuries healed without beginning to fester since they were kept clean. All the knowledge we would continue to share would be passed down through the generations, benefiting Eldred and Hilda's descendants, including my family.

Since I was back home and all had turned out well, I was no longer as upset about getting caught in the magical trap. In a way, it had been an exceptional adventure! Something that could have turned out detrimental to all of us imprisoned in the construct ended up bringing some benefit to most of us, including me!

Starting with Finna, these improvements have allowed our clan to thrive for well over a thousand years now!

When Phillipe, my parents, and I entered the chamber, my eyes immediately fell on a woman whose long curly, gray mane was as untamable as ever. It was nicely cut, and she was well dressed, but the hair was still wild. Smile lines were deeply engraved on her face, and she looked like someone who had found true happiness. The way she looked at the elderly man who was with her told me much.

I was delighted that Mæva had found such a loving and lasting connection. Had her reluctance to return to her own time had something to do with where she had ended up? From what I had learned from my mother, it seemed she had appeared out of thin air one day before I was born. Had this been a coincidence, or had she used me as a marker to home in on this era?

In any case, her sudden materialization had caused quite a ruckus, and her unconventional arrival had initially been greeted with suspicion and apprehension. But, since she was a Magnuson and willing to do what she could to further the clan's interest, she had been welcomed. Over the years, she had become a valued advisor on obscure magic that had not been seen for ages. She had settled some distance from Ny Havn but was in constant contact with the head of the archives.

As my parents, Phillipe, and I moved toward her, Mæva spotted me. She excused herself from the head of the council she was talking to and hurried my way. The moment she reached me, I was engulfed in a huge hug.

"I am so happy to see you again!" Mæva said with tears in her eyes. "Let me look at you!"

Gently, she pushed me back a little and examined me from head to toe. At first, this seemed strange, but then it hit me. What had been only a few days for me had been over 20 years for her!

"Beautiful, just as I remember. And this must be Phillipe! I heard so much about you! It is so nice to finally meet you!"

My mother was eyeing my friend strangely. Then recognition shone on her face.

"You were the midwife that brought Cara into the world!" she stuttered.

"Yes, that was my great privilege," Mæva confirmed with a smile.

At this point, the sound of a gavel repeatedly hitting the podium caught our attention. The meeting was about to begin! We would have to catch up later. Maybe my parents would agree to invite Mæva to their house?

After briefly introducing the reason for the assembly, I was called before the council. The chairman encouraged me to share every detail that I could remember. There was no telling what would turn out to be important! Careful not to leave anything out except the most private events, such as Cedric's attempts at seduction, the girls' willingness to share him, and Katrín's desperate act, I told my tale. We had to take several breaks since it took over four hours!

Once I was finished, the questions started. My husband and I shared the details we had discovered thus far. Then, Mæva was asked to join us. She confirmed those things that she was aware of and had some further insights to offer. Even though Isobel was long since dead, a sentence was pronounced. As expected, she was found guilty of casting harmful magic. But, my kin were not ogres. Due to the extenuating circumstances and Finley's abuse of her and her child, the only sentence pronounced was a warning.

Once the official part of the assembly was concluded, we were asked to join the council members in their chambers. Here, in the privacy of their sanctuary, they shared more information with Phillipe and me than we had been privy to. I realized that my actions in the time trap had quite an effect! However, I did get a talking to about the risks I had taken by giving our ancestors such advanced knowledge!

We had been lucky that the changes had turned out to be so beneficial. Each of our friends had heeded my warnings to implement things carefully so we would not alter the timeline too much. Then again, the only one who could see the difference was me! I had to think about that for a few moments and compare what I knew of our history before my disappearance to what I had learned of it since my return.

So far, the only alterations I had detected were that our records were much more detailed and that the Ny Havn area seemed much cleaner. And, maybe, the people of the clan were friendlier and kinder, but I was not going to point that out.

Once that part of the business was finally over, we joined the party. It was already in full swing. Soon, my head started to spin. It seemed everyone wanted to toast to my safe return, and I was not used to drinking that much! Even though I had been taking tiny sips, I still felt the effect of the alcohol. Realizing I needed a break, Phillipe gently stirred me outside to the pavilion. Here we sat peacefully, cuddled up together, watching the stars.

Before long, Mæva, her husband, and my parents joined us. By then, I was starting to get sick from all the drinking. With a wave of her hand, my friend eliminated the liquor from my body. I immediately felt perfectly sober, and my tummy settled down. I thanked her profusely and asked her to teach me that spell. I was sure that it would come in handy!

Phillipe suggested replacing the champagne with some sparkling water. That way, no one would be any wiser that, for some reason, my favorite drink was not agreeing with me.

Since it would have been rude to leave a party in my honor, we decided to take a break for a bit and then head back in. This gave my friend and me a chance to catch up. When I told her about my visit with the girls and Bo, she was sorry to have missed it. She had been the one to shut the spell down, and it had taken its toll. Mæva had been absolutely exhausted! It had taken her several days to recover enough to have the energy to enter the Meeting Place.

But, after that, she had been a regular visitor, and I suspected she would be there when I went next. It was so weird that she had been there on many occasions by this time! She could tell me what was to come! For one, Bo's fate weighed heavily on my heart. I hated to see him so depressed and imprisoned! He deserved to be free and happy like the rest of us! Hearing that all would turn out well was a huge relief!

It took a few years, but Mæva and the counsel finally devised a solution. Cedric had been looking for a host body for him for some time, but no one wanted to do harm to anyone else. Eventually, a spell was located for the creation of a golem he could inhabit. Mæva taught the rest of us just what to do and how to ensure Bo had free will. He would have hated it if someone else had been able to take control of him!

After some trials and errors, we created a body that looked just like Bo's adopted form. He then slipped into it, imbuing it with life for the first time. It was an incredible triumph when he opened his eyes and smiled. He was finally real! Using the energy from the leylines, he refined his new vessel until it was perfect in his eyes. And in Hilda's!

Cedric, with the help of the girls, made the preparations for Bo's arrival in Havn. No one had thought anything of it by the time he got there. Quite naturally, the young man joined the household. Eldred had done well! She had used her magic to convince all the kin that he had always been there. And no one questioned the affection Bo had for Hilda!

The only thing we could not give him was the ability to procreate. This was sad since he genuinely loved children. Once again, Cedric had come to the rescue. He had provided the seed that Bo did not have. This resulted in twins, but the delighted couple did not mind. Eldred, Cedric, Bo, and Hilda raised all the little ones together as one big happy family.

Officially, all the kids were claimed as Cedric's since Hilda was his wife. And they were his biological descendants. Unofficially, however, they were Bo's. A more doting father than him had never existed, and Mæva had been delighted to meet the children once they were old enough to come to the Meeting Place.

The house started to feel small as the family grew. So Hilda and Bo added their own wing. Many years later, when most of the offspring were out of the house, the couple decided that they would like to travel and see more of the world. But it had been hard for the loving parents to leave their children, so the two youngest came along.

The family took up residence on one of the merchant ships of the fleet. They liked that kind of life very much. Due to Hilda's ingenuity and Bo's willingness to do what needed to be done, they soon had the funds to buy the vessel. But, not being sailors, they had much to learn about running this beauty! Eventually, however, the two learned enough about the sea and their ship to become co-captains.

Hilda absolutely loved being at the helm and was good at it. Using her magic, she saw them through even the worst of the storms without a scratch. Due to their reputation of being lucky and blessed by the Divine, she and Bo had never lacked for crew.

Mæva assured me that they were going to be very happy. About anything concerning me, she was very cryptic. She told me not to worry so much about the future and my friends. I needed to let life flow more. It would all work out, sometimes in unexpected ways. How strange to talk to someone I had visited with for years in the Meeting Place, especially since that had not yet happened! What a time paradox!

My mother did invite her and her husband over for breakfast the following morning. She and Mæva had hit it off like a house on fire! That was most likely the most surprising thing that happened that day! Here was my mum, so very proper and immaculately dressed, and then, there was Mæva, a flower child if I had ever seen one. So happy and bubbly, she really fit into our century!

In contrast, her husband, Norbert MacPherson, was one of the calmest, quietest men I had ever met. But the fire that sparked between them whenever they looked at each was most certainly hot! Since Norbert had just retired, it did not take my mother very long to convince them to move to Ny Havn.

Midwifery was becoming a lost art in our area, and Mæva was one of the best. My friend and her spouse agreed to move into one of the empty cottages. She would teach other young women her skills, thus providing the clan with capable midwives for years to come.

When Mæva mentioned that maybe she would deliver Phillipe's and my child one day, we only laughed. Kids were not on our agenda! My mother and she exchanged a knowing glance that made me wonder.

But very quickly, they distracted me with questions about the witch that had cast the enchantment, not giving me a chance to figure out what that look had been all about!

All in all, it turned out to be a wonderful party. Phillipe and I danced, laughed, and talked to many people. The trick with the sparkling water worked like a charm. I felt amazing and really did not miss it. But, for some weird reason, I kept wandering over to the buffet for the herring rolls, something I am not usually that crazy about! I shrugged it off to my stomach needing something after almost getting sick and paid it no further attention.

At some point during the party, Phillipe commented that chocolate-covered strawberries and herring in cream sauce were quite an odd combination. We had a good laugh about that. Only later that night did it dawn on me that I had spent weeks in the time trap and had forgotten all about the birth control pills when I returned! And, we had not been cautious, never even thinking about that!

Not only that, but I always took them at night, right before bed. We had made love that morning before I got caught. Using my senses, I examined my womb. To say that I was shocked would be putting it mildly! I sat up in bed and started crying. Neither of us had wanted children! How would Phillipe react to this? When he felt me move and sensed my distress, my loving husband immediately pulled me in his arms to comfort me.

"Love, what is it? Did you have a nightmare?"

"No," I sobbed, unable to give voice to the thing that I had just discovered. Saying it out loud would make it real!

Phillipe, however, was no dummy. He did his own scan of my body! Suddenly, his eyes grew wide, and he looked at me with a sense of wonder. Then, his whole face lit up with a joy I had never expected!

"We are going to be parents!" he shouted, loud enough for the entire house to hear.

I don't think that I have ever seen him so excited. Here, the man who claimed he had no intention of bringing a child into this world was so happy that we just had to get out of bed and tell my parents. Once again, a celebration ensued, but we stuck to orange juice and left the champagne away this time. Nine months later, our daughter Aurora Jane was born. Phillipe was instantly hooked.

That baby had him so wrapped around her little finger that he would have spoiled her terribly had I let him. Most of the time, our daughter was a delight, but she did have her moments. Phillipe and I had to have an occasional strategy session on how to deal with some of her tantrums. We needed to be on the same page. No way was I going to let our little darling play us off against each other!

The dogs were absolutely crazy about Aurora as well. Wherever she went, they went. Hella Rose especially took to guarding her crib and had to be told that it was ok for her grandparents and our friends to pick up the child. Two years later, our son Harrison Dale came along. He, unlike his sister, was actually planned! Bear adopted the role of protector over him. The first few weeks, he was worse than a mama bear!

He would only grudgingly allow my mother to hold the little boy, but no one else besides her, Phillipe, and I could get near him. Once that huge, overprotective dog settled down a little bit, our friends came to visit, and we could continue our social life.

Most surprising of all was our move. A few weeks after my return, the clan opened a new office in Washington State in the United States. My parents decided to oversee it, and they needed a lawyer. Phillipe liked the idea of new challenges, so we flew over and went house hunting. I about fainted when the realtor showed us the home I had seen in my vision! We bought it on the spot!

While the paperwork was being recorded, we packed up our home on the Isle of Arran. Once the movers came and took the furniture away, we stayed in our quarters in Ny Havn. The house would be rented out during our absence. We thought we had everything arranged when we discovered that most airlines would not allow guinea pigs on board. For a good reason!

It seemed that their little hearts could not withstand the altitude change! The customer service representative told us that they might die in transit. That really upset me, but I could not bring myself to leave them behind. They were part of the family! Phillipe, my hero, as usual, found a way. He talked the crew of one of our transport ships into taking them along across the Atlantic!

Naturally, the young man who took charge of them was well reimbursed for his time! Phillipe verified that he was reliable before we handed Orion and Teddy over to him. I was so thrilled and immensely grateful. We picked them up in New York in our new motor home and then drove across the country. Phillipe had taken a month off, and so we took our time. There was so much to see and such a variety of landscapes!

Our trip turned into a great adventure, and the little guys and all the dogs made it safely to our new home. To my surprise, my parents were learning to delegate. By the time our daughter was born, they actually had the time to be grandparents! I had never expected them to leave the governing of the clan to someone else! However, my mother confided in me that she and my father felt they had missed out on enough of our lives.

From her comments, I should have suspected they intended to have all of us in one spot. My brother Oliver and his wife bought a house in our neighborhood shortly after! We started doing family things together, something I would have never believed possible before getting caught in the enchantment! When Phillipe and I bought the boat, we went exploring in the glorious San Juan Islands. I was hooked!

My love for our new home grew deeper with each day. On occasions, I would miss Scotland. But that was easy enough to fix. My father could usually find a reason for the company's small jet to take us back for a week or two! Phillipe and I decided to keep our place on the Isle of Arran. When Quinn ran into financial trouble, we had him move in and take care of it. This way, we can visit any time we want!

After Aurora was born, we found a way to take kids and pets to the Meeting Place. This way, all our little ones got to know and play with each other. We added more cabins and a playground so the sisters' family and mine could spend time together. Katrín, Maxwell, and their kids were frequent visitors as well. Little Kira insisted on having her own place, and all the children adored her, especially Jameson. He did not care in the slightest that she was much older than him.

One day, Katrín asked us to let her bring the horses we had rescued. They had never quite recovered from their ordeal in the time trap and were still painfully thin. However, they thrived in that little dimensional pocket, especially once Bo restored them to full health. They became the first permanent inhabitants of this beautiful space.

When Arianna began to fade a few months after she turned 13, Phillipe, Aurora, and I took her there to stay with Emla, who had moved in the previous year. Since the place was outside of time and space, Eldred, Hilda, and I used our magic to rejuvenate her. Our old girl was thrilled to be able to run and play again. She raced around us like a puppy, enjoying her youth and health.

But then came the time for us to go home. The big dog did not understand why she had to stay behind. Eventually, with rather bad grace and a lot of pouting, she accepted the inevitable. We were as heartbroken as she was and promised to bring Aurora and Harrison back to visit the next day. To our surprise, Arianna's body was gone when we got home.

She had just vanished and only existed in Meeting Place now. Teddy and Orion, our guinea pigs, joined her a short time later. While Kira looked after Harrison, Phillipe, Aurora, and I spent all afternoon creating the most fun home for them we could imagine! We left it open on one side so that they could explore the magnificence of their new world if they so desired. They did spend hours out in the tall grass but usually came back when they heard us!

It was hard not to have those three in our daily lives anymore, but we visited as often as possible. Once she got older, Aurora took to picking Arianna up from Emla's cabin and doing her homework either at Bo's house or near the guinea pig run next to our cottage. She already knew how to get back and forth all on her own! And how to carry items or beings with her, including her brother, Micha, Hella Rose, and Bear, and she was only five! Needless to say, Phillipe and I were very proud of her!

A few months later, Revna moved into another of the little homes. Our friend had become very ill, and she knew the end was near. Just like Emla before her, she decided to stay in the beautiful place we had created and explore it rather than go to the afterlife, Summerland, Heaven, or whatever awaited us after death. Leave it to these two to even do dying on their terms!

Since Emla disliked hiking and Bo was often busy, Arianna was thrilled with the company. She and Revna soon became fast friends and adventure buddies. This made up a bit for not having her humans and the rest of her pack around all the time! As far as she was concerned, Teddy and Orion were not all that entertaining. Still, she liked watching over them when they went out exploring.

To everyone's surprise, the horses loved tagging along with Revna and the dog on their daily walks in this magical space.

Having the power of foretelling is a remarkable and precious gift. I was fortunate to see far into the future of the Meeting Place. Over the years, many of the others who had access to that special space would join Emla, Revna, the horses, Arianna, and the boys. Mæva designed a spell that would automatically draw us and our pets there once death neared. That made things so much smoother! My parents, Oliver, and his entire family also intend to join us there. But, hopefully, that will be a long time from now!

Eventually, all of us, and some extras, will be together again in that glorious space of our creation! It boggles the mind to think that an enchantment designed to do maximum damage ended up bringing so many blessings!

APPENDIX

The Origin of the Magnuson Clan

The Magnuson clan can be traced back to one Viking couple and their descendants. Finna Breckingsdottir was a vølva, a seeress. Once this became known, she became the prisoner of a Viking chieftain who wanted her at his beck and call at all times. His son, Bjørn, fell in love with the young woman, and eventually, she with him. When her situation became untenable, he managed to free her. The two fled toward the northwest to Norway from what is now Denmark. Their original names are unknown since they changed them during their journey.

During their flight, Bjørn's own abilities started to emerge. The two decided to keep their magic a secret. Eventually, they were given shelter by a group that dedicated their lives to helping others like them. Many of its members were powerful warriors with arcane powers. Since folks tend to fear the unusual and those they do not understand, all these men and women had experienced persecution and challenges.

As a result, the outcasts wanted little to do with the rest of the people in Scandinavia, but they did welcome others like them. Word had spread of their willingness to aid those who did not belong. But entry into this closed-off, suspicious tribe of magic users was far from easy. They had been betrayed once. The subsequent raid had cost many a life before they could turn the battle in their favor. It had, however, provided them with several boats. And it had cemented the idea of one day creating a safe haven far away from home for those like themselves.

After learning about their history and who they were on the run from, Finna and Bjørn were quickly accepted. They were taken to the secret and well-defended location, aptly named Trygg Havn, Safe Harbor, to keep them from being found. This was the group's primary home. With their neighbors' help, the young couple built themselves a cabin and settled in. Their first son was born shortly after. Since both parents had powers, their eleven children were also gifted.

All those living in the village were taught to hide their true nature to blend in better. Nothing gives one away faster than out-of-control magic! The planned relocation would grant many a second chance at a normal life, but only as long as no outsider knew they were different. Therefore, their powers were never to be used in a manner that was flashy or could be observed.

As a result, a whole new way of utilizing their abilities was born that the clan continues to employ to this day. Around the Magnusons, things just happen, often long after they are gone. Due to marrying within the large extended family or to others like them, the abilities of the kin grew even stronger over time. By an edict dating back to Finna and Bjørn, even those who chose not to use their natural born talents must learn to control them.

A special school, the Magnuson Academy, was built for this purpose in 1809. After a few years, it began admitting other children that needed its teachings.

In the sanctuary in Norway, life was not easy. Being rather enterprising and not content just to exist, Bjørn started procuring things for their neighbors. Then, Leiv, the oldest, came up with a fabulous plan. As a result, the family employed many of the people in the tribe to make nets imbued with a slight bit of magic. Since fishing was an essential part of life along the coast, this gear was quickly in high demand.

The Magnusons' enterprise had the blessing of Olaf Gunnarsson, the chieftain of their little tribe. He saw the benefit it brought to their people. Those working with Bjørn were building up nest eggs that allowed them to buy land in far-off Scotland. Within a few years, the one ship Bjørn had started out with became several, and his sons started ranging further from home.

Often, they traveled with the Viking raiders since there was safety in numbers. The resulting trade made the family, as well as the tribe, very wealthy. This was, however, drawing unwanted attention from their neighbors. It was time to relocate to somewhere safer!

Therefore, Bjørn secretly met with the Mackay Clan on his next voyage to Scotland. He was determined to negotiate a safe haven for their people near Gairloch. After some back and forth, he was allowed to buy a forested section outright. In return, he would supply the clan with reasonably priced goods, a win-win for all.

Had they known, the Vikings already settled in the area would have eyed this arrangement with contempt. Their motto was, 'I want it, I take it!' Bjørn had never liked his father's or the raiders' brutal ways. He was smart enough to realize that the fierce Scots would eventually drive the invaders from the region. He did not want to be among those forced to leave!

Therefore, he planned to stay apart from the two factions but be useful to both. He needed the goodwill of the Vikings, or his ships would become prey, but also that of the local laird. Since the man was in need of a wife, Bjørn promised him the hand of one of his daughters. With preparations for their arrival from Norway in place, he returned to the sanctuary.

While he was gone, the rumors of an imminent invasion of their settlement had grown louder. It was time to take action. The tribe still had the boats from the last raid. Frantic packing ensued but only behind closed doors. Since they were under surveillance, outwardly, everything had to appear normal. Things could be moved about only at night and when Finna and her daughter Auga cast a spell over the village that hid their activities.

About that time, Olaf fell seriously ill. Once he realized he would never see their new home nor continue his duties, he declared his friend Bjørn the new leader. This was greeted with approval by all but a few. One man, Lars Anderson, had designs on the position himself and was not pleased. Letting anger get the best of him, he was about to betray his people to the locals when he was caught and stopped.

So, sadly, Bjørn's first act as the new chieftain was to sentence the man to exile. He gave the wife and daughter the choice to go with him or remain with the rest. Both requested to go with the tribe. No one could blame them for abandoning Lars due to what they had seen over the years. He had been a lousy husband and cruel father. His lady therefore requested and was granted a divorce. She had no intention of sharing his punishment.

Since their secret sanctuary had been located and the situation was becoming more precarious daily, one foggy, moonless night, the boats were brought in under cover of darkness. All those things that had been packed were quietly hauled aboard. The operation went off without a hitch. Long before sunrise and before the mist ever lifted, no sign remained of the longships.

Bjørn made the decision to remain behind with part of his family and a few friends. They would make it look like nothing had happened. He had tasked his son, Leiv, the oldest, who was leading the expedition, with looking after their people until he and the rest arrived. Not all had found room on the longships, however. Therefore, Bjørn hid them on the Magnuson merchant ships that left with the fleet.

Finna and her daughter Auga had used their magic to make everything appear normal during the nights. Therefore, no one had noticed that the men had hauled all the furnishings that remained into the sair, the mead hall, the center of their small village. From there, it had been transported down a tunnel leading to a cave system. One of these caverns had a direct connection to the sea and was large enough to hold several longships.

Coming and going was only possible at low tide, but it provided the perfect hiding space for the boats. Bjørn and Finna were sad to abandon the sanctuary that had been their home for over 22 years. But, it was no longer safe. By the time most of the people left, the houses were almost empty. Within a couple of days, they were totally cleared.

Those who would come raiding would find nothing of value. One of the men had suggested burning the place to the ground, but the rest had vetoed his suggestion. Let others move in! They had felt that was better than destroying what they had so lovingly built.

Olaf, who Bjørn loved like a father, died just a few days later. His most profound regret was that he would not accompany the tribe he had so fondly and wisely led to their new home. Creating the sanctuary had been his idea. He had wanted a place for others like him to be safe, live in peace, and have children of their own, something that he would never have due to the cruelty of his once master. For years, he had dreamt of the day when they finally found a spot where they could thrive and not constantly worry about garnering the envy of others around them.

His vision had been to establish safe havens for all those born with magic in Norway as well as in Scotland. Due to the greed of the chieftain of a large village a little way down the coast, their refuge on their native soil was lost to them for the moment. But they still had the caves. All the entrances were well concealed and not only with magic. They would have to serve as a hide-away and jumping-off point to kinder places until times changed.

With the old man's death, the fulfillment of his vision fell to the new chieftain, who promised to do his very best. A storm hit the region the night after setting Olaf adrift on a flaming boat in the style of the Vikings. This was a sign that it was time to abandon the settlement.

After just such a gale, Finna's visions had seen the place invaded the next morning. They had no intention of being there when the raiders arrived.

Thus, while lightning split the sky and thunder shook the earth, Bjørn and the men did one last check of the settlement. Then, they slipped down into the tunnel system. They closed the large hatch in the sair behind them and locked it in place. It was now one with the floor. A wooden door, reaching from floor to ceiling, sealed off the stairway. Quickly, additional supports were hammered into place. Another lever released the sand and gravel stored in the walls of the building, thus blocking off that entrance to the passage.

As they made their way toward the caves, Bjørn remained at the rear. Once the others were clear, he started opening the shafts all along the tunnel, allowing dirt to flow in. The rain helped tremendously. It washed in a slurry of sand and gravel. But, with the storm raging above, the water started rising too quickly in the passage. Fearing for his life, Bjørn ended up running from one lever to the next. Finna was greatly relieved when, out of breath but safe, he reached the cavern where she was waiting.

The three men who had chosen to stay behind in Norway to help others born with magic would live in the caves. They were close to the abandoned sanctuary, but with the tunnel out of commission, the hideaway could only be entered from the sea. The place was safe, especially since the emergency exit was near impossible to reach from the outside, but it would allow them to get away if need be.

The enormous cavern that hid their boats was churning and tossing during the gale. The magically concealed entrance was totally invisible and impenetrable to all but their vessels. However, it did little to tame the waves! The two remaining longships were pitching about wildly, making boarding a challenge! The refugees decided to wait out the storm in one of the dry caves further up.

The tempest battered the coast for another two days. Finna and Bjørn were keeping watch over the sanctuary from the emergency exit the first morning the sun dawned bright and clear. As she had foreseen, the invaders came sneaking in with the first light. They stormed into the houses only to find them deserted. The raiders' disappointment was the one consolation to losing their home, but it did little to offset the heartache.

The next night, hidden by a convenient downpour, the remainder of the family set out for Scotland. Within a few years, they, as well as those with them, would be recognized as the Magnuson Clan.

Once they reached safety, Bjørn filed a complaint against the chieftain who had invaded their lands back in Norway. Since he had plenty of money, he had excellent representation and ended up winning. As restitution, he and his people were not only awarded the sanctuary but they were also given the lands of the invading tribe. The love for the magic fishing nets and the protest that followed when Bjørn's customers realized what had happened to their supplier most likely had a lot to do with this outcome!

Olaf's dream had finally become a reality. From then on, no one dared to even think of making any threats toward the haven. Any magic-born who reached it were safe and off-limits, no matter who had a claim on them. In return, they spent a few hours a week helping with the thriving business of weaving nets that had been re-established.

To remain neutral in Scotland, the refugees had decided to build their homes a little apart from the Vikings as well as the local people. They called their little village Havn, which means haven in Norwegian. At first, they had a few close calls with some of the raiders who were after the much-prized nets. But, those brutes found the small community no easy victim, especially once they were protected by the local clan.

After that, they decided to pay for the goods they acquired. This was a wise choice since even the fierce Vikings feared the inhabitants of western Scotland and the Hebrides. Bjørn, using the money from their business, legally acquired a few more stretches of land from the local laird. He eventually signed a covenant accepting the hospitality of the Mackay Clan and agreed to help them fight off any invaders.

His oldest son Leiv took over the rule of the clan after him. Even more so than his father, he managed to persuade the entire village to keep their magic use and abilities a secret. To the folk nearby, they appeared just like regular people, maybe a little eccentric but otherwise no different than any of them! Anything out of the ordinary was easily forgiven and forgotten since the newcomers seemed to be bringing good luck to the region.

Once Leiv felt that his people had perfected the skill to hide who they were, he asked for volunteers to become peddlers. Why confine the clan's business only to trading by sea and with the local lairds? He also wanted to reach folk further inland and thought this was a great way to collect information and spread a tale if need be. He sent out a few to discover what their neighbors needed, wanted, and dreamed of.

Leiv, trained by his father, knew just what to do. And he had a well-thought-out plan. To keep this new venture separate from the village, he had the clan build several log houses right on the border of the Magnuson lands. He named the settlement Bytte Hjem, trade home. This became the base for the business. Here, they sold goods from many of the places the merchant ships visited.

Within weeks, the items were so popular amongst the locals that more homes had to be added to accommodate the extra kin needed to work there.

Thanks to their magic, the Magnuson clan was expert at finding items everyone wanted. Leiv made sure that his people remembered to remain cautious, even at the village when they were among themselves. The Highlanders seemed more accepting, but letting their guard down was not a good idea. Since trust came hard after their experiences in their homeland, the kin heeded his words. For one, they did not want to cause envy among their neighbors. That had not worked out so well in the past!

Being aware of human nature, they knew if they looked much more prosperous than those around them, they might get raided by the fierce Highland warriors or the Vikings living nearby. Therefore, they did not openly display their wealth. If you looked closer, it showed in subtle things like the finer quality of their clothing and fabrics. Still, outwardly, the village resembled the others in the region.

Only slowly did they improve their living conditions and always in step with their neighbors. Leiv was extremely cautious and a brilliant tactician. His peddlers kept an ear to the ground and picked up any rumors circulating in the region. Wanting better conditions for himself and his people, he started the practice of improving the lives of all those around them along with their own.

His wisdom was passed on in the clan's stories that all the children grew up with. Even Cara, well over a thousand years later, was told them and taught the importance of hiding her abilities. 'No one must ever know' was the motto. That practice proved extremely prudent during the time Cedric was chieftain. Then, witch trials took place in many parts of Scotland. As the ruler, he ensured that the Magnuson settlement at Gairloch appeared so ordinary and above suspicion that no one ever looked twice.

Another of the clan's practices that originated with Olaf was the search for individuals born with powers. The peddlers made great scouts, both in Scotland as well as in Norway. They would approach those in less-than-ideal situations and offer them sanctuary. Most of those who still had their freedom joined gladly. Some others, however, had to be rescued or bought.

The advantages of having foresight and knowing what was about to happen or who to beware of were priceless. Therefore, the dream of many a chieftain was to possess his or her own seer, seeress, or magician. Anyone with abilities was in high demand. Unfortunately, many leaders seemed to forget that these people were also human. They were often treated as valuable commodities but without regard for their feelings.

Some had been property since childhood and had developed an attachment to their owners. Only those wanting help were rescued but were never taken to the main settlement in Scotland until there was no doubt about their loyalty and affiliation. As their number grew, more houses were built around the trading post, which became a second village with no apparent ties to the clan except for the sale of some of the nets. Most of those traveling and peddling goods had their official residences there.

All that hustle and bustle at Bytte Hjem helped to make Havn seem like a sleepy backwater with little to offer. To their neighbors, it was just a community of artisans and craftsmen who produced the most sought-after fishing nets in the Highlands and Scandinavia. If you threw one of those in the water, it would bring up something to feed you! And, best of all, they were still reasonably priced despite being in high demand!

Most people could afford one of the smaller ones, and those who could not usually made a bargain of sorts. There was always work to be done around the village or on the boats. Being this fair, and willing to accommodate even the poorest among them, gained the community the protection of all those who relied on this gear. This, alone, helped to stave off raids of Havn by some of the more ambitious fellows.

If any contemplated such actions, their neighbors, including the trading post, closed ranks against them. Suddenly, they found themselves without the supplies they had come to depend on! That usually gave them pause and drove home the point that the isolated village was to be left alone.

Amazingly, even the remaining Vikings figured out that any goods they might acquire by force would not make up for what they had to lose.

When Bjørn and Finna's offspring reached adulthood, most married other magic users. It was just easier that way. Who wanted to hide their true nature in the comfort of their own home? Many of the spouses came from the clan, but three married Highlanders. One such was Signe, the daughter who sealed the bargain with the local laird. Each had several kids of their own. As a result, over time, most of the residents of Havn were related to some degree or another and had powers.

Ulf Magnuson took over after his father, Leiv. As can be expected, he was a very shrewd man. He saw the writing on the wall that the fierce Scotts would eventually repulse the Vikings and feared they might decide to drive all the Scandinavians out of the Highlands. To protect his people, the main village kept pretty much to itself. Unlike the traders, they formed few alliances with the locals but were good neighbors.

The young ruler loved his home here in the Northwest Highlands of Scotland. He thought that the Gairloch area was just beyond beautiful. Therefore, he set out to establish ties with the lairds in the region. As soon as a daughter was born, she was promised to one of the nobles' sons. This created considerable goodwill, as did the celebrations of each such event.

Unbeknownst to their neighbors, the trade the clan had been conducting had made them a lot of cash. Ulf, claiming to act on behalf of a wealthy relative, now put this money to good use. After some back and forth with the Highlanders, he worked out a deal. He bought another large section of land and started building houses. Naturally, he hired craftsmen from nearby, and he paid them well.

Once everything was prepared, he sent the ships to fetch those remaining in Norway who wanted to leave. Hearing how prosperous the clan was, many decided to make the voyage. They settled peacefully in the new village under the guidance of two of Ulf's sons. Many volunteered to help with the trade or work on the nets.

Ulf also made sure that those of his clan helped where they could. If there was trouble somewhere, his folk were the first to arrive and give a hand. He encouraged the mingling with the Highlanders, especially among the young. This aided in locating more of those having magic. Most were unaware they had powers, but any union with them was still encouraged. Some of the men marrying in even decided to adopt the Magnuson name.

Thanks to Ulf's shrewdness and foresight, his clan was well-integrated with the local people by the time the Vikings disappeared from the area. And they were connected by blood. That, to the Highlanders, carried even more weight. The newcomers finally became kin and no longer had to fear one of the lairds getting it into his head to evict them. Making the best fishing nets far and wide also helped a fair bit.

The practices instituted by Ulf continued after his death. They were passed down from father to son and eventually written into clan law.

Cedric Magnuson took over as chieftain in 1615. He was instrumental in keeping much of the witch craze that affected other regions at bay. His people, with the blessing of the local lairds, approached all those who behaved suspiciously and hid them in a safe place. Thus, life for those with the gift in the Gairloch region was not as hard as elsewhere and relatively peaceful. Thanks to his guidance, the clan prospered beyond their wildest expectations.

During this time, the kin also extended some of their ancestral lands in Norway and forged closer ties with the folks living there. As a result, ships traveled back and forth every couple of months, and some families, subtly encouraged by Cedric, decided to return to the old country.

After Cara's visit and her sharing of vital information, the knowledge the clan gained was cleverly disseminated around the region. Some popped up here, some there, but it always spread like wildfire. Magic did have a bit to do with that! Word of the innovation would reach the Magnuson village soon after. There it was adopted and instituted. The origin of the new ways could never be traced, no matter how hard some suspicious persons tried.

Geira, the enchantress, officially Cedric's advisor, taught Eldred, Hilda, and all others in Havn with powers. Things ran much more smoothly with her guidance. She was never seen doing magic by any outsider, nor was she known for potions or such. This kept her, along with everyone else, safe and above suspicion. All the local lairds loved her wisdom and would stop by to ask her advice.

Eventually, well after Geira's death, she was credited with being the source of all the innovations that had appeared in the region during her lifetime. She was admired for being well ahead of her time.

The hygienic practices attributed to her saved hundreds of lives, as did the remedies Cara had shared with her. Sanitary conditions in the homes improved drastically, as did customs about food storage.

Over the next few hundred years, the Magnuson Clan bought a few more parcels. They continued to expand their territory, but they were careful. It would not do to get too big since they were guests of the Mackays. By the time Cara is born, the clan is a large extended family scattered all over. Many return to the Gairloch area once a year for the clan's annual summer solstice celebration.

The trading village, Bytte Hjem, still exists and now sports modern houses. It has turned into a bustling town that thrives on commerce. Most of the homes remaining from the older settlements of Havn are in ruins and are now a heritage site. The stone homes were built nearby instead of on top of the village. Thus Ny Havn was born. The Magnuson Clan has tried its best to preserve what was left of the dwellings of their forefathers.

Of the original log houses, only the mead hall and the chieftain's home saw continued use and were rebuilt several times. The yearly solstice celebrations are held in the large, two-story building. The new town with its stone structures was called Ny Havn, New Haven. Some of these cottages are still in use, and a large hotel accommodates the kin, researchers, and visitors to the site.

A good number of the clan still reside and work in Ny Havn. The place is well known among the arcane community as a sanctuary for those born with magic. They can come to learn and, in some cases, be taught to hide their abilities. The number of those seeking knowledge varies wildly and depends on the political climate and times. The library alone is a huge attractant. However, most of the works there are reproductions since the originals are priceless and kept in a safe facility at an unknown location.

The Magnusons' ability to get people many of the items their hearts desired led to the establishment of the Magnuson Procurement Company, called MPC for short. To this day, it is a clan owned and run business that offers such a variety of positions that it has something for most of the youngsters. Phillipe, for example, is a successful and

well-paid MPC attorney, while Cara has chosen to follow her own bliss. She is a successful author.

THE MAGNUSON CLAN'S FIRST COUPLE AND CHILDREN

Finna Breckingsdottir-Magnuson and Bjørn Magnuson
They had eleven children:

Leiv Magnuson
Erik Magnuson
Signe Magnuson
Auga Magnuson
Torsten Magnuson
Svend Magnuson
Hilda Magnuson
Sten Magnuson
Rune Magnuson
Njal Magnuson
Yrsa Magnuson

People

A

Arthur Pickerton: An old gent, once the laird of his lands, who lost his wife unexpectedly on a walk. The shock of her sudden death sent him into such deep grief that his mind ended up totally jumbled.

Auga Magnuson: One of the daughters of Finna and Bjørn. She and her mother cast a spell over the sanctuary that makes everything appear perfectly normal. This hid their activities from those spying on them. Under cover of the enchantment, the last bits of furniture were moved to the sair, the mead hall, and from there, down the tunnel to the sea caves. The magically concealed entrances would allow for the retrieval of anything left behind at their leisure.

Aurora Jane Magnuson-Mackay: Cara and Phillipe's daughter. The little girl likes the Meeting Place, and she figures out how to get there on her own at a young age.

Ayla Sutherland: Lady Satterfield by marriage. Ayla was the daughter of Emla Sutherland and her husband. She is a very determined young woman.

B

Bertha Magnuson: Ny Havn's gossip, a rather rotund lady always looking for some tidbit she could spread around.

Bess Delande: The lady spent a long time in the construct and is in terrible shape when Cara, Hilda, and Revna find her.

Beth Magnuson: A middle-aged lady Cara, Hilda, and Revna take home.

Bjørn Magnuson: He and his wife Finna are credited with starting the family's procurement business. Bjørn freed Finna from his father's imprisonment and fled northwest with her from what is today Denmark. On the way, they changed their names. Their origin or real names are unknown. The couple had 11 children that intermarried with those in the sanctuary, thus creating the foundation for the Magnuson Clan. Bjørn discovered his own powers during their flight.

Bo: When Cara enters the time trap, the possibility of his existence is created. Her meeting with Eldred and Hilda is the catalyst for his birth. Over the next few days, he becomes ever more conscious. By pure chance, Cara makes contact with him. He chooses good and improves the lives of all the captives in the construct. Eventually, once he has a semblance of a body, he and Hilda fall in love.

Brigit Magnuson: A young lady known to Cara who gets pulled into the trap.

C

Cara Magnuson: The main character, a direct descendant of Eldred Magnuson. She is a writer, has magic, and has been trained how to use it. She can sense connections through time and just knows things, has visions, foresight, and some knowledge of healing and herbology. In addition, she can slightly manipulate the threads of fate in an emergency.

Cassandra DeLeón: Isobel's daughter with Finley. She later gets to meet her half-brother and is welcomed into the family by Katrín, who sees them all as victims of a disturbed and evil man.

Cedric Magnuson: He becomes the chieftain of the Magnuson Clan in 1616 and marries Eldred and Hilda. He is a good man and turns out to be a wise ruler who manages to keep those hunting witches from collecting any of his kin or neighbors.

Christopher Mackay: The laird who marries the Viking maiden Signe.

Cletus Magnuson: A teacher in Ny Havn and a very perceptive man. He was well-versed in the region's history and knew of the terrible things Victoria DeMonde had done and her sudden, unexplained disappearance.

D

Dorian LeClaire: The best man for Cedric at his wedding. Dorian was of French origin, but his parents fled to the Highlands when he was just a lad. Once they were located by Havn's scouts, they were invited to join the magical community.

Doug MacPherson: Takes the place of Cara's father as officiator during the summer king and queen coronation ceremony. Doug is a rather straight-laced fellow and seldom joins in with the drinking. Also, he did not attend the fetes very often.

E

Eldred Magnuson: She is Cara's ancestor and was born in 1598. In 1616, at the age of eighteen, Eldred married Cedric Magnuson. The couple has five children. She is tall and slender, with glowing skin, forest green eyes, and waist-long, shining chestnut-colored hair. The strong set of her jaw reminds Cara vividly of her mother. Eldred is almost 18 when she meets Cara. She is two years older than her sister Hilda.

Lady Emla Sutherland: An old lady caught up in the spell. She is kind to Eldred and Hilda, and they see her as a surrogate grandmother. She is the first the girls and Cara take home. Emla is a distant relation to the Magnuson Clan.

Estrid Anderson: The wife of Lars Anderson. She divorces him once his treason is discovered and goes to Scotland with her daughter and the rest of the clan.

F

Finley Delaby: He is the depraved man engaged to Isobel when he marries Katrín. He pays for his breach of a promise with his life. He has a son, Jameson, with his wife and a daughter, Cassandra, with Isobel.

Finna Breckingsdottir-Magnuson: She is the wife of Bjørn and a vølva, a seeress. Once her gift was discovered, she was taken prisoner by her future husband's father. The chieftain wanted to make sure that he was the only one who had access to her accurate predictions since this gave him an edge over the neighboring tribes. Despite the unkind treatment she received, Finna is a sweet and kind person and a wonderful mother to their 11 children. Finna is an absolutely beautiful woman. She is tall and slender, with fair hair down to her waist and piercing blue eyes.

G

Geira Sorunsdottir: A wise woman and advisor to Cedric, at least officially. In reality, she is a powerful sorceress, healer, and teacher to Eldred, Hilda, and all those in the clan who wish to learn to use their magic and conceal it. After all, being in control of your abilities is the best way to hide them! Geira Sorunsdottir is not only extremely powerful but also incredibly motherly and kind.

Gudrun: The wise woman who becomes like a mother to young Finna and teaches her the art of healing and how to hide her visions.

H

Harrison Dale Magnuson-Mackay: Cara and Phillipe's son.

Herald Magnuson: He becomes chieftain of the Magnuson clan in 1889. His engagement to Liv Magnuson almost comes to an end when Victoria DeMonde shows up in Ny Havn and decides that she wants to become his wife.

Hilda Magnuson: She is Phillipe's ancestor and was born in 1600. Then, in 1616, she marries Cedric Magnuson despite being in love with Bo. Hilda is sixteen when she gets caught in the trap where she meets Cara. She has long blonde hair and startling blue eyes. The girl is shorter than her sister Eldred and has powerful magic. She gives birth to four spirited daughters.

I

Inga Anderson: The traitor Lars Anderson's daughter with his wife, Estrid. The girl is terrified of her father and gladly takes the opportunity to be free of him when he gets caught sneaking off to commit treason.

Ingrid Peterson: Estrid's mother.

Isobel DeLeón: The witch who cast the enchantment that creates the time trap in a fit of despair and the need for revenge. Finley had systematically destroyed her reputation. Then, without even breaking their engagement, he marries Katrín. No longer having his support to count on nor being able to make enough money to survive, Isobel is forced to foster the daughter she bore him with friends. This sends her over the edge and makes her determined to get back at the man and the woman who 'stole' him.

J

Jameson Delaby: Katrín's son with Finley. The boy was conceived in a rather unorthodox way and with the help of magic.

Jensen Bixbury: A neighbor who helps Phillipe search for Cara. He is the one who walks down the path looking for her, but since he is not a Magnuson, he does not run afoul of the enchantment.

K

Katrín Magnuson-Delaby: The young lady forced to wed the depraved Finley. She and Mæva must go to some lengths to ensure the marriage is consummated and an heir conceived. Katrín is an incredible beauty with green eyes, the fairest skin Cara had ever seen, and glossy raven hair down to her waist.

Kira Magnuson: Only 13, she was as innocent as freshly fallen snow and as capricious as a fairy, an absolutely delightful mix.

L

Lars Anderson: The ambitious man resents it when Bjørn Magnuson takes over from Olaf. He intends to bring the local raiders down on the tribe but is stopped just in time. As a result, he is exiled to the Faroe Islands.

Leiv Magnuson: The oldest son of Finna and Bjørn. He is the one who takes the group to their new home near Gairloch when his father remains behind to stay with the dying Olaf.

Liv Magnuson: A lovely and intelligent young woman who is engaged to Harald Magnuson.

M

Mæva Magnuson: A powerful enchantress the girls meet in the time trap. She teaches Cara, Eldred, and Hilda more about magic and is instrumental in taking down the enchantment. The healer's auburn mane is very curly and almost untamable.

Maxwell Mackay: The young man Katrín falls in love with. They marry once her time of mourning ends, and she bears him two sons and a daughter.

N

Norene Magnuson: The elderly lady knew Eldred and Hilda's parents.

Norbert MacPherson: Mæva's second husband, a very quiet and serene individual who perfectly complements his bubbly wife. With him, she finally finds the love and spice she had been looking for.

O

Olaf Gunnarsson: The chieftain of the sanctuary in Norway. He and Bjørn Magnuson are best friends.

Oliver Magnuson: Cara's brother and the one who was supposed to take over the Magnuson Procurement Company and the other clan businesses. He prefers drawing and painting to running the clan. Eventually, he became a renowned artist.

P

Phillipe Jeremiah Mackay-Magnuson: Cara's beloved husband, a direct descendant of Hilda Magnuson, Eldred's sister. He and his wife are distant cousins and know each other as children. He is highly intelligent and exceedingly perceptive. Phillipe works as an attorney for the clan's main business, the Magnuson Procurement Company. His magic is inherent. Any time he questions someone, they find themselves unable to lie. Phillipe has gorgeous green eyes and dark brown hair; he is tall and well-built.

Q

Quinn McPherson: He is a friend to the couple and their housesitter. Quinn also looks after the garden. Phillipe calls him to help with the pets while he is out looking for Cara.

R

Revna Magnuson: everything about her reminds Cara of happiness and sunshine. The power coming off this pleasantly rotund lady is impressive. Like many with such an intimate connection to the Divine, she has a timeless quality. Her shiny, bouncy, brown curls frame a sweet, unlined face with skin so smooth and youthful that it makes her appear much younger than she is. Revna's eyes are an unusual violet color; they are kind and understanding.

Rodger Magnuson: A gentleman caught in the time trap. He is an incredibly rude individual.

S

Signe Magnuson: Signe is the daughter of Finna and Bjørn Magnuson. Despite being in severe pain, she is on the way to get water when she gets pulled into the spell. After she is healed from the injuries she sustained while scouting in Norway and free of the time trap, Signe marries Laird Christopher Mackkay. They are very happy together and have seven children.

Sten Coffers: A silver-tongued cad with the magic of persuasion who kept impersonating Laird Harald Magnuson. He was finally put on a ship and sent to some far-off place from where he never returned.

U

Uma Magnuson: Leiv's wife. She is best friends with Signe and has five children of her own.

V

Victoria DeMonde: A beautiful woman who shows up in Ny Havn one day, acting like a fine lady. No one is sure where she came from, and her behavior toward anyone who is not nobility is dismissive and cruel. She quickly focuses on Harald Magnuson, the chieftain's son. He is already engaged to a lovely lady, but this harpy still tries her best to break them up. One day, she just disappears, never to be seen again.

W

Willow Mackay: A young lady who meets the sorceress responsible for the enchantment several years before she casts it. She is from the same time as Katrín and does not live far from her.

Z

Zelda Stewart: A member of the group Maxwell belongs to. She goes home peacefully while he stays to be with Katrín.

Locations

Bytte Hjem, Scotland: The trading village founded by Leiv Magnuson. The name means Trade Home.

Caledonia: Another name for Scotland.

Gairloch, Scotland: A town near the home of the Magnuson Clan and their three villages. The oldest settlement, Havn, later becomes a heritage site.

Havn, Scotland: The settlement founded by Finna and her descendants. During Eldred and Hilda's time, most of the houses were log cabins built on the rock foundations of the previous generations. By Cara's time, Ny Havn has become the main settlement. The remnants of the original village are a heritage site that people come from afar to visit. Only the mead hall is still in use. Most of the other buildings are in ruins, but the oldest surviving intact stone structure is still covered in thatch, just like it had been during Uma's time! The clan's Viking ancestors Finna and Bjørn, their family, and all who had come to Scotland with them were the first to settle there. Over the years, their dwellings were continually upgraded or replaced. Eventually, the magnificent log homes of Eldred and Hilda's time were built. Then, in the 1800s, these handsome residences would be replaced by the charming stone houses of Ny Havn. The remains of some of these are still habitable to this day. No one lives in Havn anymore since the village has become a treasured heritage site. The entire clan works together to preserve it and still uses the mead hall. Once a year, around the winter solstice, they allow people to join them in

the celebration that follows the tours. Those parties tend to get pretty wild but maybe not as boisterous as those the Magnusons have in private!

Isle of Arran, Scotland: Cara and Phillipe have their home there. It is about halfway between Gairloch and London, where Phillipe lived when he fell in love with Cara.

Meeting Place: The dimensional pocket created for Bo to retreat to. All those invited can visit, and it later becomes a haven for those fading from life, including the horses from the construct and Cara's and the others' beloved pets.

Ny Havn, Scotland: The village Cara grows up in. It was built near the original site of Havn.

Trygg Havn, Norway: The sanctuary where Finna and Bjørn find shelter. The name means 'Safe Harbor.'

Captured People

This list includes only those individuals mentioned by name. By the time Cara is caught within, it has become a large complex holding well over a hundred prisoners. It took weeks to send them all home.

People are listed by the year they were captured.

1. Signe Magnuson, 1001
2. Finna Magnuson, 1001
3. Uma Magnuson, 1023
4. Conall Sinclaire, 1411 D
5. Bess Delande, 1553
6. Arthur Pickerton, 1561
7. Gudrun Mackay, 1567
8. Norene Magnuson, 1591
9. Eldred Magnuson, 1616
10. Hilda Magnuson, 1616
11. Mæva MacClair, 1717
12. Genevieve Magnuson, 1737
13. Elanora Dickinson, 1739
14. Heather Magnuson, 1749D
15. Zelda Stewart 1796
16. Kira Magnuson, 1798
17. Finley Delaby, 1799
18. Katrín Magnuson Delaby, 1799
19. Willow Mackay 1799
20. Rodger Magnuson, 1801
21. Rita Lindström, 1803
22. Xavier O'Rourke 1804
23. Maxwell Mackay, 1805
24. Lady Emla Sutherland 1824

25. Victoria DeMonde, 1861
26. Harald Magnuson aka Sten Coffers, 1871
27. Delilah Magnuson 1885
28. Conall Westing, 1901
29. Cletus Magnuson, 1901
30. Eileen Westerby, 1904
31. The umbrella woman, 1911
32. Revna Magnuson
33. Little Cara 1998?
34. Brigit Magnuson: 2022
35. Cara Magnuson: 2023

Many more individuals than are listed here were caught in the spell.

Eldred, Hilda, and Cara kept track of them all. A complete register of all the names and dates can be found in the Magnuson Archives in Ny Havn.

Definitions

Jarls: Earls, noblemen, the aristocracy. In Viking Society, they functioned as the local chieftains. A jarl could either be elected by the karls or take the position by force if he had enough money.

Karls: A freeman such as a farmer or a peasant in Viking society.

Magnuson Procurement Company (MPC): The trading company owned by the Magnuson Clan. Most of the employees are kin, and it is run by the heads of several of the families. The idea was conceived by Bjørn Magnuson. Using their powers, the peddlers determined what people truly desired. Then, if possible, the company would acquire it and sell it for a reasonable price. From early on, one of the goals was to improve the lives of everyone around them. To this day, MPC sells products that benefit people in mysterious ways.

Thralls: An enslaved person in Old Norse.

Sair: The mead hall, usually located in the center of the village. The one in Havn has been rebuilt multiple times and is still in use.

Magic
is in
you!

Acknowledgements

A huge thank you to Robbi Baskin for helping me with the editing! She is not only one of the sweetest and kindest people I know but also tends to find those subtle errors I have missed. Also, thank you to all my friends, family, and pets. I am so grateful for your constant encouragement, understanding, and immense patience. Your support made this wonderful book possible!

And a very special 'THANK YOU' to all my amazing readers! You motivate me to continue writing to bring you yet another of my entertaining stories!

And last, but not least, a huge thank you to the Divine for sending me this tale in a dream and helping me write it.

Author's Biography

GC Sinclaire loves to write and could not imagine her life without it. Her inspiration comes from many places. One of these sources is Sinclaire's vivid dreams. When she records the tale, her fingers fly over the keyboard. Sometimes, she feels like she can barely keep up! More facts emerge while she is typing, almost like she has lived the story. The author sees the scenes in her mind and is determined to make them as real as possible for the reader.

'An Exceptional Adventure' resulted from one of these incredible dreams and is the latest of her books. This inspiration came along when GC ran into a snag in volume 5 of the 'Child of the Ice' books. She needed something different while her mind worked on the conclusion to that tale. The first installments of that series should be published in the fall of 2023. Several other stories, including a sequel to 'Arianna,' and the third part of the 'Mystic Highlands Series' are in various stages of completion.

If you want to learn more about GC and her works, please visit her Facebook page, GC Sinclaire, or her web page at www.gcsinclaire.com. You can check on updates there and connect with the author.

www.ingramcontent.com/pod-product-compliance
Lightning Source LLC
Chambersburg PA
CBHW020454020726
47493CB00001B/28